Impact Parameter
and Other Quantum Realities

GEOFFREY A. LANDIS
WITH A FOREWORD BY JOE HALDEMAN

THIS BOOK IS THE PROPERTY OF
THE NATIONAL CITY PUBLIC LIBRARY

GOLDEN GRYPHON PRESS • 2001

Foreword, copyright © 2001, by Joe Haldeman
"A Walk in the Sun," first published in *Asimov's Science Fiction*, October 1991.
"Impact Parameter," first published in *Asimov's Science Fiction*, August 1992.
"Elemental," first published in *Analog*, December 1984.
"Ecopoiesis," first published in *Science Fiction Age*, May 1997.
"Across the Darkness," first published in *Asimov's Science Fiction*, June 1995.
"Ouroboros," first published in *Asimov's Science Fiction*, January 1997.
"Into the Blue Abyss," first published in *Asimov's Science Fiction*, August 1999.
"Snow," first published in *Starlight 2*, Tor, 1998.
"Rorvik's War," first published in *New Legends*, Legend, 1995.
"Approaching Perimelasma," first published in *Asimov's Science Fiction*, January 1998.
"What We Really Do Here at NASA," first published in *Science Fiction Age*, July 1994.
"Dark Lady," first published in *Interzone*, August 1995.
"Outsider's Chance," first published in *Analog*, December 1998.
"Beneath the Stars of Winter," first published in *Asimov's Science Fiction*, January 1993.
"The Singular Habits of Wasps," first published in *Analog*, April 1994.
"Winter Fire," first published in *Asimov's Science Fiction*, August 1997.
"Afterword: About the Stories" copyright © 2001, by Geoffrey A. Landis

Copyright © 2001 by Geoffrey A. Landis
LIBRARY OF CONGRESS CATALOGING-IN-PUBLICATION DATA
Landis, Geoffrey.
    Impact parameter and other quantum realities / Geoffrey A. Landis.
      p.   cm.
    ISBN 1-930846-06-1 (alk. paper)
     1. Science fiction, American.   I. Title.
    PS3562.A4766I58   2001
    813'.54—dc21   2001033977

All rights reserved, which includes the right to reproduce this book, or portions thereof, in any form whatsoever except as provided by the U.S. Copyright Law. For information address Golden Gryphon Press, 3002 Perkins Road, Urbana, IL 61802.
Printed in the United States of America
First Edition

Contents

This one is for Mary, with love

Foreword
by Joe Haldeman

A WORKING SCIENTIST AND SERIOUS POET, GEOFFREY Landis is one of the best "hard" science fiction writers around today; one of the best ever. He has a couple of unfair advantages, though, besides his dual preparation in physics and poetry—he's also the only person in science fiction to have actually visited Mars, although others may *think* they've been there. (Technically, it was his electronic surrogate, an experiment attached to the solar array that powered the plucky little Sojourner a couple of years ago.)

Landis writes in many genres—fantasy, "slipstream," what have you—but since most of the stories in this volume are hard sf of one kind or another, I'd like to approach introducing them in that context.

So what does "hard" mean, other than being difficult to write?

In a 1994 scholarly essay, David Hartwell said that hard science fiction "is a metaphorical or symbolic representation of the wonder at the perception of truth that is experienced at the moment of scientific discovery." That seems to me to be far too restrictive. I think only two of Landis's stories fit that Procrustean bed, and it's lumpy for them.

Peter Nicholls may inhabit the other extreme of exclusivity (in his and John Clute's *Encyclopedia of Science Fiction*), saying "While a rigorous definition of "hard sf" may be impossible, perhaps the most important thing about it is, not that it should include real science in any great detail, but that it should respect the scientific spirit; it should seek to provide natural rather than supernatural or transcendental explanations for the events and phenomena it describes." That does describe every story in this collection (except for a tongue-in-cheek one) but I think it's uncomfortably broad at the edges. Nicholls's parameters include a lot of non-genre literary fiction, as well as most detective stories and non-romance historicals.

I spent most of a morning trying to find an anecdote about Samuel Johnson and poetry, which has so far eluded me, but I can paraphrase it. Someone asked Dr. Johnson a question that seems curiously modern (since most of us, even knowing better, think of free verse and prose poetry as modern phenomenae)—"What, actually, is a poem—what's the difference between a poem and plain writing?" Johnson's answer was along these lines, probably prefaced with "Sir"—I would hesitate to posit a rule that could be universally applicable. All I can say with confidence is this: I can point at one piece of writing and say, "This is a poem," and point to another and say, "This is not."

That diffuse-yet-particular non-definition is the way I, and I suspect most sf readers, feel about the hard and soft sf. We know when we're reading a hard sf story, even when it's about things contrary to scientific fact, like telepathy or Victorian steam-powered computers.

(None of Landis's stories fit into the all too common subgenre "hard sf where the science is unintentionally bad." I've done that. It generates mail.)

The two Landis stories that fit into Hartwell's scholarly definition are two of my favorites, "Dark Lady" and "Beneath the Stars of Winter." Without giving anything away, I'd like to point out that neither story is particularly upbeat—and that these are stories about "scientific discovery" by a person who does scientific discovery for a living.

I think that's relevant and interesting. Primitive hard sf goes back to Hugo Gernsback's pulp scientifiction magazines of the '20s and '30s—where his declared primary purpose was not to entertain, but to encourage boys and girls to become scientists and engineers. These two stories are accurate portrayals of scientific minds at work. But there are real human beings attached to the minds, and sometimes the sense of wonder is elusive.

His "A Walk in the Sun" is a particular kind of hard-sf writer's dream—it takes a universally known scientific fact and turns it into a completely original story. The science in this story has been around since before Gernsback's pulp magazines—but it took most of a century before Landis looked at it from his unusual perspective and turned it into an affecting human drama.

The small wry "Ouroboros" does take an ancient Gernsbackian concept, but makes it eerily real by applying modern but mundane computer technology to it.

The award-winning "Approaching Perimelasma" flings an adventurer down into a black hole, and Landis uses his familiarity with esoteric astrophysics to explain carefully and convincingly what happens to his character there.

"Outsider's Chance" is pure hard science fiction, an Analog-type "problem" story. The avoidance of melodrama is typical of Landis's writing. A conventional writer couldn't have resisted making this an adventure story with a zinger ending.

"Winter Fire" is a curious hybrid of hard science fiction and mainstream. The same story—in terms of the relations between people—could have been told, with mundane technology, about many wars in the present and the recent past. To my mind, though, it's quintessential hard science fiction, because the story is much more effective with the futuristic technology at its center, resonating with the central moral problem of doing science that can be used in war, even when there's no doubt that your cause is just and the enemy must be defeated at any cost.

I hasten to note that all is not seriousness here—There are a couple of light and even silly stories in the volume. "The Singular Habits of Wasps" is a delicious Sherlock Holmes pastiche, and "What We Really Do at NASA," well, is hard to describe. It can't possibly be the truth, or they wouldn't have let him live. And he did show up at a party a couple of months ago.

Of course it could have been a clone, or worse. When I asked him what he'd like to drink, he asked whether I had any WD-40.

Human or not, Geoffrey Landis has written a book that's a real treasure, modern in its literary values and at the same time infused with the fascination and love for science that characterizes classic science fiction.

Joe Haldeman
Gainesville, Florida
February 2001

Impact Parameter

And Other Quantum Realities

A Walk in the Sun

THE PILOTS HAVE A SAYING: A GOOD LANDING IS ANY landing you can walk away from.

Perhaps Sanjiv might have done better, if he'd been alive. Trish had done the best she could. All things considered, it was a far better landing than she had any right to expect.

Titanium struts, pencil-slender, had never been designed to take the force of a landing. Paper-thin pressure walls had buckled and shattered, spreading wreckage out into the vacuum and across a square kilometer of lunar surface. An instant before impact she remembered to blow the tanks. There was no explosion, but no landing could have been gentle enough to keep *Moonshadow* together. In eerie silence, the fragile ship had crumpled and ripped apart like a discarded aluminum can.

The piloting module had torn open and broken loose from the main part of the ship. The fragment settled against a crater wall. When it stopped moving, Trish unbuckled the straps that held her in the pilot's seat and fell slowly to the ceiling. She oriented herself to the unaccustomed gravity, found an undamaged EVA pack and plugged it into her suit, then crawled out into the sunlight through the jagged hole where the living module had been attached.

She stood on the grey lunar surface and stared. Her shadow reached out ahead of her, a pool of inky black in the shape of a fantastically stretched man. The landscape was rugged and utterly barren, painted in stark shades of grey and black. "Magnificent desolation," she whispered. Behind her, the sun hovered just over the mountains, glinting off shards of titanium and steel scattered across the cratered plain.

Patricia Jay Mulligan looked out across the desolate moon-scape and tried not to weep.

First things first. She took the radio out from the shattered crew compartment and tried it. Nothing. That was no surprise; Earth was over the horizon, and there were no other ships in cislunar space.

After a little searching she found Sanjiv and Theresa. In the low gravity they were absurdly easy to carry. There was no use in burying them. She sat them in a niche between two boulders, facing the sun, facing west, toward where the Earth was hidden behind a range of black mountains. She tried to think of the right words to say, and failed. Perhaps as well; she wouldn't know the proper service for Sanjiv anyway. "Goodbye, Sanjiv. Goodbye, Theresa. I wish—I wish things would have been different. I'm sorry." Her voice was barely more than a whisper. "Go with God."

She tried not to think of how soon she was likely to be joining them.

She forced herself to think. What would her sister have done? Survive. Karen would survive. First: inventory your assets. She was alive, miraculously unhurt. Her vacuum suit was in service-able condition. Life-support was powered by the suit's solar arrays; she had air and water for as long as the sun continued to shine. Scavenging the wreckage yielded plenty of unbroken food packs; she wasn't about to starve.

Second: call for help. In this case, the nearest help was a quarter of a million miles over the horizon. She would need a high-gain antenna and a mountain peak with a view of Earth.

In its computer, *Moonshadow* had carried the best maps of the moon ever made. Gone. There had been other maps on the ship; they were scattered with the wreckage. She'd managed to find a detailed map of Mare Nubium—useless—and a small global map meant to be used as an index. It would have to do. As near as she could tell, the impact site was just over the eastern edge of Mare

Smythii—"Smith's Sea." The mountains in the distance should mark the edge of the sea, and, with luck, have a view of Earth. She checked her suit. At a command, the solar arrays spread out to their full extent like oversized dragonfly wings and glinted in prism shades as they rotated to face the sun. She verified that the suit's systems were charging properly, and set off.

Close up, the mountain was less steep than it had looked from the crash site. In the low gravity, climbing was hardly more difficult than walking, although the three-meter dish made her balance awkward. Reaching the ridgetop, Trish was rewarded with the sight of a tiny sliver of blue on the horizon. The mountains on the far side of the valley were still in darkness. She hoisted the radio higher up on her shoulder and started across the next valley.

From the next mountain peak the Earth edged over the horizon, a blue and white marble half-hidden by black mountains. She unfolded the tripod for the antenna and carefully sighted along the feed. "Hello? This is Astronaut Mulligan from *Moonshadow*. Emergency. Repeat, this is an emergency. Does anybody hear me?"

She took her thumb off the TRANSMIT button and waited for a response, but heard nothing but the soft whisper of static from the sun.

"This is Astronaut Mulligan from *Moonshadow*. Does anybody hear me?" She paused again. "*Moonshadow*, calling anybody. *Moonshadow*, calling anybody. This is an emergency."

"*—shadow, this is Geneva Control. We read you faint but clear. Hang on, up there.*" She released her breath in a sudden gasp. She hadn't even realized she'd been holding it.

After five minutes the rotation of the Earth had taken the ground antenna out of range. In that time—after they had gotten over their surprise that there was a survivor of the *Moonshadow*—she learned the parameters of the problem. Her landing had been close to the sunset terminator; the very edge of the illuminated side of the moon. The moon's rotation is slow, but inexorable. Sunset would arrive in three days. There was no shelter on the moon, no place to wait out the fourteen day long lunar night. Her solar cells needed sunlight to keep her air fresh. Her search of the wreckage had yielded no unruptured storage tanks, no batteries, no means to lay up a store of oxygen.

And there was no way they could launch a rescue mission before nightfall.

Too many 'no's.

She sat silent, gazing across the jagged plain toward the slender blue crescent, thinking.

After a few minutes the antenna at Goldstone rotated into range, and the radio crackled to life. "Moonshadow, *do you read me? Hello,* Moonshadow, *do you read me?*"

"*Moonshadow* here." She released the transmit button and waited in long silence for her words to be carried to Earth.

"*Roger,* Moonshadow. *We confirm the earliest window for a rescue mission is thirty days from now. Can you hold on that long?*"

She made her decision and pressed the TRANSMIT button. "Astronaut Mulligan for *Moonshadow.* I'll be here waiting for you. One way or another."

She waited, but there was no answer. The receiving antenna at Goldstone couldn't have rotated out of range so quickly. She checked the radio. When she took the cover off, she could see that the printed circuit board on the power supply had been slightly cracked from the crash, but she couldn't see any broken leads or components clearly out of place. She banged on it with her fist — Karen's first rule of electronics, if it doesn't work, hit it — and re-aimed the antenna, but it didn't help. Clearly something in it had broken.

What would Karen have done? Not just sit here and die, that was certain. Get a move on, kiddo. When sunset catches you, you'll die.

They had heard her reply. She had to believe they heard her reply and would be coming for her. All she had to do was survive.

The dish antenna would be too awkward to carry with her. She could afford nothing but the bare necessities. At sunset her air would be gone. She put down the radio and began to walk.

Mission Commander Stanley stared at the x-rays of his engine. It was four in the morning. There would be no more sleep for him that night; he was scheduled to fly to Washington at six to testify to Congress.

"Your decision, Commander," the engine technician said. "We can't find any flaws in the x-rays we took of the flight engines, but it could be hidden. The nominal flight profile doesn't take the engines to a hundred twenty, so the blades should hold even if there is a flaw."

"How long a delay if we yank the engines for inspection?"

"Assuming they're okay, we lose a day. If not, two, maybe three."

Commander Stanley drummed his fingers in irritation. He hated to be forced into hasty decisions. "Normal procedure would be?"

"Normally we'd want to reinspect."

"Do it."

He sighed. Another delay. Somewhere up there, somebody was counting on him to get there on time. If she was still alive. If the cut-off radio signal didn't signify catastrophic failure of other systems.

If she could find a way to survive without air.

On Earth it would have been a marathon pace. On the moon it was an easy lope. After ten miles the trek fell into an easy rhythm: half a walk, half like jogging, and half bounding like a slow-motion kangaroo. Her worst enemy was boredom.

Her comrades at the academy—in part envious of the top scores that had made her the first of their class picked for a mission—had ribbed her mercilessly about flying a mission that would come within a few kilometers of the moon without landing. Now she had a chance to see more of the moon up close than anybody in history. She wondered what her classmates were thinking now. She would have a tale to tell—if only she could survive to tell it.

The warble of the low voltage warning broke her out of her reverie. She checked her running display as she started down the maintenance checklist. Elapsed EVA time, eight point three hours. System functions, nominal, except that the solar array current was way below norm. In a few moments she found the trouble: a thin layer of dust on her solar array. Not a serious problem; it could be brushed off. If she couldn't find a pace that would avoid kicking dust on the arrays, then she would have to break every few hours to housekeep. She rechecked the array and continued on.

With the sun unmoving ahead of her and nothing but the hypnotically blue crescent of the slowly rotating Earth creeping imperceptibly off the horizon, her attention wandered. *Moonshadow* had been tagged as an easy mission, a low-orbit mapping flight to scout sites for the future moonbase. *Moonshadow* had never been intended to land, not on the moon, not anywhere.

She'd landed it anyway; she had to.

Walking west across the barren plane, Trish had nightmares of blood and falling. Sanjiv dying beside her; Theresa already dead in the lab module; the moon looming huge, spinning at a crazy angle in the viewports. Stop the spin, aim for the terminator—at low sun angles, the illumination makes it easier to see the roughness of the surface. Conserve fuel, but remember to blow the tanks an instant before you hit to avoid explosion. That was over. Concentrate on the present. One foot in front of the other. Again. Again.

The undervoltage alarm chimed again. Dust, already?

She looked down at her navigation aid and realized with a shock that she had walked a hundred and fifty kilometers.

Time for a break anyway. She sat down on a boulder, fetched a snack-pack out of her carryall, and set a timer for fifteen minutes. The airtight quick-seal on the food pack was designed to mate to the matching port in the lower part of her faceplate. It would be important to keep the seal free of grit. She verified the vacuum seal twice before opening the pack into the suit, then pushed the food bar in so she could turn her head and gnaw off pieces. The bar was hard and slightly sweet.

She looked west across the gently rolling plain. The horizon looked flat, unreal; a painted backdrop barely out of reach. On the moon, it should be easy to keep up a pace of fifteen or even twenty miles an hour—counting time out for sleep, maybe ten. She could walk a long, long way.

Karen would have liked it; she'd always liked hiking in desolate areas. "Quite pretty, in its own way, isn't it, Sis?" Trish said. "Who'd have thought there were so many shadings of grey? Plenty of uncrowded beach—too bad it's such a long walk to the water."

Time to move on. She continued on across terrain that was generally flat, although everywhere pocked with craters of every size. The moon is surprisingly flat; only one percent of the surface has a slope of more than fifteen degrees. The small hills she bounded over easily; the few larger ones she detoured around. In the low gravity this posed no real problem to walking. She walked on. She didn't feel tired, but when she checked her readout and realized that she had been walking for twenty hours, she forced herself to stop.

Sleeping was a problem. The solar arrays were designed to be detached from the suit for easy servicing, but had no provision to power the life-support while detached. Eventually she found a way to stretch the short cable out far enough to allow her to prop up the array next to her so she could lie down without disconnecting the power. She would have to be careful not to roll over. That done, she found she couldn't sleep. After a time she lapsed into a fitful doze, dreaming not of the *Moonshadow* as she'd expected, but of her sister, Karen, who—in the dream—wasn't dead at all, but had only been playing a joke on her, pretending to die.

She awoke disoriented, muscles aching, then suddenly remembered where she was. The Earth was a full handspan above the horizon. She got up, yawned, and jogged west across the gunpowder-grey sandscape.

Her feet were tender where the boots rubbed. She varied her pace, changing from jogging to skipping to a kangaroo bounce. It helped some; not enough. She could feel her feet starting to blister, but knew that there was no way to take off her boots to tend, or even examine, her feet.

Karen had made her hike on blistered feet, and had had no patience with complaints or slacking off. She should have broken her boots in before the hike. In the one-sixth gee, at least the pain was bearable.

After a while her feet simply got numb.

Small craters she bounded over; larger ones she detoured around; larger ones yet she simply climbed across. West of Mare Smythii she entered a badlands and the terrain got bumpy. She had to slow down. The downhill slopes were in full sun, but the crater bottoms and valleys were still in shadow.

Her blisters broke, the pain a shrill and discordant singing in her boots. She bit her lip to keep herself from crying and continued on. Another few hundred kilometers and she was in Mare Spumans—"Sea of Froth"—and it was clear trekking again. Across Spumans, then into the north lobe of Fecundity and through to Tranquility. Somewhere around the sixth day of her trek she must have passed Tranquility Base; she carefully scanned for it on the horizon as she traveled but didn't see anything. By her best guess she missed it by several hundred kilometers; she was already deviating toward the north, aiming for a pass just north of the crater Julius Caesar into Mare Vaporum to avoid the mountains. The ancient landing stage would have been too small to spot unless she'd almost walked right over it.

"Figures," she said. "Come all this way, and the only tourist attraction in a hundred miles is closed. That's the way things always seem to turn out, eh, Sis?"

There was nobody to laugh at her witticism, so after a moment she laughed at it herself.

*   *   *

Wake up from confused dreams to black sky and motionless sunlight, yawn, and start walking before you're completely awake. Sip on the insipid warm water, trying not to think about what it's recycled from. Break, cleaning your solar arrays, your life, with exquisite care. Walk. Break. Sleep again, the sun nailed to the sky in the same position it was in when you awoke. Next day do it all over. And again. And again.

The nutrition packs are low-residue, but every few days you must still squat for nature. Your life support can't recycle solid waste, so you wait for the suit to dessicate the waste and then void the crumbly brown powder to vacuum. Your trail is marked by your powdery deposits, scarcely distinguishable from the dark lunar dust.

Walk west, ever west, racing the sun.

Earth was high in the sky; she could no longer see it without craning her neck way back. When the Earth was directly overhead she stopped and celebrated, miming the opening of an invisible bottle of champagne to toast her imaginary traveling companions. The sun was well above the horizon now. In six days of travel she had walked a quarter of the way around the moon.

She passed well south of Copernicus, to stay as far out of the impact rubble as possible without crossing mountains. The terrain was eerie, boulders as big as houses, as big as shuttle tanks. In places the footing was treacherous where the grainy regolith gave way to jumbles of rock, rays thrown out by the cataclysmic impact billions of years ago. She picked her way as best she could. She left her radio on and gave a running commentary as she moved. "Watch your step here, footing's treacherous. Coming up on a hill; think we should climb it or detour around?"

Nobody voiced an opinion. She contemplated the rocky hill. Likely an ancient volcanic bubble, although she hadn't realized that this region had once been active. The territory around it would be bad. From the top she'd be able to study the terrain for a ways ahead. "Okay, listen up, everybody. The climb could be tricky here, so stay close and watch where I place my feet. Don't take chances — better slow and safe than fast and dead. Any questions?" Silence; good. "Okay, then. We'll take a fifteen-minute break when we reach the top. Follow me."

Past the rubble of Copernicus, Oceanus Procellarum was smooth as a golf course. Trish jogged across the sand with a smooth, even glide. Karen and Dutchman seemed to always be lagging behind or running up ahead out of sight. Silly dog still followed Karen around like a puppy, even though Trish was the one who fed him and refilled his water dish every day since Karen went away to college. The way Karen wouldn't stay close behind her annoyed Trish—Karen had *promised* to let her be the leader this time—but she kept her feelings to herself. Karen had called her a bratty little pest, and she was determined to show she could act like an adult. Anyway, she was the one with the map. If Karen got lost, it would serve her right.

She angled slightly north again to take advantage of the map's promise of smooth terrain. She looked around to see if Karen was there, and was surprised to see that the Earth was a gibbous ball low down on the horizon. Of course, Karen wasn't there. Karen had died years ago. Trish was alone in a spacesuit that itched and stank and chafed her skin nearly raw across the thighs. She should have broken it in better, but who would have expected she would want to go jogging in it?

It was unfair how she had to wear a spacesuit and Karen didn't. Karen got to do a lot of things that she didn't, but how come she didn't have to wear a spacesuit? *Everybody* had to wear a spacesuit. It was the rule. She turned to Karen to ask. Karen laughed bitterly. "I don't have to wear a spacesuit, my bratty little sister, because I'm *dead*. Squished like a bug and buried, remember?"

Oh, yes, that was right. Okay, then, if Karen was dead, then she didn't have to wear a spacesuit. It made perfect sense for a few more kilometers, and they jogged along together in companionable silence until Trish had a sudden thought. "Hey, wait—if you're dead, then how can you be here?"

"Because I'm not here, silly. I'm a Fig Newton of your overactive imagination."

With a shock, Trish looked over her shoulder. Karen wasn't there. Karen had never been there.

"I'm sorry. Please come back. Please?"

She stumbled and fell headlong, sliding in a spray of dust down the bowl of a crater. As she slid she frantically twisted to stay facedown, to keep from rolling over on the fragile solar wings on her back. When she finally slid to a stop, the silence echoing in her ears, there was a long scratch like a badly-healed scar down the glass of her helmet faceplate. The double reinforced faceplate had held, fortunately, or she wouldn't be looking at it.

She checked her suit. There were no breaks in the integrity, but the titanium strut that held out the left wing of the solar array had buckled back and nearly broken. Miraculously there had been no other damage. She pulled off the array and studied the damaged strut. She bent it back into position as best she could, and splinted the joint with a mechanical pencil tied on with two short lengths of wire. The pencil had been only extra weight anyway; it was lucky she hadn't thought to discard it. She tested the joint gingerly. It wouldn't take much stress, but if she didn't bounce around too much it should hold. Time for a break anyway.

When she awoke she took stock of her situation. While she hadn't been paying attention, the terrain had slowly turned mountainous. The next stretch would be slower going than the last bit.

"About time you woke up, sleepyhead," said Karen. She yawned, stretched, and turned her head to look back at the line of footprints. At the end of the long trail, the Earth showed as a tiny blue dome on the horizon, not very far away at all, the single speck of color in a landscape of uniform grey. "Twelve days to walk halfway around the moon," she said. "Not bad, kid. Not great, but not bad. You training for a marathon or something?"

Trish got up and started jogging, her feet falling into rhythm automatically as she sipped from the suit recycler, trying to wash the stale taste out of her mouth. She called out to Karen behind her without turning around. "Get a move on, we got places to go. You coming, or what?"

In the nearly shadowless sunlight the ground was washed-out, two-dimensional. Trish had a hard time finding footing, stumbling over rocks that were nearly invisible against the flat landscape. One foot in front of the other. Again. Again.

The excitement of the trek had long ago faded, leaving behind a relentless determination to prevail, which in turn had faded into a kind of mental numbness. Trish spent the time chatting with Karen, telling the private details of her life, secretly hoping that Karen would be pleased, would say something telling her she was proud of her. Suddenly she noticed that Karen wasn't listening; had apparently wandered off on her sometime when she hadn't been paying attention.

She stopped on the edge of a long, winding rille. It looked like a riverbed just waiting for a rainstorm to fill it, but Trish knew it had never known water. Covering the bottom was only dust, dry as powdered bone. She slowly picked her way to the bottom, careful not to slip again and risk damage to her fragile life support system. She looked up at the top. Karen was standing on the rim waving at her. "Come *on!* Quit *dawdling*, you slowpoke — you want to stay here for*ever?*"

"What's the hurry? We're ahead of schedule. The sun is high up in the sky, and we're halfway around the moon. We'll make it, no sweat."

Karen came down the slope, sliding like a skier in the powdery dust. She pressed her face up against Trisha's helmet and stared into her eyes with a manic intensity that almost frightened her. "The hurry, my lazy little sister, is that you're halfway around the moon, you've finished with the easy part and it's all mountains and badlands from here on, you've got six thousand kilometers to walk in a broken spacesuit, and if you slow down and let the sun get ahead of you, and then run into one more teensy little problem, just one, you'll be dead, dead, dead, just like me. You wouldn't like it, trust me. Now get your pretty little lazy butt into gear and *move!*"

And, indeed, it was slow going. She couldn't bound down slopes as she used to, or the broken strut would fail and she'd have to stop for painstaking repair. There were no more level plains; it all seemed to be either boulder fields, crater walls, or mountains. On the eighteenth day she came to a huge natural arch. It towered over her head, and she gazed up at it in awe, wondering how such a structure could have been formed on the moon.

"Not by wind, that's for sure," said Karen. "Lava, I'd figure. Melted through a ridge and flowed on, leaving the hole; then over the eons micrometeoroid bombardment ground off the rough edges. Pretty, though, isn't it?"

"Magnificent."

Not far past the arch she entered a forest of needle-thin crystals. At first they were small, breaking like grass under her feet, but then they soared above her, six-sided spires and minarets in fantastic colors. She picked her way in silence between them, bedazzled by the forest of light sparkling between the sapphire spires. The crystal jungle finally thinned out and was replaced by giant crystal boulders, glistening iridescent in the sun. Emeralds? Diamonds?

"I don't know, kid. But they're in our way. I'll be glad when they're behind us."

And after a while the glistening boulders thinned out as well, until there were only a scattered few glints of color on the slopes of the hills beside her, and then at last the rocks were just rocks, craggy and pitted.

Crater Daedalus, the middle of the lunar farside. There was no celebration this time. The sun had long ago stopped its lazy rise, and was imperceptibly dropping toward the horizon ahead of them.

"It's a race against the sun, kid, and the sun ain't making any stops to rest. You're losing ground."

"I'm tired. Can't you see I'm tired? I think I'm sick. I hurt all over. Get off my case. Let me rest. Just a few more minutes? Please?"

"You can rest when you're dead." Karen laughed in a strangled, high-pitched voice. Trish suddenly realized that she was on the edge of hysteria. Abruptly she stopped laughing. "Get a move on, kid. Move!"

The lunar surface passed under her, an irregular grey treadmill.

Hard work and good intentions couldn't disguise the fact that the sun was gaining. Every day when she woke up the sun was a little lower down ahead of her, shining a little more directly in her eyes.

Ahead of her, in the glare of the sun she could see an oasis, a tiny island of grass and trees in the lifeless desert. She could already hear the croaking of frogs: braap, braap, BRAAP!

No. That was no oasis; that was the sound of a malfunction alarm. She stopped, disoriented. Overheating. The suit air conditioning had broken down. It took her half a day to find the clogged coolant valve and another three hours soaked in sweat to find a way to unclog it without letting the precious liquid vent to space. The sun sank another handspan toward the horizon.

The sun was directly in her face now. Shadows of the rocks stretched toward her like hungry tentacles, even the smallest looking hungry and mean. Karen was walking beside her again, but now she was silent, sullen.

"Why won't you talk to me? Did I do something? Did I say something wrong? Tell me."

"I'm not here, little sister. I'm dead. I think it's about time you faced up to that."

"Don't say that. You can't be dead."

"You have an idealized picture of me in your mind. Let me go. *Let me go!*"

"I can't. Don't go. Hey—do you remember the time we saved up all our allowances for a year so we could buy a horse? And we found a stray kitten that was real sick, and we brought the shoebox full of our allowance and the kitten to the vet, and he fixed the kitten but wouldn't take any money?"

"Yeah, I remember. But somehow we still never managed to save enough for a horse." Karen sighed. "Do you think it was easy growing up with a bratty little sister dogging my footsteps, trying to imitate everything I did?"

"I wasn't either bratty."

"You were too."

"No, I wasn't. I wasn't. I adored you." Did she? "I *worshipped* you."

"I know you did. Let me tell you, kid, that didn't make it any easier. Do you think it was easy being worshipped? Having to be a paragon all the time? Christ, all through high school, when I wanted to get high, I had to sneak away and do it in private, or else I knew my damn kid sister would be doing it too."

"You didn't. You never."

"Grow up, kid. Damn right I did. You were always right behind me. Everything I did, I knew you'd be right there doing it next. I had to struggle like hell to keep ahead of you, and you, damn you, followed effortlessly. You were smarter than me—you know that, don't you?—and how do you think that made me feel?"

"Well, what about me? Do you think it was easy for *me*? Growing up with a dead sister— everything I did, it was 'Too bad you can't be more like Karen' and 'Karen wouldn't have done it that way' and 'If only Karen had . . .' How do you think that made *me* feel, huh? You had it easy—I was the one who had to live up to the standards of a goddamn *angel*."

"Tough breaks, kid. Better than being dead."

"Damn it, Karen, I loved you. I love you. Why did you have to go away?"

"I know that, kid. I couldn't help it. I'm sorry. I love you too, but I have to go. Can you let me go? Can you just be yourself now, and stop trying to be me?"

"I'll . . . I'll try."

"Goodbye, little sister."

"Goodbye, Karen."

She was alone in the settling shadows on an empty, rugged plain. Ahead of her, the sun was barely kissing the ridgetops. The dust she kicked up was behaving strangely; rather than falling to the ground, it would hover half a meter off the ground. She puzzled over the effect, then saw that all around her, dust was silently rising off the ground. For a moment she thought it was another hallucination, but then realized it was some kind of electrostatic charging effect. She moved forward again through the rising fog of moondust. The sun reddened, and the sky turned a deep purple.

The darkness came at her like a demon. Behind her only the tips of mountains were illuminated, the bases disappearing into shadow. The ground ahead of her was covered with pools of ink that she had to pick her way around. Her radio locator was turned on, but receiving only static. It could only pick up the locator beacon from the *Moonshadow* if she got in line of sight of the crash site. She must be nearly there, but none of the landscape looked even slightly familiar. Ahead—was that the ridge she'd climbed to radio Earth? She couldn't tell. She climbed it, but didn't see the blue marble. The next one?

The darkness had spread up to her knees. She kept tripping over rocks invisible in the dark. Her footsteps struck sparks from the rocks, and behind her footprints glowed faintly. Triboluminescent glow, she thought—nobody has *ever* seen that before. She couldn't die now, not so close. But the darkness wouldn't wait. All around her the darkness lay like an unsuspected ocean, rocks sticking up out of the tide pools into the dying sunlight. The undervoltage alarm began to warble as the rising tide of darkness reached her solar array. The crash site had to be around here somewhere, it had to. Maybe the locator beacon was broken? She climbed up a ridge and into the light, looking around desperately for clues. Shouldn't there have been a rescue mission by now?

Only the mountaintops were in the light. She aimed for the nearest and tallest mountain she could see and made her way across the darkness to it, stumbling and crawling in the ocean of ink, at last pulling herself into the light like a swimmer gasping for air. She huddled on her rocky island, desperate as the tide of darkness slowly rose about her. Where were they? *Where were they?*

Back on Earth, work on the rescue mission had moved at a frantic pace. Everything was checked and triple-checked—in space, cutting corners was an invitation for sudden death—but still the rescue mission had been dogged by small problems and minor delays, delays that would have been routine for an ordinary mission, but loomed huge against the tight mission deadline.

The scheduling was almost impossibly tight—the mission had been set to launch in four months, not four weeks. Technicians scheduled for vacations volunteered to work overtime, while suppliers who normally took weeks to deliver parts delivered overnight. Final integration for the replacement for *Moonshadow*, originally to be called *Explorer* but now hastily re-christened *Rescuer*, was speeded up, and the transfer vehicle launched to the

Space Station months ahead of the original schedule, less than two weeks after the *Moonshadow* crash. Two shuttle-loads of propellant swiftly followed, and the transfer vehicle was mated to its aeroshell and tested. While the rescue crew practiced possible scenarios on the simulator, the lander, with engines inspected and replaced, was hastily modified to accept a third person on ascent, tested, and then launched to rendezvous with *Rescuer*. Four weeks after the crash the stack was fueled and ready, the crew briefed, and the trajectory calculated. The crew shuttle launched through heavy fog to join their *Rescuer* in orbit.

Thirty days after the unexpected signal from the moon had revealed a survivor of the *Moonshadow* expedition, *Rescuer* left orbit for the moon.

From the top of the mountain ridge west of the crash site, Commander Stanley passed his searchlight over the wreckage one more time and shook his head in awe. "An amazing job of piloting," he said. "Looks like she used the TEI motor for braking, and then set it down on the RCS verniers."

"Incredible," Tanya Nakora murmured. "Too bad it couldn't save her."

The record of Patricia Mulligan's travels was written in the soil around the wreck. After the rescue team had searched the wreckage, they found the single line of footsteps that led due west, crossed the ridge, and disappeared over the horizon. Stanley put down the binoculars. There was no sign of returning footprints. "Looks like she wanted to see the moon before her air ran out," he said. Inside his helmet he shook his head slowly. "Wonder how far she got?"

"Could she be alive somehow?" asked Nakora. "She was a pretty ingenious kid."

"Not ingenious enough to breathe vacuum. Don't fool yourself—this rescue mission was a political toy from the start. We never had a chance of finding anybody up here still alive."

"Still, we had to try, didn't we?"

Stanley shook his head and tapped his helmet. "Hold on a sec, my damn radio's acting up. I'm picking up some kind of feedback—almost sounds like a voice."

"I hear it too, Commander. But it doesn't make any sense."

The voice was faint in the radio. "Don't turn off the lights. Please, please, don't turn off your light. . . ."

Stanley turned to Nakora. "Do you. . . ?"

"I hear it, Commander . . . but I don't believe it."

Stanley picked up the searchlight and began sweeping the horizon. "Hello? *Rescuer* calling Astronaut Patricia Mulligan. Where the hell are you?"

The spacesuit had once been pristine white. It was now dirty grey with moondust, only the ragged and bent solar array on the back carefully polished free of debris. The figure in it was nearly as ragged.

After a meal and a wash, she was coherent and ready to explain.

"It was the mountaintop. I climbed the mountaintop to stay in the sunlight, and I just barely got high enough to hear your radios."

Nakora nodded. "That much we figured out. But the rest— the last month— you really walked all the way around the moon? Eleven thousand kilometers?"

Trish nodded. "It was all I could think of. I figured, about the distance from New York to LA and back—people have walked that and lived. It came to a walking speed of just under ten miles an hour. Farside was the hard part—turned out to be much rougher than nearside. But strange and weirdly beautiful, in places. You wouldn't believe the things I saw."

She shook her head, and laughed quietly. "I don't believe some of the things I saw. The immensity of it—we've barely scratched the surface. I'll be coming back, Commander. I promise you."

"I'm sure you will," said Commander Stanley. "I'm sure you will."

As the ship lifted off the moon, Trish looked out for a last view of the surface. For a moment she thought she saw a lonely figure standing on the surface, waving her goodbye. She didn't wave back.

She looked again, and there was nothing out there but magnificent desolation.

Impact Parameter

1. Parameters of the Problem

THE TERMINAL WHISTLED FOR HIS ATTENTION, A theme by Paganini in E-flat. Ben got up and stretched, trying to clear the fuzz out of his brain. He hadn't even realized he had been napping. It seemed that he was just about to say something to Barbara, something important, and now he had forgotten what it was. He shook his head and smiled as he walked over to the coffee pot. He hadn't been married to her for well over five years.

It was almost four in the morning. His guaranteed-observer time, two hours on the three-meter gamma ray observatory, came when scheduling bureaucrats said it came, not when it was convenient. Smooth-talking astronomers with billions in grant money and lecture fees got the convenient times. With the low priority and ragged funding of Ben's project, he was lucky to get on the GO list at all.

Time to get moving. He started the coffee dripping and went to his computer. While the previous run was finishing, he put a request into the satellite's command queue for it to locate and lock onto his guide stars with the finder scope. He pulled the celestial coordinates out of disk and uplinked them to the satellite, then sat back to wait.

As soon as he leaned back in the chair, Rajiv walked in. Ben looked at the clock. Four on the nose. "Right on time."

"We are working together so long, are you still thinking I would be late?"

"You, late? Never."

The console whistled again, a theme from Paderewski in a minor key. He looked at the message. The computer had found his guide stars, but one of them was not quite in the position he had specified. He downlinked a visual. There was his guide star, Omicron Ceti, with the reticule showing its starchart position in the center of the screen. The star was noticeably off the crosshairs — five microradians, maybe more. Ben pounded his fist on the console. "Damn you, why can't you work right just one time, just one lousy time?"

"What is the problem?" asked Rajiv.

"Damn star in the wrong place."

"Oh, but that is not possible, surely, no? How could a star be moving places?"

"Oh, the star's in the same old place, Raj, you can bet on it. The damn satellite is out of alignment." Most likely the satellite position sensors had drifted again.

Rajiv frowned. "We will be recalibrating? Or perhaps we just observe and let the maintenance people do their job on their own shift?"

Ben looked at the schedule. Recalibrating would take half an hour, a good quarter of his week's observing time, and it wasn't his job. The maintenance and calibration people had huge blocks of time, why couldn't they do their job right? Damn it, the telescope had been calibrated just three days ago. It wasn't fair. Every instinct told him to let it slide, to let somebody else do it. His project didn't require absolute positions anyway. He was searching for modulated gamma-ray laser signals from alien intelligences, and his search area was big enough that it really didn't matter if the absolute pointing was off by a tiny bit. When he found a signal, a real signal, *then* he could go back and calibrate the scope.

But in twenty-two years of searching they had never found a signal.

He'd been with the old radiotelescope SETI group at Arecibo, listening in to the stars for alien radio messages, hearing only the ocean-roar of static and the atonal singing of hydroxyl radicals. He'd been part of a fruitless search at optical wavelengths, looking for alien lasers. Infrared and UV, no luck either. Slowly the search had progressed up the spectrum. Not very many astronomers were left in the SETI camp; most of them had drifted off into other fields when success never came. Ben was one of the last. He had made a case that aliens could be sending their messages at the extremely high energy end of the spectrum, using gamma-ray lasers to send narrow-beam look-I'm-here messages. It was enough of an argument that he'd gotten GO status on the gamma ray satellite, but not enough to climb the priority queue.

But knowing there was a problem with the telescope, and not fixing it, was something he just couldn't do. It would just shuffle the problem onto the next observer, who likely needed the time just as badly as he did. He sighed. "Boot up the calibration procedure, Raj. I'll message the institute, tell them we're using a chunk of our time to do their job. Maybe they'll look fondly on us and give us some time out of the TOO register later in the week, huh?"

Rajiv brightened up. "Really, you are thinking so? That would be very considerate of them, yes indeed. Surely that is what they will be doing, you are quite right."

Right, hell. There were a hundred observers fighting for scraps of time on the satellite.

But it had to be done. He might as well feel virtuous about doing it. He and Rajiv buckled down to work.

Half an hour later Omicron Ceti was still out of position. The telescope was working flawlessly. Rigel, Aldeberan, Fomalhaut; all the calibration stars were rock steady. But Omicron Ceti was still out of place.

He sighed. He'd never succeeded in recalibrating his ex-wife, either.

"It is maybe a software error?" asked Rajiv.

"Maybe," said Ben. "I can't make myself believe it, though. A software error that would just move one star? Unlikely. Next to impossible."

"Is there something peculiar about this star?"

"Nothing I can think of. Red giant, maybe seventy, eighty parsecs away. Not the type of star we'd ordinarily look at—if it had planets, it swallowed them thousands of years ago when it went into the giant phase."

"Nobody could be moving this star?"

Ben laughed. "No. No way the star could move."

"And so what we are doing next?"

Ben sighed. "Hell, I don't know. Check it on one of the other 'scopes." He called up the listing of astronomical satellites and printed out a hardcopy of the list. "Looks like we could request target-of-opportunity time on Herschel." He shook his head. "Buddy, we sure are going to look like fools if there's something obvious we missed." He picked up the phone.

The scheduler was obliging. "Omicron Ceti? No kidding? Sure, we can get you TOO time—it's a snap. Why don't you ask Harvard Astrophysical, though? They just requested target-of-opportunity scheduling on Herschel twenty minutes ago to look at Omicron Ceti. What is it with this star, anyway? Can you tell me? Hello? Hey, are you still there?"

Ben put down the phone and crumpled up the hardcopy. "Looks like we're on to something. And we've been scooped." He sighed. "Might as well go ahead with what's left of the usual session, Raj. Maybe we can salvage something out of the morning."

The Harvard astronomer was Janilee Stormer, an old gamma-ray astronomer from the pre-satellite days when they still put telescopes on the peaks of mountains. He knew her slightly from seminars. He arranged to meet her for lunch in Harvard Square. He spent the morning calling up archived photos of the region, trusting her to make the proper measurements during her observing run.

She'd already ordered when he arrived. She handed him a stack of hardcopy without a word, and started her lunch as he leafed through her data.

At last he dropped the data on the table and looked up at her. "Any idea what it is?"

"None at all," she said. "You saw the spectra we took. Normal."

"We got some old pictures out of the archives for comparison."

"Good. I put in a request for that, but I've been too busy to get to them. Find anything?"

"Yeah. It's right at the limit of resolution, but by my best guess, this has been going on for five years, maybe a bit more. Right about five years ago the star started drifting slowly out of position."

"Hmmmm. Funny." She sipped her hot chocolate. "Have you checked the background stars yet?"

"No, I haven't. Why? Have you?"

"Just an idea. Tell me what you find, will you? Get together again about eight?"

"Right-o."

"Good." She gathered up her data and left. He hadn't even ordered yet. He decided that he wasn't interested in lunch anyway, and went back to his lab.

He compared the most recent star photo with an old photo from the archives. When he overlaid the two, it was quite obvious that all the stars in the region were affected, even background stars thousands of parsecs away. In a tiny region of space, only a few seconds of arc across, some cosmic hand had nudged all the stars away from one spot in the sky. More peculiar, one faint star had disappeared entirely. It would have been exactly in the center of the avoided zone.

He had Rajiv print out an extra hardcopy of the overlays, and brought the photos with him when he met again with Stormer. She brought out her own data, a computer plot where the distance of displacement had been plotted against the distance from the extrapolated center of the anomaly. Clearly, the closer the stars were to the center, the more they had been moved to the side.

"What about the missing star? What happened to it?"

She smiled. "Take a look at this one. I had the Herschel integrate the photon count over a ten minute interval, editing out the foreground stars." She showed him a photograph. The background was a chaos of irregular brightness. He could almost see the pattern, stars toward the center smeared away in a thumb-sized circle. "And the missing one?"

She reached over with a fork and traced out an arc. "Here."

Once it had been pointed out, he could see it clearly. A narrow ring surrounded the blank spot, so faint as to be almost indistinguishable from the noise of the photo. He traced the circle all the way around. "My god. An Einstein ring."

"Bingo. We've found ourselves a big ol' gravitational lens."

"It must be incredibly massive."

"Or incredibly close. But what's causing it? Brown dwarf? A neutron star?"

"My god, Jan, that's not the real question." He spread out his photos, ordering them from oldest to most recent. Over the last five years, the anomaly had been growing stronger, but the center stayed firmly in the same region of Cetus. "No proper motion. Whatever it is, *it's coming right at us.*"

"Have you told anybody yet?"

Ben shook his head. "My graduate assistant Rajiv knows."

"Same here. Let's keep this quiet a bit longer, okay? Until we know a bit more?"

"We'll need to bring an astrophysicist in on it."

"I have one in mind. A relativist, too. What I meant, let's not spread it around too much outside just yet. Maybe there's something we're missing."

Ben shook his head. "I hope so. I really hope so."

Ben reserved a small conference room in the physics center for the discussion. One by one the various participants arrived. When the last had entered, Dr. Stormer closed the door, walked to the front of the table, and started the discussion without any preamble. "We have now searched for an object in the center of the gravity lens in every wavelength range available," she said. "If it were a brown dwarf, we'd see it in the IR or microwave. A neutron star would shout out across the spectrum. Nothing. I think we can confidently eliminate everything except a black hole."

"Everything we know of, that is," said Ben.

"It's invisible, it's massive, it bends light—what else could it be?"

"I don't know. Just covering the bases."

"But a black hole would be having an accretion disk," Rajiv said. "Such a thing would be jumping with gammas, no? Are we seeing nothing in the gamma ray spectrum?"

"No." Dr. Stormer sketched a circle in the air with her forefinger. "Nothing there but cosmic background."

"Doesn't mean anything," said the astrophysicist, Tim Deloria. He was a tall, dark-haired postdoc wearing a gold earring and a leather vest. "If it's a mature hole, and hasn't passed through a dense gas cloud in the recent past, it might not have anything to accrete."

Isu Yokomono, the relativist, cleared his throat and spoke. "I have plotted the gravitational lensing effect against theory." He tapped his keypad to flash a slide onto the screen. "As you can see, the agreement is excellent, except at very low impact parameter. Tim suggests this may be a refraction effect from compression of the interstellar medium near the hole. He's working on a model. I can't give you a good value for the mass until you can give me a distance, but the best guess would be between point one and point oh one solar masses, which I am told is unusually low by astrophysics standards."

"Ben?"

"Right. It's hard to measure distance of something we can see only by looking at where it *isn't*, but we've managed to make tentative parallax measurements from the archive data. About a thousand astronomical units."

Somebody whistled. "That close? Are you sure?"

Ben shook his head. "I'm sorry, folks. It doesn't matter just exactly how far it is. What matters is how fast it's coming."

"And that is?"

He put his graph on the screen. The line showing the projected trajectory neatly cutting across the Earth's orbit. "Give or take a small margin of error, in ten days the black hole intersects the Earth."

"How much is the margin of error?"

Ben shook his head slowly. "Not enough, gentlemen. Not enough by half."

When evening fell Ben went out into the apartment's tiny back yard. The lawn was unkempt and the grass choked with weeds. No point in fixing it up now. He set up his little telescope next to an abandoned washing machine and with little difficulty found Cetus low in the east. Cetus was more familiar to him than the yard was; for decades they had searched the star Tau Ceti at every frequency for every modulation scheme they could think of. Omicron Ceti was lost in the haze of the horizon and the skyglow from the city. It didn't matter; there was nothing there to see with his little telescope anyway.

Day by day the anomalous region grew larger. The amount of distortion in the starfield was minute, far too small to be visible with the naked eye, but knowing exactly what to look for, the effect was enormous and ominous.

They met four days later to discuss their most recent results.

"Can you tell us just what, exactly, is going to happen?" Ben asked. "Tides? Earthquakes? What?"

Tim looked at Isu. "It's coming a little too fast for us to see much in the way of prelude effects, I think. The exact details will depend on the impact parameter. For all of the scenarios, we'll get the atmosphere ripped off first, of course."

"And the oceans," said Isu.

"The planet then gets stretched out like a sausage."

"Like pulling on silly putty," said Isu. He smiled. "At this point viscous mantle material oozes out through the cracks in the crust, like stepping on a tube of toothpaste."

"More likely the frictional effect just melts the crust," said Tim. "After this, at low impact parameter, the planet breaks up. Somewhere between half and ninety percent of the material forms a ring around the hole and gets slowly swallowed, while a small portion gets sprayed out into space in the form of droplets of magma. Presumably these then cool into asteroidal material, unless they're flung entirely free of the sun. At higher impact parameter the planet simply gets stretched out into a sausage and breaks up into droplets. This effect is rather interesting, actually—"

"I think I get the picture. Any chance of surviving?"

Tim shook his head. "Even at the three sigma point, the atmosphere gets ripped off."

"Oh."

The room was quiet for a moment.

"It's too damn unlikely, you know?" said Tim. "To be coming right at us, right exactly precisely at us—give me a break, will you? That's not coincidence, that's conspiracy. Here's what I think. I think that we've been polluting the galaxy with radio waves, old *Happy Days* reruns, *My Favorite Martian, Days of Our Lives*, that crap, and I think that somebody out there just got pissed. In the radio spectrum the Earth is brighter than most stars, you know that? We put out megawatts, gigawatts of garbage. I think somebody got so tired of old *Gunsmoke* reruns that they just lobbed a black hole our direction, no offense buddy but just shut up permanently, okay?"

"You don't really believe that, do you?" said Ben. "Any civilization that had the ability to push around black holes. . . ."

"I know, I know. You'd think they'd talk to us first, and you've been looking, and they're not talking. Hell, maybe they're just the silent type. Maybe they're critics. I don't know."

Isu cleared his throat. "In any case, I think we have quite enough data to publish," he said. "Should we prepare a press release first? I think on this one we may get some attention."

Jan looked at him with contempt. "It's a bit pointless to do that, don't you think?"

Isu shrugged. "I don't see why not."

"I can," said Tim. "Why get everybody upset over something they can't do anything about? I'd say we should very definitely *not* tell anybody. Keep it close, or there'll be panic in the streets. Chaos."

"Heck, that's not half of it," said Jan. "Do you really want to spend your last days giving interviews to reporters? Think carefully. You know what it's like being followed around by cameras? Explaining the same basic principles of physics over and over to people who wouldn't understand them if you pounded it into their skulls with an air-hammer? Living without any privacy at all, with reporters camping in your living room, following you everywhere, into bed, into the bathroom?"

"Yeah," said Tim. He made a face. "Interviews on television shows with psychics who said that they predicted this ten years ago and it will go away if we all think rosy thoughts and chant Om."

"And holy-rollers who say that it was all revealed in the Bible, but don't worry because the faithful — of their particular faith, that is — will be saved," said Jan. "Dimwits who tell you that it's all the scientist's fault; if we had never invented black holes in the first place everything would be fine. No, thanks."

"I didn't think of that," said Isu. "You really think people would panic? Okay, okay, maybe you're right. It's too bad, though — the first thing I've ever been on really hot. It just seems we ought to tell *somebody*."

Jan shrugged. "Anybody else think we should go public? Take a vote on it?" She looked around. Nobody spoke up. "I think it's settled, then."

"But this thing, it is going to kill us," said Rajiv. "Is there nothing that we can be doing?"

The room was silent. Finally Ben answered him. "Afraid not, Raj. It's just too big. There's no handle, no way to get a grip on it. We're like an ant about to get stepped on by an elephant — maybe we can see what's coming, but that's not going to stop us from getting squished."

"It's the cosmic lottery," added Tim. He shook his head. "And we just went bankrupt."

2. Just Before the End

And then there were only a few days left. The project team has stopped meeting regularly. There was nothing left to do. "It's the end of the world, Ben," the astronomer Jan said. "What are you going to do?"

"Party?" he answered. "I don't know. How about you?"

"Abandon my diet, that's for sure." She laughed. "Clean my desk. I'd like to face my maker with a clean desk."

"Think you'll find anything interesting?"

"I don't know. That's what's so exciting. On the other hand,

I've been thinking that maybe I'll just clean it right out the window. What the heck.

"And after *that*, I think there are a few people over in administration I'm going to tell exactly what I think of. Something they've been needing for a long time." She smiled. "I thought about taking my pistol—I shoot every weekend, did I tell you? Third in the state championships—I was thinking about some live target practice using administrators for targets. But I figure, why bother? They'll be dead in a week, too."

Ben laughed. There was a bit of life in the old astronomer after all. "You going to tell anybody? Your family?"

"God, no! It would only get them upset—why make their lives miserable now? Hell, if I tell anybody, I'll tell somebody I detest."

"Makes sense. How about you, Raj? What are you going to do?"

"I am going home to India. I will see all my friends again, my cousins and grandparents and my two little nieces. I will bring many many gifts for them. Oh, they will be so happy to see me! Yes."

"Yeah?" Ben raised an eyebrow. "Where'd you get the cash to buy a ticket?"

Rajiv smiled. "I am borrowing money on my credit card. Low interest, two years to pay."

"Why not? Guess you can do anything you want. Rob a bank. Why not just steal a Learjet—what are they going to do, kill you?"

"Oh, no—I would never rob a bank. That would be quite dishonest. How could you think that of me?"

Ben patted him on the arm. "I know, Raj. Have a good trip home."

As he was leaving, Ben ran into Tim and Isu. Tim was holding a bottle of wine, Isu a pile of books and papers. "I'm just in to pick up some of my stuff," said Isu. "Guess I won't be around for the rest of the week—for the rest of my life, for that matter."

Ben shrugged.

"I wrote a haiku. You want to hear it?"

"Sure."

Tim handed Isu the bottle of wine.

"Thanks, pal." He took a sip, handed the bottle back to Tim, and cleared his throat. "Singularity:

'This is it.
"Nothing else you ever did matters
"The place where all your words mean nothing
"Doorway to forever.'"

Isu paused and looked at Ben. "You like it?"

Ben shrugged. He never could find much to say about poetry. "Aren't haiku supposed to have only three lines?"

"So I'm not a purist. You don't like it, sue me."

"Hey, no problem. So—you have plans yet how to spend the last week?"

"Sure. Yesterday I went to church. The Baptist church on Boylston, and the Epis— Episcip— Episcopalian church downtown. Tomorrow I'm visiting the Bahai temple and the Quaker meeting. Sunday I'll get baptized."

"Covering all the bases, huh?"

"Oh, no, there are many more. I have much studying to do." He smiled ruefully. "The final exam is coming, and I've been skipping my homework."

"Yeah. Well, I guess it's your last final, anyway. Hope you do well on it." They shook hands.

"How about you, Tim? You going with Isu?"

"Heck, no. I've already *got* religion." He winked. "Her name is Candy—can you believe that? Candy? No baloney." He shook his head, and took a sip of wine. "For the rest of the week, you can bet your ass I intend to worship at her shrine as often as possible and in as many different positions as I can think of. When the end of the world comes, we're not even going to *notice* it."

"Uh, I'd think that there was only so much of that you'd be able to do."

"Yeah, maybe—so I'm going on an all-oyster diet. How about you, Ben? You got some body-heat you can turn to for a little comfort for the dying?"

"Uh, guess not. No."

Tim clapped him on the shoulder. "Hey, no crime, buddy. Some guys got it, some don't. Tell you what you do. Find yourself a high-priced downtown call-girl, one that takes plastic, and rent her for a *week*. You know what I'm saying? I tell you, you will forget all about the end of the world, guaranteed."

"It's a thought."

"Righto. Gotta go, got something to put in the oven, so to speak."

"See ya."

"I doubt it. Have a good life." He left.

Ben walked out the door, and realized that there was nothing he wanted to do, no place he wanted to go.

He could go home, he supposed. Tell his family he loved them, tell them goodbye. They'd be surprised to see him, but glad, of

course, in their low-key fashion. But what would he tell them?
Was there any real point in telling them the world was ending in
a week? It could only upset them.

Religion wasn't for him, either. Try Tim's solution? One of the
graduate students, maybe? That kind of thing was rather frowned
on by the admin, but what could they do, fire him? But the
students had lives of their own that he was mostly ignorant of. He
wouldn't even know where to start.

On an impulse he called up his ex-wife Barbara.

"Ben? I don't believe it. Are you drunk or something? High?"

"Is there some law that says I can't call you? I just thought I'd
like to see you again. Is that a crime?"

She was silent for a long time. "It's been a long time, Ben. I
don't know. Are you sure you want to stir up those old ghosts
again?"

"I remember some good times. Don't you remember the time
we went walking down the old boardwalk on Revere—"

She laughed. "Gosh, I haven't thought about that in years.
And the abandoned roller coaster. You think it's still there?"

"I think it got washed away a long time ago, when the water
started to rise."

"Yeah. A lot of things got washed away. Too many things."

"So, how about it? For old times?"

"I just don't know. I don't think it's such a good idea, Ben. I
mean, but, well. . . ."

"Uh, I guess I should have asked. Are you, ah, seeing somebody?"

"Well . . . yes. Sure, lots of people. Not the way you mean it,
though. I've got my circle of friends. It's enough."

"So, why not? Just this one time, I promise. Please?"

"Well . . . okay. You know where I live now?"

He stopped on the way for a bouquet of flowers. He picked out
two dozen lilies, all colors, charging them on his card.

She was a little older, a little more weathered than his memory.
Her hair was long now, a thick braid tossed casually over her left
shoulder, but still as deep a shade of black as ever. He handed her
the flowers. "You're looking good."

She hesitated, but finally took them from him. She thrust her
face into the bunch and inhaled deeply. "I always liked lilies."

"I remember."

"Here." She handed the flowers back to him and went into the
kitchen for a vase. He looked at the posters. They were different

from the movie posters she had when he married her, but the same types of old movies. *Casablanca. Gone with the Wind. Jewel of the Nile.* She came back with an enameled brass vase, one he'd brought back for her once long ago when he'd gone to India for a conference.

"You still have that? You said you threw out all my stuff."

She shrugged. "I lied. I always liked that one."

"I know something else you always liked." He took her in his arms. As he leaned over to kiss her she turned her face aside.

"Oh, Ben . . . I'm not sure this is a good idea. We don't have that type of a relationship any more. Ben. . . ."

He brought his hand up and traced the line of her jaw with a fingertip. lingering at the hollow of her throat. "Just this one last time."

"Well . . . okay." She tipped her head back, and he kissed the tip of her nose. She giggled. "I guess sometimes maybe I do miss you. A little bit."

The morning sunlight was faded and tinted vaguely pink. The cat sleeping on the windowsill stretched, blinked, turned around to center herself more fully in the faded sunbeam, and went back to sleep. Barbara looked at him. "That was nice. You can be so nice sometimes, I almost miss being married to you."

He didn't say anything, just continued stroking her breast slowly, almost absently, with his hand.

"But you were always self-centered. Sometimes you would just ignore me, treat me like an object."

"I guess I was busy."

"Oh, yes, busy watching for your aliens. Busy? You were obsessed. Imagine, fifteen years ago I thought that a man with an obsession was sexy. All that intensity. Damn, I was naive." She rolled out of bed, searched around on the floor for her panties, pulled them on and then looked around for her bra.

"In the living room, remember?"

"Oh, yeah."

"Barb? Would you stay with me?"

She walked back into the bedroom and looked him in the eye. "No."

"Please? Just for a while?"

"You always were a little hard of listening, Ben. No. I remember too much of what it was like. I'm finally doing what I want, and I like it fine. No. Period. Final."

"Please?"

"Five years, Ben. So why all of a sudden?"

"Because the end of the world is coming, and I don't want to be alone." His voice sounded childish, even to himself. He hadn't meant to say it. It had just sort of slipped out.

She laughed. "I can't believe it. You, getting religion? You always were one to go diving off the deep end. Remember what the marriage counselor told you, way back? That you ought to try talking with a therapist, it would do you good? Maybe she was right. You might think about it.

"I told you, Ben. The night was fun, it really was. You can be sweet sometimes. Don't spoil it, okay? If I stayed with you, we'd only get back into the same old rut. I couldn't take it again. So let's just say goodbye, okay?"

He sighed. "Okay." He paused. "Then one last breakfast at the Crêpe Stop?"

"No more talking foolish? No pressure on me?"

"Not if you don't want to."

"Okay. But after that, I'm going."

The day had not yet built up to the furnace heat of a Cambridge summer, and they found an empty table out on the boardwalk. It was built up almost a foot above the old street level. He looked out across the water.

"The blue of the sky," he said, suddenly.

"Huh? What about it?"

"How blue, so poignantly blue it is. Nothing else is quite that color, so vibrant, so full of life."

She shrugged. "I suppose it is. Not any more than any other day."

"I never notice. Every day I walk to work, the miracle of sky is luminous above me, and I never even look up. So many things. Look." He gestured at the buildings across the way. They were dilapidated brick apartment buildings, the upper stories faced with wood. "Look at them, really *look*. Look at the color and texture of the brick. The brickwork. Look at the carvings on the lintels, on the cornices. Just old buildings? Look at the work some ancient stonemason did, long ago. You can see the love and care he put into the job."

"Irish," she said. "The old stonemasons were Irish and Italian. My mother told me that once. I guess you don't see workmanship like that any more. Today it's all aluminum and plexi boxes."

"And we walk by it every day. That building, that tired build-

ing with peeling paint and clotheslines on the roof flying somebody's flowered sheets, that's what it is to be human. It's beautiful,
beautiful.

"And listen." He was silent for a moment. Behind the traffic
noises, the babble of conversations around them, the lapping of
wavelets against the boardwalk, was a soft trilling chireep, chireep,
chireep. Tiny frogs. Spring peepers? He'd heard them every
spring, but never bothered to look up what they were. Since the
waters had started to rise they were peeping all through midsum-
mer. "The sounds of life, just singing its joy at being alive."

"My, aren't you poetic today." She was silent for a moment.
"You really believe it," she said softly. "You really do believe that
the world is coming to an end."

He nodded. He couldn't trust himself to say anything. His eyes
were full of tears.

"What will you do when it doesn't? When the end of the world
comes, and the world doesn't notice, just keeps on going?"

"I wish I could believe that, Barbara. But it's coming. There's
nothing we could do to stop it."

"But what if, just suppose, it didn't? You won't do anything
foolish, will you? You'll see a professional then, won't you? Please?
Promise me?"

He smiled. "Barbara, if the end of the world doesn't come, I'll
laugh out loud. I'm going to hug everybody I know. I'll parade
naked down the middle of the street in front of the State house
playing a trombone, at noon. And I'll never, not for one day, forget
to be glad I'm alive."

She shook her head, vagrant wisps of hair blowing across her
face. "Sometimes I really like you, Ben, in spite of all the bad
times. I really do. Take care of yourself, will you?" She blew him
a kiss and walked away. A block down the boardwalk, almost lost
in the morning pedestrian traffic, she hesitated and looked back.
He waved, and she turned and disappeared into the crowd.

"Goodbye," he said. She'd left her crêpe untouched.

He'd spent so long at the telescope listening for voices. They
weren't there. Or if they were, they weren't talking. Maybe everybody was listening, nobody broadcasting.

He'd had an uncle who had spent his life looking for little
green men; under the bed, behind the curtains, in the bottom of
a whiskey bottle. He'd said they were beaming messages into his
brain, that he heard them every day. "Eccentric," the family had

called him on good days. "Crazy" on the worse days. He'd finally allowed himself to be put away. But at least he had heard the voices he'd spent his life searching for.

The facility at Arecibo had been mostly shut down by the time he'd left. There was little it could do that couldn't be done better by one of the radio interferometers in space. But he still had the access codes from his time there, and he doubted that they would have changed them.

They hadn't.

He had trouble deciding what to broadcast. At first he thought the Encyclopedia Brittanica would be best, but at the last minute, after accessing the Arecibo computer and programming his request, he changed his mind. Somehow something as dry as the encyclopedia didn't fit his mood. He chose Mahler, the crazy, romantic old Austrian, to tell the universe that once there had been a planet with life and intelligence, and occasionally a little bit of wisdom. As the Earth slowly turned, it would be broadcast out across the entire sky. Maybe sometimes we did make a mess of things, he thought, but we could love life, too. The universe may crush us, but we had style, damn it. We were here. Where were you? Where the hell were you?

One day left. He tried calling Barbara again, but there was no answer. Perhaps she'd unplugged the phone. He called his parents, and his sister, but found he didn't have anything to say. He had never been very good at long phone calls. He settled for just telling them that he loved them.

"Why, thank you, Benjy," his mother said. "That's very nice. And we love you, too."

He walked the streets of the city, not going anyplace in particular, just taking in the sights and sounds of life. It really was beautiful, he thought. Even the discarded papers swirling in the wind were beautiful.

Mists rose from the canals as night fell over the city. He was in a part of town he wouldn't ordinarily think of walking in at night. Neon flashed from the bars at every street corner. Fragments of music and rapid women's conversation in some foreign language spilled out of open doorways. Three Cambodian men in T-shirts sat on a doorstep drinking wine and talking. They stopped talking to watch him pass, and one of them called out. "Hey, brother, how's it going?"

"Fine," he said. "Everything's fine. How about you?"

"Doing okay, yes, think I'm doing okay, thank you."

He walked on.

He thought for a moment that perhaps he should be at the observatory, taking notes on the approach of the black hole right up to the end. Like a good scientist. Hell with that.

He'd never been much of a drinking man, even in grad school, when the Friday night parties were about the only entertainment around. But it seemed he had to do something to celebrate, no, to *memorialize* the last night of the world. He stopped in at a liquor store. He wasn't sure what to get. Champagne, certainly. He wasn't sure if he could tell one from another, but he picked the most expensive. It was a week's salary. Some hundred year old brandy. Bailey's Irish Cream—that had always been Barbara's favorite. Why not? He grabbed a dozen other liquors, picking them for the oddly shaped bottles and interesting names. He'd never get another chance to try them. He brought the collection to the front.

"End of the World Coming, Says Harvard Astronomer," proclaimed the tabloids at the checkout counter. "Black Hole Will Swallow Earth." He laughed, quietly at first and then with an almost hysterical energy. So Isu had spilled the news after all—and nobody cared.

The cashier looked at him, and at the assortment of liquor, with a dubious stare.

"A going-away party," he said. "So to speak."

She shook her head. "Odd selection. Some party—you started early, eh? Well, hope y'all have fun, y'hear?"

"I hope so, too. Say, you do take credit cards, I assume?"

3. The Day the World Ended

He woke up groggy and nauseated. Painfully bright sunlight was streaming in the window, and the doorbell was ringing insistently. It took him a moment to realize that the ringing was real, and not part of the painful confusion in his cranium.

He hadn't expected to wake up at all. After a moment he recognized the voice of his neighbor from upstairs, an old Mexican immigrant who sometimes came over on Sundays to share the newspaper.

"Hello? Hello?"

"What is it?" he shouted back. His voice was more of a croak. He found his pants and pulled them on.

"Aren't you awake? God, you missed it! It was incredible!"

"The black hole?" he said, confused. It just passed by? How could it?

"What are you talking about? The parade! I thought everybody in Boston was there!"

"Parade?" Now he was more confused than ever. "What parade?"

"Haven't you even seen the news? Join the real world, Ben! They're here! Aliens! From outer space!" He went over to the window and flung back the curtains. "Look!"

In the distance, something floated over Boston harbor. Ben squinted. A giant balloon? It was hard for him to focus. Then he caught the scale of it. It was floating behind the towers of the financial district, and, whatever it was, it was *huge*. It was no balloon the world had ever seen. He suddenly realized the *alienness* of it. It was nothing at all the world had ever seen. He felt an uneasy feeling in the pit of his stomach. All his life he had spent searching for aliens, and here they were. He turned away from the world, childishly afraid to show his tears. They were here. Nothing would ever be the same again.

"But . . . the hole," he said, stumbling over the words. "What about the black hole?"

"Hole? Oh, you must mean the loophole? That's right, I remember. The teevee man explained something about the loophole. They brought it with them. It's a, uh, a 'loophole in the theory of relativity', right. What allows them to travel. I forgot the details. They said it would be parked somewhere out by Saturn or something, we could use it if we want to."

He remembered now. Wormholes, he'd heard them called. A wormhole was precisely the same as a black hole from the outside, but deep inside, at the throat, a wormhole connected to another wormhole somewhere else, instead of to an infinitely dense singularity. Back in the 'eighties a couple of physicists had claimed that a sufficiently advanced civilization might be able to make a wormhole and keep it open, use it to travel across interstellar distances. It had caused a stir at the time, but was eventually forgotten.

It made sense. It all made sense. While he had wasted his life listening to the sky, desperately listening for a distant voice, all that time they had been coming. Why beam radio waves when you can just bring a loophole and get there in an instant?

On an impulse he hugged his neighbor. The old man was surprised, but after a moment he hugged Ben back. "It's wonderful," Ben said. "It's the end of the world, it really is."

"Ah, the world ends every day," the old man said. "The secret of it is, it is made anew every morning."

"That's deep."

The old man nodded. "Something my father used to say, long ago."

Ben realized that the job he'd been doing all his life had become obsolete overnight. He could do whatever he wanted. Sail around the world. Climb Mount Everest. But first he had a promise to keep.

He hadn't missed the parade. He'd be a little late, that's all. He would be his own parade, down the steps of the state house at noon, celebrating the way the world had been born again.

"Say, you wouldn't happen to have a trombone, do you?"

The old man only gave him a puzzled look. Skipping to the tune of an old childhood song, Ben danced out the door, laughing like the world was new.

And it was.

Elemental

1. Ramsey

FIFTY KILOMETERS SOUTHEAST OF NAPLES, TWO MEN sat waiting in the bright fluorescent-lit power control room of Napoli Spaceport. In front of them glowed an array of green lights and computer consoles. Behind them, outlined on the floor in a violet glow only faintly visible in the brightness of the room, was a complex five-fold symmetric figure: a pentacle.

The younger man watched the array of dials intensely, occasionally touching a knob to make some infinitesimal adjustment. The older man watched him work. What he saw seemed to satisfy him, for he strolled over to the window and gazed out across the landing field.

Without looking up, the younger man spoke: "Luna shuttle's about ready to lift, Mr. Layr."

"Ready for it, Carlo?"

"Running steady at a hundred ten percent, sir."

"She's all yours." Christian Layr walked over to a monitor screen where he could watch the youth's performance and take over if necessary. He doubted that any such necessity would arise. There is a certain skill to controlling magic, a skill of balance and timing not unlike that of a juggler, and the boy had it. Layr almost wished something would go wrong, so he could see how the boy would handle it. The youth had the talent, but Layr would feel uneasy about certifying him until he saw how he tackled a real problem, one of the minor emergencies that make power control a job for men with skill and courage, rather than a simple task for machines. Despite Layr's unspoken wish, though, for the last ten days the station had operated smoothly.

Almost too smoothly.

Layr heard the nearly subsonic rumble of power build-up and directed his attention back to the display. Power level a hundred fifteen percent; there would be no problem with this one.

"Here it goes."

Layr glanced up to the window. As if by magic, the blunt-nosed spacecraft appeared from the launch pit to hover for an instant before his eyes. Slowly it began to inch upward, then to hasten forward with an implacable urgency, finally to rush with a clap of thunder headlong into the morning sky, as if all the demons of hell chased after it.

In a sense, they did. Behind him the control pentacle lit the room with a brilliant violet fire as it transmitted the energy flux to shove the thousand-ton shuttle up to parking orbit. Far beneath his feet, the main pentacle glowed, not violet, but gamma. No human eye could ever look upon it in its full glory. Within the impenetrable walls of the protecting spell was confined a more powerful magic yet: two hundred kilograms of pure antimatter.

In Chicago it was 7 A.M. Yawning, Ramsey Washington looked out the window of his third-floor apartment. A soft wet snow fell steadily. It masked the outlines of the tenements and weighed down the branches of the evergreen that struggled to grow in the building's entrance courtyard. He cursed softly.

Perfect Christmas weather—in April. Some bureaucrat at the weather service must have thought it a good April Fool's joke. More likely, he reflected, they'd needed a blizzard here as the best way to equalize a water imbalance elsewhere in the world. Africa or Antarctica or Alabama or somewhere. Maybe it had been announced and he'd just missed.

He dug through the cluttered drawers of his desk and came up with a usable piece of blue chalk and a battered secondhand hardcopy of the *Handbook of Thaumaturgy*, 2052 edition. He cleared the accumulation of dirty clothes and half-written papers from a one-meter circle on the floor, then carefully chalked a pentacle, copying exactly the diagram in the book. He chanted the book's recommended spell sequence and stepped inside. Spell completed, he grabbed his data microdisc and headed outside.

As he entered the snowstorm, a circle of warm air formed around him. Although by now the snow was nearly twenty centimeters deep over the walk, where he stepped and for a one-meter circle around him the snow vanished, reappearing magically behind him again as he walked onward.

Modern thaumaturgy — usually simply called "magic" — was the logical outgrowth of quantum field theory. The basic premise of thaumaturgy is that "reality" is merely an abstract mathematical construct. Therefore, it can be controlled by the manipulation of abstract symbols — provided that the correct symbols can be chosen. The snow ward which Ramsey took for granted was only one of many changes wrought by the consequent technology.

Protected by his home-made ward, Ramsey ignored the snowstorm swirling about him. As he walked under the low-hanging branch of the evergreen in the courtyard he ducked his head instinctively. Anyone as tall as Ramsey quickly learns to duck without ever really noticing it. As walked under the tree, the snow on the branch above vanished, exorcised by the snow ward. Freed, the branch sprang up, smacking the branch above it and shaking loose a new mound of snow. In a chain reaction of unleashed branches, the whole tree shook itself free of its burden of snow.

Ramsey's low-power spell had been designed to protect against a pretty heavy snowstorm, but it had never been intended to stop an avalanche. The spell overloaded with a loud pop. He abruptly found himself up to his armpits in snow.

Ramsey heard a giggling somewhere behind him, and whirled around to see who was laughing. Unfortunately the snow was rather more slippery than he'd anticipated. His feet skidded out from under him, and he landed flat on his back in a flurry of snow. Helpless, he heard the giggling rise into a robust laugh.

He pulled himself carefully to his feet. "Have you no respect for the mortally wounded?" He shook himself off and glanced surreptitiously at the girl standing on the sidewalk laughing.

"Oh!" The girl rushed over. "I'm sorry! Are you hurt? Where?"

"My dignity, woman, my dignity's taken a mortal wound. I may never recover."

"Oh, poor baby!" she replied in mock seriousness. "Shall I kiss it and make it better?"

"Hey, that's the best offer I've had all day," said Ramsey. He looked up at the girl and grinned. "Say, you mind if I ask a dumb question? What's your name? I've seen you around, but I don't think I know you."

"Susan Robinette," she said. She had just a trace of a French accent. "I work in a lab about two doors down from you."

"Oh! So that's why you seem so familiar! But you're not a physics student, are you? I thought I knew everyone in the department."

"Oh, no; thaumaturgical engineering. My lab just happens to be in the Physics building." She paused. "Say, Ramsey, I apologize for laughing at you. You just couldn't believe the funny look on your face when all that snow started to fall on you."

"Yeah." He thought about it for a second. "Now that you mention it, I guess it was pretty funny. At least in retrospect." He grinned. "Well, if I have to look silly in front of somebody, I guess it's better you than Doctor Williamson." Suddenly he realized he was standing in a snowstorm, and it was cold. He started to shiver.

"Here, come over and share my shield before you freeze to death! Walk with me, and you won't have to make a new shield."

"Yeah, I'd appreciate that. Thanks."

The two of them had to press together in order to both fit into the single snow shield. Ramsey decided he didn't mind at all.

By the time he'd finished breakfast, Ramsey felt more like his usual self. He looked across at Susan. She was nearly as tall as he was, which was surprising right there, and thin. Rather thinner than he usually liked, but pretty in a rather unsophisticated way, with dirty blonde hair and bright brown eyes. He noticed her watching him watch her, and quickly dropped his gaze down to his now-empty plate.

"Well, I gotta run. I got an appointment at nine, and I better not keep Dr. Williamson waiting." He lingered for a moment, trying to think of something else to say. "I'm lucky enough to have her for an advisor; I wouldn't want—"

A booming voice interrupted Ramsey's speech.

"Susie, there you are!" It was a short, rotund man in a dusty tweed jacket. "I've been looking for you. The papers for the Venus project just came in, and we've got to get them turned around. We've got work to do, *liebchen*."

"Professor Kirschmeyer! I'm sorry; I've been dawdling. Do you know—"

"Ramsey Washington. Yes, yes, Janie's protégée. Quite the bright young man, she tells me. Maybe even good enough for my young genius here, no?" He winked.

Ramsey started to say something, but Susan beat him to it.

"Now, Hans, don't let your dirty mind run away with you. I barely know him, and already you're marrying us off."

Kirschmeyer laughed. "Well!" Turning to Ramsey, he said, "You must excuse us, young man. I must steal your pretty girl away, even if she does claim she doesn't even know you. There is much to do, and too little time." He offered his arm to help Susan up.

"See you around, Ramsey," she said, ignoring Kirschmeyer's offered arm. "Good luck with your meeting."

"Thanks." Kirschmeyer and Susan walked out of the restaurant, already deep in conversation. "I'll need all the luck I can get."

In Italy it was early afternoon. The sun beat down warmly, as might be expected on a day in early April. In the fields, two farmers stopped working the rich volcanic soil to rest in the shade of a solar array. One of them brought out the midday snack of bread, wine, and cheese, while the other hooked the tractors up to recharge.

"Explain once more to Giuseppe how it is that your vines produce so bountifully this year?"

"It is because of this amulet of my wife's mother." Luca held up a small piece of carved volcanic rock suspended on a silver chain. Giuseppe looked at it dubiously.

"That? It is no different than the one my wife wears about her neck to ward off the evil eye. Yet my vines do not produce like yours."

"Ah," said Luca smugly, "*wearing* is not enough. You must know how to use it."

"Ah," said Giuseppe. "So tell me, how is it done, to use this thing?"

"And why is it I should say to you?"

"Come, Luca. Did we not grow up together? Are we not friends? How is it that you would now hold out on your poor friend Giuseppe?"

"Indeed," said the other, "I would not. This is what is to be done. Each morning before going into the fields you must take the amulet and make with it this gesture . . ." he demonstrated with his hands ". . . and say the following chant . . ." he intoned a short series of nonsense-sounding syllables.

Giuseppe was still dubious. "That's all?"

"Indeed."

"It would be simple enough for me to try. Father Corsi would not approve, though. He would call it witch-work."

"There is no deed for Father Corsi to know. Besides, he is surely aware of how many of his flock wear charms against the evil eye, no?"

"Yes. And he calls it idolatry, too."

"But he does not forbid it."

"This is true, he does not. But tell to me, how is it that you know this thing?"

"My cousin Roberto, who was in the navy, learned it from a sailor who had a brother who went to the university to learn science. This sailor knew many things to do with such charms, but only the one of any usefulness."

"So," said Giuseppe. "This does not sound like the devil's work. Indeed, I will do it. Perhaps my vines too will become as bountiful as yours."

"I wish you luck." Luca looked at his wristwatch. "Time now for us both to be back to work." He walked over to his tractor. "Do you remember well the gesture and the words?"

Giuseppe repeated the words, making the gesture Luca had shown. Luca nodded. "Good. I wish you prosperity, my friend."

"And you."

As Giuseppe drove the tractor that afternoon he repeated in his mind the words and the gesture. If it worked he would show it to his brother-in-law, who also grew a small plot of grapes behind his fields. And perhaps to his cousin Rafaelle? Yes, he decided. Such a useful thing should not be kept to one's self, but had to be shared with others.

Ramsey looked down at his stack of notes, licked his lips nervously, looked at his watch, and then knocked at the door. Without waiting for a response, he walked confidently in. Doctor Williamson looked up from her desk computer.

"Ah, yes, Mr. Washington. Right on time. I'll be with you in a moment." She turned back to the qwerty.

Ramsey walked over to one of the plush lounge chairs and sat down. He looked at the expensive glass sculpture on the table next to him, then let his eyes wander over to watch her work. What a woman, he thought. She had light brown hair, almost a shade of blond, cut fashionably short. Today she wore a light green sweater with a gold and green silk scarf wrapped casually around her neck. Dressed in impeccable taste, as always, he thought. I bet she never falls down in the snow on her way in. She flicked the Save switch on the computer and turned to him.

"That outfit looks very good on you, Dr. Williamson," Ramsey remarked casually.

"Thank you, Mr. Washington," she replied curtly. "Now let's get to work, shall we? I presume you've finished the data analysis on your recent run, right?"

"Well, not exactly," Ramsey said. "I've been having a slight problem with the data in the third and fourth quadrants. Nothing important, I'm sure."

"Let's have a look at it." Doctor Williamson reached out a hand. Ramsey quickly dug out his microdisc and gave it to her. She popped it into the receptacle on her computer and studied the screen for a moment.

"I see," she said. "What do you think this signifies?"

"I'm not really sure," Ramsey replied. "Maybe some localized anomaly in the Earth's field?"

"Yes, I suppose that's a possibility. Rather unlikely that no one previously ever mentioned it, though, don't you think? After all, people have mapped the magnetic field for several centuries now."

"Maybe it wasn't there before?"

"Now, that seems rather far-fetched, doesn't it? Just where do you suppose such a change would come from? It looks to me much more like the characteristic signature of a magnetometer which has not been properly degaussed before the measurement."

"I calibrated and degaussed the equipment every two hours," Ramsey said.

"Well, Mr. Washington, it certainly looks here as if you missed one, doesn't it? Don't be too glum about it—if we didn't make mistakes, we wouldn't learn anything, now would we? It's the kind of simple mistake everybody makes when just starting out in experimental work. You'll learn to be more careful.

"In the meantime, though, it looks like you'll have to re-do the measurement from about here . . ." she touched the screen, ". . . on. The rest of the measurements, excepting of course that part, are simply marvelous. Fine work."

Ramsey smiled ruefully at the compliment. "Thank you."

"I expect that you'll be able to have the whole thing done right by the time I get back from Rome." She walked over to her desk and touched the keypad beside her chair. A calendar appeared on the screen. Looking at it, she said, "I'll expect to see you at 9 A.M. on the sixteenth, a week from Monday. We'll have another little chat then."

She tapped the appointment time onto the computer and it appeared dutifully on the calendar.

"Thank you for taking time to see me, Dr. Williamson." Ramsey tried to smile pleasantly. Two weeks of work down the pipes. "Have a good conference."

"I intend to," she said cheerfully. "I'll send you a postcard."

Ramsey walked out and shut the door behind him. Damn, but she'd laid it on him good. He shook his head in dismay. Still, he couldn't help thinking about how she'd looked today. She certainly was one roxy fox! And cool as well. Cooler than a cryostat. Now, if she ever warmed up toward him, even a little. . . . But that wasn't about to happen. Better get back to thinking about what to do next.

He knew damn well his data was right. Wasn't it? He flipped quickly through his lab notebook.

As he'd thought, he had carefully degaussed the magnetometer, checked for residual magnetism, and recorded it carefully in the notebook.

Maybe the magnetometer itself was faulty? Ramsey walked back deep in thought.

Susan sipped her coffee slowly and looked across at him. "Your main difficulty comes in subtracting out the Earth's magnetic field?"

"Yeah," said Ramsey. "My results don't agree with what everybody else gets."

"Can I see?"

"Why not?" Ramsey handed her the stack of hardcopy. She paged through it silently, sipping her coffee. She stopped at a map of Italy. Superimposed on the map in deep red were a series of concentric circles.

"Very pretty," she commented. "I tell you what. I'll be passing over that area Thursday. If I see any giant red circles painted on the ground, I'll be sure to give you a call."

"Huh? You're going to Italy?"

"Yep."

"Why?"

"Just passing through." She smiled, and her eyes glowed. "I'm going to Venus."

"Venus?" he said in surprise. "How come?"

"I've pretty much done all I can here," she said. "I'm studying the Earth elemental—the magical force incarnate in the core of a planet. Very little is actually known about it. It normally takes an earthquake or a volcano to manifest it with any power. It's hard to get permission to create earthquakes, even small ones, though."

"You actually create earthquakes?"

"Well, tiny ones, anyway. Not big enough to measure without extremely sensitive equipment, but big enough to manifest the elemental."

"So how come you're going to Venus, if you're studying the Earth?"

"Hans and I think that we could learn a lot more about the nature of the elemental by invoking the elemental of another planet for comparison. He's managed to talk the NSF out of enough funds to send me to Venus to try it."

"But isn't it rather dangerous?"

"Manifesting the elemental? Yes, I suppose it is, but I've been working with it for years, and there's a lot of controls built in. Actually, it's pretty well confined to the Earth's core. I don't expect any trouble."

"No, no — I mean Venus. Isn't Venus rather dangerous?"

She laughed. "You've been watching too many dramatapes. Venus is about as safe as Earth. Maybe safer. Same technology as your little snow-spell, but a whole lot more reliable, keeps the heat and atmosphere out.

"My only real worry is that I might accidentally forget the rules against incidental magic and get myself booted out."

"Rules?"

"Venus base has very strict laws forbidding any use of 'incidental' magic. Lighting cigarettes, untying knots, that sort of thing. It's a sensible enough rule. It's the ward spells that keep the whole place from being uninhabitable, so it's understandable that they'd be a bit picky about anything that could conceivably result in an accidental cancellation of a key spell. But I'll miss being able to play."

She snapped her fingers. A tiny ball of pink fire popped out of the air and settled in her palm. "All us thaumaturges like to play with spells."

She tossed the ball of fire to her other hand and grinned wickedly. "But wanton magicing is a bad habit to get into. After all, if too many people start playing with magic without the strict safeguards built into commercial spells, the side effects could add up, and who knows what could happen?" She snapped her fingers once again. The tiny fireball flashed blue, then vanished with a pop.

"You mean, like, if I made my snow spell wrong it could cause an earthquake in Katmandu?" asked Ramsey.

"A snowstorm more likely, unless you've got a pretty unusual snow ward. For an earthquake you'd need to awaken the Earth elemental. That's my job."

Walking to the lab after lunch, Ramsey heard a low roar. As he approached, it got louder.

Now he could hear a voice, barely audible above the roar. Susan? It sounded like she was in trouble.

He ran to her lab. Unlocked. He shoved the door open, and a spray of water rushed out at him.

Inside was chaos. He looked down into the lab. Susan stood in front of a computer terminal, waist deep in swirling brown water. Her hands flew about frantically as she intoned a rapid series of spells. In front of her a fountain of water gushed out of midair two meters off the floor. Arranged in a circle around this strange waterfall burned six candles in arcanely carved copper stands.

Ramsey ran down the steps and waded into the room.

"Susan! What's going on?"

She looked up. "Ramsey! Thank God! I've got a runaway! If the water rises up and puts out the candles, we're in big trouble!"

The candleholders were already submerged. The water level was about ten centimeters below the flames, rising slowly.

"What can I do?"

"I don't dare move. Find some way to stop the flow! But for God's sake, don't put out any of the candles!"

"How do I stop it?"

"I don't know! Figure something out!" She went back to chanting.

Ramsey grabbed a book, waded over to the fountain, and pressed it against the stream of water. Water spurted around the edges unimpeded. He pressed harder. The book passed right through the source of the waterfall. Ramsey, unprepared for the sudden loss of resistance, nearly fell on his face.

This wouldn't work. He needed another approach.

A fire extinguisher caught his eye. Good against fire, not water. Or was it? He grabbed it off the wall and tried it. Yes; the right type. He aimed it at the fountain and blasted. The frigid blast froze the water where it struck, but the torrent rushed the ice away as fast as it formed. No good.

He walked around the fountain, looking for a weak spot. The

water was now about three centimeters from the candle flames. Susan had paused in her chanting and was watching him.

From the back, he could see that the water came from a one-centimeter hole suspended in midair. If he could block it, the flow would stop. He tried the extinguisher. By directing the cold blast around the edges of the hole, he found he could create a ring of ice, hanging in the air, through which the torrent passed. But the hole wouldn't freeze closed; the water was moving too fast.

Holding the extinguisher on the hole with his left hand, he rummaged through his pockets with his right until he found a coin of the right size. He pulled it out of his pocket and carefully placed it up against the ring of ice from the back. The water pressure pushed it up against the ring and held it. He used a blast from the fire extinguisher to freeze it into place.

The torrent stopped.

"Great!" said Susan. "Hold it there while I reverse the invocation." She tapped something into the qwerty behind her and then made a gesture. The water started to drain. "Okay, now extinguish the candles."

When Ramsey blew out the last candle there was a soft pop. The ice-coated coin fell into the water. He walked over and passed his hand through where it had been. Nothing there.

Somewhat later they sat in the coffee lounge sipping hot chocolate. "You were quite the sorcerer's apprentice today," Ramsey commented. "What was going on back there, anyway?"

"I don't know exactly," replied Susan, "but I can guess. That lab is also used for Kirschmeyer's intermediate thaumaturgy course. I think one of the students set up to summon the air elemental and screwed up. Instead of calling air, he somehow got the water elemental. Rather than abort the summons, he panicked and ran. He must have left a latent connection with the nearest large body of water: Lake Michigan.

"I should have done a latency check before I started work. I was in a hurry, though—not much time left before I leave—and skipped it. So when I invoked the Earth elemental, I inadvertently opened the portal at the same time.

"That's about it. The portal was within the pentacle I'd made for the Earth elemental; so I couldn't dismiss the Earth elemental until it was closed. I couldn't close it until there was nothing flowing through it. And I couldn't leave my own pentacle, or I'd lose my control of the Earth elemental. So I was stuck."

"What would have happened if I hadn't come along? Kept on gushing until it drained the lake?"

"Oh, no. After an hour or so the portal would have phased out. By that time the water would have made quite a mess, though."

"Oh," said Ramsey. "So there wasn't ever any real danger?"

"No," said Susan. "Actually, the water elemental is pretty tame. That's about as far out of control as I've ever seen it. "The one I'm working with—the Earth elemental—is quite a bit more powerful. In fact, if it was ever fully summoned it would be rather awesome. Since its power is concentrated at the center of the Earth, though, it's pretty hard to awaken it fully. The research I do invokes its presence without really fully awakening it. Tickling the toes of the sleeping giant, so to speak."

"That's not dangerous?"

"Not really. Remember, the center of power *is* seven thousand kilometers away. Here at the surface the Earth elemental is pretty weak. It would be different if we were near a power locus, like an active volcano or an earthquake zone."

"I see," said Ramsey. "Tell me, what exactly is an elemental? It's something you've talked about, but I don't really know just what it is. Something to do with Earth, Air, Fire, and Water; right?"

"Something like that." she said. "Any sufficiently complex ensemble of symbolically interrelated objects, when interacting with a symbol-manipulating object, such as a man or a large computer, will exhibit non-stochastic behavior—"

"Thanks a lot," Ramsey interjected. "How 'bout doing it in English?"

"Sorry," she said. "Let's see. Inanimate objects sometimes react to magic as if they had intelligence of their own. No, that's not quite right . . . call it volition. They react as if they had a will of their own."

"Sure," said Ramsey. "That's just Murphy's law. I used to have a '34 Sparrowhawk that damn sure had a mind of its own, I'll tell you."

"Well, that's partly it. In general, this only applies to really large systems, though. Things much more complicated than a car. The ocean, the atmosphere . . . the Earth. In terms of thaumaturgy, we can deal with these almost as if they were separate, quasi-sentient entities.

"Whenever thaumaturgy is done on such complex systems, portions of the system which you don't intend to disturb are still necessarily affected by the magic. This excess power—call it the side effect if you want—is free to be manipulated by the 'volition' of the entity, which we call an 'elemental'."

"So an elemental isn't something that's already there. It's something you create when you do magic."

"Not really. The elemental is inherent to start with in any complex system. But until that system is acted on by symbol manipulation—magic—the elemental is constrained to obey statistical laws. The use of magic can remove these constraints, and thus unleash the elemental."

"Oh," said Ramsey. "So what do you do? Talk with it? What's it good for?"

"You can't really talk with an elemental. It has no true intelligence. At least not as we know it. You can communicate with it somewhat, using a symbolic meta-language. Aside from studying the elemental for research, like I'm doing, there's several things that elemental magic is practical for. For one thing, it's very useful for power control. An elemental has direct, fine control over huge amounts of power. The energy has to be already there; the elemental just gives you the control."

"I see," said Ramsey. "Kind of like a light switch."

"Right. Or a detonator."

Over the next couple of days Ramsey recalibrated all his equipment, changed his instruments, took readings at every time of day, and tried every trick he knew to eliminate any noise in his readings. Finally convinced his data was right, he set out to map the disturbed region in detail.

"Need help?" Susan's voice drifted in from the open door.

"Oh, hi, Susan," Ramsey said. He was perched precariously on top of a stepladder, positioning little probes over a four-meter plastic sphere representing the Earth. "Yeah. Watch the display screen and shout whenever the position marker goes over a hundred. That way I can focus all my attention on the vernier."

"Sure thing."

After a while the readings stopped. "There! Now let's take a look at what we got." Ramsey got down, walked over to the terminal, and called up a plot.

"Hey, best data I've got in a long time. Wanna stay on and be my assistant?"

"Love to," said Susan, " 'long as you work fast. I'm leaving tomorrow morning."

"You're leaving tomorrow? But I thought you weren't leaving until. . . ." He stopped and thought for a moment. Could it be Wednesday already? "Huh! It doesn't seem like so much time has gone by!"

"No, it doesn't," she said in a small voice. She hesitated and started to say something, stopped and looked at him for a moment, then glanced away quickly.

"So what does this new data show, anyway?" she asked.

Ramsey looked it over. "The anomaly has localized and grown somewhat more intense." He walked over to the screen and touched a control. A map of the world superimposed itself on the data. "Just south of Rome."

"What's this?" Susan asked, pointing to a squiggle at the bottom of the screen. "Looks almost like the signature of the Earth elemental."

"There's a quick modulation superimposed on the steady anomaly field." Ramsey touched the screen and a scale appeared on the axis.

"Well, how 'bout that!" she said. "It *is* the characteristic of the Earth elemental. Wonder why you should pick that up? You wouldn't believe the sorts of things we do to get that clean a signal. Some people just have all the luck."

"Luck!" said Ramsey. "What luck? How do I get rid of the damn thing?"

"Well, it's not coming from my lab. I haven't manifested the elemental since the day we had that problem with the water elemental. Why don't you ask Kirschmeyer? I'd bet that either he's running something that's interfering with you or else he knows who is. Can't think what it might be, though.

"Anyway, I've gotta go. I have a ton of stuff I got to take care of by tomorrow, or else. You take care of yourself now, okay?"

Before Ramsey could reply, Susan ran up to him, stood on her tip-toes, put her arms around him, and gave him a quick kiss. Then she turned and ran out of the room. Ramsey stood there startled for a moment, staring at the open door.

"But how do I get this elemental out of my system?" he called after her.

"You have problems, see Hans," came the faint reply.

Giuseppe looked out in amazement at the vineyard behind his house. Grapes as big as a man's fist! Who had ever heard of such a thing? He pulled out the amulet and looked at it dubiously. He had *la paura*, the feeling of something bad about to happen. But what person stops just when things start to go well? He shook his head and once more began to make the now-familiar set of gestures. As he started the chant, he could feel the power begin to draw itself about him.

Away in the distance, a plume of steam ascended from the mountain into the clear blue sky. Just as it had done on afternoons like this for thousands of years.

Late Wednesday night, Ramsey was still trying to pinpoint his problem. About midnight he ran into Susan outside her office. "Susan! You're still here? I thought you left hours ago."

"I should have. Just one more thing to finish off before I leave. You ready for a break? Want to get some coffee?"

"Sure."

Over at the coffee lounge, Ramsey asked about something Susan had mentioned earlier. "The reason the ancients never got their magic technology to work is that they never learned that most spells change with time?"

"Partly. So on the rare occasions somebody wrote down a working spell sequence, in a decade or so it would be useless anyway. The so-called 'magicians' back then were pretty secretive about what they did. They didn't write down very much. Also, even when they learned that a spell sequence had changed, they had no method to figure out what it changed to."

"How's that done now?"

"You can get good approximations by analytic methods. To get a spell exactly, we do an exhaustive computer search. We just have the computer try out every possible variation on the initial approximation until we get the answer."

"You mean computers can do magic?"

"*Mais oui.* Of course. Magic is just a form of mathematics. Anything that can manipulate symbols can do magic." She looked down at her coffee. Cold. She muttered a spell and snapped her fingers. "Want yours warmed up too?"

"Warmed up? It's just barely cooled down enough to drink," he said. "So if they had computers in medieval times, all the would-be witches and sorcerers would have been able to do real magic?"

"Unlikely. They had a lot of other misconceptions too. One or two might have lucked onto a spell that worked, but mostly they didn't go about it in the right way. First, they expected their spells to make sense. They thought the symbols used in thaumaturgy should mean something in English, or at least in Latin or Sanskrit or something.

"Second, a whole lot of what they tried to use magic for back in the Middle Ages simply can't be done by thaumaturgy. Turning lead into gold, coal into diamond; that's easy. We do that routinely. But things like eternal youth, or love potions, those you can't easily do using magic. Biological systems are just too complex. For that sort of stuff you need a biochemist, not a magician."

"You don't say. Know any who can get me some of that elixir of eternal youth?"

" 'Fraid not. I know a few who are working on it."

"Figures. How about a good love potion, then?"

"That can be arranged. But what would you need a love potion for, though?" She looked at him coyly.

He missed her look, or else ignored it. "Oh. . . I'm sure I could find some use for one."

"It turns out that you can't actually make a love potion. Love isn't something you can turn on and off." She sighed. "Unfortunately."

She looked up at him. "But sex, now. . . that's something simple, and relatively well understood."

Ramsey laughed. "Well understood? It darn well ought to be, considering all the time people spend thinking about it."

"Oh, Ramsey, you're impossible," she said. "Won't you let me keep any dignity at all?"

Ramsey laughed. "Sorry," he said. He walked over and cradled her face in his palms. Then he kissed her.

"That's more like it," she said.

2. Susan

When Layr came on shift he immediately felt something was wrong. The violet glow from the transfer pentacle lit the room almost brighter than the fluorescent lights, too bright to look at directly. He looked at the total power indicator. One hundred eighty percent of nominal power. He'd never seen it so high.

Carlo came in a moment later. "Something's wrong, sir," he said immediately.

Layr's opinion of the boy went up measurably. "I know. Do you know the shutdown procedure?"

"Of course."

"Drop her down to standby level."

Layr walked over to a control phone, picked it up, and pressed a button.

"This is power control. We've got a possible malfunction; we're going off-line until we can do some diagnostics. No, I don't know what it is yet or if it's going to be serious. I can't say how long. Better cancel all lift-offs for today. I'll call if it looks like there'll be any danger to the spaceport. So far we're just being cautious. Right. Will do. With any luck, we'll be back on line tomorrow morning. Hold tight. Bye."

The spaceport launch system perfectly exemplified the synthesis of the old technology with the new. Antimatter power source held in check with thaumaturgical wards; computer-generated spells regulating the fire elemental that controls power flow to the bank of positronium lasers that boost the shuttles; the whole complex located at a thaumaturgical nexus to enhance the effectiveness. Simple enough in concept, although rather complicated in the actual working details. What could be going wrong?

He put down the phone and walked over to Carlo. "Well, my friend, it looks like we've got a job to do today."

MUCH later, the sun was just beginning to peep into Ramsey's apartment when Susan slipped out from under Ramsey's arm and began to quietly put on her clothes.

"I'm sorry, my love," she whispered, kissing him lightly on the forehead. "I wish we could have had more time. *Adieu, mon amour, et au reuoir.*"

When Ramsey awoke she was long gone.

THREE hundred miles off the coast of New Zealand, a small group of puzzled geologists tried to determine why the cone of Manatla had recently and unexpectedly gone dead. Manatla was the newest of a chain of tiny volcanic islets on the edge of the Pacific ring of fire; it had sprouted out of the ocean floor in a burst of flame and soot in the summer of 2053.

Its arrival had been predicted well in advance; and it was not expected to stop erupting until well after 2100. The failure of the tiny volcano was an unexpected surprise.

Of course, the geologists were looking for the problem on the wrong side of the world entirely, but that was not at all obvious. Not yet.

*   *   *

Susan arrived in Naples tired, but too excited to sleep. The Venus ship left the next morning from the Napoli spaceport. The NSF had provided a room at the spaceport Hilton for the night. She tried to read, but somehow couldn't concentrate. She found a sliding door that opened onto a tiny balcony and went outside.

Looming out of the cloudy night was the immense bulk of the mountain Vesuvius. The European spaceport had been built practically atop it, she recalled, because the presence of the volcano made the spot a thaumaturgical nexus. This made it easier to control the fire-elemental spells used to boost spacecraft.

The volcano would also make this a dandy place to invoke the Earth elemental, she thought. But dangerous. She remembered how she had told Ramsey about the indiscriminate use of magic. Should she call him? What could she possibly say to him, after last night?

Instead she undressed and went to bed, dreaming inchoate fantasies about earth and fire, volcanoes, spaceships, and pentacles.

She was wakened at ten by a call from the spaceport. Her Venus flight had been postponed a day due to some unspecified problem with the launch system. They were terribly sorry. In the interim, her hotel room and meals would be paid by the spaceline, and if she chose to amuse herself by taking any of the many tours and day-trips offered by the hotel—she thanked them and hung up.

She did not care to amuse herself with tours and excursions, but found she couldn't get back to sleep. She thought about calling Ramsey. Instead she called Kirschmeyer's office. He wasn't in. What time was it back in Chicago, anyway? Oh . . . five A.M. No wonder nobody was there.

She ended up spending the day lounging around the hotel pool, sunbathing and organizing her notes on the Earth elemental, working out some ideas to put into action when she got to Venus.

At five in the evening she got another call from the spaceport. The Venus flight was postponed again . . . she'd half expected it. She went over to the tours desk to look for a tour to the Vesuvius crater. None on Saturday. Since she couldn't see Vesuvius itself, she settled on a tour to see the cities it had buried, Pompeii and Herculaneum.

Without thinking about what she was doing, she punched out Ramsey's number. She held her breath as she waited for an answer. When there was no answer after fifteen rings, she didn't know whether to be relieved or annoyed. Kirschmeyer wasn't in either. She left a message with the prof's computer telling that the flight had been delayed, then went back to the pool and read the brochures on Vesuvius.

Although technically dormant rather than extinct, she read, geologists had determined that the volcano would not be likely to be active for several centuries at the very least. In the meantime, tourists climbed its slopes and marveled at the occasional puffs of steam emitted from crevices in the crater, while below, farmers grew olives and grapes on the fertile lower slopes of the mountain.

She spent the rest of the evening on the balcony, watching the volcano and daydreaming. By daylight, the crown of Vesuvius was covered by an immense plume of steam. As the sun set, this turned a vivid orange. Even in full darkness, the base of the plume remained faintly luminous, as if lit from below by unseen fires.

Professor Kirschmeyer had Ramsey's hardcopy spread across the floor of his office. He knelt over it, studying intently. A trail of colored chalk dust showed which sheets had been examined. Ramsey looked on from a more dignified position, sitting on Kirschmeyer's desk. After a while the professor stood up. He pointed at one of the papers with the stem of his pipe.

"Well, mine friend, here we see a steady base beat of the elemental presence. It flares up to a higher level from time to time, but these occasional flare-ups stopped suddenly, at about the same time my Susie left us. Other than the fact that this very definitely is the signature of the Earth elemental, I can see no connection to my work. I wish Susie was here — she might have some ideas. Me, I'm lost."

"If it's not interference from your work, why did it stop when she left?"

"Coincidence. Something else must have stopped, or started, at about the same time."

"Like what?"

"If I knew that, my boy, most certainly I would tell you, and we'd have the problem solved."

"So what do I do now?"

"Next we all go home and get some sleep and think it all over. In the morning I meet you in your lab, *ja?* and maybe we have some better ideas then."

"Right."

As Ramsey and Kirschmeyer left the office, the 'incoming call' light on the terminal started flashing. Kirschmeyer reached out and flicked the switch over to 'not receiving.'

"Shouldn't you answer that? What if it's important?"

"I rather doubt it. Besides, I have a reputation to keep up. I answer too many of my calls and people might think I have nothing better to do, no? If it's important, let them leave a message with the computer."

In Rome it was almost morning. When the conference on interstellar winds ended, Dr. Williamson had intended to spend the weekend in Rome with Count Raminski, but he had unexpectedly taken ill. Might as well see something of Italy, she thought. It's been ages since I've been here.

She wandered into the Sheraton lobby and gathered a handful of the pamphlets advertising tours and attractions of Roma and vicinity. One with a picture of a flaming volcano on the cover caught her eye. "Pompeii: a City Entombed."

The drive from Rome to Naples was beautiful but hair raising, even in her little sportster, which was both smaller and more maneuverable than most of the vehicles she passed. The Italian drivers more than made up for the difference by the gusto with which they drove, bordering somewhere between hysterical and insane. South of Naples the road to Pompeii snaked along volcanic cliffs at the edge of the brilliant blue sea. Far below she could see sheltered coves and fishing villages, along with occasional empty beaches of brilliant white sand.

Even on the twisting mountain roads the drivers raced with insane verve. All she could do was hope that when one of them finally managed to push her off the narrow road, she could eject before the car started tumbling. It was a long way down.

Somewhere between Naples and Pompeii the skies changed from the oppressive grey clouds of the city into a brilliant sunshine.

"First, make a list, in order of correlation, of all activities or natural phenomena occurring within one hundred kilos of the campus which match the timing of the activity in your data," said Kirschmeyer.

"Right." Ramsey turned to the qwerty, started typing, paused for a second, then typed fast. The viewscreen across from them lit up with a list. Both of them studied it.

"Not much significance, is there?"

"*Nein.* Phone calls to Iceland; purchase of medical textbooks
. . . look hard enough and you'll find seeming correlations in any
large enough set of random events." He looked over at his pipe.
"*Tibura naal*" The pipe lit with a blue spark. He picked it up and
puffed thoughtfully. "Let's try another approach. Your anomaly
centers around Rome?"

"Closer to Naples."

"Okay. Try a correlation to activities there."

"Data bank won't be as complete."

"Can you hook an Italian data bank?"

"I can try." He started typing.

"Got it," he said after a moment. The screen blanked and then
lit up with a shorter list.

"Jackpot! There's our correlation: launches from the Napoli
spaceport."

"*Stimmt.* Right enough. It accounts exactly for the sporadic
signal, even for the stopping thirty hours ago." Kirschmeyer
paused and looked at Ramsey. "Ramsey? Why did the spaceport
stop launching thirty hours ago?"

Ramsey typed the question into the computer. " 'Unscheduled
maintenance', prof. Beats me why."

Professor Kirschmeyer looked up. "Ramsey, my friend, I am
beginning to get frightened."

"Why? Looks like I'm just picking up interference whenever
they launch a shot from Naples. Probably an electromagnetic
pulse that just happens to resonate my detector."

"Ah, my friend, I wish I had as little imagination as you. We
still can't account for why noise shows up as the signature of the
elemental. Do me a favor? Call up a plot of your magnetic anomaly, centered over a map of the spaceport."

Ramsey did so. "Huh! Look at that. It's not even close to
exactly centered on the spaceport." He typed another command.
"Center is . . . 23 kilometers off, bearing 342 degrees. Another map
. . . got it. It's centered on a frigging mountain. Vesuvius."

"As should have been obvious to me as soon as we agreed that
it was indeed the Earth elemental we saw, not some random noise
signal. Ramsey, a signal that strong only could come from an
earthquake or an active volcano."

"Active? Isn't Mount Vesuvius extinct?"

"Dormant, my friend, only dormant. Sleeping. But I don't
think it will stay asleep for long."

"You think it's about to erupt?"

"Yes. Ramsey, this data makes sense only if the Earth elemental has left the center of the Earth and is rising slowly toward Italy, dragging a portion of the Earth's magnetic field with it. Somehow, by someone, it's been summoned. Not merely manifested, like we do here for to study it, but fully awakened and called. Of course, I can't say for certain, but I can't see any other way to interpret this."

"Then we gotta do something. Stop it! Warn people!"

Professor Kirschmeyer put his hand on Ramsey's shoulder. "Hold on a moment, my young friend. Let's get some better data before we start rushing around like fools, eh? Who stirs up a hornet's nest had best be prepared for the stings.

"First, we can connect up your magnetometer to one of my spells invoking the elemental, which will give it a lot better sensitivity for this application. Next, activity on the part of the Earth elemental will be mirrored in the other elementals, particularly ocean and fire. We can set up some kind of monitor on that. Also, it should be possible to triangulate on the Earth elemental using your technique. Then we can find out for sure whether the elemental is actually surfacing."

"How much time do we have? Shouldn't we get a warning out as soon as possible?"

"That's the first thing we need to find out. I'm hoping that we can figure that out when we triangulate. The elemental is rising from the core toward Vesuvius; we need to know how deep it is and how fast it's moving. Until we can give a definite time and estimate how bad the eruption will be, it's worse than useless to try to make anyone heed a warning. If they evacuate prematurely on the basis of a quick guess, people will come back to their homes after a day or so when they see nothing happening. Then when the *real* warning comes, they'll ignore it. We'd do more harm than good."

"So let's get to work!"

"*Doch, doch,* we shall. I just wish . . . I wish we had Susan here. This is really her field, not mine."

"Not your field? Aren't you her advisor?"

"Oh, yes, her advisor I am. But Susie's work is really pioneering. There're very few people who understand the Earth elemental, and I don't doubt that Susie's the best of them. Certainly she has the 'feel' for it. Myself, I can work with it when I need to. My real skill, though, is with the water elementals — ocean, lake, rivers, that sort of thing.

"But our Earth elemental expert is merrily on her way to

Venus, so I guess we'll just have to muddle through the best we can."

"No," said Ramsey. "I don't think she is on her way to Venus. She couldn't be."

"Do you know something I don't know? She left two days ago."

"No she didn't. The spaceport's shut down, remember? No flights."

"That's right. So she must be stuck in Naples. But wait . . . if she didn't leave, I know she would have called me."

"Maybe she did. You don't answer your calls, right?"

"*Stimmt.* Right. She would have left a message with the computer. And I didn't check my office this morning. Let's go. No, you stay here and start programming. I'll go up and see if there's a message from Susie. No, better yet, you go up and see if there's a message, I'll stay here and start working—"

Kirschmeyer turned around. "Ramsey?"

But Ramsey was already gone.

Pompeii was tranquil and peaceful. Susan had expected to see a blasted ruin of rock and volcanic ash, but instead she found a sunny clearing in the midst of fields of olive trees and vineyards. The tour guide went on to take the group past varied excavations and ruins. Susan quietly slipped away from the horde of would-be guides, souvenir sellers, and vendors of 'authentic' relics surrounding the group and found a low stone wall overlooking the site to on sit and contemplate.

Up the dirt road in front of her zipped a sportscar, a sleek late-model Tigershark, gold with black trim stripes and a tinted canopy. As it came by her it abruptly slowed and skewed around in a cloud of dust. The fans revved down and the car settled to the ground. When the canopy popped open, Susan was surprised to recognize Ramsey's advisor, Doctor Williamson.

"Excuse me," said Doctor Williamson. "Don't I know you?"

"Susan Robinette. Yes, I work for Hans Kirschmeyer, down the hall."

"Oh, yes, of course. You're the one Hans always talks about, doing the work with the elemental. How unusual to run into you so far from home! But, of course, you must be on your way to Venus. Right?"

"Right," said Susan. "The flight was delayed; I'm killing time until it gets rescheduled."

"What a nuisance. You know, sometimes I think I've spent half my life in airports, and spaceports, waiting for flights, waiting for people to arrive, waiting for people to pick me up. I'd give up traveling entirely, if it weren't the only way to get from here to there."

"You travel a lot, Doctor Williamson? To conferences and such, I suppose."

"Please, call me Jane. No, I was traveling long before I ever got invited to conferences. My parents were both diplomats, you know. When I grew up, I hardly knew which continent to call home, much less which country."

"That sounds so wonderful," said Susan wistfully. "I never went even a hundred kilos from home until I left for school in Ontario."

"You're from Quebec, I take it?"

Susan pouted. "Is my accent still that obvious? Yes, I'm from Saint Andre. It's well north of Montreal, on Lac St. Jean."

"Ah, yes. Beautiful country, that. Well, I can tell you that growing up in hotels and embassies around the world may sound fabulous, but the reality is quite the opposite, I assure you. For one thing, I never had any friends my own age. Just about the time I just started making friends somewhere, we'd move, or I'd be sent off to live with my father on another continent, or something."

"Your parents were divorced?"

"Oh, no!" Jane laughed. "But they did hardly ever see one another. Except at occasional diplomatic balls and suchlike. I think they really did love each other, in their own way. You had to be very close to them to be able to tell, though."

"That seems so different from my family," Susan said. "I grew up on a farm; my parents hardly ever got out of sight of each other."

"How did you end up doing thaumaturgy?"

"In high school we had a physics teacher who knew a little thaumaturgy as well. He used to do demonstrations in class. I'd stay after school and help him set them up. I guess I was just naturally good at it. I know that as soon as I tried it was what I wanted to do with my life."

"Your parents must have been very pleased."

"My parents were furious. They thought that magic was no fit occupation for a girl; I should learn tractor repair or something practical I could use around the farm. So I could become a good farmer's wife. And if I hadn't won a scholarship to Waterloo that's all I ever would have been.

"You say you never had any friends your own age. Well, you weren't missing much. It's hard not to know people in such a small town, but there isn't anybody worth knowing."

Jane smiled. "You think you had it rough. My parents didn't ordinarily pay very much attention to me, but when I was sixteen, it somehow dawned on my mother that I didn't have any boyfriends. So my parents somehow got together and arranged a big debutante party for me at my uncle's mansion in New Canaan. A big, high society affair; people flying in from all over the world. They had a lot of fun planning it; they discussed it for months. They never bothered to ask me, of course. I was terrified. When the big day finally came, I couldn't do it." She giggled at the memory. "I couldn't face it. So I ran away. Hitchhiked right across the country in my formal. This big coming-out party, people arriving from all over, and the star attraction didn't even show up. It was talked about for just ages."

Jane threw back her head and laughed. After a moment, Susan joined in.

"So what happened when you finally returned home?"

"But I never did. I worked in 'Frisco over the summer, and in the fall I enrolled in Berkeley. I was too frightened to go back, you see. It's all rather funny now, of course."

"Still, it's all made you into a very cosmopolitan woman."

"Yes, I suppose it has," Jane said. She shook her head. "If you think that's worth the price."

"Ramsey is in love with you, you know."

"Ramsey Washington? Yes, I know," Jane said. "He doesn't think I know it, though. How well do you know Ramsey?"

"Pretty well. Not well enough, I guess."

Jane looked hard at Susan. "You're in love with him?"

"Very much."

"Oh. I see." She sighed. "There's very little I can do about his infatuation with me, you know. All I can do is to avoid encouraging him as much as I can without actually being rude to him or hurting him too much. But he'll have to grow out of it himself."

"I know. It just seems so unfair, somehow."

"The world isn't fair, dear. We just have to live with it the way it is."

Jane stood up. "Anyway, we're both here thousands of miles from home, we might as well see a bit of it. Shall we?"

3. Elemental

Layr put his wrench down and looked at Carlo. "We're in deep trouble," he said.

"I know."

Fifty hours after the power control had been put into automatic shutdown mode, the power meters still read a hundred and thirty percent. What was more frightening, though, was that the needles had stopped showing a decrease and were now very slowly inching back up.

"What bothers me most," said Layr, "is not that the control isn't working. It's that I don't have the slightest idea *why*. I can think of only one thing left to try."

"Questioning the fire elemental?"

"Yeah."

"This is a dangerous place to summon fire."

"I know it. Have any other ideas?"

"No."

"Then we'll just have to be very careful. Make a subsidiary pentacle for yourself and be prepared to take over if I'm overpowered."

"Right."

Layr walked over to the main terminal and tapped in a sequence of requests. Two projectors near the ceiling lit up, projecting three unusually complex pentacles onto the floor. Carlo knelt down and began to outline them in paint in case of power failure. Meanwhile Layr called up a review of the spell sequence required and checked it against his own dog-eared manual.

"Sir? Are you planning to have the computer do the invocation, or are you going to do the invocation yourself?"

"Doing it myself."

"Might be better to have the computer do the summons; leave you free to concentrate on contingencies."

"I thought about it. Under the circumstances, I'd rather have the invocation directly under my control. I'd like to be able to switch spells fast if there's any trouble. If I'm harmed, well, that's what you're here for."

"Thanks."

"The antimatter's protected by its own pentacles. I don't anticipate anything threatening it; it should be safe even if the backblast wipes out the whole rest of the spaceport, God forbid. If something does happen to me, though, maintaining the integrity of the confinement pentacle is your number one priority."

"Right."

Layr looked over at Carlo, who had finished outlining the pentacles and was now cleaning the brushes. "Give it another five minutes for the paint to set, then light the candles." He walked over to the control console and picked up the phone.

"Control, this is power. We're ready to summon the fire elemental, at minus five minutes, mark. This should be routine, but I suggest you have your people sheltered just in case." He put down the phone. "Wish I felt as confident as I sound."

Layr positioned himself in the center of one of the smaller pentacles. Carlo lit the five candles circumscribing the large pentacle, then retreated into his own pentacle. Layr looked at his watch, then at Carlo.

"Here goes.

"Diiratah kiimatahi na naratah na diir," he intoned in a smooth cadence. "Kiimatachi, kanahatau'illannaghani. Nehobeth! Na naratah na diir. Diiratah!"

A blue glow formed in the empty pentacle. Layr made a complicated gesture and spoke once more. The glow consolidated into an eerie violet flame.

"Sassilloe fsartha?" said the flame with a soft hiss.

Layr watched the computer screen, not the elemental. "Naal tenepah. Anada. Tnillipa pesardathi!"

"Psillissasi," replied the elemental. "?! Ness, simiss ksissith saar. ?! Simmolayah na."

"?!"

"Ness, simassis ksaar. 'illissis."

"?!"

"Ness, simallahi sis."

Layr turned from the output screen and looked directly at the elemental. He made an abrupt gesture, the reverse of the one he'd made to summon the elemental. "Diir na hataran na ihatamiik hatariid!" He made another gesture.

"Ssimiloth? Prissathi iss." The violet flame grew wider, brighter, reaching to the edges of the pentacle and seeming to push outward, as if testing the walls of an invisible prison. The candles surrounding the pentacle flickered. Layr stood motionless, watching.

"Sissarthi."

The flame vanished with a thunderclap. It took a moment for the eyes of the two watchers to readjust to the room's light.

"I've never seen the manifestation so weak!" Layr said. "There was hardly any power at all. Damn. We should have expected this. We're so well warded against fire that we should have known that it wasn't causing the problem."

"But what is, then?"

"I couldn't get that. Another elemental. What's next most likely?"

"From the amount of power involved," said Carlo slowly, "it's got to be one of the primaries. Ocean, atmosphere, biosphere . . . Earth. It's the Earth elemental. Right?"

"Yeah. That's the way I figure it, too."

"But the Earth elemental is supposed to be the most stable of all."

"Yeah. And the hardest to control. Somehow it must have been awakened. But by whom?"

"I repeat, this is an emergency. It is absolutely essential that she get in touch with me. Make every effort to have her found. Thanks." Kirschmeyer hit the kill button on his console and turned to Ramsey.

"No luck. The tour bus returned from Pompeii half an hour ago, and she wasn't on it. She's not in her hotel; she's not at the spaceport. I'm having the police watch for her. In case she comes back to her hotel room, I left a message for her with the computer there. What else can I do?"

"How long before we get the data to triangulate the elemental?"

"Rosenblum promised to call with the data in," he looked at the screen, "exactly forty-five minutes."

"Then I see only one thing left for us to do," said Ramsey.

"What's that?"

"Get some breakfast."

"Good idea. First we breakfast. *Then* we panic."

"Jane! Stop the car! Quick!"

Doctor Williamson slammed on the dragskids. The car skewed around in a cloud of dust.

"What's wrong?"

"Those farmers. Hold on here a sec, huh? I want to watch what they're doing."

Jane killed the lift fans and looked out across the field to where Susan had pointed. In the distance, two men stood by a tractor, facing the sun and waving their arms in a complicated pattern.

Jane recognized the sight of people casting a spell. What was so unusual about that?

"What—"

"Quiet!" whispered Susan, gesturing with her left hand. "Maybe I can hear what they're saying."

Now that the fans had revved down, Jane could barely hear words coming from across the field. They made no sense to her. She reached across into the glove compartment, got a pair of field glassed from under the seat, and handed them to Susan without comment.

"Huh? Oh, thanks." Susan grabbed the glasses and peered out across the field. "*Merde.* Just what I thought I saw. I'd recognize those gestures a mile away. They're invoking the Earth elemental!"

"So?"

"Jane, that's an *active volcano* over there. The only reason I can think of to invoke the Earth elemental at this particular spot would be if you wanted to commit a particularly spectacular form of suicide! Just what the hell do they think they're doing?"

"Let's ask. Climb back in." Jane shoved the lift fans into high, and the car bobbed into the air. "Hold tight." She twisted the wheel and gunned it. The car shot off the edge of the road, jumped across the roadside ditch, and skittered across the field.

"I don't expect they'd speak English," Susan said doubtfully.

Jane laughed. "So what? Susan, I can't even count how many languages I know. If they don't speak English, I'll translate for you."

"I guess there is one advantage in growing up on five continents after all." The car bounded across another ditch and skidded to a halt beside the surprised farmers.

Layr completed his spell and watched the needle swing over. "Mother of God!"

"What is it?"

"The Earth elemental presence should be barely detectable through all our shields. Instead it's off the scale! That's at least fifty thousand percent amplification!"

"You're summoning it?"

"Hell, no! Do I look stupid? I can get a reading without doing a full invocation. At these insane power levels, even that could be risky. What in hell's name is going on?"

"Sure the meter's working?"

"Yeah. Anyway, it all fits. It explains where our excess power is coming from. We're tapping the Earth elemental via Vesuvius. But how can it be that powerful? It's over seven thousand kilometers away!"

"Could it have moved closer?"

"Seems awful unlikely. It would take half a dozen thaumaturges to coerce it to the surface . . . still, that would explain the readings . . . if the power level is correct, it must be, let me see . . . 300 kilometers away? And getting closer every minute."

"What if it were a lot of untrained magicians instead of a few trained ones?"

"It would take a lot more. Hundreds. And why would they want to do it?"

"Terrorists? Maybe they want to destroy the spaceport?"

"No. Doesn't make sense. Carlo, any terrorists with the capability to summon the Earth elemental to the surface could just as easily make an antimatter bomb . . . Holy God, the antimatter! Carlo, what s the current reading on the antimatter level?"

"213 kilograms, Mr. Layr."

"We're in a lot worse trouble than I thought. If the elemental really is surfacing, the volcano is going to erupt."

"Erupt? You mean like Pompeii?" Carlo turned white. "My God! That would kill fifty thousand people!"

"A lot worse than that, Carlo. That was just an ash cloud; a natural eruption. This would be a forced eruption. These days the vent of Vesuvius is pretty well plugged. It won't just erupt, Carlo. It'll explode. Like Krakatoa. But that's not the worst of it. . . ."

Carlo was silent for a moment. "Oh, gods . . . the antimatter. The wards might not hold. Sitting on top of a volcanic explosion? They're not designed for that kind of stress. They'd overload. We'll be sitting right on top of two hundred kilos of unshielded antimatter . . ."

"Do you know how big an explosion that would make?"

"No. I can't even imagine it. Let's see . . ." Carlo turned to the computer. "Total conversion, 426 kilos . . . $E = mc^2$ . . . Ten thousand megatons. Holy mother, that's a million times bigger than Hiroshima! Why, that's . . . that's a fireball fifty kilometers across!"

"Pretty close," said Layr. "You've got to figure that only about half of the energy will be absorbed, the rest will be radiated directly into space as gammas."

"That's still pretty catastrophic," said Carlo. "Let's see, five PSI overpressure radius, 90 kilometers. Praise the gods, it won't take out Rome, at least."

"Wrong. We're almost on the sea. The blast will raise a tidal wave, I can't begin to calculate how high. It'll splash the Mediterranean dry like a puddle stepped on by a giant. I don't think there'll be much left of Rome after the tidal wave hits it. I don't think there'll be much left of anything south of the Alps."

"What do we do?"

"Neither one of us is qualified to handle this one. We need to find someone with some experience in handling the Earth elemental. And we need to do it fast . . ."

"Still no luck in contacting Susan?"

"No."

"What then?"

"According to your data, the elemental is going to surface at Vesuvius in seven hours. No way to stop that. If someone were right there when it happens, and if they had your data, and if they had enough experience with the elemental, then there would be a chance that they could calm it."

"Yeah?"

"Yeah. Maybe."

"Who has enough experience?"

"Susan. Me. Maybe four, five other people in the world. Nobody we could contact in time. Susan knows it best."

"But she's out of touch."

"Right."

"So it's gotta be us."

"Right."

"Let's hope there's a flight. We don't have any time to spare."

The gold Tigershark sped down the twisted road at almost two hundred klips. Some of the turns were rather wide; hovercars are designed for speed, not for maneuverability. When the road turned too sharply, Jane just cut across the fields, dodging between the olive trees, rather than slowing for the turn.

"I've been pretty dense," Susan said. "It should have been obvious to me from the start . . ."

"What?" replied Jane. "That a bunch of Italian peasants were inadvertently calling up the Earth elemental while trying to improve their crops? Why should that have been obvious?"

"I should have figured that *somebody* was messing with the Earth elemental. That should have been obvious as soon as I saw Ramsey's data."

In front of them the tiny dirt road joined up with the highway. "Which way?" asked Jane.

"Vesuvius," replied Susan. The car shot to the left. "No, wait . . . first the spaceport Hilton!"

Jane slammed the stick to the side, and the car spun around backward without slowing down. Then she hit both the dragskids and the turbos at the same time. The car stopped as if it were suddenly nailed to the ground, then shot off in the opposite direction.

"I've never seen anybody drive like that before!" Susan said. "Where in hell did you pick up that trick?"

"Used to play polo for Berkeley," said Jane. "What were you saying about Ramsey's data?"

"His data showed the signature of the Earth elemental."

"His equipment wasn't calibrated right."

"I think it was. I was just too blind to see what it meant."

"You looked at his data? You really think it was real?"

"Absolutely."

Jane was silent for a moment. "How bad is the situation? You're sure that just getting them to stop using that spell won't be enough?"

"Quite sure. The elemental's been called; it's just taken a long time to respond. But when it gets here, all hell is going to break loose over this part of the world."

"Then it's all my fault. I was working so hard at ignoring Ramsey that I hardly even looked at his data."

"But you didn't know what to look for, and I did."

"That doesn't matter. It was my job to know what he was doing, not yours."

The spaceport Hilton appeared suddenly on the right. Jane cut across a couple of corners and screeched to a halt in front of the door. They both jumped out of the car.

Upstairs, Susan dumped open her suitcase and started to grab out various items of magical paraphernalia.

"You've got a bunch of urgent messages waiting on the room console," Jane called back to her.

"Who from?"

"Four from Hans Kirschmeyer . . . One from Ramsey . . . One from the spaceport ticket office . . . One from Christian Layr . . ."

"Who?"

"Somebody called Christian Layr . . . the message says he's the chief engineer of power control at the spaceport. He wants you to get in touch with him, as soon as possible, urgent."

Susan laughed. "I'll bet it is! Looks like somebody else has figured out what's going on."

"Shall I call him?"

"No time! If anybody else calls, put a message in the computer saying I'm heading for Vesuvius." She grabbed a portable console from the desk and threw it on top of the stack. "Let's get out of here!"

As they reached the car, Jane asked "How likely do you think it is you'll be able to control it?"

"I give it about a fifty-fifty chance," Susan said. "But I've got to at least try."

"Think you can handle the car?"

"Not the way you can."

"But you can drive it?"

"Sure."

"Take it then. If things are as bad as you think, I'd better warn the authorities."

"What can they do?"

"They can start evacuating the area, for one."

"You trust my judgment enough to start a full scale evacuation?"

Jane looked at her for a moment. "You seem pretty certain."

"Oh, yes, I'm pretty damn sure. Okay, go to it. If it's as bad as I think, though, you only have a few hours left. That's not enough time to get everybody out of Italy even if you could convince them to go."

"True," Jane said. "But we're morally obligated to at least give the warning. The rest is up to them."

Kirschmeyer's car was a battered BMW *Landstreicher,* but he drove with every bit as much verve as Doctor Williamson. He drove up onto the walkway in front of the terminal and parked.

"You're just going to leave it here?" Ramsey asked.

"Why not? So they tow it away. We've more important things to worry about, *nein?*"

"Right." They ran into the terminal.

"*Flight 119, Naples and Spaceport Europe, boarding in ten minutes gate 99. Flight 119 to Naples, boarding in ten minutes.*"

"That's us," said Ramsey.

"*Ja.* And just enough time to try once more to get a hold of Susie," Kirschmeyer replied, heading for a public terminal.

A moment later he shouted. "Bingo!"

"You got her?"

"No! I got her computer. She left a message for us. She's figured out what's going on; she's headed for Vesuvius to try to turn it back! Good girl; she's worth the two of us put together."

"What now?"

"We still have to go there. She's out of contact again, but she needs the data and the equipment I've brought if she's going to have much of a chance of stopping it. We don't both need to go. One of us is enough. Are you sure you want to do this?"

"No way I'm staying out of the action, prof."

"It'll be damn dangerous to be there, even with what I brought for her. Damn near impossible without."

"I'm going," Ramsey said. You're going, he thought, how could I do less?

"I can't talk you out of it?"

"No way."

Kirschmeyer clapped him heartily on the shoulder. "Good lad! I thought I could count on you! It warms my heart to know that young men are still brave and foolhardy. My Susie could have picked a lot worse for herself, *ja*. I wish you both the best of luck in dealing with the volcano."

Ramsey suddenly had a sinking feeling in the pit of his stomach. "You mean you're going to stay behind?"

"Only one of us is needed to get the stuff to her. With you there by her side to give her support, what use am I? All I ever knew about elementals I have taught her, and well she learned, and far more besides. She has no need of me. With you, her brave young man, there at her side, if there is any way for her to stop the volcano from blowing you both into little teeny bits, I am sure she will find it. She will have the motivation, no?

"But for me, I have my own work for me. I have another flight to try to catch. To New Zealand."

"New Zealand!" Ramsey said. "You're running clear to the other side of the world?"

"*Ja, ja,* New Zealand it is. And I must run. Give Susie my love, yes? And, absolutely, without failure, be sure to tell her where I went. Tell her she can count on me if she needs me." Kirschmeyer turned and ran.

"Coward!" Ramsey shouted after him.

"No time to explain! Ask Susie!" Kirschmeyer shouted back over his shoulder, then, dodging pedestrians, disappeared into the corridor.

"Flight 119, now boarding at gate 99. Flight 119, Naples and Spaceport Europe, gate 99." Ramsey turned away from watching Kirschmeyer and walked over to board.

The prefect of Naples put down the handset with a scowl.

"Bad?" asked his chief of staff, a rather serious, hard-working young man without whom the governor would not be able to get anything done at all.

"I don't know," said the governor slowly. "If it weren't for the coincidence, I'd probably just dismiss them as crackpots. . . ."

"What?"

"I just got two calls, from two entirely different people, both urging me to evacuate Naples and the entire surrounding country-side."

"But that would be impossible! Why?"

"One of the calls was from a rather well known professor at the University Padua. A colleague at the University Chicago, name of Kirschmeyer, informed him that data they'd collected indicated Mount Vesuvius was about to become active again, probably with a rather large explosion."

"Vesuvius? That's ridiculous."

"Maybe so. He said that he could personally neither confirm or deny the prediction, but what data he could take showed something unusual was happening, or about to happen, on or near Vesuvius."

"He suggested you evacuate?"

"No. He said he was only passing along the information, and that whether to evacuate the area or not was a decision only I could make."

"And the other call?"

"Was from a woman, an American, also a professor at the University Chicago. A Doctor Guenevere Williamson. Rather well known in planetary physics, you may have heard of her. She happens to be visiting Naples. She stated that one of her students had evidence that Vesuvius was about to explode. She suggested in the strongest possible terms that I give the order to evacuate the entire area."

"But such an evacuation would be a major disaster, chief! And keep in mind that one of the things that American university students are famous for is the pulling of pranks. . . ."

"True. It could be just a prank. But if so, one in extremely poor taste. Or it could be simply a mistake."

"You're thinking about Pompeii," Ben stated.

"No. We've lived with the memory of Vesuvius and Pompeii for many centuries. I'm thinking more about another volcano. Peleé, a mountain on the tiny French island of Martinique. It's been one of my nightmares for many years. In 1902, or so, I don't remember exactly, Peleé started to make noise and shoot out sparks. The population of Saint Pierre, at the foot of the mountain, was terrified. But the governor-general, feeling that a panic would be worse than the risk of an eruption, put out the word that nothing was wrong, that the people should go about business as usual. Later it got still worse. Ignoring the governor's orders, people began to flee the city and head for the highlands, far from the smoking mountain. To maintain order, the governor ordered the soldiers to bar the streets and to close the port, to prevent anybody from leaving."

"And?" prompted Ben.

"So the evacuation was halted, and a panic in the city prevented. Order prevailed. Twenty-nine thousand people were in the city when the mountain exploded. When rescue ships finally arrived, three days later, there was only one survivor. Only one in the whole city."

"Oh."

"That was long ago, of course, and on another continent. But, Ben, there are three million people in greater Naples. And I'm responsible for all of them. Until now, I've never regretted going into politics. I've always felt I was needed, that I could do a good job, better than—or at least as good as—anybody else could do. I like to make the city run smoothly, to try and make the lives of my people a little better, a little happier.

"I can't let all that go to waste, Ben. I may make a name for myself as a foolish old man who let a rumor panic three million people. But still, I can't make any other choice.

"We'll make the evacuation as smooth and orderly as humanly possible. But, right or wrong, I'm going to evacuate the city."

4. Volcano

Carlo shut off the terminal and turned to Layr.

"Still no luck in finding someone qualified to work with the Earth elemental, eh?" Layr asked without looking up from his qwerty.

"Not exactly," Carlo replied wearily. "The data bank lists only seven people in the world as being qualified. One of them turns out to be here at the spaceport right now."

"Here? Who? Where at the spaceport?"

"Listed as being at the Spaceport Hilton. A Susan Robinette. I've been trying to contact her for the last half-hour, without success. I just got a message from her computer, though. She's right now on her way to Vesuvius. . . ."

"Vesuvius? Then she's already aware of the problem!"

"Unless it's just a sightseeing trip."

"Have you looked outside? Nobody sane would go sightseeing to Vesuvius today. We'd better hope she stops the eruption. We can't worry about that, we've got to do something about the antimatter."

"If she can stop the volcano, we don't have to worry about the antimatter."

"But maybe she can't. I've been keeping power readings on the elemental; it's powerful, unbelievably powerful. At this stage I'm not sure there even *is* any way to stop it."

"What is there we can do about the antimatter? Can we invert it?"

"I wish it were just that easy."

"Why not? It's a simple spell. About the simplest there is. Reverse antimatter into matter; should be about as simple as turning a left shoe into a right one."

"Oh, it's a simple enough spell, all right. But there's two reasons we can't use it. You've heard of the UN Commission on Peaceful Uses of Thaumaturgy? They've set a ward spell over the entire Earth to prevent matter/antimatter inversion spells from working. Can you imagine what would happen if any backyard thaumaturge decided to make some antimatter just for kicks?"

"Yeah. But couldn't we circumvent that somehow?"

"Yes, we probably could. All they can do is try to slow down amateurs; they can't stop a professional. It would take us some time, but we could do it.

"The second problem is that in order to invert our antimatter, we'd first have to take down our own wards. . . ."

"Oh," said Carlo. "Of course. And to do that would initiate the very disaster we were trying to avoid." Carlo thought for a moment. "What if we were to set up a pentacle around the whole power control? Then invert everything inside: the building, the air, the computers, even ourselves? Turn it all into antimatter. All but the antimatter, which is warded itself, so would stay unchanged. If we ourselves are antimatter, we can release the inner wards without any harm. Then we can do another inversion, and we're safe." Carlo grinned.

"Clever," said Layr. "Just one problem. What happens if the volcano goes off when we're halfway through?"

"Oh," said Carlo thoughtfully. "Then the disaster would be magnified a million fold."

"Right. It would split the Earth open like a clamshell. Yes, it would work, Carlo, but we don't even dare *think* of trying it." He stared off into the distance. "Still, it's basically a good idea. If we survive this, it wouldn't be hard to rig up some sort of automatic spell to invert the antimatter in an emergency. Something like that should have been built in right at the beginning. Damn poor engineering." He looked up at Carlo. "Anyway, we have to live through this first."

"You have an idea?"

"Yes," said Layr grinning. "We're a spaceport, right? Let's act like one. I say we just lob that son of a devil clear into orbit, pentacles and all!"

"Of course. Why not?" Carlo grinned back. "It'll sure make a mess of the spaceport, though. We'll have to keep the pentacles intact; that means orbiting about half of power control with it."

"True. But it'll make even more of a mess if it goes off."

Just as the suborbital entered the atmosphere over Italy, Ramsey heard an announcement. Naples port was closed to all incoming flights. Nobody would be allowed to leave the shuttle. They would pick up as many outgoing passengers as they could and boost out immediately. Naples was being evacuated. Ramsey cursed softly.

On the ground, Ramsey could see through the window that they were serious about the evacuation. Behind a rope barricade, a huge crowd milled about, waiting for a turn to board one of the suborbital transports, any one, just to get away from the city. . . and the volcano. A few policemen armed with electric stunners kept the evacuation from becoming disorderly.

Ramsey got up and walked nonchalantly down the aisle. One of the other passengers looked up at him inquisitively. "Just stretching my legs," he remarked casually. "Looks like we won't even get a chance to step outside." He stopped walking at a panel marked EMERGENCY EXIT. He looked around. Nobody else was paying any particular attention to him.

TWIST KNOB, PULL HANDLE. REMOVE ALL SHARP OBJECTS FROM POCKETS BEFORE SLIDING DOWN CHUTE. Ramsey reached out and twisted and pulled in a single smooth motion. The door popped open and the escape slide inflated with a loud pop. Before any of the startled passengers could react, he scooped up the briefcase Kirschmeyer had given him and dove headfirst down the chute. One of the guards saw him just as he hit the ground. "Hey! *Non autorizzato* — " Ramsey dove into the mob, clutching the case firmly to his stomach, keeping his head down so his height and color wouldn't give him away. The guard started after him, but a second policeman grabbed the first and said something in rapid Italian. The first guard answered back, then shrugged his shoulders.

After all, they were trying to keep the evacuation orderly, not to keep people from coming in. If some crazy American walked into the danger zone voluntarily, what was it to them?

Once outside, Ramsey quickly discovered that he had three major problems. He couldn't speak Italian. Even if he could, no one, but *no one* would be willing to take him anywhere *near* Vesuvius, for any amount of money . . . and he had no money anyway.

Kirschmeyer should have thought of these things before sending me off, he thought. Damn cowardly fool. He could have at least arranged to let somebody to know he was coming.

He walked over toward the entrance. The road leaving the 'port was empty; the one entering was jammed. Thousands of abandoned cars were parked over the sidewalks and overflowing into the plaza. Ramsey grinned. It had been a long time since the old days on the south side . . . but he figured he could still remember how to hot-wire a car.

It was easy enough to find the volcano. A huge plume of black smoke, lit from below with a lurid red light, rose into the evening sky like a giant pillar. As he got closer, hot ash began to fall out of the air.

Ten miles away he was stopped by a roadblock. A policeman stepped out of a hastily-constructed shanty and shouted something in Italian, took a good look at Ramsey, then repeated it in English. "No passage! The road closed. Go back!"

"I've got to get through!" Ramsey shouted back. "Urgent! Important!"

"Road closed!" the policeman repeated. "Dangerous! No passage!"

He could go back until he was out of sight, Ramsey thought, then try cutting across the countryside.

"Ramsey! Ramsey, is that you?"

"Doctor Williamson! What on Earth are you doing here?"

"No time to explain. Where's Hans?"

"Not here. He sent me with some stuff." He held up Professor Kirschmeyer's briefcase.

"Good! Susan said he'd come through for her."

"Susan!" said Ramsey. "Where is she?"

Doctor Williamson pointed at the mountain. From here it was barely visible through the clouds of soot and ash. "There! See that outcropping, just below the lip? Just to the left of that."

"Gods!" said Ramsey. "How can she survive up there?"

"She's warded, naturally."

"Right," said Ramsey. "Can you get them to let me through to her?"

Doctor Williamson turned to the policeman and said something in Italian. The policeman went away for a moment and brought back another man, who she also talked to. He raised the barricade and waved Ramsey through. "Better hurry," she said. "Good luck."

The drive up the volcano was like a drive through hell. Twisted trunks of burned trees loomed out of the clouds of ash like the souls of the damned. Red-hot rocks whizzed out of the sky and smashed to earth all around him. He drove as fast as he dared through the strange murky twilight. A flying rock *zing!*ed off the hood. Close behind it came another, smashing into the windshield. Through the cracks the stench of sulfur suffused into the car.

Ahead he saw an island of relative calm. The eye of the storm? Eyes stinging, he headed for it. As he approached, he saw it was a pentacle. Susan was inside, making an invocation. Near the pentacle Ramsey saw the pitted ruin of an expensive sports car. He put his stolen car next to it, grabbed the briefcase, and dashed through the ash storm to the safety of the pentacle.

"Susan!"

"Ramsey! You made it!" Susan threw herself into his arms and kissed him. "Oh, Ramsey!" She looked around. "But where's Hans? Didn't he come?"

"No."

"No? No? Why not?"

Ramsey was strangely reluctant to tell her that Kirschmeyer had chickened out, headed for the exact opposite side of the globe. "Well, he, uh. . . ."

"What?"

"When I left him he was headed for New Zealand," Ramsey said.

"New Zealand? Why— Oh, I see. So he doesn't think I can do it, huh. Thinks I can't calm it enough to stop the eruption. *Merde!* I wish he were here. I could sure use his touch."

"He said you knew everything he did."

"Balderdash. I'm damn good, but he's still better. Well, I gotta make due with what I got, I guess. So, how long do we have?"

"Huh? Oh! The data!" Ramsey opened the briefcase. Under the pile of magical equipment were two microdiscs. Susan picked them up and plugged them into the portable next to her. She looked at the display.

"Well. Not much time, is there? We'd better get to it!"

At Wellington 'port, Hans Kirschmeyer was trying to rent a vehicle. "Don't you have any hovercars? I have to travel over water."

"Sorry, all we have at the moment are wheelies. Try back in an hour."

"Is there anywhere else I can try? I'm desperate."

"Maybe dockside."

At the dock Kirschmeyer found only one rental place open. The proprietor, a lean blond kid in a sheepskin jacket, leaned against the counter. "WE RENT ANYTHING" said the sign.

"Got any hovercars I can rent?"

"Nope," the proprietor said.

"Aircraft? A seaplane, perhaps?"

"Nope."

"Motorboats?"

"Nope."

"Sailboat?"

"Nope."

"Well, what have you got?" The proprietor nodded down at the water. "Rowboat."

Kirschmeyer looked down. A tiny skiff bobbed up and down in the swell. "I'll take it. How much?"

"You want it? She's yours."

"Thanks." Kirschmeyer threw in his bag, jumped in, and tossed off the mooring line.

" 'Course," continued the proprietor laconically, "she ain't got no oars. . . ."

Kirschmeyer wasn't listening. He balanced in the boat, facing the rear and chanting, waving his hands wildly.

The rental proprietor leaned even farther over the counter to watch. Behind the skiff, a wave rose out of the sea, picked up the boat, and hurled it forward. For a moment it seemed as if Kirschmeyer would fall face first into the water. He finally caught his balance, and continued his chanting. As the boat disappeared over the horizon it was still accelerating.

Susan stood facing the volcano, speaking in a loud, commanding tone, occasionally glancing down at the portable console at her feet and scowling. Once Ramsey started to say something, but she gestured him to stay silent without ever breaking the cadence of her chant. Outside the tiny circle of calm, a nightmare scene of swirling black ash and streaks of orange flame writhed around them.

From out of the writhing ash, a deep, resonant voice seemed to speak unintelligible syllables in response to Susan's chants. Susan abruptly changed her chant, and made a new gesture with both hands. The voice got louder and deeper, almost turning into an inaudible subsonic rumble. Susan hit a key on the computer with a toe.

"Got him," she remarked conversationally.

"*Naach forsitthanna quanne,*" stated the voice in a cold, dispassionate tone. Outside the pentacle, the whirling clouds of ash seemed to form into a shape. Not exactly a face, but an inhuman presence. Ramsey felt as if some giant pair of eyes was behind him, watching him with bored indifference.

"Naal tenepaah," Susan said in the same dispassionate tone. "Suumayeh anada. Tiiratah na! Sooranala na! Tiir!"

"*Doonoro tiir,*" the presence said. "*Na ksissith, doon.*" Outside, flames shot up and swirled around the pentacle.

"Nadillil nabokikok," said Susan, and made a gesture. Deep violet flame shot from her hands and circled the pentacle.

"*Doon,*" said the presence. The violet flame vanished. "*Toorah.*" A sheet of deep orange flame formed around the pentacle and began to constrict. Susan waved one hand casually. The orange flame vanished.

"We're pretty evenly matched," Susan said to Ramsey. "So far I can't drive him back, but neither can he destroy me."

"What then?"

"Niiratah doowl," said Susan. "Kirilak!"

"*Doon, sibborkah,*" replied the low voice dispassionately.

"Sims na nabolith," she said. "Damn. That didn't work either."

Kirschmeyer was right. I don't quite have the control or the power to hold it. Almost, but not quite."

"What now?"

"It's going to erupt somewhere," she said calmly. "I don't have the power to hold that back. Not for long, anyway. But right now I still have a little control over exactly *where* it will erupt."

Suddenly Ramsey got it. "You mean, you can make the eruption happen somewhere else? Where there aren't any people? Like, say, the middle of the Pacific? Or, maybe, New Zealand?"

"Yeah. Something like that. Only I can't make it happen exactly anywhere. What I can do, though, is invert the eruption exactly. Make the eruption happen at precisely the other side of the Earth."

"Which is?"

"I checked it on the computer before we started. About 500 kilometers east, and maybe a hundred north, of the Chatham Islands. In the middle of the ocean. Off of New Zealand."

"Where Professor Kirschmeyer is waiting to handle it."

"So I hope."

She raised both hands over her head, and this time her voice was strong and confident. "SIBBOLAH! DIIRATAH! KAARANATATH TIIR! RAMANAH!"

She made a final, sweeping gesture.

"*Tiir.*" The voice died away into a gentle sigh, almost too low to hear. Outside the pentacle, the ashes swirled up once again, then began to settle. In moments the sky was clear.

Susan slumped down and gave a sigh of relief. "It's over."

Far to the south, there was a sudden flash of light. A tiny speck of fire hurled into the night sky, chased by a bolt of brilliant violet lightning. A moment later they heard the thunderclap. Ramsey jumped.

"What in the hell was that!?"

Susan looked south speculatively. "The spaceport. That must have been the spaceport. They couldn't know we would be able to stop the eruption. I'd say that they just jettisoned their antimatter pile, to protect the city just in case we failed, in case the volcano blew."

"A little late, weren't they?"

Susan looked at her watch. "No. They had another ten seconds left. Ten seconds until it would have blown."

*　　*　　*

Five hundred kilometers from any land, on a tiny rowboat alone in the midst of the south Pacific, Hans Kirschmeyer felt strangely at home. He had no way to draw a pentacle, and no need. The ocean elemental he thought of as his friend, a friend that he knows so well that they had no need for words.

Intellectually, he knew, that was complete nonsense. Elementals are forces of nature; they have friends no more than do the wind and the stars. But who says the wind and stars do not have friends? He looked at his watch and stood up in the boat.

"*Ksirrith, Kisirrith na diir*, my friend," he said. "*Na naratah na diir* for me, old friend. *Diiratha, tegah! Naboleth, tegah! Diiratah!*"

He looked at his watch again. Soon, soon. There was no way to stop the coming eruption. He wasn't even going to try. In mid ocean, he knew, a sudden volcanic eruption would be a much worse disaster than one on land. Instead of blowing away air, the shock wave would raise a great wall of water, a tidal wave, which could roll across a thousand miles of ocean as easily as across a bathtub, and still smash cities like toys. Still, he wasn't worried. He couldn't stop the eruption. But he could make his friend, the ocean elemental, ready for it.

He looked at his watch one final time. "Now," he whispered softly.

In the distance, a massive dome of water lifted into the air, fragmented into a thousand droplets, and started to arc slowly back to earth. From below it a bright plume of fire shot out, reaching into the clear sky, followed slowly by a huge cloud of black ash.

Still there was no sound. He could see two waves, one traveling out from the gash in the ocean floor, the other traveling inward to fill in the place splashed dry by the eruption. When it hit the plume of fire, a cloud of purest white rose into the air, challenging the cloud of black ash for dominion of the sky.

"Magnificent," he whispered softly.

The shock wave hit, and almost bowled the tiny boat over. Hans fought to remain upright. He whispered a word to the elemental he thought of as his friend. The boat righted itself. The tidal wave loomed in front of him, ten, twenty, fifty feet tall. It picked up the boat like a piece of straw.

"Gently, gently, my friend," Hans murmured. "*Nakonah nadoran, nakonah na diir*. Calm, calm." The boat shot along like a board riding the crest of some surfer's fantasy. Hans smiled softly as another idea occurred to him. He would calm the tidal wave, yes . . . everywhere except behind the boat. The proprietor of the rental place had looked surprised to see how he left. Just wait until he saw him return!

On top of the still smoking volcano two twisted lumps of metal lay slowly cooling in the moonlight. Ramsey could no longer even tell which one had once been the sports car. He found a boulder which was cool enough to touch, brushed the volcanic ash off, and sat down. Susan came over and sat next to him.

"I guess I still don't understand why this . . ." he gestured across the devastated mountainside ". . . had to happen. You say it was just a few grape farmers trying to improve their crops?"

"Not a few. I don't know how many. Thousands, I'd guess. Maybe millions. Once one found a spell that worked, he told somebody else. It must have spread exponentially. Individually, none of them mattered. All of them together, well, together they woke up something none of them asked for."

"Just ignorant farmers . . ." said Ramsey.

"Ignorant? Not really. No more than you, or anybody who uses a technology without really understanding it, or its consequences. Only in this case the consequences turned out to be a little worse than just having a little snow dumped on their heads. They just happened to know the wrong spell, at the wrong time, and in the worst possible place."

They sat in silence for a while.

"Well, I suppose somebody will come for us sooner or later," Ramsey said at last. "Probably not for a while, though."

"Well, I don't think I'm in any hurry," said Susan. She smiled and looked across at him. "Are you?"

Ramsey looked back at her. Her hair was a tangled mess. Her dress was ripped and streaked with ash that had somehow managed to leak in past the ward. She was still trembling slightly, either with left-over fear or with exhaustion. She was the most beautiful thing he had ever seen. "I can't think of anybody I'd rather be marooned on top of a volcano with," he said.

Ecopoiesis

"**I** WONDER WHY THEY CALL THIS THE RED PLANET?" I asked. The rebreather made my voice sound funny in my ears. "Looks like the brown planet to me."

"You got a problem with brown, boy?" Tally said. Her voice was muffled by the rebreather she wore as well.

I turned, but Tally wasn't looking at me; she was watching the opposite direction, standing in a half crouch. That position surely couldn't be comfortable, but for her it looked completely easy and natural. Her head turned with a quick birdlike grace to glance now one way, now the other. Guarding our backs, I realized. Against what?

"Nothing wrong with brown, my opinion," she said.

The more my eyes got used to the terrain, the more colors came out. Brown, yes, barren rocky brown plains and brown buttes and a brown stream frothing over a tiny waterfall. The hills were sharp-edged, looking as if they had been blasted out of bedrock the day before, barely touched by erosion. But in the brown were hints of other colors; a sheen of dark, almost purple, echoing the purple-grey of the cloudy sky, and even patches on the rocks where the amber shaded off to almost army green.

"It's beautiful, isn't it," said Leah Hamakawa. She was, as

always, two steps ahead of us. She was down on one knee in the dirt, her nose right up against a rock. She'd taken both her gloves off and was scraping the surface of the rock inquisitively with her thumbnail.

I knelt down and scooped up a handful of rocks and dirt in my gloved hand. Close up, I could see that the brown was an illusion. The rocks themselves were the color of brick, but clinging to them were blotches of purple algae and tiny, dark amber specks of lichen. I pulled off one glove so I could feel the texture. Cold, with a rough grittiness. When I rubbed it between my fingers, the blotches of purple had a slimy feel. I was tempted to try pulling off the rebreather for a moment so I could put it right up to my nose and smell it, but decided that, considering the absence of oxygen in the atmosphere, that would not be wise.

"Beautiful, yeah, right," Tally said. "You got rocks in your head, girl. Stinks. I seen prettier stinking strip mines."

"It used to be red," Leah said. "Long ago. Before the Age of Confusion; before the ecopoiesis." She paused, then added, "I bet it was beautiful then, too."

I looked at the handful of dirt in my palm. Mars. Yes, perhaps it was beautiful. In its way.

My ears and the flesh of my face in the places not covered by the rebreather were getting cold. The temperature was above freezing, but it was still quite chilly. The air in the rebreather was stale, smelling slightly rotten and distinctly sulfurous. That indicated a problem with the rebreather; the micropore filters in the system should have removed any trace of odor from the recycled air. I thought again about taking the rebreather off and seeing what the air smelled like.

"Shit," said Tally. "Anyway, you and Tinkerman about done gawking the scenery? We got a murder to solve. Two murders."

"They've been dead for well over a year," Leah said. "They can wait another day. God, isn't this place *magnificent?*"

"Stinks," said Tally.

The lander was bulbous and squat, painted a pale green, with the name *Albert Alligator* in cursive script next to the airlock door. Leah and I cycled through the airlock together. Langevin, the pilot who had shuttled us down, was waiting for us in the suiting atrium when the inner lock opened. He opened his mouth to say something, and then abruptly shut it, gagged, and turned away, his hand going up to cover his mouth and nose. He scrambled out of the atrium abruptly. I looked at Leah. She shrugged, and reached up to unfasten the strap of the rebreather from behind her head.

"Let me get that," I said, and she turned around and bent her neck. Any excuse to touch her. Behind me, I could hear Tally cycling through the lock. The strap unfastened, and I gently took a finger and ran it along Leah's cheek, breaking the seal of the rebreather to the skin.

Suddenly she broke away from me. "Oh, god!"

"What?"

"Take off your rebreather."

Puzzled, I reached up, snapped the strap free, and pulled it forward over my head. The silicone made a soft "poik!" as the seal popped loose. I took a breath, and gagged on the sudden odor.

The smell was as if I'd been wading through a cesspool in the middle of a very rotten garbage dump. I looked down. My shoes were covered in brown. My hands were brown. One leg, where I'd knelt on the ground, had a brown spot on the knee. Leah was even dirtier.

Shit.

Tally popped through the lock, accompanied by a fresh burst of fecal odor. I held my nose and suppressed my instinct to gag.

"Of course," said Leah. "Anaerobic bacteria." She thought for a second. "We're going to have to find some boots, and maybe overalls. Leave them outside when we come in."

I started to giggle.

"What's so goddamn funny?" Tally said.

"I've decided you're right," I told her. "Mars stinks. Take off your rebreather. You'll see."

The utility landing platform was a hexagonal truss plate with small rocket engines mounted on three of the six corners. The hab-and-lab module that Spacewatch was delivering for our stay was strapped on the top. It hovered in the cloudy sky like a flying waffle iron. Langevin guided it in by remote control, setting it down in the sandy valley a hundred meters from the ruins of the earlier habitat. His landing was as neat and as unconcerned as a man passing a plate of potatoes. Still operating by remote control, he unstowed the power crane, lifted the habitat off of the landing platform and lowered it gently to the ground. The habitat itself was an unpainted aluminum cylinder, fixed with brackets onto a platform with an electromechanical jack at each corner to level it on uneven ground. It was a small dwelling for three people, but would be adequate for our stay.

"Man, I don't envy y'all," he said. He delicately pinched two fingers over his nose. "No surprise nobody comes here." He shook his head. "Anything else y'all need?"

"How about the rover?" Leah asked.

"It's still in transit from the Moon; won't arrive for a few more days. When it gets here, I'll send it right down."

Tally was first one inside the habitat, of course. Even though it had just come down from space, like a cat, she had to sniff it out herself. After five minutes she waved us in.

The interior of the habitat was brand new, the fixtures molded to the interior. Across from the airlock atrium was the air regeneration equipment, with three spherical pressure tanks painted blue to indicate oxygen, and three green-painted tanks of nitrogen to provide make-up gas. To the left was a combined conference room and kitchen area, and behind that the sleeping cubbies.

"Only two cubbies," Tally said, "and a mite cozy ones at that. Guess we girls bunk down in one; give you the other all to yourself, Tinkerman."

I couldn't breathe for a moment. Somehow I managed to sneak a quick glance up. Tally wasn't looking at me. She hadn't yet realized that the silence was extending a bit too long. Leah glanced across at me. Her expression was neutral, curious, perhaps, as to what I would do. I couldn't read her intention. I never could.

In a very small voice, I said, "I volunteer to share a bunk with Leah."

Tally looked up sharply. Leah gazed back at her, her expression unreadable. But she didn't voice an objection.

"Huh," said Tally. I don't think I'd ever seen Tally at a loss for words. "Well. Guess I get a cubby to myself." She paused, and then added, almost to herself, "Lucky me."

Terraformed Mars had an atmosphere half as thick as Earth's. That was enough pressure for a human to survive, but with no oxygen to breathe. With rebreathers to recirculate exhaust carbon dioxide back into breathable oxygen, we could survive outside comfortably without a vacuum suit. For that matter, you could survive outside stark naked, as long as you had your rebreather, and didn't mind the cold.

Outside again, this time with boots and coveralls to keep the worst of the stinking dirt out of our habitat, we walked in silence across the rock-littered landscape the hundred meters to the place that the earlier habitat had been. Ragged edges of aluminum stuck out from the platform like ribs. Pieces of the habitat had been scattered across the plain by the wind, a fantail of shining metal and shards of composite sheeting visible against the brown all the way to the horizon.

There were two bodies, one within the remains of the exploded habitat, one out on the plain. Not much was left of them. The bodies were barely more than piles of dirt with a rib cage and part of a pelvis protruding, even the bones covered with the purple-brown of the Martian microbiota. I was glad for the filtering effect of the rebreather. I made videos of the bodies in position while Leah knelt down to examine them and take samples: clothing, hair, skin, tissue. After she examined the one in the habitat, she rose without speaking and went to the one outside. Unlike the other one, the clothing on this one was partly eaten away by bacteria.

Leah's long black hair blew around her face as she worked, but the carbon-dioxide breeze wasn't strong enough to move the pieces of aluminum framework. The wind must have been much stronger to have spread the wreckage so far.

Tally stood, as always, a dozen paces away, eyes restlessly scanning the horizon for enemies.

"We really should have had a doctor to do this analysis," Leah said, standing up. "But a few things are obvious. For example, the man in the habitat had a fractured skull."

"What?"

"But this one," she nodded down at the body she was standing over, "shows no apparent sign of trauma. No rebreather, either, so I'll hazard a guess that carbon dioxide poisoning was what did for him." Leah put the tissue samples into her sample-pack and took a step toward the habitat. "I'll have to let the computer analyze the samples to verify that, of course." She looked around. "Who could have killed them? Why?" She looked up the plain, following the trail of debris. "I think we've seen enough. Tinkerman, you have enough pictures? Does your checklist have anything else?"

I looked down at the list. "No, as far as forensics is concerned, we're done."

"Then, unless you have any further suggestions, do you think maybe we could get them decently buried?"

When there's a fatal incident in space, of whatever kind, there needs to be an investigation. If it was an accident, the cause has to be found so that Spacewatch Authority can take appropriate measures to prevent its recurrence, and deliver warning to anybody else with similar equipment.

We were that incident investigation team, Leah and I. Tally, a freelance survival specialist, was our protection. If somebody had killed the two researchers, deliberately blown up their habitat for some as-yet-undetermined motive, whoever it was that had killed them might come back.

But nobody cared about Mars. The exciting horizons were light-years away, where relativistic probes lasercast back terabits of images, giving the excitement of vistas that anybody could access on optical disk without the danger and discomfort of leaving Earth, and with far stranger life-forms than any mere microbes. Mars was such an uninteresting location that it took over a year before Spacewatch Authority noticed that a scientific team that had gone there to study microbes hadn't returned. They were the first researchers to bother with an on-site investigation of Mars in over a century.

"It doesn't make sense," I told Leah, back in the habitat. "Why would anybody want to murder two researchers on a stinky planet too close to Earth to even be interesting?"

She shrugged. "Kooks. Bacteria-worshipers. Or, maybe one of 'em had an angry ex."

"It's not as if the planet were exciting," I said. "They tried to terraform it. They failed. End of story, go home."

"Failed? Tinkerman, you have it all wrong. You should go learn a little history before going on a trip." I could hear her switching into lecture mode. "They didn't try to terraform Mars. They *never* tried to terraform Mars. What they did was ecopoiesis, and they succeeded spectacularly, more than anybody had a right to expect."

"Ecopoiesis," I said, "terraforming, same thing."

"Not at all."

The way Leah told it, it was part epic, part farce.

It's hard for us, now, to imagine what it was like in the age of confusion, before the fusion renaissance and the second reformation, but the people of the twenty-first century had a technology of chemical rockets and nuclear reactors that, although primitive, had its own crude power. By the middle of the twenty-first century, Mars had been explored, cataloged, and abandoned. It was too cold to harbor life, even of the most primitive sort; the atmosphere was closer to vacuum than to air, and there were far more accessible resources in the asteroids. Mars was uninteresting. It didn't even make good video. The largest canyon in the solar system—so big that if you stand in the middle, the walls on both sides were out of sight over the horizon. The biggest mountain in the solar system—but the slope so gentle that it meant nothing on any human scale. Ancient fossil bacteria—but not even a hint of anything that hadn't been dead and turned to rock a billion years before trilobites crawled the oceans. A hundred spots on Earth and across the solar system were more spectacular. Once somebody had climbed Olympus (and in the low gravity of Mars it wasn't a hard climb), and had placed flags at both poles of Mars, why go back?

The ecopoiesis of Mars was done by a band of malcontents from one of the very first space settlements, *Freehold Toynbee*. Habitats—they called them "space colonies" back then—were crowded, dangerous, under-supplied, constantly in need of repair, and smelly. They were haven to malcontents, ideologues, fanatics, and visionaries: the vanguard of humanity, the divine agents of the manifest destiny of mankind into the universe. More succinctly, the habitats were home to people who couldn't get along with their fellow humans on Earth. Arguments were their way of life.

It was an engineer named Joseph Smith Kirkpatrick who proposed that *Toynbee* could transform Mars. The people of *Toynbee* debated the question for a year, arguing every conceivable point of view with a riotous enthusiasm. At the beginning, the consensus of the colony seemed to be that since human destiny was in space, even to consider living on planetary surfaces could only be idiocy, or some deviant plot to subvert that destiny. But Kirkpatrick was more than just a maverick engineer with wild dreams, he was a man with a divine mission. A year later, the quibble about living on a planetary surface wasn't even part of the argument. *Toynbee* decided that the right of Mars to remain unchanged was preempted by the imperative of life to spread into new niches. They had convinced themselves that they had not merely a right, but a divine duty to seed life on Mars.

Mars, back then, was completely inhospitable to life. The atmosphere was less than one percent of the Earth's, and the average temperature was far below freezing, even at the equator.

But their analysis showed that the climate of Mars just might be unstable. The surface of Mars showed networks of canyons and run-off channels, dry lakes and the seashores of ancient oceans. There had been water on Mars, once, a billion years or more ago, and plenty of it. All that water was still there, hidden away. The old scientific expeditions had proven that—frozen in the polar ice caps, locked into kilometer-thick hills of permafrost in the highlands. They convinced themselves that there was, in fact, far more water on Mars than previously suspected, frozen into enormous buried glaciers under featureless fields of sand. Enough to form whole oceans—if it could be melted. All that was needed was a trigger.

It's not easy to heat up a planet, even temporarily. They did it by setting off a volcano. There were a number of ancient volcanoes on Mars to choose from; after many geological soundings to determine magma depth, they picked a small one. Or rather, a volcano small by Mars standards, still a monster by the standards of any Earthly mountains. Hecates Tholus; the Witch's Teat. To set it off, they determined, required that they drill five kilometers deep into the crust of Mars.

Just because it was clearly impossible was no reason they wouldn't do it. Mars has no magnetic field, and so the solar wind impacts directly on the planetary exosphere. A thousand miles above Mars, currents of a billion amperes course around the planet, driven by the solar wind-derived ionization. Joseph Smith Kirkpatrick and his team of planetary engineers short-circuited this current with a laser beam, ionizing a discharge channel through the atmosphere, creating the solar system's largest lightning bolt. They discharged the ionosphere of Mars into the side of Hecates, instantly creating a meter-deep pool of molten rock. And then they did it again. And again, as soon as the ionospheric charge had a chance to renew. And again, a new lightning bolt every five minutes, day and night, for ten years.

One million lightning discharges, all on exactly on the same spot. They melted a channel through to the magma chamber below, and a volcano that had been sleeping for almost half a billion years awakened in a cataclysmic explosion. The eruption put carbon dioxide and sulfur dioxide into the atmosphere; more importantly, it shot a hundred billion tons of ash directly into the stratosphere. Over the course of several months, the ash settled down, blackening the surface.

The new, darker surface absorbed sunlight, warming the planet and releasing adsorbed carbon dioxide from the soil. The released carbon dioxide thickened the atmosphere, and the greenhouse effect of the thicker atmosphere warmed the planet yet more. The resulting heat evaporated water from the polar ice caps into the atmosphere. Water in the atmosphere is an effective greenhouse gas, even more effective than carbon dioxide, and so the temperature rose a little more. Finally ice trapped underground for eons melted. A whole hemisphere of Mars was flooded, eventually to form the vast Boreal Ocean, as well as innumerable crater seas and ponds. But that was much later. In the beginning, in Joseph Smith Kirkpatrick's lifetime, only on a band around the equator was water actually liquid all year round. But that was enough for what they wanted to do. Slowly, the eons-frozen permafrost of Mars was melting.

The atmosphere was still thin, and still almost entirely carbon dioxide. But Mars is a sulfur-rich planet. Sulfur dioxide frozen into the soil was also released, and rose into the atmosphere. Ultraviolet light from the sun photolyzed the sulfur dioxide into free radicals, which recombined to form sulfuric acid, which instantly dissolved into the new equatorial oceans . The new acid oceans attacked the ancient rocks of Mars, etching away calcium carbonate and magnesium carbonate, releasing carbon dioxide. In a few years, the acid oceans had been once more neutralized — and the atmosphere was thick, fully half a bar of carbon dioxide, enough for a greenhouse effect, warm enough to keep the new oceans liquid year round.

Mars had been triggered.

But how to keep this new atmosphere, to keep the planet warm? Not even Joseph Smith Kirkpatrick could keep a volcano erupting forever, and already the Witch's Tit was settling down from an untamed explosion of ash to a sedate mound of slowly-oozing lava.

Joseph Smith Kirkpatrick's answer was bacteria. Anaerobic bacteria, to live in the oxygen-free atmosphere of Mars.

"Sewer bacteria," I said.

"You got it, Tinkerman. Anaerobic bacteria — modified sewer organisms. Yeasts, slime-molds, cyanobacteria, methanogens and halophiles as well; but all in all, bacteria closer to gangrene than to higher life."

"No wonder it stinks." I shuddered. "They were crazy."

"Not so. They were, in fact, very clever. They engineered a whole anaerobic ecology. The bacterial ecology darkened the surface, taking over the job of the volcanic ash. It burrowed into the rocks and broke them apart into soil, releasing adsorbed carbon dioxide in the process. The methanogens added methane, a vitally important greenhouse gas, to that atmosphere, and raised the temperature another few degrees. They didn't dare establish too many photosynthetic forms, of course, because if the carbon dioxide in the atmosphere were to be converted into oxygen, the greenhouse effect that kept the planet warm would vanish, and the planet would return to its lifeless, frozen state.

"But terraforming Mars hadn't been their goal in the first place; in fact, terraforming was the very antithesis of what they intended. Their goal was ecopoiesis, the establishment of an ecology. They were Darwinists, and diversity was their creed. They looked down in contempt on unimaginative humans who believed that humans were the pinnacle of creation; they saw humanity as only agents of life, spore-pods by which life could jump from one world to another. They believed that once life, however primitive, could establish a toehold on Mars, it would adapt to its environment, and flourish, and someday evolve. Not to make a copy of Earth, but into something new, something indigenously Martian."

"So they wanted to be gods."

Leah shook her head. "They wanted to be men."

"So they're responsible for this place. Great."

"The ecopoiesis was a wonder in its day, Tinkerman. It spawned debate across the Earth and cis-lunar space: was this the greatest feat of engineering in history, or was it a crime against nature? The year of arguing at *Freehold Toynbee* was nothing compared to the cyclonic fervor that was released when Joseph Smith Kirkpatrick proudly announced to the Earth what they had done.

"Kirkpatrick was kidnapped from *Toynbee* and put on trial in Geneva as an eco-criminal. The question the High Court argued was, Do Rocks Have Rights? Can it be a crime to destroy an ecosystem that contains no life? The trial took three years, and ended in a hung jury. Kirkpatrick was eventually acquitted of all charges, but he was never allowed to leave the Earth again, and died an angry, bitter man.

"*Freehold Toynbee* claimed ownership of Mars, and passed a law making it illegal for any human to land on it for the next billion years—but nobody paid any attention to their claim. For decades, Mars was the subject of intense scientific scrutiny. In a few more years *Toynbee* went bankrupt, for ecopoiesis paid no bills. Technologically obsolete, the colony itself was ripped apart for scrap; the colonists scattering to a hundred colonies and asteroid settlements. And then, after a few decades of fame, Mars was ignored. Bacteria or no bacteria, there were far more abundant resources elsewhere in the solar system."

"And if two researchers hadn't decided to die here, it would still be uninteresting today."

"Not uninteresting, no. Ignored, maybe. But not uninteresting."

"To you."

Leah smiled. "To me."

Langevin took the lander back upstairs, flying the utility platform in formation with him, leaving us alone on the planet. We were in the tiny kitchen area of the habitat, sitting around the only table large enough to serve as a conference area. Leah spoke first. "Tally, did you learn anything?"

"After almost two years," Tally said, "did you really seriously believe any footprints of the perpers would be left preserved? Well, surprise." She grinned. "Yeah, I found some boot prints. Took me some looking, let me tell you, but I found 'em."

"So tell," Leah said. "What did you get?"

"A few places in the lee of the rocks didn't get washed away by rain or blurred by wind." Tally shook her head. "But I checked them all; every damn print matches the size and patterns of one of the boots in the hab. Either whoever did it used the same boots as our late friends, or, more likely, whoever did it didn't leave any boot prints. That's all I've got. You?"

Leah spoke slowly. "The one in the hab died from being hit in the head. The other one died outside. No rebreather in evidence, and he wasn't dressed for outside. Just a thin robe. Carbon dioxide poisoning, as I expected."

"Hmm," said Tally. "Two guys sleeping in the same cubby. Ask me, I'd call it as a lover's quarrel gone violent. The one guy bashes the other in a fit of rage, probably didn't mean to hit quite so hard. Then, realizing what he did, he blows up the habitat and walks outside to die."

"Could be," Leah said. "It's a hypothesis, anyway. Can't prove it one way or another with the evidence we have so far. One odd thing, the man who died outside had charred clothing."

That explained the ragged appearance of the clothing of the man who had been outside. His clothes hadn't been eaten by bacteria; they had been charred.

"Maybe caught alight when he blew the habitat?" Tally suggested.

Leah shook her head. "Carbon dioxide and methane atmosphere. Nothing burns, outside."

"Um," Tally said. "Guess I don't have an explanation for that one."

"Tinkerman?" Leah said. "You get anything?"

I shook my head. "I collected as much of their records as I could find, but so far I can't read them. A lot of their opticals were damaged by fire, and on the ones that weren't, the surfaces are pretty corroded by exposure. I've started cleaning them off, and I may be able to get at some of their records, but, even if I can do it, reading it will be pretty much a bit by bit process. They weren't very conscientious at making backups and putting them in a secure location, I'm afraid."

"Pity. If we could read their diaries, it would help, let us see if anything was going wrong before the blow-up. Oh, well. Do what you can, and we'll get together again tomorrow and check progress."

As we talked, Leah's face had slowly been reddening. Her eyes were pale circles; her nose and lips and chin, where the rebreather had covered them, a pale diamond. The rest of her face slowly turned a brilliant scarlet, deepening even as I watched. She raised a hand and brushed her hair away from her face. "Ouch." She looked puzzled.

Reflexively, I raised a hand to my temple. My own touch was like a whip, a brilliant stab of heat.

Tally looked at the two of us, grinning. "Well, well, aren't you two the sight. Look like you're wearing warpaint. Painted up like two owls, you are."

Tally's dark skin showed nothing, but Leah reached over and gently touched her face.

"Yow! Hey, that hurts! Shit!"

"Ultraviolet," Leah said. "It's the hard ultraviolet. CO-two is too difficult for UV to split; it doesn't form an ozone layer. The climate is cloudy and cold, but the hard UVs still get right down to the surface. I'd say, we've been a bit stupid, going out unprotected. Good thing we weren't out much longer."

"Shit," said Tally. "Why didn't you say something sooner?"

"The hab has to have some kind of a med kit," Leah said. "Maybe we'd better see if it has any sunburn ointment."

At night, in the cubby. I didn't know what to expect.

She wasn't in the bunk. She was sitting in the cubby's one

small chair, staring into space. I got into the bunk, on one side, making a space for her.

She didn't move. Fifteen minutes. Half an hour.

I'd done something wrong. But she hadn't objected! I thought —

Damn.

The silence in the cubby was oppressive.

At last I said, "Leah?"

She said nothing.

"Leah, I'm sorry. I didn't mean to try to — "

In the dark it was hard to tell where her eyes focused, but I could see the slight movement of her head and knew that she was looking at me.

"David." She paused for a moment, and just before I was about to speak again, to apologize to her, she continued, "I've seen bodies before."

It was not what I'd expected her to say. "Bodies?"

"I thought I was used to it." Her voice was tiny in the darkness. "I thought I could handle it. I can handle it."

It was odd. The bodies hadn't bothered me. They had been so far decomposed that they were barely recognizable as having been human at all. And they hadn't seemed to bother her, not in the daytime.

"I've seen too many bodies." And then she came into bed, turning to face away from me. I held her. Her body was rigid, but she turned her face and pressed her head into my side. "Too many, too many." Her breath was warm against my shoulder. "It wasn't even anybody I knew. I'm sorry. I'm sorry. I'm going to stop crying now."

I touched her face. Her eyes were dry, but somewhere inside she seemed to be crying.

"I don't even know why I'm still alive," she said. "Everybody else died."

I didn't know what to say to her, so I stroked her hair and said, "I know, I know."

"Careful how you touch me, you idiot," she said, and her tone was back to normal. "My whole face feels like it's on fire."

I knew so little about her. She never talked about herself; she so deftly managed to always avoid the subject. She had always seemed so much in control. But suddenly she was asleep, and the time for asking questions had passed.

*   *   *

I've heard that some people fall in love at first sight. It took me about three classes.

The first one, I don't think I even noticed her in particular, just another face among the many. I was teaching a class on trouble-shooting. There are two techniques to troubleshooting equipment. The first is, you know the equipment so thoroughly that you have a sense of it, you know it as a friend, and when it's down, you can feel what's wrong by pure instinct. That method is rather hard to teach.

The other way is to be simple, thorough and logical; to home in on the problem by pure mechanical elimination, a matter of dogged and willfully unimaginative technique. That was the technique I was teaching. It means teaching how to be methodical, how to structure a grid to let no combination of symptoms escape detection.

The Institute has simple rules: everybody teaches, everybody learns. Every year, during the Earth's northern-hemisphere summer, the Institute holds a month-long convocation, and this year I was teaching. My class lasted only a week, and it was almost half over before I really noticed Leah.

But, once I'd noticed her, I couldn't get her out of my mind. The breeze rustled across pine needles, and I heard the sound of her voice, asking a question, precise, cogent, perfectly phrased. I'd see the way she cocked her head, listening. I became suddenly self-conscious, worried about how I presented the material, whether it was clear and precise.

So, when I finished, I sat in on her course, although it was somewhat out of my usual feeding range. Soliton-wave solutions of the Einstein field equations. I'm slow; my lips move when I solve field equations in four dimensions. She was a lot faster than the class, so smooth that it was obvious that she knew the material so well she didn't even bother to review it before she started talking.

I knew that once the convocation had ended, I would never see her again. The thought made me desperate, although I'd not spoken more than a half dozen words to her beyond what was required of a student. I knew absolutely nothing of her other than her name, Leah Hamakawa, and the obvious fact that she knew more about general relativity than I would be able to learn in a lifetime. I had to do something that would get her attention.

I invited her to come with me to visit old Los Angeles.

The month after the convocation is traditionally a time for

vacation and independent study, before we went back to our individual lives, hiring out as Institute-bonded technicians or consultants or troubleshooters. I had no idea whether she'd be interested in a trip to OLA; it was a wild shot to try to impress her. But her eyes had suddenly flared with interest, and, for the first time, she looked at me and actually saw me. "Old LA? Interesting. Have you been there?"

I didn't want to admit that I hadn't, so I temporized. "I know a good guide."

OLA was one of the most dangerous, and certainly the oddest, of the ecosystems on the Earth. Back at the end of the second Elizabethan age, the doomed city had been the home of a dozen or more gene-splicing laboratories, corporations that had made synthetic retroviruses to replace flawed DNA with custom-designed synthetic, right inside the chromosome of the target organism. Other cities had such labs, too, of course, and Los Angeles hadn't even been the most prominent of them. Just the unluckiest.

The virus that had gotten free was a generic gene-splicer. It would copy snippets of genes at random out of any host organism it happened to infect. As soon as it vectored to another host, it would make a billion copies of itself, and of its copied DNA, copy the genes back into a likely spot in the genome of the new host, and then start over again from the beginning by grabbing a snippet of DNA from the new host. As a parting gift to the new organism, it would then trigger the cell's own enzyme promoters to express the DNA.

The fact that retroviruses copy DNA from one organism to another is a natural process, of course; just a part of the mechanics of evolution. The rogue virus had the effect of a million years of evolution, set loose in a single day: chaos.

Most of the additions to the genome were meaningless changes, genes which coded neither useful nor harmful proteins. Most of the changes that had effect were dysfunctional, and killed the hosts over the course of a few days or weeks, if they were lucky, or produced an explosion of cancers that killed the host over the course of months, if not so lucky. Over the course of the first year a great die-off occurred.

The things that survived were—strange. The rogue virus had indiscriminately cut and pasted genes with no notion of species; what came out of the mingling were neither humans nor animals nor plants, but weird mixtures: predatory plants, octopuses with hands, tiger-sized raccoons that knew how to use guns, social bacteria that drew recondite, hypnotic patterns across deserted beaches. The thrown-together quarantine barriers held, barely, and the hastily-mobilized scientific effort to combat the virus devised a specific antiviral protein that knocked out the rogue virus's ability to reproduce. The plague was stopped before it spread outside the boundaries of what had been Los Angeles.

Inside the hundred-mile ring, surrounded by scorched sand and silent, instant death, what had once been Los Angeles was still evolving toward a new ecosystem. There was no place more deadly, or more strange. The retrovirus itself was gone, but the creatures it had spawned remained. You could go there, if you signed a waiver indicating that you knew the danger and were aware that there was no guarantee that you would come back.

The guide I had been told about was a mysterious survival specialist and weapons expert named Tally Okumba. Nobody, I was told, knew more about OLA, or about any of the odd, dangerous corners of the Earth, than Tally did; and nobody knew more about staying alive, on Earth or elsewhere.

"Old LA," Leah said. Her eyes were veiled, dreaming. "When do we leave?"

In the light of the dawn, Tally was dancing, high kicks, spins and backflips in the low gravity. Over her rebreather, her face was covered with a bone-white warpaint that, after a moment, I realized was an improvised sun-block. I watched her through the habitat's window, and wondered how long she had been at it. Her flexibility was astonishing.

Leah did not mention what she'd said the night before, and I didn't bring it up.

The task for the day was to gather up shards of the shattered habitat and as much of the wind-scattered contents as we could find. Leah and I worked mostly in silence, occasionally pointing out to each other pieces in the distance. Aerial photos taken as we had landed helped locate the more distant fragments, but didn't substitute for plain, dogged walking.

The job took a lot of walking. The camp was located on the Syrtisian isthmus. This was a broad saddle that separated the Hellenian Sea from Gulf of Isidis, a bay of the Boreal Ocean which covered nearly the entire northern hemisphere of Mars. To the northwest the land sloped gently upward toward the Syrtis caldera, an ancient shield volcano, dead now for well over a billion years. An endless series of lava-etched rilles corrugated the landscape from northwest to southeast, each with a tiny brown stream at the bottom. The wind that scattered the pieces of the habitat had, in accord with Murphy's law, been crosswise to the rilles, meaning that we had to trek up and down innumerable gullies to collect the fragments.

"It must have been some wind," Leah said. "Blowing pretty constantly from the Hellenian Sea toward the Gulf, apparently."

The carbon dioxide atmosphere was still now, with barely a trace of breeze.

By local noon we had made a large collection of pieces. I took a break and sat on a rock by one of the streams. The brook foamed as it rippled over submerged rocks. Amber bubbles clumped together, then detached and floated downstream. The stream looked like an alcoholic's vision of paradise: a river of ice-cold beer, flowing down into a lake of beer, emptying somewhere into a frigid ocean of beer—

"Well, yes—what did you think that the rivers are?" Leah said, when I mentioned the thought to her. She was wearing a make-shift sunbonnet constructed from piloting charts; even with her face hidden by a rebreather and caked with burn ointment, she was stunningly beautiful. I wondered what it would be like to peel off her winter garments, to make love to her right there by the stream. "By any practical definition, it *is* a river of beer. Yeast is an anaerobic microorganism—the stuff that the ecopoiesis team seeded this planet with will ferment just about everything. Naturally carbonated, too: five hundred millibars of carbon-dioxide atmosphere is going to dissolve a hell of a lot of carbonation into the water at this temperature. I'd bet that if you brought a glass of that stuff inside it would develop a pretty good head."

"You mean I could drink this stuff?"

Leah looked at it critically. "Hmmm. You know, you just might be able to. Full of bacteria, I expect, but if our anti-biologicals aren't working, we're already dead anyway, so I doubt it's a problem. Tell you what." She looked up at me. "You try it, and let me know."

I didn't.

By mid-afternoon, we had gathered as much of the debris as we could find. Everything that looked like it might have originally been part of the habitat pressure vessel, Leah set out in a array next to the site of the explosion. Each piece was numbered, and then Leah began fitting them together like a jigsaw puzzle.

"There are some minor pieces missing, but I think we've pretty much got everything important," she said at last.

I walked up behind her and looked at the neatly-indexed array of scrap. "What have you learned?"

She shook her head. "It doesn't tell me a story, yet." She picked up a piece and handed it to me. "Tell me what you think about this one."

It was a curved piece of aluminum, forty-centimeters long, somewhat bent. "Exterior habitat pressure-vessel wall," I said.

"Right so far. What else?"

The piece had broken at a seam at one edge. Shoddy workmanship? Probably not; the other end had ripped jagged right across; the weld had probably never been designed for the stress it must have taken. It was bent in the middle. The jagged end had a scrape of paint on the raw metal. "Blue paint chips on the end here," I said.

"Right," she said. "And the bend?"

It took me a moment, but suddenly I saw it. "Bent the wrong way," I said. "It bowed in. The explosion should have blown it out." I thought for a moment. "Could have been bent by the wind, later."

She nodded, thoughtful. "Possibility. There are other pieces bent the same way, though."

"How much overpressure would it take to bend it that way?"

"Good question," she said. "If we could figure the overpressure as a function of position, we can guess the locus of the blast. Turns out, though, that it doesn't take much blast pressure to make the habitat structure fail this way. The pressure vessel was designed to hold an interior pressure; it's not well designed against an external overpressure."

"So, what do you think?"

"It might have failed in the rarefaction rebound following the overpressure of an explosion," she said. "Microstructural examination might tell. Might not."

"Or the explosion was outside the habitat." That would make sense. If somebody had wanted to kill the team, the easiest way to do it would have been to put a bomb next to the shelter.

Leah shook her head and chose another piece to hand to me another. "Carbon deposits," she said.

I looked at it and nodded. The burn marks were on the concave side, the interior. "Fire after the blast?" I suggested.

She nodded, but slowly. "Could be, I suppose. But after the habitat breach, everything vents to the reducing atmosphere. Fire goes out pretty quick."

*   *   *

"If it was murder," Leah said, "Who might have done it?"

We were sitting back in the little conference room. My whole face itched now, despite the ointments that Tally had devised for sunburn. My face felt like I was still wearing the rebreather.

"Hard to say," Tally said. "I suppose either one of 'em might have had enemies. If it wasn't personal, I've got a few possibilities. First, before they went, turns out they got a couple of anonymous messages saying not to go. The point was, Mars was property of *Freehold Toynbee*, and it was reserved for the Martians, however long it took them to appear. Humans were expressly forbidden to land."

"Toynbee!" Leah said. "They were dissolved more than a century ago. Bankrupt and sold for scrap. Besides, lots of researchers have visited Mars."

Tally nodded, slowly. "A century ago, yes. I doubt anybody been here in the last hundred years, though, except our poor friends. Seems hard to believe anyone would still care. A nut, I'd say. Still, a nut might be what we're looking for."

"And the other possibilities?"

"Turns out that there are still some people," Tally said, "as think that ecopoiesis is usurping the role of God. And some as think that ecopoiesis is, or was, a crime against the ecosystem. And there's been talk that if Mars could be triggered, then other planets, in other solar systems, could be. Some of these have life of their own, incompatible with terrestrial life. So, some radicals, they don't want Mars studied. They're scared that any studying of Mars is a step to triggering planets in other solar systems. There are those as would like to stop that. Stop it early, and stop it at any cost.

"And, finally, there are those as worry about Mars, worry that this ecopoiesis might just be another LA waiting to happen." She shrugged. "Me, I rather like old LA. Got that kind of raw charm you don't see much in other cities nowadays. But I know that not everybody thinks like me."

"I see," said Leah. "And which of these would have set a bomb?"

Tally shrugged. "Any of them. Or all of them, working together."

"Working together? Logically, the Toynbees and the eco-radicals are enemies."

Tally smiled. "Logically, we're not precisely talking rational people here."

"So what do we have?"

"See, are we even sure it was a bomb?" Tally said. "Tinkerman, you find any suspicious pieces of pyrotechnic?"

I shook my head. "Nothing yet. But I don't know much about bombs. I might have missed something."

"Me neither," Tally said. "And I do know about bombs, I do. A bit."

Leah Hamakawa was completely opaque to me. I never had a clue what she was thinking, what she felt or thought about me. Sometimes her gaze would wander over me and stop, and she would look at me, not with a question, not with an invitation, just a look, calm and direct. I wished I knew what she was contemplating. I wished I knew why I was so attracted to her.

The trip to Old LA had been a cusp in our relationship. On the trip we had just been fellows, co-adventurers and nothing more. Afterwards, Leah accepted the fact that I tagged along after her as just a facet of the environment, hardly worth commenting on. We're not, actually, a team, although it must seem like it to others. Leah was the hotshot scientist, and, well, every team needs a tech and a pilot.

Eventually she had noticed.

"Look," Leah had said. "You're as skittery as a colt, you're stammering, I can't get one full grammatical sentence out of you in a cartload, and you're so nervous I'm sure you're going to break something. Do you want to sleep with me? Is that it?"

Her gaze was direct. It was always direct.

I couldn't say anything. I had trouble closing my mouth.

"If you do," she said, "fine, do it, or don't do it, I don't care, just will you quit stumbling around."

And, later, after she'd taken off her clothes, she said, "Just don't think it means something, okay? I couldn't stand that."

But it did. Maybe not to her, but to me.

And so we came to Mars. When the authorities had finally noticed that the missing science team had stopped filing status reports to Spacewatch, and the orbital eye they sent to report got a break in the heavy Martian cloud cover and saw pieces of the habitat spread across ten kilometers of landscape—a "presumed fatal malfunction," as it was reported, Spacewatch had asked for Leah; she had a rep for unraveling tough balls of fur, and I scrambled to rate the slot to go along. Not that this was so hard; I had my skills, piloting and mechanicing and, yes, troubleshooting, and most crews were glad to have me aboard. In this investigation, the third slot on the team was special, in case the accident we were investigating was no accident at all, and the perpetrators might not be finished. The third slot needed a professional paranoid.

We both knew exactly the survival expert who was right for that place.

"Still hanging 'round with that long-legged white girl, I see," Tally had greeted me, when I came to ask if she wanted to join the team. "Give it up, boy, she's too good for you."

"Don't I know it," I'd said.

But that was the past, and brooding over the past wasn't going to get me to bed, or explain Leah Hamakawa to me. She had undressed without the least trace of self-consciousness and gotten into the cubby's tiny bed. I undressed, with a lot more trepidation, and lay down beside her. She turned and watched me with a pellucid gaze, free of any emotion I could interpret. She wouldn't let me understand her, but for whatever reason of her own, she would let me love her.

For the moment, that would have to be enough.

The next day I worked on decoding the data from the damaged opticals, while Leah put together the jigsaw puzzle of the exploded habitat pieces, and Tally ranged in ever-wider loops from the habitat, exploring. I succeeded in getting large blocks of data, but nothing was of any evident value: lengthy descriptions of bacteria, lists of bacteria count per square millimeter in a hundred different habitats.

"Here's something," Leah said. "Take a look at my collection of pieces. What's missing?"

I looked over the junk pile. Skin, electronics, window fragments, plastic shards. "What?"

"Don't you see it? Aluminum, titanium, carbon-composite, plastic—anything missing here?"

Now that she had given the hint, I could see it, too. "Steel. Nothing out of steel, or iron. Is that surprising? Steel's heavy." Hardly anything in a space-going technology is made out of steel. In space, every extra gram is paid for over and over again in fuel.

"There's not a lot of steel on a hab module," Leah said, "but there is some. Look around our hab, not everything is made of the light metals. But, no steel in the pieces here. And, take a look here." She chose a piece out of the pile and handed it to me. It was a damaged recording unit. The capstan flopped loose in the absence of the steel axle it should have rotated on. She handed me another, a piece with a neat hole where a steel grommet should have fit.

"Does that mean anything?"

She shrugged. "Who can tell? Probably not."

"Any steel fixtures hold pressure?"

Leah shook her head. "I checked the plans. No, all the iron and steel parts are incidentals. No steel penetration of the pressure hull."

Tally came back from her scouting, and looked at us both. "You are working too hard," she said. "It's time for a break. Way past time, you ask me. And I know just the thing."

"What do you have in mind?" I asked.

"Here." She handed me a sheet of aluminum. It was about a meter long, slightly curved, one side coated with a carbon composite facing. In a corner "117 Outer" was written in Leah's neat printing. A panel from the outer skin of the exploded habitat. A mounting flange with a hole for bolting interior fixtures was at one end. She handed another one to Leah. "Sure you don't need these panels, now?" she asked Leah.

"Already looked at them." Leah shook her head. "That was the side opposite the explosion. Nothing but junk, now."

After we had suited up for outside and smeared one another's faces white with sunblock, we each took a panel, and Tally led us up to the top of the ridge that rose above the habitat. The hill surface was comprised of sand held in place with a thin veneer of purple-brown algae, slick as powdered Teflon. We had to choose our footing carefully to avoid skidding back down.

It was a gorgeous day. From the ridge, the marscape appeared striped, brown and purple strips in alternation all the way to the horizon. The purple was the algae, covering the sunnier face of each ridge; the brown anaerobic scum colonizing the shadier back face. The characteristic north-south wind pattern was clearly manifest in the form of long streaks trailing behind each of the larger boulders. Today, though, the wind was once again slight, erratic light gusts of no fixed direction.

We reached the top, and Tally smiled. She threaded a lanyard through the bolthole on her aluminum sheet, dropped it on the ground, and put one foot on it. "You might try this sitting down first," she said. Holding the lanyard in one hand like a set of reins, she pushed off down the hill.

At first she didn't move very fast. As the sled gathered speed, each bump sent it increasingly higher. Her balance seemed precarious, but in the one-third normal gravity of Mars, she had plenty of time. As she leaned to control the sled, her movements were a slow-motion ballet. We could hear her shout, muffled by her rebreather, trailing behind her.

"Yahoo!"

I looked at Leah. She looked back at me, then shrugged. She dropped her sled on the ground and pushed it with her toe, testing how well it slid over the scum. Then she sat down on it, grasped the lanyard with both hands and pulled it taut, and looked back over her shoulder. "Give me a push," she said.

It took a little more skill than Tally had let on, but after a few spills, we got the hang of it, and organized scum-sledding races. Tally on one sled and Leah and me together on another, then Leah and Tally together, then finally all three of us on one sled, Leah and I sitting docked together and Tally standing with her knees gripping my chest from behind.

At a rest break, sitting exhausted from climbing, I said to Tally, "So this means that you think there's no danger? I mean, nobody trying to kill us?"

"Never said that." Tally shook her head. "No, I'm not about to be calling all-clear, not quite yet. But I'm pretty sure that there's no danger right exactly this instant. Not unless these killers are invisible and don't leave footprints." She paused. "And, 'sides," she continued, "this is pretty much the tallest ridge in the area. If they were coming for us, we'd see 'em miles away."

"But what if we did? What could we do? We'd be sitting ducks."

Tally grinned a broad grin. "Sitting ducks, you say? Take a peep that ridge over there." She pointed.

I looked. Nothing special, no different than any other ridge. "So?"

I had glanced away for only an instant, but suddenly Tally had an omniblaster in her right hand, a knife in her left, and a projectile rifle with an infrared targeting scope resting at her feet. I had no idea how she could have concealed such armament on her.

"How bout you?" she said. "Don't tell me you're naked?"

I was far from naked—the temperature couldn't have been more than a few degrees above freezing—but I wasn't carrying a weapon.

"Didn't I tell you to always wear a gun?" she said. "Dangerous out here. Who knows who might want to shoot you?"

"Carry an omniblaster? No, I don't think you ever told us that."

"Yes I did. Told you both. Back in OLA." She paused for a second. "Shit. I bet Leah's walking around naked, too." She shook her head. "You two just a bunch of children. I'm surprised you've lived this long, I really am."

"Say, look," said Leah, coming up behind us. "The sun's out."

We both looked up. The sky had been steadily overcast ever since we had landed, but the clouds were breaking up, and between them we had a glimpse of the sun.

"Take a look at that sky!" Tally said. "Isn't that gaudy!" Behind the clouds, the Martian sky was a startling blue, a bright, nearly turquoise shade that I'd never seen on Earth. I couldn't think of a reason offhand why the sky should be a different color, but, naturally, Leah could.

"Methane," she said, after a second of thought. "After carbon dioxide, methane is the main atmospheric component here. Strongly absorbs red light, so the sky color is a deeper blue than just the Rayleigh scattering would predict."

"Oh," I said.

"Explains why the colors here are so muted," Leah said.

With the sunlight, the wind had picked up as well, a steadily rising wind out of the north. Suddenly the coveralls we had on weren't enough to keep us warm. We ran for the habitat.

The overcast had cleared completely the next day. The sky was preternaturally blue, and the wind had become a steady near-gale from the north. Leah and I worked inside. Tally still did her reconnaissance patrol outside, but I think that even she must have spent much of her time huddled in the windscreen of one or another of the boulders. Now we knew what had scattered the pieces of the habitat.

The missing iron, as it turned out, wasn't a mystery at all. Once Leah realized what to look for, she found it easily enough, in the form of grit scattered in with the rest of the habitat pieces.

"It's a sulfur rich planet," she said. "I should have thought of it. In the year and a half of exposure, everything iron or steel got converted to iron sulfide. It looked just like part of the regolith, so I overlooked it the first time."

"In just a year?" I asked. "Isn't that kinda fast?"

Leah shrugged. "Seems fast to me, too, but don't forget the UV. The surface here is more reactive than we're used to."

I worked on deciphering their electronic records. They hadn't kept personal logs, or perhaps if they had, they were on some optical I hadn't found yet. The opticals I had were mostly data, with occasional notes about where or how the samples were collected. By afternoon I had enough to determine when the last data had been recorded, and could at least put a date to the disaster.

"Sometime on August tenth," I told Leah. "Two years ago."

"Really," Leah said. "That's interesting."

"Interesting?" I said. "Not really. But you asked me for a date."

"No, but it is interesting," Leah said. "Today is June 23rd."

"So?"

"That's Earth reckoning, of course. The Mars year is 687 Earth days long—one year, ten months and a few weeks. So, in Mars reckoning, it's nearly the first anniversary of the disaster. Five days from now, in fact."

"Spooky," I said.

"No, I wouldn't call it spooky," she said. "But it is an odd coincidence."

I marked it on the calendar.

I liked working alone with Leah, with Tally outside on patrol. I didn't exactly resent Tally, but I did sometimes envy her effortless camaraderie with Leah. I welcomed the chance to be alone with her, even though, for the most part, we worked in silence.

"Tinkerman," Leah said.

"Yes?"

"Once you start getting the data you've recovered indexed, do a search on weather for me."

I shrugged. "No problem." I looked at her. "You think it's relevant to the investigation?"

She shook her head. "Just curious."

They had, I discovered, not taken detailed observations of the Martian weather. But occasionally there was a mention of conditions outside. Their own experience mirrored ours. About the same time in the Martian year, the overcast had cleared, and a steady wind had arisen out of the north. The day before the disaster, data had been marked with a note that samples from two sites had been missed; the wind had blown away the stakes marking the site locations.

On another optical I found satellite photos of Mars. I looked at these with interest. The weather clearing we'd seen wasn't local to the Syrtisian saddle; the photos showed the northern hemisphere completely obscured by cloud cover, and then a sudden clearing across the entire hemisphere. The view must have been an infrared falsecolor, since the ocean was white and the land areas, in contrast, looked nearly black. I checked the dates on the photos, and converted them in my head into Martian season. The clearing started at just about the end of northern hemisphere spring.

Leah nodded when I showed her what I'd recovered. She'd already radioed up to ask Langevin for orbital photographs, and he'd confirmed that the clearing of the clouds we'd seen was ubiquitous, starting with breaks in the cloud cover at northern mid-latitudes, then slowly spreading south. "Apparently it's a seasonal thing."

Langevin had also mentioned that the rover had arrived, after a long slow transit from the Moon. Did we still want it? Where should he set it down?

Oh, yes, we still wanted it.

"Time for a vacation!" Tally said, when the unpiloted utility lander had dropped the rover off and I had checked out the systems and declared it fully functional. The rover was the same awful shade of yellow-green as the lander had been, a color chosen for maximum contrast against the browns and purples of Mars. It had six webbed wheels mounted on a rocker-bogey suspension that would give it incredible hill-climbing ability; I had little doubt that it would have been able to crawl right over the hab-lab, if an incautious pilot had tested poorly on navigation. I said as much to the team after the brief test drive.

"Are you seriously suggesting that the habitat was crushed by a rover?" Leah said. "No tread marks were found on any of the pieces we found."

"A rover would have left tracks," Tally said. "Even after two years, we'd have see them."

I shook my head. "No," I said. "I was just giving an example of how robust the suspension is."

"I see."

"So," Tally said. "Time for a trip."

"A trip" Leah said. "Why not? Where did you want to go?"

"Why not go to the beach?" Tally said. "Head north. See what a Mars ocean is like."

"Mmmm," Leah said. "Not today. I'll still be busy tomorrow, too, I think. Maybe the next day."

"Copacetic," said Tally. "I wouldn't mind a day to do some long-range recon with the rover, anyway. That is, if Tink says it's checked out okay?"

"All systems in perfect shape," I said. "No reasons for you not to drive around a bit."

A lot of the work Leah asked me to do seemed to have nothing to do with the investigation of the accident. She was conducting her own investigation, I decided, a scientific investigation of the progress of terraforming—no, ecopoiesis—on Mars. She had me decipher all the data I could out of the opticals; data on bacteria counts and atmosphere, and checked it against the measurements she could make herself. "Cripes, I wish I were a biologist," had become her favorite phrase, muttered as she stared into the screen of a microscope, counting bacteria, but she was clearly happy doing the work, and I was happy to assist, to do anything that made Leah happy.

More methane in the atmosphere, she said, at a break. Some ethane, ethylene, even acetylene. And quite a bit more oxygen than expected.

"Oxygen and methane? Isn't that explosive?"

"No, oxy is still way under one percent; all in all, it's still mostly a reducing atmosphere. The hydrocarbons are all greenhouse gases."

"Gaia," I said, suddenly realizing what she was getting at.

"Gaia," she agreed, a soft smile creeping slowly across her face. The bacteria were producing greenhouse gases, warming the planet up. Making it a better abode for life.

I was getting bored with the claustrophobic spaces of the habitat, and the sameness of the landscape, and I was sure that Leah and Tally were as well. We were all looking forward to the jaunt north to the shores of the Boreal Ocean. So I was rather surprised when, as breakfast on the morning designated, Tally shook her head, and said, "It'll be just you two loverbirds. I'm not coming."

I pretended interest in my food. I never could guess how Leah would react. For me, the idea of a trip in the pressurized rover, a thousand-kilometers alone with Leah, was as close to heaven as I was likely to ever find.

"Why?" Leah said.

Tally smiled. "A trap."

Despite assiduous searching, Tally had found no evidence whatsoever of sabotage. Anybody else would have said, that means it was an accident. Tally said: that means that they were clever.

We made a great show of our departure, deliberately packing the rover slowly and openly with all the supplies for three people to take an extended trip. Then all three of us got in. From outside, through the bubble canopy, it would be clear that three people were in the piloting compartment, eagerly watching the terrain. It would be impossible to tell that one of the three was no more than a dummy constructed of spare clothing.

Once abroad, I powered up the rover, and it rose up from its squatting position to its full height above the Martian terrain. I checked all the systems one more time, testing each wheel in turn for forward and reverse power, making skid-marks through the brown grit and tossing muck across the landscape. The bacteria would not care; they would thrive in one spot quite as well as another.

If somebody had bombed the first habitat, and was clever enough and subtle enough to betray no sign of themselves, they must be flushed out of hiding. They might be complacent enough to try the same trick again, if they were thoroughly convinced that nobody was watching. Tally wanted to give them that chance. Tally wanted to watch them set the bomb.

Systems all functional. I had a wild urge to wave goodbye to Tally, but that would never do. We set off with no ceremony.

For hundreds of kilometers we looked at brown rocks, covered with a thin veneer of slime.

The wind got stronger as we drove north toward the ocean. The landscape was monotonous; rocks and rilles and tiny rivers, broken by lakes, each lake in the form of a perfect circle, reflecting the too-blue sky. To our left, the ground sloped gently up toward the ancient volcano whose flanks we were skirting. The actual summit of the volcano was invisible over the horizon. When we crossed the peak of the Syrtis saddle the wind was coming straight at us at well over a hundred kilometers an hour. It was enough to slow the rover's progress considerably, and at places I almost worried that the wind would pick us up and blow us backwards, but the rover's six huge wheels held traction superbly, and kept us moving.

Once across the pass, the wind dropped a bit, but never let up entirely. It was constant, unwavering from the north.

The rover drove itself, if we let it, with infrared laser-stripers searching out obstacles in front of it and a mapping program in its computer brain that continually compared the view against the inertial navigation and the stored satellite maps, to compute an optimal traverse across the rippled terrain. For most of the first day, Leah and I took turns driving, following the computer's suggested path sometimes, diverting to a different route that looked smoother or more interesting when the whim struck. By the afternoon, the novelty of the drive had slackened, and we let the rover pick its own path.

Langevin had left Mars orbit days earlier, but he had left behind him a little areosynchronous communications relay, so we could have stayed in touch with Tally at the habitat if we had desired to. We kept radio silence, though, by agreement: Tally had said that we should assume that any radio communications we made would be heard by the enemy. The relay had enough power to let us send reports directly to Spacewatch. We transmitted our daily report back, essentially just a "yes, we're alive" verification, and in the report we included a recorded snippet of Tally's voice, to maintain Tally's deception to her hypothesized snooping ears.

In the middle of the afternoon, the rover crested a rise and angled off to the west, finding a smoother traverse down the slope to avoid a field of boulders the size of skyscrapers. Leah was in the aft cabin, analyzing data she had brought with her, and I was alone in the cockpit. At first I didn't know what I was seeing, looking north. The horizon was white.

This was the highest ridge between us and the ocean, so, looking north, I ought to be able to see the ocean. Was the ocean covered with ice? I overrode the autopilot and parked the rover for a moment, rummaging for binoculars to get a better view. Leah came up from the cabin.

"The ocean's white," I said.

"Odd." Leah looked at it, pondering. "Not ice; it's nearly northern summer, and the ice melted months ago. Whitecaps, from the wind, maybe. We'll see soon enough, if we keep driving."

I took that as advice, and brought the autopilot back on line. The rover started to roll. Leah reached out an arm to steady herself against a handbar, and kept on standing, looking out the bubble at the horizon.

We didn't reach the Boreal Ocean that evening. The autonavigation on the rover was perfectly capable of continuing its traverse after dark, but we were no more than thirty kilometers from the ocean, and we elected to shut down for the night, so that our arrival at the ocean would be in daylight.

After nine hours of motion, the cabin still seemed to rock with the motion of an imaginary traverse, although I had squatted the rover in the lee of a hundred-meter escarpment.

The workstations of the aft cabin folded away into panels on the walls, and two narrow cots folded out from the bulkhead, transforming the cabin into a small but cozy bedroom. I looked at the cots, and at Leah. The cots were narrow, but looked like they might be wide enough for two, if the two slept close. Leah gave me no hints. I folded the second cot back into its niche, and convinced myself that I saw just the faintest trace of a smile on Leah's face. In any case, she slid over silently, and I nestled myself in next to her.

We reached the ocean a bit before noon of the next day. The final few kilometers was a steep traverse down the bluffs, not quite steep enough to be called cliffs, but steep enough that the rover picked its way slowly, sidling nearly crabwise down the last few hundred meters. There wasn't much of a beach; just rocks. From above, the ocean was white. It moved with something more than just the rhythmic swell of waves. It writhed, and humped, looking almost alive. As we got closer, a fine spray peppered the bubble in erratic spurts. The spray dried to milky white flakes, smearing but not totally obscuring the view.

"Salt?" I said.

Leah shook her head. "Magnesium sulfate, mostly," she said. She spoke louder than normal to be heard over the whistling of the wind and a sudden patter of spray. "The ocean's got tons of it. It's another reason the ocean doesn't freeze solid in the winter; lowers the freezing point a few degrees."

I squatted the rover down behind a boulder, where it would be out of the worst of the spray, and we suited up with rebreathers and sunblock to go outside.

Outside, the constant wind was warm and damp. Between the wind and the spray, I think that it was the most miserable place on Mars. Leah, though, laughed and ran like a little girl, arching her back and spreading her arms, daring Mars to do its worst.

I took off one glove, raised my hand and caught a bit of spray on my fingers, then pulled up my rebreather mask slightly to put it to my tongue. It was slightly bitter. Leah looked back at me over her shoulder, and laughed. "Don't eat too much of it," she shouted.

"Why?" I shouted back. "It's not poisonous."

"You might regret it," she shouted back. "You know what they used magnesium sulfate for in the old days?"

"What?"

"Laxative for infants! You're standing right next to the universe's largest dose of baby laxative!"

With that she turned back, and started to pick her way past the rocks toward the ocean. I scrambled to catch up with her. I could hear the ocean now, but it wasn't the rolling of waves that I heard. It was a stranger sound, hissing and popping and splatting.

In a few moments we reached a final set of rocks, right at the edge of the ocean, and at last we could observe what we had been unable to see from further away.

The ocean was boiling.

From the pools at our feet to the farthest horizon, the entire ocean was aboil, bubbles rising up and breaking, spattering spray everywhere. Enormous bubbles rose burping out of the depths with a thunderous roar followed by a tremendous splatter; smaller bubbles rose with blurps and pops from everywhere; infinitesimally tiny bubbles fizzed and hissed in rocky pools.

A huge bubble burst in front of us, not five meters distant, and I instinctively flinched, anticipating being hit with scalding spray. Leah laughed with delight. She pulled her glove off and, when the slosh came toward her, bent over and dipped her bare hand into the boiling water. Before I could scream at her, she cupped a handful of water and, with a grin so large I could see it even behind her rebreather, she dashed it in my face and giggled.

The water was lukewarm.

When we got back in the rover, our coveralls were so stiff with dried spray that it was difficult to peel them off. Our faces and hands were red from the wind, and itchy with dried ocean. Leah was still in her puckish good mood, and as we peeled down to undergarments, she was laughing.

"You know what?" she said, pulling off her rebreather, and she didn't bother to wait for an answer. "You know the great thing about it? Makes it worth the whole trip?"

"What's that?"

"You don't stink!"

I opened my mouth to say something, and suddenly realized she was right. The stench of Mars that we had gotten so used to every time we came in from the outside, was missing.

"What a great planet," she said.

We both stripped, and gave one another sponge baths. The water recycler would have the devil of a time pulling sulfate out of the water, but that was what machinery was for. I took a lot longer cleaning her off than I had any right to, and with one thing leading to another, it was nearly dark before either of us dressed.

I knew she was waiting for me to ask. At last I did. "Leah? The water was warm, but it wasn't hot. Why was it boiling?"

"That's an easy one. It wasn't."

"But—"

"Carbon dioxide," she said. "I should have known, but it wasn't obvious until I saw it. Mars has mostly carbon dioxide in the atmosphere, so it should have been obvious that the oceans would be saturated with dissolved CO-two. It wasn't boiling—it was *fizzing*."

That made sense, all but one thing. "But, wouldn't it be in equilibrium? Why should it be fizzing?"

"Summer. The ocean is warming up in the summer sun. Carbon dioxide has a solubility in water that strongly decreases when it gets warmer. So, as summer comes to the northern hemisphere, the Boreal Ocean releases carbon dioxide."

"Oh."

And it wasn't until the middle of the night that she suddenly stiffened and sat bolt upright. "Oh," she said, in a tiny voice. I opened my eyes and watched her sleepily. "The wind," she said. "The wind."

She got up, and in a moment there was a glow as her computer came alight. She was beautiful, limned in pale fire by the glow cast by the screen backlighting.

"What is it?" I said.

"Nothing. Go back to sleep."

"It must be something."

"Just—I had a thought, that's all."

"What?"

"I wonder." She bit her lip. "Just how much carbon dioxide, exactly, do you think *is* dissolved in the Boreal Ocean?"

By the time the sky started to brighten with dawn, Leah was distinctly bedraggled, but she had it mostly worked out. The answer was, a lot. A hell of a lot.

Over the long Martian winter, the temperature of the northern ocean dropped to near freezing, and the ocean had served as a sponge for carbon dioxide. A peculiar convection served to stir the ocean as it cooled: as the surface layers cooled and became saturated with carbon dioxide, they got denser, and sank, turning over the ocean until the entire ocean was uniformly cold and saturated with carbon dioxide.

When the spring began, the surface layers of the ocean warmed up, and the dissolved carbon dioxide began to come out of solution. But the warmer water, free of its heavy carbon dioxide, stayed on the surface; the cold, saturated water stayed below. With only two tiny moons, there was little in the way of tides to stir the deeps. The water got warmer, but in the deep water the dissolved carbon dioxide was under pressure. The water warmed a little, but the supersaturated carbon dioxide stayed in solution. But it was an unstable situation, and ever more precarious as the season moved toward summer. Eventually, something must trigger the inevitable. Somewhere, a little of the carbon dioxide came out of solution, at pressure, and formed bubbles. The bubbles stirred the water, expanding as they rose, and the stirring let more carbon dioxide out of solution. The warm surface waters turned over, and supersaturated cold waters from the depths warmed up. Like a chain reaction, the release of supersaturated carbon dioxide was almost explosive, and it took only days for the reaction to spread across the entire width of the Boreal Ocean. A whole winter's worth of atmosphere was coming out of the ocean, and coming out with vigor.

The wind. We had felt the wind from the ocean, a clue blowing right in our faces, and we'd ignored it.

"They weren't murdered, Tinkerman," Leah said. "They were—my god, Tally's still back there, in the habitat. She doesn't know—The radio. We can get her on the radio, warn her."

"Doesn't know what?"

"I'll explain everything when I talk to her. Quick, what day is it?" She grabbed my calendar and looked at it. In neat letters, on the bottom corner of the square marked June 28, I had completely forgotten that I'd written a note: *One Martian year. RIP.*

But Tally didn't answer the radio, not the regular channels, not the emergency channel.

"Damn," I said. "It's Tally and her blasted radio silence. She won't answer."

Leah shook her head violently. "I know Tally better than that. She would listen to the emergency channel no matter what, and she'd answer when she heard us break silence. Tinkerman, I think the wind must have torn away the radio aerial. The hab was designed for space, not for Mars, and the antenna wasn't that strongly mounted. Probably blew over the high-gain antenna as well."

"So?"

"So how fast do you think this thing can go?"

It took longer to get moving than I had expected. The autonavigator wouldn't come on line. Over the night the spray had fogged over the lenses of the laser stripers, and the autopilot wouldn't budge without its obstacle-recognition system working.

As I took the rover up the bluff on manual control, climbing only centimeters at a time over the rough spots, Leah fidgeted with clear agitation, but she stayed silent, knowing that distracting me from piloting would only slow us down. As soon as we had climbed a few hundred meters above the ocean, I put on a rebreather and, using half our supply of clean water, I carefully washed the laser striper and the bubble.

The steel parts of the rover looked matte, almost corroded. When we got back, I would have to take the rover down for inspection and overhaul. In fact, I would have preferred to do a thorough inspection right then, but I knew Leah wouldn't let me stop for that. The rover's autodiagnostic checked out green, so I put the autopilot back on line and punched for speed.

There was nothing more we could do. There was no way that I could out-pilot the autonavigation system over a course it had run before; it had all the bad terrain memorized in detail and had learned exactly which parts to detour around and which were smooth running. The ride was bumpy, but that was only to be expected. I turned to Leah, and waved a hand.

"I'm ready to listen," I said.

"It was all there in front of us," Leah said. "All the clues, if only we'd really seen them. The pieces of the habitat, that should have tipped us off right there. The habitat modules, they weren't originally designed for Mars. We knew that. Nobody ever goes to Mars, so how could there be hab modules designed for it? It's a lunar habitat design.

"The air pressure on Mars is five hundred millibars, just about half that of Earth. So we set the pressure in the hab to five hundred millibars, and forgot about it. With a nearly fifty-fifty mixture of oxygen and nitrogen in the air mixture, the oxygen in the habitat was just what it is at standard conditions, and after a week I bet you didn't even remember that it wasn't Earth standard.

"But there's one critical difference. Lunar habitat modules are designed to withstand pressure from the *inside*. They're plenty strong, against internal pressure. But what about external pressure?"

"It imploded."

"Right. The air pressure on Mars is not a constant! All that gas dissolved in the northern sea—when it comes out of solution, the air pressure rises. It rises a *lot*. The wind, that constant wind from the north—that was our second clue. The habitat was set to maintain a constant pressure of five hundred millibars inside. Nobody ever designed it with the idea that the outside pressure might increase. Somewhere there was a weak joint, maybe a seam that wasn't reinforced against an unexpected pressure from outside. It blew."

"But there was an explosion. We saw the marks."

Leah shook her head. "You saw the piece, the one with the tiny scrape of blue paint on it. What does blue paint mean to you?"

I only had to think for an instant. "Blue. Oxygen."

"Right. The implosion must have punctured an oxygen tank in the habitat. Pure oxygen, under pressure, spurting out into the Mars atmosphere . . . the Martian atmosphere is mostly carbon dioxide, but a good component is methane, and it's got noticeable amounts of other hydrocarbons as well. In a pure oxygen leak, of course it will burn."

"It must have happened at night," I said. "They never knew what hit them. The one man was killed instantly. The other was tossed out of the hole in the side of the habitat, without a re-breather, to die of suffocation."

Leah nodded. "And now the same thing is happening. The atmospheric pressure is rising. Tally's there in the habitat, alone . . . and she's waiting for the wrong enemy."

We were over the peak of the Syrtis saddle and a good way into the long, slow downhill toward the Hellas basin, only a hundred kilometers from the hab, when the wheel fell off. Leah was on the radio, in the unlikely hope that perhaps the synchronous relay was the problem, and now that we were approaching line of sight conditions, direct communication might raise Tally. The wheel came off with a resounding *snap*, and the rover lurched.

The autopilot diagnosed the problem, instantly rebalanced the suspension to keep the weight away from of the missing wheel, and smoothly braked us to a stop, blaring alarms.

The alarms were a little late.

We both went outside to look. It was the right rear wheel that had failed; we found it a few dozen meters further on, where it had rolled up against a rock. The wheel itself was a titanium-alloy mesh, light enough to carry in one hand, for all that it was nearly two meters in diameter. The wheel bearing was steel. Or, it had originally been steel, when it had been there at all. There was little left of it.

"Well," Leah said.

"Well," I said. There was no way to replace a wheel; they weren't supposed to come off. "I think maybe we can rebalance the rover. Shift the loading to the front left side. Five wheels ought to be enough. We might have to go a bit slower."

Leah nodded. "It's a plan."

We piled rocks onto the rover, and strapped them down with bungees, to move the center of gravity forward off of the missing wheel. Then we piled more rocks inside the rover, in the front left pilot's seat. I didn't mention that we would never get the Mars stink out of the rover; it was too late to worry about that, and we barely noticed it by then anyway. The autopilot refused to budge so much as a meter without an overhaul, so I piloted it on manual. This was good for less than a third the speed of the autopilot, but still, even that pace covered ground. Leah went back into the aft cabin to examine the samples she had scraped off of the wheel.

It was only a hundred kilometers. We finished more than fifty of them before the second wheel fell off.

We were going more slowly this time. There was no lurch, and no noise. The rover just slowly careened to the right, and kept on rolling until it slid to a stop on its side.

Leah came out of the hatch after I did. She didn't bother looking at the axle, or at the rover. No need; it was obviously not going anywhere, even if we had a crane to put it back right-side up. The rocks we had piled onto the rover had cracked the bubble when it rolled. "Sulfur-reducing bacteria," she said.

"Say again?"

"Sulfur-reducing bacteria," she said. "Convert iron to iron sulfide. There's energy in free iron; in the presence of free sulfur, enough energy for a bacterium to exploit. The lack of iron at the site; I should have figured that ordinary weathering wasn't enough to account for it."

"Oh," I said.

"Not that it matters now," Leah said. "We don't have time to waste. We've got to get to Tally and warn her." With a matter-of-fact attitude, she hopped up onto a rock and stared across the horizon. "So how far do we have to walk?"

I tried the radio one more time. Come on, Tally. What was she doing, I wondered. Did she even know that the antenna was down, or did she just think we were scrupulous in keeping radio silence? Was she standing at the door of the habitat with a gun? Hiding behind the rocks, waiting for enemies that would never come? If only she would answer; it would only take an instant to tell her about the dangerously low habitat pressure.

Fix the antenna, Tally, I thought, just fix it, and listen to the radio. But she wouldn't. Fixing the antenna would be too obviously a sign that the habitat was still occupied. I threw down the radio.

The inside of the rover was a mess, but we managed to scrounge two spare sets of replacement packs for the rebreathers. I downloaded the bearing to the hab out of the rover's computer, and set the inertial compass. Once we got close, we would be able to use the habitat's come-hither beacon to home in. I grabbed a set of portable radio transceivers and checked that they were working. I couldn't think of anything more to carry. Before we left, Leah snipped two pieces of titanium sheeting away from internal partitions of the rover, and snapped them free.

"Ready," she said.

We ran.

The Mars gravity makes it easy to run, and the unwavering wind was, for a change, on our side. Still, after an hour of running I was winded, and the second hour was more trudging than running. Our cold-suits trapped sweat all too well, and it ran down my back and down my legs, like ants with clammy feet.

Mars narrowed in on us. Ridges, followed by valleys; valleys followed by ridges. Another hour.

"Bear further to the right here," Leah said.

"That's not the most direct route."

"I know."

We were walking pretty slowly by now. Her route followed the contour, instead of cutting downhill, and was a bit easier, even if it was less direct. I was beginning to worry that we wouldn't make it to the habitat by nightfall. It would be impossible to continue after darkness fell—Mars's moons shed almost no useful light—and by the morning, we couldn't even be certain that the habitat would still be there.

In another hour we had reached the edge of a long downhill. There, tiny in the distance was a glint of metal: our goal, the habitat.

It was impossible to tell from the gleam whether it was still in one piece.

Without a word, Leah handed me one of the two sheets of titanium. I looked at the downhill. It was a long, smooth grade, with the usual cover of Martian slime. I grinned, and Leah grinned back at me, her face in the rebreather mask like some painted mechanical demon, and then we both stood on our sleds, grasped the lanyards, and, at the same moment, pushed off.

We would arrive in style.

My sled skidded to a stop in a spray of slime a hundred meters or so from the habitat, and Leah stopped close behind me.

The habitat was apparently empty. But at least it was still apparently in a single piece. I ran toward it, shouting for Tally. I reached the airlock, and was just reaching out for the handle when I felt the gun pushed gently between my shoulder blades.

"Moving *real* slowly, friend, keep your hands in sight, and turn around. Slowly."

Tally was painted the same color as the Martian slime, bits of sand and rock sticking to her randomly. The projectile rifle was in her left hand, aimed steadily at my middle. I could see the crinkling at the edges of her eyes as she smiled behind the rebreather. "Tinkerman. Welcome home."

She lowered the gun, and turned to greet Leah. "Didn't expect you to come back on foot. What brings y'all back so sudden?"

"The air pressure," Leah said. "It's going to—"

"Yeah," Tally said. "I noticed something going on with the air. Could feel it in my bones, like a thunderstorm. Fact, I had to dial up the pressure in the hab three times in four days."

Leah stopped, thunderstruck. "You increased the hab pressure?"

"Why, sure," Tally said.

We just looked at each other.

"What?" Tally asked. "Something wrong with that? I figured that if the hab pressure wasn't increased, there could be trouble."

Leah shook her head. "No, nothing wrong. Nothing at all."

It was our last night on Mars. We had filed a preliminary report with Spacewatch, and in the morning Langevin would bring the lander down to take us home.

I was looking out the tiny window of the hab at the Martian landscape. In the evening twilight the browns had turned to purple. Tiny puddles of water caught the skylight and reflected it back at us. Even the slime looked fragile and ethereal "It is beautiful," I said, "in its way."

"Ask me, it still stinks," Tally said.

"It's dying," Leah said.

"Dying?" I turned away from the window.

Leah nodded slowly. "I've been finishing up the work from the data they had stored to optical before the accident. They got enough data to fully model the ecology. It's dying."

"How?" I asked. "Why?"

"Oxygen," she said. "The oxygen level in the atmosphere is rising, slowly but inexorably. The photosynthetic forms simply outcompete the anaerobes, and the result is that oxygen is gradually accumulating in the atmosphere."

"But that's good," I said. "That's what happened on Earth. The biosphere is evolving."

Leah shook her head. "But Mars isn't Earth. The oxygen is starting to scavenge hydrocarbons out of the atmosphere, and after that it will begin to displace carbon dioxide. Just like on Earth, but for Mars, that will be catastrophic. A few tens of millibars less carbon dioxide, and—" she clapped her hands. "Frozen solid. End of story."

"But the Gaia hypothesis—doesn't the presence of life regulate the temperature?"

She shook her head. "Bacteria are dumb. Gaia is a hypothesis; it's never been a proven theory. In this case, it happens to be a wrong theory."

"You're sure?"

Leah nodded. We were silent for a moment, and then I asked, "How long?"

"Hmmm? Well, couldn't say precisely. Not enough data."

"Give or take."

"I'd give it few thousand years at the outside. Probably less than a thousand." She saw me smiling, and added, shaking her head, "The time may be uncertain, but the fact still is, it *will* happen."

That put a little different spin on it. We would all be dead before the planet returned to bare rock. No need to mourn for Mars, not for quite a while yet.

Later, alone with just Leah in the tiny sleeping cubbyhole, I made love to her slowly and deliberately. She closed her eyes and arched her back as I stroked her, in her own way sensuous as a cat, but still I couldn't tell what sort of feeling she had for me.

When it was over, and we were lying in the dark, I had to ask. "Do you feel anything for me? Anything at all?"

Leah turned over. "Quit asking meaningless questions. I unask your question. Mu."

Much later, after I thought she had fallen asleep, she said

softly, "It looks like I'm stuck with you. I suppose there are worse people I could get stuck with. Don't get in the way."

It was all I could ask for. I will follow her as long as she will allow it, love her, ask nothing in return. Maybe some day I will mean something to her, maybe some day as much as a comfortable pair of slippers or a favorite chair.

In the mean time, though—It was a large universe. There would be places to go, no end of places to follow her to. That was enough.

In the morning, the lander would come, and I would follow her home.

Across the Darkness

*O*UR SHIP *SANTA LUZIA* HAS THE WIDE EYES OF A saint etched onto her foremost fuel tanks, though how the eyes of even a saint could see to guide our path in the absolute darkness between the stars, I could not say. *Santa Luzia,* and we within her, must see ahead only with the eyes of hope. We pass through the darkness at a speed almost unimaginable, five humans in a titanium bubble that seems far too fragile protection against the unending vacuum.

Eleven months out, the fusion drive began to lose efficiency.

I first became aware that there was a problem when Jeanne started acting grumpy and distant. After a day and a night of this, I asked her what was wrong. "It's nothing, Beth," she said. "Nothing at all. The damn drive has been losing power, and I don't know what's causing it, and it's not an important loss yet but if it keeps getting worse at this rate it could get real bad and we might not have enough fuel to slow down at the other end, but I don't know if it will keep getting worse, but I don't know that it won't, either, because I don't know what's causing the damn thing to lose power, and it has me worried, so it's nothing you should worry about, so why don't you go away and leave me alone?"

"You don't have to snap at me," I said, but I went away.

On a starship with five crew members and only a hundred cubic meters of living space, it's not possible to go away very far. I did my best to stay out of Jeanne's way. In this case, that meant hiding out in our sleeping niche. The space, usually cramped, seemed large and empty without her lanky body next to mine. But Jeanne was our fusion engineer, and if there was a problem, I wanted her to have the best conditions possible to solve it. That night she stayed up working on the ship's computer, and didn't come to our sleeping niche until very late. I opened my eyes, and in the dim red-tinted light that symbolized the ship's night I watched her wriggle out of her shift, stretch, and toss it over a hook. If she had wanted me, she would have spoken, but she said nothing, just settled slowly into the bed in a smooth, controlled collapse, and lay without touching me, close enough that I could feel her heat.

Jeanne had dark brown hair, cropped short, as we all wore it. Her deep brown eyes were always focused far away, even when she was talking to you, even when we were making love. Her body was spare, and she moved with a lean economy of movement. Sometimes when she slept I would compare my squat, stocky body to her lean perfection. She was everything I was not; she completed me, and I completed her.

The whir of the air circulation and Jeanne's regular breathing was a lullaby that gentled me into sleep. In the morning I asked her again about the drive.

"Beth, I still don't know, so don't bother me. The degradation in performance is still under one percent, but it's definitely getting worse, but only slowly, so we don't have anything to worry about except I'm worried because I don't know what's going on and I don't like it, and nobody has ever run a fusion drive this long at such high acceleration so we don't really know a damned thing about what might be happening, and I'm worried, and I think maybe we should shut the drive down and check it out, but that might be just me worrying too much, and I don't know what to do, and I'm going to shut down the drive to see what's going on just as soon as we empty the tertiary drop tank." She took a long breath. "Are you satisfied?"

That evening we shut down the drive.

A hundred years ago, the fusion-powered prospectors of the Federação Católica do Sul sifted the gravel of the asteroid belt and brought back riches, making Brazil the center of an industrial empire that dominated half the globe. At the height of the Brazilian expansion, they sent tiny fusion starprobes out into the long dark, knowing that they would not receive the results in their lifetimes, trusting that when the results came back, someone would have starships ready to use them. Their faith in the future was naive, unwavering, and completely Brazilian. They had the dream.

The empire of the Católica do Sul faded without actually falling, marking the globe with the rhythm and the complex shade of the Brazilian spirit even as it ebbed. Their attentions turned back inward, but their dream lived on. After years the results came in, and dozens of telescopes across the planet listened eagerly for the faint flickering of the lasercast reports. In a few hours of flyby after decades of emptiness, the Brasileiro probes told stories of frozen balls of methane, of empty deserts baking under nitrogen skies, of ringed gas-giants and colossal granite mountains on desolate, airless worlds. Of nearly a hundred probes sent to the stars close enough to reach, only one found a planet hospitable to any form of life. The star was Delta Pavonis, the eye of the peacock. It was twenty light years away.

A fusion-engine rocket can traverse the solar system in months. The stars were a thousand times further away, but in that year when the probes sent back their spectacular pictures, the stars had seemed barely out of reach, so close that they could be grasped with only a little more effort. Billions had seen the photographs of a cloud-streaked blue-and-amber world that the Pavonis flyby probe had lasercast as it sped past on its voyage across the endless night; where a probe could go, how could humans fail to follow? That fusion power put the stars almost in our grasp was a lie so plausible that entire nations were convinced.

A collaboration of a dozen nations built the ship. It was the largest single object ever built by humankind, larger than any pyramids or dams, more expensive than wars. Governments fell, and rose, as politicians debated intangible benefits against very real costs. Getting it built had been my father's career, and his obsession. The fuel supply for the fusion reactor alone, ten cubic kilometers of helium-deuterium mixture frozen into balloon-like disposable tanks, would have been beyond the resources of most governments. The resources of the entire world were driven to the edge of bankruptcy to build it; the surface of the moon raked in an attempt to distill rare helium isotope from tons of dust. They had promised the nations that built it that there would be three ships, each with a crew of a hundred. Even with the best Brasileiro engineers in the world working on the design, that proved impossible. In the end they constructed a single ship, designed to carry the minimum crew needed to successfully start a colony. The mission engineers scrambled to design a new mission plan to assure the genetic diversity necessary for survival.

The starship we'd imagined had been spacious and gleaming with polished metal. The one we had, after less than a year of habitation, was dingy, stinky, and cramped. We'd imagined an unparalleled view of the stars. We flew in a windowless crew compartment surrounded by balloon-tanks of HeD fuel. The crew we'd imagined had been efficient, unshakable, superhuman. The people I flew with had trouble with pimples, got irritable a whole lot more than just once a month, and were a little too quick with sarcasm and witty put-downs. We were merely human.

The mission planners had been great visionaries and superb engineers but, as we learned, not as good psychologists. They had chosen a minimum crew of five. This number was debated vigorously, with talk about required skills and degree of redundancy, and heated arguments about level of maturity versus age at destination. The crew structure was unusual in that the ship had no captain. All the crewmembers were professional; all given the same rank, and all had an equal voice in running the ship. We'd been given exhaustive training in how to resolve problems by workshopping and reaching a consensus, but the mission designers demanded an odd number to be sure the crew wouldn't ever deadlock. The engineer assigned to psych issues had concurred; a team of four might splinter into two antagonistic groups of two.

Instead we split into two groups of two, with one left over. The engineers had been naive about one critical factor: sex.

Relativistic time dilation at ninety percent of the speed of light would shorten our travel time a bit, but not by enough. Even with relativity — and if the drive could be cajoled into working properly — it would take us over twelve years to get to Pavonis. After less than a year in cramped quarters, we were barely getting along. I wondered how we would be able to make it.

We were five girls just become women, who had been chosen to leave the world forever. We had not yet truly become a team, for all that we had been training together since the day we had been selected from the thousands of applicants, and, at fifteen, decided to give our lives to a one-way voyage for the sake of a dream we could barely articulate.

We had jettisoned the two high-thrust primary stage boosters three months back, and the single fusion sustainer engine must serve us for the rest of the voyage. Our acceleration had dropped from half a gee to a tenth of a gee when the boosters dropped away, but as we used and discarded fuel tanks, the acceleration slowly crept back toward a half gee again.

Losing the engine would be disastrous.

In principle, making extensive use of the exhaustive documentation in the computer archives, any of us should have been able to take apart the fusion drive. We'd all done it, alone and in teams, in training. In practice, we all had specialties. Rosa and Jeanne were the two crewmembers with primary training as drive engineers. Consuela and Katerina and I could only watch.

I disliked Rosa for my own reasons. Her father had been the last and the most devious of political opponents of the project, and I'd heard the story that the price of his support for the project had been that one of his daughters be put on the crew list. My disdain of her was only compounded by the fact that she was big, bony and awkward. She was bright and competent enough—she had to be, political influence or no—but icily aloof of any hint of sexual expression.

And, besides, she had acne.

Every day that the drive was off added about half a day to our travel time. Neutron activation from stray D-D reactions made the drive chamber too radioactive for humans to enter. With Rosa helping—iron maiden Rosa, engineer, and reserve pilot—Jeanne disassembled the drive using tiny remote-control inspection robots. It was a long, painstaking job, and even after the reaction chamber had been disassembled, it took the two of them about six hours to figure out what had been happening. Stray fusion plasma had been slowly sputtering metal off the walls of the reaction chamber. Most of the sputtered debris got exhausted with the fusion flame, but a tiny bit had been redepositing elsewhere in the drive chamber. Some of it was getting in the way of the laser collimation. If left alone, it would continue to get worse, until the drive eventually failed.

With thrust cut off, zero-gee was a novelty to us. For all that we'd been in space for eleven months, we'd been under the effective gravity of continuous thrust. In zero gee, with the continuous rumble of the pulsed fusion engines absent, and with a real problem to focus our attention away from each other, the spirit was like Carnival—at least, for the three of us not involved in designing a fix. I got along well enough with Consuela and Katerina, when they weren't wrapped up in each other. While Jeanne and Rosa worked, we stripped naked and played gymnastics in zero gee, trying to see who could do the most flips before drifting into a wall, holding a race to see who could propel herself across the width of the common module by the reaction force of blowing air, and giggling enough to almost make up for the adolescence we'd never had. We were having a great time, at least until Rosa poked her head back and shouted at us to cut the racket; they were trying to work.

For Jeanne and Rosa, it was no Carnival.

In the evenings, I rubbed the tension out of Jeanne's muscles while she talked nonstop. Eventually she would wind down, her energy spent, and we would just float in silence, our bodies barely touching.

The first day after the drive shut down, Jeanne and Rosa were optimistic about fixing it. In a few days they managed to modify the computer model of the thrust chamber to simulate the problem, and soon after that they designed a makeshift barrier that, along with a reconfiguration of the magnetic field, would work to keep the sputtered material away from the collimators. They gathered us all together to critique it, but none of could find any fatal flaws in the design. The next day they started cleaning away the deposits with the remotes.

Then one of the two remotes failed.

Rosa was on duty when the robot failed. She used the other robot remote to bring the first one in, and they both checked it out. It had failed because of cumulative radiation damage to the CPU. The chips were big bipolar jobs, and well shielded, but the drive chamber was so hot that it eventually fried the robot nonetheless. They replaced the part, and we all started to worry. There was only one set of replacement parts, and after cleaning the drive, they still had to realign the lasers.

The repaired robot failed the next day. They managed to finish the cleaning with the other, but the hardest job was still to come. The lasers could only be aligned with the drive on. Not at full power, but there had to be a plasma.

The remaining remote failed on the first day of realignment.

They shut the drive down. Jeanne pulled Rosa into a sleeping niche, and they conferred in low whispers for a moment. Then they came out, and Jeanne suited up and went EVA to retrieve it. She was only in the hot zone for two minutes, not long enough to pick up a heavy dose. "It doesn't matter much," she said, trying to smile. "The children I have won't be mine, anyway. You know that." I wanted to tell her that it wasn't the babies that mattered, that all I cared about was her. But I knew that she had problems enough already. I remained silent.

Jeanne and Rosa cannibalized one robot to fix the other. After only two hours of service, the fixed one lost control and floated into the plasma core. The lasers vaporized the robot, spraying metal vapor over the laser optics and across the drive chamber. All the work they had done was erased. The drive was now completely non-functional. We were traveling at three-quarters of the speed of light. With the drive broken, we had no way to slow down.

Jeanne did not cry, not even a little; her iron self-control would not let her. But, when she told me what she would have to do, I spent all that night crying on her shoulder and trying to convince her to find another plan.

"It's not fair," I told her. "Don't do it. We don't need to stop. We can stay like this, forever traveling."

Jeanne hugged me. "No, love. I wish we could."

"But why not? We've got all we need here. Forget the plan. Let other people colonize Pavonis."

"There will be no others," she said. "Even before we left, the coalition was ripping itself apart, you know that. The ship was too expensive." Jeanne smiled wistfully. "And, even if we wanted to, without the fusion engine, we will run out of power to keep the life support up. You know that, too."

I did know that, though I had tried to forget it. "But we don't need full power. Can't we get it running just enough to stay alive?"

Jeanne shook her head. "Let's sleep. Time enough to make plans in the morning."

But I slept very little, staring blankly into the darkness.

The next day Jeanne was calm and completely professional when she called together the crew to discuss our options. The five of us workshopped the problem all that day, and kept arguing well into the ship's night, but we could find no solution other than the one Jeanne had told me the night before. In the end, we let her do what she had already decided had to be done.

That night, for the first time since we met, Jeanne let her self-control slide away. She told me about her life. I had known her ever since we both entered the mission-training regimen that would wash out nine out of ten of the girls who had made the finalist position. On the voyage, I had been intimate with her for nine months. In all that time she had never told me her secrets, and I had been content enough not to pry.

She had always known she was different, she told me, staring into the dark. She'd realized from the start that she had to conceal her difference and pretend to be like other girls. Only by accident, when she overheard a girl tell a friend that another girl was *despercibida*, and then giggle, did she realize that there was a word to codify her difference. It was a Brasileiro word that meant, literally, "unseen," but the way the girl had exaggerated each syllable and then made a kissing gesture toward the other girl had made the meaning obvious. When Jeanne whispered the word to herself, a shiver went through her. If there was a word, then somewhere there must be others.

At thirteen, it had been an easy difference to hide. There were other pursuits besides boys—athletics, and astronomy; the wonders of learning calculus, and above all that wonder of wonders, a starship almost completed circling barely a thousand kilometers above her head, visible in the hour after sunset as a tiny crystal of light slowly creeping across the heavens. At fourteen, when she volunteered for the program, there was no time for other pursuits. It was to be the greatest adventure in the history of mankind, and she had the dream. She was determined to let nothing keep her from becoming a part of it.

From there her path paralleled my own. For all of our pride in our intellects, the mission planners picked us more for our pedigrees than for our minds. Over the twenty light-years of the journey, we would be beyond the shielding atmosphere and magnetic field of Earth, traversing an interstellar void that was permeated by cosmic radiation. As the ship reached relativistic speeds and coasted between the stars, time dilation would shorten the trip to barely over twelve years, but even with the shielding provided by burying the crew behind tanks of helium-deuterium, the radiation dose would be immense. The mission planners searched first for candidates that had minimum susceptibility to radiation-induced cancer. People vary drastically in their tolerance to radiation; some have lived in perfect health for decades after tolerating doses that had killed in hours workmates that received identical exposure. Any candidate with a family member who died of cancer was rejected. The remaining candidates were subject to exhaustive genetic screening for each of five hundred known proto-oncogenes that could cause radiation-induced cancer. Our minds were important, too, but secondary. Our bodies were what they wanted.

Jeanne's fate was dealt by tests she had no control over. She passed, as did we all, and two dozen other girls as well. We were trained, and selected, and trained more, until at sixteen we all had the equivalents of a doctorate in our specialties; I in biology and she in fusion engineering. And then the remaining candidates were selected down again, until at last the crew of five was picked.

"And all that time," she said, "I hid my secret like my most precious treasure, because although they never said anything, I knew that they would find an excuse to wash me out as psychologically unfit if they ever suspected. I think half of the girls in the final selection were lesbians, a few of them even quite openly, and I never gave any one of them a hint that I'd like to know them closer, because I knew it was too dangerous. One at a time they washed out, as I had expected, and I studied psychology in secret, practiced making all the right answers on their tests, and stayed.

"And then, Beth," she said, "I met you. It's funny; I never even noticed you in the beginning of training, and then we were together more and more. It felt so natural, so right. But you were so straight. I kept wondering if it was just a facade, like mine, but I was too afraid to ask."

I smiled in spite of myself. "But eventually you did."

"After the launch, of course, when it was a little too late for the old men to change their selections." She laughed, her eyes twinkling. "Oh, Beth, you should have seen the expression on your face! You were so innocent, you really were! Completely naive, and I loved you all the more for it. It was then that I knew I had to have you, no matter what."

"And you did." I stroked her cheek.

"Yes. I'm glad. Even if I'm going to die, I'm still glad. It was worth it, love, it was all worth it."

So Jeanne had known all along what she was! I was awed by her perfect self-confidence. I wondered if Katerina and Consuela had known it, too; if I was the only one who had never guessed what I was. I hadn't even dreamed it.

I had dreamed of other things.

In the darkness I told her about my father, how he'd had the

dream, how he'd used his position as senator and later as commissar of spaceflight to bull the starship project through in the
days when every new estimate by the design engineers tripled the
cost, how it cost him his career, and eventually his life. I'd been
raised with the dream of spaceflight. My father had never expected other than that his daughter would make the final cut, no
matter how tough it would be. He'd given me his dream, and I'd
believed that it was worth the sacrifice of any number of lives,
including my own.

But then, I'd never been in love.

In the morning I didn't want her to go.

"I have to, love," she said. "I'm sorry."

"Why couldn't it be Rosa? Why does it have to be you?"

"I'm better with hardware, Beth, you know that. Rosa's a
wizard running remotes, but she's clumsy with hardware, you
know that."

"So what? It would maybe take her a little longer. We can spare
her, and we can't spare you. She's nothing but trouble anyway."

Jeanne put her hand on my shoulder. "Rosa's smart and level-
headed, Beth; I bet you'd probably even like her, if you ever decided to leave Earth behind and gave her a chance. And you'd
better learn to trust her sense for machinery, whether you like her
or not. We can't spare anyone, but we can't afford to screw up this
repair. I've got the fingers for it, and Rosa doesn't, and that's that.
Now, would you please be good and come help me suit up? I'd like
to have you there with me."

I helped Jeanne wriggle into her suit for the repair, and then
kissed her long and hard, not caring about discretion—let Rosa
watch, floating in the perfect safety of the piloting cubicle. Let
her be thoroughly disgusted, the bitch. I didn't want to let Jeanne
go. At last she gently pushed me away, placed a fingertip on my
cheek to wipe away my tears, and then pulled on her helmet.

Iron-maiden Rosa monitored her as she entered the chamber.
The rest of us, helpless, watched her on the big monitor, holding
our breath at critical moments, knowing that there was nothing
we could do to help. It was a job that should have been done by
robots, but we had no more robots left.

I have no faith in saints, not now or then, but in desperation
I prayed to Santa Barbara, who stills the lightning, and for once
the voice of my father in my head was silent. I promised her that
if she would do for me just this one miracle, I would believe.

Jeanne was inside for a total of twenty hours, cleaning the optics and then, with the lasers on, aligning them. Toward the end she was working very slowly, with long rests between, but she made no mistakes.

The instant she got back inside I rushed to her. She managed a weary smile for me. With trembling fingers, I unclipped the radiation monitor from her suit. I turned the screen slightly away from her and pressed the readout button.

The numbers were too high to have any meaning. The summary graphic showed completely black.

I tapped it lightly with my finger, hoping the summary might change to yellow, or at least show a hint of red. "It could be wrong," I said, and whacked it hard against the palm of my hand. "Radiation monitors are never completely accurate. They design these things to be conservative."

Jeanne put her hand over mine and shook her head slightly. "Thanks, Beth, but it's no use trying to fool me. I was in there for twenty hours. I can calculate the dosage as well as you can."

"But it's just not fair."

Jeanne shook her head. "So when has that had anything to do with it?"

We buried her in space. The fusion engine that took her life even now thrusts against us, a steady vibration against our feet. When we will reach our destination, Jeanne will travel on ahead of us. At seventy-three percent of the speed of light, Jeanne will travel farther than any of us.

Baby machines, that's all we are. Pilots, engineers, biologists, medics, as well; but all this is secondary. Genetic diversity was the god of the mission designers, and the mission designers our own uncompromising masters. In return for the gift of the starship, they demanded of us not just our loyalty and our competence, but our bodies and our lives. Above us, far from the stray radiation of the drive, is our irreplaceable cargo, the bank containing the supercooled sperm and ova that are the true colonists. Our bodies are no more than hosts, although we work and die to finish the hundred-trillion-mile journey to reach what will one day be their home. We are being used, and we name ourselves honored, for the sake of the dream.

After a few days I stopped crying, but the ache within me kept gnawing deeper inside, and there was nowhere to go, no private place I could bury myself for a while and try to heal. Katerina came to me to offer a shoulder to cry on, but I hated her for still having Consuela, and told her to leave me alone.

I curled in our sleeping niche, and tried not to think of Jeanne. Once, before we had become lovers, she had come to my sleeping niche. She'd officially been on night watch, but the watch formality didn't require her to remain in the piloting niche; only to be awake and prepared for any action. I had been restless. I stayed up with her, talking, and she she aimed her intense, far-away gaze at me, through me. I hadn't known what to feel. We talked about horses — her parents had kept horses, and she'd been a rider, as a child — and about books, and then about boys. "Did you have a boyfriend?" she'd asked. I had to admit I hadn't. "Me neither," she said. "You know, Rosa did. She told me once while we were training."

—And I hated Rosa even more. Nobody would have ever wanted me for a girlfriend.

"Do you wish you'd had one, now?"

"I don't know," I said. It had never seemed important to me. "I guess."

"If you'd had a boyfriend, how would he have kissed you?" I shook my head and looked away, embarrassed. No one had ever kissed me, except for my father, who kissed me on the forehead before I went to bed, on the days when he was at home.

"Would he have kissed you like this?" She turned my face toward her and kissed me lightly on the lips, closing her eyes for a moment. I felt the tip of her tongue dart against my lips and jerked back, startled. Jeanne laughed, and after a second I laughed too. "You're wicked," I said.

"I know," she said. "Or, maybe like this?" I closed my eyes this time, and she kissed me on the tip of my nose. She rubbed the tip of her tongue up and down, and then nibbled gently. It tickled, and I started to giggle.

"Or like *this.*" She reached around and pulled me against her, hard. Then she turned her face until we were almost at right angles, and kissed me hard. Her mouth tasted funny; like velvet, like almonds, like dandelions.

At last I pulled away. I didn't know what to think. I was an expert on biology, but real people were an enigma. "You shouldn't."

"Did that feel good?"

"I don't know."

"You didn't pull away."

"I did too."

Jeanne had smiled, and raised a finger. "Not very fast."

And I'd spent the rest of the night, and the next day, wondering when—if—Jeanne would kiss me again; wondering whether I would let her; wondering how I would be able to stand the wait without the electricity inside me melting through my belly.

That was long ago, months ago, a lifetime past. I tried very hard not to think of Jeanne.

A day later Consuela came to talk to me, and that time I was desperate and lonely enough to talk. I told her how Jeanne had had the dream, and died for it, and how beautiful it was.

Consuela rolled her eyes. "If you tell us one more time about the dream," she said, "I'm going to rip your tongue out and shove it up your butt. Can't you talk about anything else?" She suddenly clapped her hand over her mouth, and her eyes squeezed shut. "Oh, no. I didn't say that, did I? I'm sorry."

"Would you do me a favor, Connie?" I said. "Would you kindly go and jump out the airlock? And take Katerina with you. Why are you here, if that's the way you feel about it?"

"I'm sorry! All I meant was, we've heard it already. But you can tell me again. Please. I really don't mind."

"Just leave me alone, okay?" I buried my head in my mattress. She put a hand on my back, but I refused to look up. After a while I was alone.

Rosa pretended a sudden, intense interest in the scientific instruments, or would spend hours hiding in her sleeping niche practicing her little flute, the single personal possession she had brought. I hated her too, of course, and plugged my ears to keep out even the faint streamer of sound that filtered out, but I was glad, in a perverse way, that at least she was sensitive enough to leave me to myself.

I thought I'd known what I was doing. When I left I'd sworn that I would never feel homesick for grass, for weather, for unfiltered air or sunburn or the common cold. I didn't know how much I would crave simply a chance to focus my eyes on something more than three meters distant. To meet people I could say anything to, knowing I'd never see them again. To see animals. We should have brought a cat, I thought suddenly. There was margin designed into the life support system, not enough for another person, but we could have had a cat. My father had always liked cats. Why didn't they let us have a cat?

I spent a week in silence, lying in our—my—sleeping niche without sleeping, trying to remember why I'd fought to be allowed to spend my life breathing the recycled air of a spaceship far smaller than a prison cell, for the sake of a dream my father had had.

Consuela had been right. I'd been slave to his dream for all my life. It had seemed to me to be a beautiful dream, but it demanded too much. I waited until the others had gone to sleep. Consuela and Katerina were twined together in their sleeping niche. Rosa slept alone, curled into a tight ball in her cubby. I was careful to sneak past them quietly. I wanted to say goodbye, but could not. The note would have to do.

I should have made my confession and received my peace and absolution, but the compromise that the engineers and the priests had agreed to, of our confessing to a computer terminal, had never seemed right to me. And there was one sin that could not be forgiven. We had been blessed and received forgiveness before we'd left Earth. That would have to be enough.

The sleeping niches open out onto the main room. Above is the piloting cubicle; below the library access room and exercise booth. Below that is storage and access to the life support. I headed all the way down, where the spacesuits were kept.

All I needed was a helmet. If you turn off the carbon dioxide recirculation, you go quietly to sleep, and never awake. I picked the red one, the one that had been Jeanne's. Still slightly radioactive, it was carefully kept separate from the others. The choice seemed appropriate. I ripped a handful of wires out of the air recirculation, put it on, and looked around me.

There, standing in the doorway silent as iron, was Rosa.

"Beth."

I jumped. Of course it would be Rosa, the lone wolf of the crew. She'd been asleep, damnit. I thought I'd been quiet. Had she been watching all along?

"Don't do it."

"It's none of your business," I said. My voice echoed oddly inside the helmet. I'd thought it might smell of Jeanne, at least a little, but it had only the faint scent of silicon sealant. "Leave me alone."

Rosa shook her head. "We're all in this together. We need you."

"I don't want to be needed any more." I pulled the helmet off, dropped it on the floor, and kicked it, hard enough to hurt. It felt good. "I'm weary of being used, sick of being a pawn for someone's grand design. You just need my body, another baby machine for the grand plan."

Hearing myself say that I felt like a stranger, as if the Beth I had been had floated away and another, unknown person stood there talking. Hadn't the old Beth been one of the most vigorous advocates of the plan, long ago? Yet I was only saying what all of us, in one way or another, must have felt.

"Beth, please. Isn't one death enough? If there is anyone on the crew who's not wanted here, it's me."

"You? You don't need anybody. You like being by yourself. You resent it whenever one of us even talks to you."

"Maybe when we first boosted. But not now."

"Then why do you act like such a bitch?"

Rosa stepped backward, apparently surprised. "Me? *I* act like a bitch? What do you want me to do? You all fit together so smoothly. Consuela and Trina, you and Jeanne. What was I supposed to do? What can I do, except to pretend I don't see it, pretend I don't care?

"Do you think you were the only one who cried when Jeanne died? You don't even care how I felt, do you? You think that you're the only one allowed to have feelings. When Jeanne and I worked together all day fixing the drive, when every night Jeanne would crawl into her sleeping niche with you, and you would soothe away her tensions, and I would have to crawl back to my sleeping niche alone, don't you think I wasn't even a little jealous?"

"You?" Now I was the one surprised. "You, jealous of me? That's ridiculous. You've never needed anybody. You're straight as an arrow."

"I hide my feelings because I have to, not because I want to." Rosa reached forward to put her arm on my shoulder, and I jerked away from her. "Do you think that just because we never had sex, I couldn't love her too?"

"You? But you're the only one on the ship who's not a, a—" The word stuck in my throat. "Not a *pervert*. You couldn't love her—you're *normal*."

"Oh, Beth. Is that what you think you are? No wonder you're so confused." She hugged me. I stiffened and started to pull away from her, and then I realized she was crying too. "Nobody on the ship is a pervert, Beth," she said. "Nobody."

I let out my breath slowly, and all at once the tension drained out of my muscles, leaving me weak. Suddenly it was hard to remember why I had believed that there were no solutions for me other than death. I held her and rocked her in my arms and comforted her as best I could.

"I'm sorry, Rosa. We've both lost someone we loved," I said, almost whispering. I stroked her hair softly—bristly and tightly curled, so different from Jeanne's—and then I told her about the dream. "It owns us, Rosa. We gave it our souls, and we gave them freely. It's something that grabbed you when you were a child and believed in wonders, when you looked up into the dark at those tiny points of light so far away. It's a thing that won't let go, no matter how you long to be like the others, a thing that makes you wake up sometimes in the middle of the night with tears in your eyes, knowing that there is something you desperately need and that you can't ever reach."

It had been my father's dream, yes, but it had been mine, too, and surely it must be Rosa's as well. She, too, had given her life. We all had.

"Jeanne wasn't the only one to die for the dream. It demands everything we have, and one day it will demand from us more than we've got to give. Then it will kill us, too." I stroked her hair, caressed her back, shoulder, face, and I saw how much Rosa was like Jeanne, how much she always had been. "Did you ever have a boyfriend?" I asked, and she nodded without saying anything. I took her face gently between my hands, and turned it toward me. She had her eyes closed, and I saw with surprise that they were wet. "Did he kiss you?" I asked. "Did he kiss you like this?" I kissed her gently on the lips.

"No," she said. Her eyes were still wet, but she had a faint trace of a smile. "He kissed me like this." She put her arms around me and pulled me close to her, crushing her breasts against mine, and this time she kept her eyes wide open.

I took her back to my sleeping niche. We didn't do anything but talk, and cuddle, and finally drift into sleep.

But I couldn't sleep.

I couldn't blame Rosa. It was me; I was the problem; I could see that now. Oh, Jeanne, I'm sorry, please forgive me I'm sorry, I'm sorry.

Oh Jeanne, Jeanne, I wish you were here but you're gone and she's not. I'm sorry. I'll never forget you, never, and she will never take your place not ever but, may Blessed Luzia forgive my sins, I can't help myself. You're gone and I still want to live.

I want to live.

And after a long while I convinced myself that Jeanne would forgive me for what I wanted, and I slept.

In the morning I saw both Katerina and Consuela sneaking

sidelong looks over at us when they thought I wasn't looking. I knew that they were wondering just exactly what had happened the night before, and just how much things had changed between us. They were smart enough not to ask. Let them wonder for a while. The next time I caught Consuela giving me the eye, I turned and stuck my tongue out at her.

Sometime that day Katerina found the helmet where I'd dropped it, and I overheard her whispering to Consuela. After a brief conversation, the two of them came my direction, clearly intent on having a talk. I braced myself for confrontation, ready for a fight. "You want to talk, Beth?"

I crossed my arms and gazed into the wall. Anodized titanium reflected a blurred image of the cubicle. "No."

After a long look at my face, Katerina nodded. "We're here, Beth."

"Fine. I know it. Thanks." I was still getting used to being alive again, and really didn't want to talk with them about it. Rosa was enough. But I knew I was being too abrupt. "Another time, okay?"

They walked away.

Another night. Without asking, Rosa crawled into my sleeping niche and curled beside me without speaking, and I pressed up against the warmth of her back. One of her hands found mine. It had been a week since I'd slept in more than fits and starts. At last, I slept long and deeply.

I awoke to Rosa nudging me in the ribs. "Wake up. Wake up. We're having a crew meeting. You're the only one who's not up yet." Rosa started to tickle me.

"Okay, okay, I'm up. Can't this wait?"

"No. Ready? Let's start the meeting."

I swung up, dangling my legs out of bed. The main lounge was right outside the sleeping niches; so we were already effectively gathered for the meeting. I looked across at them, at the faces that I would see every day of my life, and could summon no feeling for them at all, not camaraderie or love or even contempt. They were the faces of serious and competent women who had made a choice that they would have to live with for the rest of their lives.

"We're slowly going crazy," Rosa said. "We're packed into too small a space, without anything important to do, except wait."

"Wait one second," said Consuela. "We *are* doing important things. What about the measurements of the interstellar medium? What about the magnetic field measurements? What about monitoring the drive?"

"And our studying," Katerina said. "And the simulations and drills."

Rosa shook her head. "Come on. Makework. Except for monitoring the drive, it's completely makework, and I'm sure all of us have figured that out by now. How much time do the measurements really take? An hour a day? And we've got eleven years for studying. If we keep on like this, we'll never make it to Pavonis. We'll never make it to turnover. We'll end up killing ourselves."

Katerina and Consuela both glanced up at my face, and then quickly away. "We know that, Rosa," said Katerina. "But what do you suggest we do about it?"

"We have been following the plan as if we were slaves to it," said Rosa. "I think it is time for us to admit things have changed. I think we should start planning for ourselves."

"Now you're the one being ridiculous," Consuela said. "Isn't it a bit late to change the mission plan?"

"We already changed the mission plan once," Rosa said. "Sleeping arrangements."

I looked away, and saw that Katerina and Consuela also had the grace to look ashamed. The original mission schedule had the crew stand watches, with three sleeping niches for the three crew in the off-duty rotation. Jeanne and I had decided—without asking Rosa—on sleeping two in a niche, and when Katerina and Consuela did likewise, had left Rosa the odd member out. There was nothing to watch for, anyway. Space flight is boring.

"Then just what," Katerina said, "do you think we should do?"

"I think we should have a baby," Rosa said.

Katerina and Consuela and I all started talking at once. After a while, Rosa managed to quiet us down and explain. Her suggestion wasn't as impossible as it sounded. The life support system was one of the most carefully designed pieces of hardware on the ship. Every kilogram of extra mass required a thousand tons of hydrogen to boost it. The life support system was engineered with no margin to keep any more than the minimum crew alive. We all knew that. But now we were only four. We had room for another.

"More than that, though," Rosa continued. "The mission plan tells us what to do for every single hour after touchdown. I think we should take that plan, and toss it out the airlock. We should make our own society, not remake theirs."

"We can't. We owe the world. . . ."

"Nothing. We left them behind, and they left us on our own. We can."

For the first time since the discussion started, I spoke up. "We will."

The sperm and ova bank were not designed to be accessed from the ship in flight, but everything that could conceivably fail had maintenance hatches. Rosa and Katerina managed to get in by cutting through the spare refrigeration control unit. We picked a random number to decide who would. I don't know whether it was by luck, or by some connivance of the others behind my back, but I won the draw.

We named her Estrela. She is our hope; the dream we dreamed together.

It was Estrela who really kept us sane, those long nine years. Oh, she nearly drove us mad, too—I had never have imagined how much work a baby would be!—but even in depriving us of our sleep and our freedom, she gave us a focus and a reason, and so kept us sane. Over the voyage, in the too-cramped and smelly crew compartment, we bickered and despised one another alternately, and it is the worst kind of feeling there is, to hate those whom you love and admire most, who you know love you. When things got worst, in the afternoons during naptime we would gather around her, watching her silently as she slept. One of us— usually Consuela, but sometimes Rosa—would whisper, "What kind of world shall we make for her?"

"A world without war," Katerina would say.

"A world where women can live together as friends and equals," Rosa would say.

"A world that always remember the dream," I would say, and remember Jeanne. But there is no pain now.

"A sane world," says Consuela. Then she would get out her *cavaquinho*, and Rosa her flute, and we would sing, or sometimes just close our eyes and listen. For a brief moment, the ship would not feel cramped at all.

That was many years ago, when we were still at the very beginning of our journey. It was not the only crisis we had, but when we had weathered that, we knew we could take the worst and survive.

I've come to terms with myself. I don't need labels for sexuality any more. Rosa explained it to me, once, when I asked her. "You love who there is to love," she said. "How could it be otherwise?"

Now we are eighteen light-years from Earth, with the ship's magnetic fields braking hard against the solar wind from Pavonis, decelerating us toward our goal. The eyes of our ship *Santa Luzia* look behind us now, but our own eyes look ahead. Estrela is nine. She has never known any world but the spaceship. She is annoying sometimes, demanding to know what this is for, and why that, and why not another thing; but we spoil her, because she reminds us always of why we are here. In two years we will reach our destination.

In two months Rosa will have a baby of her own. We will land before Estrela is fully grown; there is just enough margin in the life support system to support a new infant.

"What kind of world shall we make for her?" asks Rosa, patting her bulging belly.

"A world of strong, happy people who love the land they live in," says Consuela, strumming softly on her *cavaquinho*. Estrela is curled up against her hip, nearly sleeping. With her free hand, Consuela rubs Estrela's back.

"A world where after working long and hard, the people will come home and know that all they have done is worth the effort," says Katerina, her brown eyes unfocused, staring at nothing.

"A world that will always remember the dream," I say, and look around me at the people I love.

Ouroboros

"**B**UT THIS IS INCREDIBLE," SAID DUNN. HE WAS wearing his Celtics cap, since it was still officially basketball season, but the jacket draped over the back of his chair showed that he was ready for baseball just as soon as it came. "What your math says is, that since quantum mechanics is completely deterministic after all—"

"Right," said Professor Beatrice. "That means an entire universe can, if we want, be perfectly simulated on a computer." She wore a tweed jacket and a wool skirt; apparently in the mathematics and computer sciences department, basketball season didn't count for much.

"But we—"

"We, ourselves, are composed of atoms and energy levels, nothing more. If we simulated a universe on a computer, we could simulate ourselves—or people just like us—perfectly."

"But it would be just a simulation."

"No, no. From the *outside*, you would know it was a simulation. But if you were the simulated grad student, there would be no conceivable way that you could know, no possible test you could perform, that would reveal to you that you were a simulation. The laws that govern your universe would be exactly the same as the laws that govern our own."

"But that means, if we just had the computer power—"

Beatrice smiled. "Haven't you been following developments in supercomputers? I just put in a purchase order. That's the next step."

Dunn seemed thunderstruck. "No! But if that's true, then we ourselves really *could* be just—"

✻✻✻

"Hey, look at this," Betsy said. She had been following the progress of the computer world with rapt attention for days now. "This is really something! The computer-model universe has people in it who just figured out that they could be a computer model!"

Dr. Torrez scrolled back the output Betsy had set her pointer to, looked at it, and smiled. "And why shouldn't they? After all, they are just as complicated as we are."

"But—" said Betsy. "But, can they really do that, and make it work? What happens when our computer tries to model another computer with as much computing power as it has?"

Dr. Torrez smiled. "That's the wonder of efficient data compression. A data set can contain within it a data set that has as much complexity in it as the original data, by encoding it within the redundancies of the original data. And the real universe is full of redundancy."

"Neat," Betsy said.

"And haven't we talked out that issue in exhaustive depth? How do *we* know that our own universe isn't just an algorithm running on a—"

ccc

"Hey, check this out, dude!" Samuel said. "This sim you're running is fan-freaking-tastic! Not only are the sim people running their own sim, but, get this—their *simulation* is talking about doing its *own* simulation of a universe!"

Fredrickson smiled. His roommate wasn't a computer jock, but Fredrickson got a kick out of showing off the output to him, just to hear his reactions. And he'd known that this one would really knock his socks off. "Pretty amazing, isn't it?"

"Amazing? That don't say half of it! It's like, fractal, dude! Fan-freaking-tastic!"

"Well, I would say that it's not so surprising as all that."

"Dude, open your eyes. Like, you gotta let yourself dance to the music of the implicate order. This is just so freaking cosmic, it's like, it's Zen, dude! I mean, think about it. They're simulating a world . . . we're simulating a world . . . somebody's up there right now, simulating us. Brahma dreams the world into being, man, and the world dreams Brahma."

"Somebody's simulating us, you say?" Fredrickson looked around with theatrical exaggeration. "Really? Well, suppose somebody was. How would we ever—"

aaa

"This simulation is something more than merely incredible," Chen said, looking at the fast-scrolling output almost in disbelief. "It's absolutely uncanny. I *know* people who talk like that."

"Don't call them simulations," Professor Mohlenbrock said. "By every definition, it is, each one, a real universe. Even though it lives inside our own supercomputer, it's quite as real as our own. Our universe is the manifold encompassing a deterministic working out of natural laws, and so is theirs."

"I'm surprise that it doesn't slow the program down to simulate a computer which is itself running a simulation."

"Well, it does slow it down a little. But, mainly, the program just compensates by approximating the calculation of unimportant details, like the insides of rocks that nobody's looking at."

"It doesn't bother you that we could just be simulations, too?"

"Should it? The universe follows laws programmed into it. Does it matter whether there's some external machine it runs on?"

"Damn right! I want to be real, not some lines of code!"

"But it's *all* real, Chen." Mohlenbrock shrugged. "Well, somewhere there has to be a real, physical universe. Ultimately, I suppose, there's got to be an actual machine to run code."

"Say," said Chen, "our simulation runs a thousand times faster than real time. That third level was talking about running a simulation. I bet by now they've—"

666

"It's amazing," said Dunn. "Every time I check your universe simulation, it's twice as surprising as the last time." Dunn was fully into baseball season now, with a Red Sox cap and T-shirt. "I never thought it would evolve people. Then I never thought that they'd think of running their own universe simulation. And now not only are they running a simulation, but their simulation is running a simulation that's running a simulation! Where will it stop?"

"Why should it stop?" Professor Beatrice said. "Maybe we're just a simulation on *their* machine." She still wore a tweed jacket, although, since the weather warmed up, the wool skirt had switched for a cotton one.

"Or on the simulated machine that their simulation is running," Dunn said. "Say, do you think that we could just scroll the output and see ourselves talk? Or, better yet, you think we could make them tweak the parameters on their sim and maybe let the Sox win one for a change?" They both laughed, and then Dunn said, "Hey, what happens when we take the machine off-line for maintenance?"

"Hey yourself." Professor Beatrice shrugged. "Nothing at all. We just run them again when the computer comes back up."

"But—they'll cease to exist!"

"Not to themselves—the simulation will pick right up where it left off."

"And their simulations," Dunn said. "Those people will cease to exist, too. And their simulation's simulations—"

"Yes, yes. And so forth. They'll all be restored when the program comes back online. Does it matter?"

Dunn thought for a moment, then shrugged. "Guess not. It just seems sorta weird, that they could just cease for a while, and not even know."

"Just as long as nobody turns off the computer that's simulating *us*," Professor Beatrice said, "they'll never know."

They both laughed at that, and so did the people watching them on the screen, even though, really, it shouldn't have been funny to any of them.

Into the Blue Abyss

THERE IS NOTHING QUITE LIKE THE COLOR OF A hydrogen atmosphere tinted with methane. Deeper than sapphire; milkier than turquoise, Uranus was an indescribable luminous hue. Over the weeks, it had swollen from a dim, watery speck to the featureless blue pearl that hung below us.

Supported by an invisible microwave beam, the base station lowered into the edge of the stratosphere, and the moment came.

Wrapped in a cocoon of diamond and steel, safe within our technology, we readied ourselves to drop.

"Two questions," I had said. "Why Uranus? And why me?"

God, who would ever go to Uranus? Way out in the big dark, nearly as far beyond Saturn as Saturn is from the sun. It is cold and dark and, for the most part, uninteresting.

Stodderman was a thin man, neatly dressed, intense; a natural team leader. Some women would have found him sexy, I think. I was not one of them.

We had been in the common lounge of an orbital habitat with the improbable name of Wat Benchamabopit. That suited me; I hadn't wanted to go down to Earth quite yet anyway. I had unfinished business there which I was not quite ready to face.

The Wat Benchamabopit habitat had been chosen as a pragmatic place to meet: it was in an eccentric trans-lagrangian orbit that placed it at an energy convenient for both of us to rendezvous. Like many orbital habs, it rented out a common area for the use of transients. The recycled-air odor was covered over with the faint scent of some flowery fragrance, perhaps incense. Entry to the main part of the habitat was through the wide-open mouth of a blue-faced demon, elaborately carved with huge bulging eyes and protruding tusks. The symbolism seemed, to me, to be ominous.

Stodderman chose his words carefully. "The ice moons of the outer solar system are beginning to attract some attention. You know that there's a lot of prospecting going on right now. Uranus is far from the commercial belt, but there are people who think that the moons may be valuable soon."

"I've heard the rumors," I told him. "But you weren't talking about the moons, you were talking about the planet itself. Cut to the data-dump. Uranus? Why?"

"One of the prospectors. An old coot, a miner. The kind with wild hair and huge eyes and UV-hardened skin, been alone a little too long with only her p-buggy and computer for company. Those outer-moon prospectors are all half-crazy, Dr. Hamakawa."

"Leah," I said. "Please. Go on."

"Leah. Right," he said. "The prospectors. They've got tools, you know, some pretty good prospecting tools, and they've got a lot of free time. So, this one had a hobby: she took to sending some of her prospecting probes out, instead of down. Looking at Uranus from orbit. Something she saw got us interested. Down in the atmosphere. Deep down. We seem to be seeing some, ah, call it disequilibrium chemistry."

"Disequilibrium chemistry" I said. "You mean, life? You're saying that there's life on *Uranus?*"

"Call it, possible indications of organic molecules of unknown origin," Stodderman said. "Hydrocarbons and so forth. We'd prefer not to suggest anything about life right now. You're too young, I expect, but I remember the Zeus expedition."

The Zeus expedition had been an expedition to Jupiter's moon Europa. It had been an enormous, extravagant mission, as expensive as an interstellar probe. The expedition leaders had publicly vowed that they would return with proof that there was life in the oceans below Europa's icy crust.

Two hundred people, in habitats magnetically-shielded from

the deadly radiation of Jupiter's belts, had landed on the shattered ice-plains of Europa and bored with a fusion drill twenty kilometers through the ice to the secret ocean beneath. They brought arc-lights to depths that had not seen sunlight in a hundred million years, and explored the fantastic seascapes with submarines, bottom-crawlers, sub-surface drillers, and telerobotic probes. They found wispy structures of precipitated limestone, pale and fragile and intricate as a lace curtain, extending for hundreds of kilometers. They found strange chemistry, undersea volcanoes, a fascinating system of global oceanic currents driven by tidal stretching—but they found no life: no hydrothermal-vent communities, no bacteria, not even pre-biotic molecules.

The Zeus mission had scouted and cataloged the resources of Europa. The infrastructure that Zeus set up had opened up the moon to human habitation. Europa was now the largest human settlement in the Jupiter system, and the largest of the Europan cities was Zeus, honoring not the god, but the mission. But in the public mind, the Zeus mission was still a synonym for an expensive failure.

The solar system, except for the Earth, was dead. From the sulfur ice caps of Mercury to the fairy-castle frost of Charon, a hundred expeditions had searched for life, and had failed to find it. No one except the crazies and the fanatics looked any more.

"That's why we're keeping this low key," he said.

The first Uranus expeditions had looked for life, of course. Humans had not explored the planet itself in person—that idea was crazy—but Uranus had been investigated with robotic probes that floated on hot-air (or rather, hot-hydrogen) balloons in the cloud layers. That was the obvious place to look for life; up where there was still sunlight, where the pressure was only one or two atmospheres.

"Nobody has looked down deep," Stodderman said. "The atmosphere is fifteen hundred kilometers thick. They only looked at the very top."

"It seems terribly unlikely," I said. "Where's the energy?" Life is a solar-driven heat engine—regardless of how strange life might be, it would need energy. "Does any sunlight penetrate the atmosphere?"

"No," he said. "There's not much sunlight even above the clouds. Below? Nothing. Where the oceans are, it's dark."

"So what drives the life? Heat from the interior?"

Stodderman shook his head. "No. Turns out Uranus is odd—

it's the only one of the gas giants that has no detectable heat coming out of its interior."

"Then, what?"

"That's what we're looking to find out."

"Fair enough," I said. "And my second question? Why me?"

"Several reasons," he said. "One is that we're looking for somebody with skill as a submersible pilot."

As a student, I had worked for a fish farm. We corralled the fish with submersible vehicles, mechanical fish piloted by a virtual reality link. A school of fish doesn't have a leader—its motion is a perfect example of a self-organizing chaotic system—but with a computer providing real-time feedback, a single mechanical Judas fish could subtly influence the motion of a school and, over time, lead it anywhere. I had gotten to be good at it. It was a popular job for university students, something that could be done from a dormitory, where I was a student anonymous among ten thousand others. I had never needed to be within a thousand kilometers of the ocean.

I nodded. "OK. So, out of maybe fifty million people who had jobs as fish-pushers in college, why do you want me? I'm a physicist. Seems to me that you want a biologist."

"Oh, we have a biologist on the mission, of course. But what attracted us was the fact that, although you're a physicist now, you have some background in biochemistry as well."

"That was years ago."

"No matter. You seem to dabble in many subjects, and you're not afraid to stick your neck out and speculate a little. We're going to dive into an ocean where the pressure is well over fifty thousand atmospheres. It's a realm that's never been explored; we have no ideas what we might find. We thought a physicist might be a good thing to have along."

I nodded.

The reward that he hadn't bothered to state aloud was a tempting one.

I was not a member of an institute, but a freelancer, a mercenary scientist, desperate to get in an institute—but not willing to sell my freedom for it. If I went on the expedition, and if we were to find life, I could return not merely an associate, but a full fellow of any one of the great institutes. That would give me my freedom.

But that didn't matter. I had been hooked before he said a single word. There was no way they could keep me off this expedition.

Uranus! I was on my way.

Stodderman had put together his expedition on a budget of hopes, promises, and the discarded oxygen canisters and recycled detritus of earlier missions. He had hired transport to Uranus on the fusion-powered transfer ship *Astrid* that brought supplies to the prospector's camp on Oberon. He had arranged the use of the fusion motor on *Astrid*, and on a second freighter, *Norge*, for a full week after our arrival.

The expedition base station hung from a hundred-kilometer long tether, dangling into the fringes of the stratosphere below a V-shaped sail made of thin metallic mesh. Thousands of kilometers away, in a stationary orbit, two fusion-powered masers generated beams of microwaves that reflected off the sail, producing the upward force which held the base station up, lowering us slowly. At the lowest point, barely dipping into the fringes of atmosphere, the base station would drop the two exploration pods into the depths.

The maser idea had seemed crazy to me, and I'd told him so. Why not descend with rockets? Or balloon in the atmosphere?

Stodderman shrugged. "We looked at that. The balloon would have to be enormous. The atmosphere is mostly hydrogen, so a balloon doesn't have much lifting power."

"But on Venus they have whole cities floating in the clouds."

"On Venus they don't drop the cities down a gravity well, float them for a while, then try to launch them back out. The gravity is less than Earth's, but the well is twice as deep.

"Turns out our way is simpler. The ships are here anyway; *Norge* isn't heading back for weeks, and *Astrid* is staying even longer. Twenty kilometers per second into the gravity well, and another twenty out again, that's a killer task even for a fusion rocket. But it's not hard to reconfigure fusion engines to make a maser. And a mesh sail weighs almost nothing; it's like lowering a spiderweb down. It sounds complex, but really it's the low-cost solution."

"Doesn't sound complex; it sounds risky," I said. "What if the maser fails when you're lowering the station? Or when you're hovering for the drop-off?"

"If the maser fails," Stodderman said, "we'd better hope like hell that the crew on the ships are working to restart it. In two, maybe three minutes, we hit the atmosphere hard enough to pick up frictional heat. About six minutes, give or take, the base station is moving so fast that even if the maser could reacquire the sail, we can't accelerate fast enough to pull out. In eight minutes, the sail hits the atmosphere."

"And then?" I asked.

Stodderman shrugged. "It's a toss-up. Either the atmospheric pressure crushes us, the tether melts, or the mesh sail hits the atmosphere and disintegrates. I don't think anybody is taking odds." He looked at me. "This bother you?"

"No," I said. "I don't understand much about people. But I do know one thing. People die."

Of the four of us in the expedition, two of us were to descend through the atmosphere into the Uranian ocean. Over the eight weeks spent on *Astrid* in transit to Uranus, we had trained on the use of the Uranus hydrosphere mobility pods in the simulator. We crawled into it in a fetal position, bodies slick with transceiver gel, wearing neural pickup gloves and skinsuit. In the actual vehicles, we would be intubated for oxygen and liquids, but in the simulator, this final step was skipped.

Hanita Jayavel and I were the most adept at the intricate set of skills required in piloting the pods. To call the skill "piloting" was to understate the task; the mobility pods fit around us like a second body, a body with a diamond shell, steel muscles and electronic senses that taste the chemicals in the water and see sonar echoes.

Exploring the oceans of Uranus in person, and not by telepresence, was crazy. The expedition pods were the reason that it was possible at all.

The two pods had been specially designed for the Uranus ocean, and were the most expensive objects on the expedition. Tiny, self-contained submarines with full life-support systems and independent power, they had an ovoid pressure vessel, grown from diamond fiber, to protect us from the enormous pressures beneath the Uranian atmosphere. Around the pressure capsule, the body had been designed on the model of a dolphin, with dolphin's flexibility to its steel fins and tail. Attached to the diamond bodies were a thermophotovoltaic isotope power supply and canisters filled with chemicals that, when our mission was over, would generate the hot gas that would fill the buoyancy floats to bring us to the surface. From the surface, balloons inflate to bring us into the Uranian stratosphere, where we could ignite solid rocket motors to hop back to the hovering base station. The pod also had a sample acquisition arm, slender and jointed, which retracted fully into the body.

Over the long transit, Hanita and I had talked for a long time, and she told me of her life.

Hanita Jayavel had been the daughter of a Kuiper habitat. I had known little about the fringe habitats that were scattered deep out in the far dark, only that they were inhabited by anti-social fanatics and isolationist religious factions; they were unimportant to the politics and economics of the inner solar system. Hanita's birth habitat had been a communistic one. They lived on an icy body in the Kuiper belt, a body with plentiful water and nitrogenous volatiles, and, most important, one that was far from everybody else. Their economic system was to share and share alike, and their credo that nobody in the habitat was any better than anybody else. There were other colonies in the Kuiper diaspora, a thousand groups seeking to distance themselves from the crush of humanity, but with a hundred million kilometers between outposts, commerce between them was slight.

And then the fusion renaissance expanded outward. It swallowed the Kuiper diaspora without even a gulp, destroyed them not by war, but by a surfeit of riches. The children of the commune saw the wealth that the robber barons brought. They had been taught that the robber barons were evil, but what they saw was the robber barons financing institutes, art, science. The laws of Hanita's habitat had not been restrictive; they were proud to allow their inhabitants to leave freely, and, free, their children had drifted away.

Hanita's family had been one of the last to leave, when the settlement had lost so many of the younger generation that it had become clear that there would be too few to sustain it. More of an immigrant than a refugee, Hanita had studied chemistry in one of the inner belt communities, and joined on to the expedition as much for her background in the outer solar system as for her expertise in chemistry.

After three weeks of the mental and physical exhaustion of training together, Hanita had confided in me further. Unknown to Stodderman, she had a personal reason for joining the expedition, a secret reason for her fierce dedication to mastering the piloting simulation. She was making certain that she would be one of the two chosen to dive into the unknown ocean.

Hanita Jayavel wanted to reinvent paradise.

Uranus is four times the diameter of the Earth, but the density of the planet is so low that the surface gravity is actually slightly lower than Earth's. Above the clouds, the temperature is frigid— seventy degrees Kelvin, cold enough to freeze oxygen. Down below the cloud tops, though, the temperature rises. It rises only slowly, because the interior of Uranus produces almost no heat. At the ocean, it was calculated that the temperature was moderate, in the range of three to four hundred Kelvin: the range required for human biochemistry.

The search for life motivated Stodderman, but did not excite Hanita. As a chemist, she had long ago concluded that in the absence of either sunlight or interior heat there was no entropy gradient for life to exploit.

In the warm dark ocean, Hanita Jayavel wanted to make a new colony of humans. Hidden a thousand kilometers under the opaque atmosphere of Uranus, she would set a secret colony far from the numerous habitations of humankind. A colony free of the economics of the solar system.

Humans don't need sunlight; the Kuiper colonies in the cold dark had proved that. With an infinite supply of hydrogen and deuterium from the ocean waters, with helium-three from the atmosphere, humans could create their own sun. The oceans of Uranus had everything needed, except life.

She would bring that.

She explained her plans to me, showing me how she would modify the human genome to make oceanic life. She drew a fantastic picture of life in a three-dimensional ocean, spreading out across a world with a surface area sixty times larger than the land area of the Earth. To her, the expedition into Uranus's oceans was not a search for life—it was a scouting trip.

Hanita was a fanatic, I realized, and, when I told her so, she admitted it. I will stop at nothing, she said.

"Even killing?" I asked.

"Without hesitation," she said.

OK. I could live with that.

Inwardly, I agreed with Hanita; with no plausible source of energy, we were unlikely to find life. For me, curiosity alone was sufficient reason to drop into the seas of Uranus.

But I, too, had motivations that I kept to myself.

In the inner solar system my life had been becoming com-

plicated. I was not sure how to deal with romance. I didn't know
what to think. I had never learned how to love. Was this love, what
I felt? Would I even know it?

And yet, though I had made no encouragement at all, he
wanted me.

The meat was nothing to me. People died. There was no point
in getting close to them; they die and leave you alone. This was
what I knew.

In some vague, abstract way, I wondered if I was even capable
of this thing, love, that others find so all important. Probably not.
But if I were, if I were a whole person, if I'd never experienced
what I had experienced, in the camps, in the war, I would not be
the same person. Perhaps growing up as a child of the war had
burned something out of me, something that others thought
precious, but it also had forged me and shaped me into the person
I now was. This was the price I had paid, for being what I was.
And the price was cheap.

The situation was too complicated for me. Uranus was conveniently far away from Earth. A mission to Uranus uncomplicated
my life.

As for basic facts about Uranus—before the expedition, I had
known little more than the dumb jokes ("Hey, there are rings of
dirt around Uranus!"). It's true: the rings of Uranus are unlike
Saturn's gleaming particles of ice; they are dark, the color of coal.
Rings of dirt. What else was there to know about Uranus, other
than that it was cold and dark? An oddball among the planets, it
orbits on its side, with the north pole pointing sunward for half
of its 84-year orbit, the south pole sunward for the other half.

Below the clouds, way below, was an ocean of liquid water.
Uranus was the true water-world of the solar system, a sphere of
water surrounded by a thick atmosphere. Unlike the other planets, Uranus has a rocky core too small to measure, or perhaps no
solid core at all, but only ocean, an ocean that has actually
dissolved the silicate core of the planet away, a bottomless ocean
of liquid water twenty thousand kilometers deep.

The microwave jockeys tweaked their masers, and inch by inch
lowered us down the gravity well. There were four of us in the
station; Hanita and I to pilot the pods, Stodderman as the expedition leader, and our technician Kamishinay. Kamishinay was a

spindly guy from a zero-grav habitat, limbs as thin as chopsticks with small hard muscles protruding like walnuts. He was quiet, but superb with equipment.

At last the expedition base station hung in the most tenuous wisps of the Uranian atmosphere. The base station was smaller even than the quarters on the *Astrid*, barely large enough for the control center and the two exploration pods docked in their slings. It smelled of metal and oil and the acetic-acid odor of outgassing silicone seals. After the rancid sweat and the organic smell of the recirculated air in the transfer ship's cabins, the new-equipment smells of the station were welcome. We worked elbow to elbow, getting ready. Hanita and I stripped, and our technician Kamishinay assisted in pasting sensor electrodes over our bodies, checking each one as it was placed, adjusting it minutely for the best pick-up of muscular signals. Unexpectedly, although he had just run his hands over nearly every square decimeter of our naked bodies, Kamishinay was squeamish about inserting our catheters, and so I lubricated the tube and insert it for Hanita as he averted his eyes, and then spread my legs and held myself rigid to let her reciprocate for me. Despite the grease, the catheter stung like a rasp as it slid in. Finally, with Kamishinay again helping, we inserted the intravenous monitors—another sharp sting—and nasal tubes, until both of us seemed to be cybernetic organisms as much as biological.

Through this all, Stodderman had been ignoring us, concentrating on details of piloting and reading the external sensors for clues to the environment below. To him, we had become little more than two pieces of the mission's equipment. His intensity was reserved for his machines.

The Uranus exploration pods were tiny, and slithering inside was a tough proposition requiring a liberal application of gel. Once inside, in the tight dark, with the sense-net hugging your body closer than a lover, the bile taste of the tongue control and the scratching, choking itch of the tubes down your throat, it felt like some medieval torture—until the system was energized.

With the power on, your senses came alive, the diamond shell became your skin, the sonar senses your second eyes, the chemical sensors your smell and taste and touch, a thousand times more sensitive than the crude chemical instruments that humans call their senses. The fins flexed to our slightest touch. Mechanical dolphins, we squirmed and fidgeted, itching for release from the docking harness that held us.

The moment came. Our systems had been tested, the tests checked, the checks rechecked and verified, and the verification checked. We were ready.

First Hanita, and then it was my turn: we were jettisoned from the expedition base station, and fell — plummeted — into the pearly blueness of Uranus.

We dove into the infinite abyss.

An unmanned probe, operated by telepresence, would have been less crazy, but that solution turned out to be unworkable. Under the enormous pressure of the hydrogen atmosphere, hydrogen atoms are forced into solution, and dissociate into ions. This made the water conductive enough to block electromagnetic transmissions. If we wanted to know what lies below the surface of the ocean, we had to explore it in person.

Even further down, the pressure becomes so high that the water itself became liquid metal. Slow currents flowing in the water gave Uranus its magnetic field. But that was farther than we would ever go. To explore the upper ocean would be enough for any one expedition.

Above us, the base station, lightened by the loss of the exploration pods, rose on its microwave wings back into orbit.

We fell, shrieking, down through the hydrogen atmosphere.

At the edge of the atmosphere, the sunlight was like a late afternoon, not noticeably dim, Uranus a huge blue ocean below us.

The blue slowly deepened from sapphire into cobalt into the deepest shade of midnight.

The atmosphere thickened. In the stratosphere, there were winds of a thousand kilometers per hour; but here below the clouds, the atmosphere was still. If there were any winds at all, they were below the level of detectability.

Down, into the deeper blue. Dark blue. Pastel, then ink.

Down.

We fell through clouds: first methane clouds, then ammonia clouds, then ammonium hydrosulfide, and into the darkness. Oddly, we didn't even need parachutes. As the atmosphere thickened, by slow degrees our fall slackened speed. We fell for hours; a thousand kilometers, and continued to fall. We were falling in utter darkness now, and incrementally the atmosphere had become so dense that our fall slowed to a crawl.

And, in the darkness, below a thousand kilometers of atmosphere, as slowly as an ant falling through the thick air, we splashed in slow motion into the ocean.

We were now buoyant: no longer falling, we were swimming. Sweeping across the darkness, our spotlights saw only a waveless obsidian surface; our sonar saw nothing at all but its own reflection. Only the taste had changed, from methane-laced hydrogen into water.

We were fishes in the Uranian sea.

But the tantalizing hints of disequilibrium chemistry that had drawn us across the vast darkness and down through the clouds had not been here at the surface. We swam, making measurements, taking the measure of our diamond and steel bodies, checking the systems that had been checked a thousand times before, leaving wakes across the waveless sea.

And then we dove.

The ocean was the temperature of blood. Encased inside mechanical dolphins, we swam in the dark. I chased Hanita, laughing, and tagged her; then she turned and chased me, and then together we dove deeper into the darkness of the Uranian sea.

I had left myself behind.

We tasted the water, we heard the sounds. Sound? We reconfigured, boosting the amplification on our electronic ears. Sonar showed nothing there, but something was making a chirruping, faint but (to our amplified ears) quite clear. A sound oddly like the serenade of spring peepers. We turned our floodlights on to the brightest setting, but they showed nothing, only water. There was no discernible directionality to the sound, and nothing there to see.

Deeper.

There were no currents in this sunless sea, or if there were currents, they were so sluggish that we could not detect them. No bubbles, no form to the water. It was so clear and dark that we had almost no sense of immersion; it was as if instead of diving we were hanging motionless, suspended in nothing.

And then, as we dove—a kilometer below the surface, by my pressure gauge—suddenly there was something in our lights. A layer, as thin as a soap bubble, iridescent in the glow of our floodlights, giving a visible surface to the formless deep. It undulated sluggishly. We penetrated through it, and it offered no barrier to our passage. Slow oily ripples spread out from the area of penetration, pieces breaking off and floating free, oscillating in shape, dancing like tiny butterflies in a way that was almost lascivious. A layer of thin, oily scum. Organics. Biological in origin? Maybe. But what could be the energy source? We had been measuring thermal lapse as we penetrated deeper, and we had found only a minuscule heat flow, just enough to keep the oceans from freezing. There was no trace of free thermal energy. Where there was no free energy, there could be no life.

I schooled myself not to be excited, so I would not be disappointed. I hadn't wanted to be a fellow anyway.

Hanita's chemical analysis showed the scum to be tangled chain molecules; hydrocarbon, primarily, with small amounts of nitrogen and traces of sulfur. "Not really biological," she informed me, "but in some ways similar to biological chemistry. You might call it pre-biotic molecules. Primordial slime." The organic slime from which, on Earth, life had arisen.

Despite the lack of an identifiable energy source, the organic molecules were slowly replicating, but they assembled nothing of interest: no cells, no complicated structure, just endless copies of hydrocarbon ooze. Was ooze life? I didn't want to be a fellow, all it would give me was freedom, and I didn't need or care about freedom.

The molecules catalyze their own formation, Hanita reported. Out of dissolved methane, hydrogen sulfide, and ammonia, they formed molecules which serve as catalysts to form more of themselves. Was this life? Perhaps by the simplest definitions — it replicated — but with no structure, with no metabolism, it would hardly serve to excite those above.

Meanwhile, I had been trying to analyze the sound. My working hypothesis was that the sound was meteorological in origin. The vortices of storms hundreds of kilometers overhead were filtered by the layers of atmosphere, turning noise into eerie music. It was odd, but no odder than stratospheric whistlers.

Then a fish swept by us. It was huge. It was a filter-feeder, grazing on the hydrocarbon layer.

It was singing.

The fish was wide and flat and thin, an irregularly shaped pancake. It moved slowly, creeping along at the pace of a carpet of ants. It had no sense organs that we could detect, no eyes, no sonar.

It didn't mind our floodlights; why should it? How could it have evolved photosensitivity, a thousand kilometers below any possible trace of sunlight? We circled it, photographing, documenting the fish in the Uranian ocean. This changed everything.

It was perhaps the ugliest fish ever imagined, a lumpy grey tortilla, undulating languidly as it munched its way across the oily slime. Our sonar showed—nothing. It was the same density, apparently the same composition as the scum that it ate.

This changed more than just the way the solar system would view our expedition, I realized. Hanita wanted to recreate her childhood paradise in the oceans of Uranus, but this could only be possible if humanity ignored Uranus. Uranus wouldn't be ignored if life was reported.

But if Stodderman's mission reported nothing, no one would ever return to Uranus, not soon, not perhaps for hundreds of years. Long enough for a colony to flourish.

Under conductive ocean, we weren't able to report our results. No one would know what we found until we surfaced. There was only one solution: Hanita must try to kill me before we reach the surface.

I was suddenly aware of my body, cramped into fetal position, packed in gel and penetrated by tubes, unable to do more than twitch, separated from crushing pressure by only a thin eggshell of diamond filament. We had been training on the mobility pods for weeks; we both knew hundreds of things that could go wrong, weak points that could be exploited to let in the deadly pressure. Death would take only a moment.

OK. I could deal with that.

We privately tagged the layer of hydrocarbons "plankton," although compared to terrestrial plankton, this was unthinkably more primitive. The filter-feeder crept along like a lawn mower, and the oily layer imperceptibly oozed closed behind it, leaving a trail of slightly disturbed hydrocarbon. The trail was invisible in sonar and in visible light, but by polarizing our floodlights, we could see a curved line that faded in the distance, faintly extending back as far as our floodlights would reach. At irregular intervals it was crossed by other paths through the slime layer, even older and fainter.

By following the other trails, we found other fish. They were the same in everything except size, identical as clones, equally flat, equally lumpy, equally ugly. They were only sparsely populated across the ocean; I estimated a density of only a single fish in every twenty square kilometers.

"But this is impossible," Hanita said. "Where the hell is the energy source?"

While she had been photographing the fish—the fourth one we had found, identical in all particulars to the other three—I had been thinking. While I thought, I had been analyzing the water, the organics, the electrochemical potentials.

"I can tell you that," I said.

Water rises in the atmosphere, I explained. Rises into the stratosphere, and when it gets high enough it is photodissociated to free oxygen and hydroxl radicals. High in the stratosphere, the radicals recombine into oxygen and to hydrogen peroxide. Heavier than the hydrogen, these cool and fall, tiny cold droplets of oxidant raining slowly into the ocean. No photosynthesis was needed. The oceans were plentiful with dissolved hydrogen, so there was fuel and oxidizer. The pre-biotic molecules self-assemble, fueled by the energy of the oxygen; the filter-feeders subsist on them.

The life was driven by the oxygen cycle, which was, ultimately, driven by sunlight.

"But that can't be very efficient!"

"My quick calculation is that it's about a million times less efficient than the photosynthesis that powers the Earth," I said. "So? It's slow-motion life. Where there is energy, there is life."

And then a predator. Of course, there would be predators, I realized; predation was a cheap way to harvest energy—let somebody else do it—and such a rich ecological niche wouldn't stay empty. Sharks, a pack of them. In slow motion, the filter-feeder banked as if to flee, rising up out of the slime layer, but the sharks were inexorable.

The ease with which they ripped the fish apart showed that the filter-feeding life form had no bones, no detectable muscles, no internal structure. It must be more like a motile jellyfish than any sort of true fish, I realized. I swam around, keeping the floodlight on the scene, as Hanita photographed the slaughter. With scoop-like mouths, the sharks suctioned the shreds down their gullets. A few of the fragments, too small for the sharks to bother with, gradually contracted into pancake shape, becoming fingernail-sized copies of the fish that had been torn apart. They settled toward the slime layer, and then begin to feed.

Then a shark turned on us.

Its mouth was huge. Hanita kept photographing right up to the moment it swallowed her.

Like the filter-feeder, the sharks were transparent to sonar. I turned just a moment too late to see the one that grabbed me.

We cannot possibly be its natural food. The shark had made an unfortunate mistake, and swallowing us was most likely going to poison it.

I was unable to shake free of it. Our diamond bodies were already under hydrostatic pressure of fifty tons per square centimeter, and designed with considerable safety margin, they could withstand far more than that. It was unlikely that the shark could directly harm the craft. Still, trying with futile vigor to rip into us, the shark produced an erratically varying, non-uniform pressure far different from anything that the pod had been designed for, and it would not be very wise to let it continue.

I was briefly sorry for the shark, but there was no choice.

The balloon inflated sluggishly with hydrogen. The shark was disoriented, and attempted to swim, to hold its position, but hydrostatic pressure and Archimedes' law were unforgiving. It was inexorably pulled to the surface. Unwilling, or more likely with too little brainpower to let us go, it bloated and came apart.

As I rose, I grabbed with my manipulator arm, and with a lucky swipe, managed to snag a piece of flesh. A sample.

Bobbing at the surface of the ocean, we were again in electromagnetic contact with the hovering base, bathed in a flood of welcome microwave energy.

I was still alive.

"Wow," I said. "What a ride."

We were floating in darkness on a warm, stagnant sea. "I expected you to kill me," I said.

"It was a dream, all my life, to return," Hanita said, slowly. "And since there was no place to return to, I dreamed I would make a place. It was a nice dream."

"Why?" I said.

"Why didn't I kill you? I don't know." Encased in her pressure shell, she was invisible to me, but in my mind's eye I could see her shake her head. At last, she spoke again. "Can you ever really go back?" she said.

*   *   *

We have found life in the cold dark, life that could never even conceive of the stars. The gravity is lower than the gravity of Earth, but the well is far deeper. Life in a realm with no metals, no fire. Life that could never escape.

Uranus is ocean, all ocean, an ocean twenty thousand kilometers deep. We have barely seen the outermost skin of the Uranian ocean. What life could there be, in the incalculable depths?

We fire the pyrotechnic separators to sever us from the now-useless steel exostructure of our dolphin bodies, leaving only the naked eggs of our pressure vessels, and the balloons and rockets that will take us home. By burning hydrogen into helium and using the waste heat to fill and then stretch taut the gas-bags, the balloons tug us sluggishly free of the ocean.

Side by side, we rise like jellyfish through the thick air toward the stratosphere. It will take days to reach a height where we can ignite our solid rockets, as the base station, suspended below its microwave-lit sail, dips to meet us. There is still the split-second rendezvous to accomplish, still a thousand things that could go wrong, but for all that, nevertheless the mission is over. We have transmitted the most important parts of our results, the photographs and the chemical analyses, and the base station is broadcasting them across the solar system. In a few hours, everyone will know.

"What will you do now?" I ask her.

"I don't know," she says. She could have asked me the same question, but she doesn't.

But I know.

Life can exist even in the most extreme environment. It is not fragile. It can feed on only the tiniest scraps of energy.

There will be other missions, and beyond them yet other missions. I will let things happen, as I always have, as I always would. The events will flow over me, and I will be unchanged.

Outward, to the farthest horizons, I thought. And beyond them, other horizons, never ending.

Home.

Snow

THE SNOW WAS COMING DOWN HARDER NOW, NOT A gentle snow like memories of childhood Christmases that had never been, but wet gobbets plummeting out of the heavens like saliva, puddling half-frozen on the pavement. The temperature was continuing to drop. Before midnight, Sarah calculated, it would start freezing. The night would be a deadly one for anybody who didn't have shelter.

For a moment Sarah let herself slip into her other world, her private world that had no rain, no weather, no rummaging through dumpsters or begging for quarters. The crystalline beauty started to build itself around her. It was so tempting . . . she shook herself, hard, and stomped her feet. If she let herself go there now, she would die. It was that simple.

Stamping her feet had made Christie start to cry. Sarah pressed the baby closer to her and made soothing noises, but, once awake, Christie was not so easily satisfied. She really needed warmth, shelter. Sarah quickly ran through her options. Steam vents around Public Square . . . but lately the police had been rousting anybody who lingered too long. A mayoral election was coming. The shelter . . . but after what had happened the last time, she would never go back there. Even if they let her. That left various doorways and alleys that she knew. But it was going to be awfully cold for that.

Christie started crying again, this time wailing with all her energy, and Sarah gave up on trying to shush her. Let her cry; she had a right. The world was mightily unfair, and she had every right to complain about it.

Once Sarah's voices might have come to her aid with their unworldly advice, but for the last few months the voices had deserted her. That was something to think about, the fact that the voices had, for now, gone away from her. Was it a good thing or a bad one? The voices had rarely offered practical advice, but they often told her how important she was, how the National Security Agency wanted to steal her brain; they had warned her about agents plotting against her, pretending to be social workers or psychologists or stray dogs. (But stray dogs don't have radios implanted in their heads; she had seen that, she had!) Had the voices left her for good? Was that even possible? The psychologist had said that the voices wouldn't go away unless she took the special medicines, but then, the psychologist was an agent. The voices had told her so.

But the voices sometimes lied, too.

In any case, she had no choice. Tonight she would need a room.

Shifting Christie to her left arm so she could examine her pockets with her right, she came up with a crumpled bill and fifty-eight cents in change found on the sidewalks. She uncrumpled the bill eagerly, hoping it might be a twenty, or even a fifty—it was possible, it was—but it was only a single. A dollar and a half. She'd need twenty for the cheapest room.

Two blocks down Superior she found Old Mother Rags huddled in her doorway. She was wearing what must be the remains of at least five different dresses, and was surrounded by more, a veritable department store of tattered plaids and patterns and corduroy. Sarah plumped Christie down among them. "Take the kid for me, okay?"

Mother Rags smiled, showing yellow and uneven teeth. "Ten dollars."

Sarah shook her head. "Two."

"Five," said the old woman slyly. "Five, and not dollar less."

"Okay, three," Sarah said. She pulled out her bait and held the crumpled bill out, dangling from her fingers. "I'll give you one now."

Mother Rags's smile grew wider. "Give," she said.

"Take the kid. Three dollars."

"Deal!" said Mother Rags, smiling greedily. "Now, give!"

Sarah dropped the bill into her lap, and Mother Rags scooped it up, the bill and the child together.

Christie would be warm and safe, for a while at least, and Sarah would be free to do what she had to. Besides, let Mother Rags deal with the kid for a while. Do them both some good.

The air was even colder, snow coming down like bullets through the yellow glow from the streetlights, and Prospect Street was as empty as an alien planet. Sarah huddled in a doorway, waiting. As she waited, she allowed her other world to creep into the edge of her mind. In her pocket she had four envelopes scavenged from trash cans, business-reply envelopes from some advertising promotion, one side beautifully blank. The cold made the other world clear, and she let it play in her mind, but refused to let herself go, despite the temptation of those beautifully pristine envelopes.

A car. She heard it before she could see it, tires ripping the wet asphalt, like tearing an envelope in two. She stepped out into the circle of light cast by the streetlight. A big Lincoln Towncar, tinted windows, power everything. It slowed slightly as it cruised past, but didn't stop. It turned at the corner. She waited, miserable. Half a minute later it came around again, slowed to a stop by the streetlight. Motionless, the car looked less pristine; the bumper slightly skew, the rear door-panel dented with patches of rust showing. A window purred down.

She leaned in. "Hey there, mister," she said, trying not to let her teeth chatter, trying to look pretty, not the least bit soaked and bedraggled. The car's heater caressed her face. "You looking for a party?"

She clutched the three crumpled ten-dollar bills. The guy had given her an extra five; a big tipper. She wondered if she'd ever met him before. Maybe he knew her, maybe that was why he gave her the extra five. Or maybe he just didn't have any fives. Either way, she had been almost sorry to leave the warm car.

On her way back to Superior she detoured to a gas station to change the ten. The kid in the armored booth didn't want to change it unless she bought something, which she wasn't about to do, but he didn't want her lingering in his station, either, so he did it, peeling out the singles slowly and methodically, never letting his eyes off her. Maybe he was an agent, assigned to watch her. Could they have guessed she'd visit that gas station? Maybe. Or maybe he was just worried that she'd pocket a handful of Lifesavers.

Christie was sleeping, almost buried under the mountain of rags. Old Mother Rags was dozing as well, but snapped out a palm as soon as Sarah touched the pile. "Give," she said.

It was worth the price. Sarah dropped two singles into the outstretched palm, and Mother Rags deposited them into some hidden cache under her fortress of cloth.

"Thanks," said Sarah.

She'd been in the hotel before, and the room clerk didn't even look up when she dropped the twenty on the scarred mahogany counter, just slid a key across the desk. He didn't ask her to sign the book, and she didn't offer; there was little chance that her twenty would ever show up on an accounting ledger.

The room was clean, if a bit threadbare. Long ago, it had been elegant. There was soap in the bathroom, and even, to her surprise, hot water. Sarah put Christie into the bed, tucked her in, and went back to the bathroom. She thought about washing her clothes in the sink, but reluctantly decided against it. The radiator was putting up a valiant, and quite noisy, effort, but she couldn't take the risk that it might not dry her clothes by checkout time.

But she could take a bath. A bath!

Later, her skin as wrinkled as the face of old Mother Rags, but with the cold of the streets steamed out of her bones, Sarah sat at the tiny desk. Christie was fast asleep, oblivious to the banging radiator. No stationery in the drawer. She had hardly expected that she would be so lucky, but when she pulled the drawer all the way out, and inspected behind it, she found two paperclips and a pencil. A pencil! The tip was broken, but she could deal with that.

She gnawed at the point, humming with contentment. A warm room, Christie asleep, and she still had eight whole dollars, and almost the whole night left. She had never needed very much sleep, only an hour or two, and when she had the pencil tip gnawed to a needle-like point, she had four envelopes to work with. A night's worth, at least; maybe more if she wrote very very small.

She took out the first envelope, and carefully spread it open. Her other world was very close, the world that she created out of herself. She knew that somewhere, somewhere out in the world there were other people who knew how to enter that other world. Sometimes she wondered if she had ever met any of them. But, she decided, that really didn't matter. What mattered was that other world.

She checked once more that Christie was sleeping soundly, and then, writing in almost invisibly tiny script, she started.

"Theorem 431. Consider the set of non-singular connections mapping an 8-dimensional vector space onto a differentiable Hausdorff manifold. . . ."

She paused for a moment, picturing the simple beauty of the eight dimensional complex mapping, and wondering for a second if there might be a straightforward extension of the theorem to arbitrary dimensionality. She smiled. Might that be theorem 432?

The snow fell outside the window, mapping a divergenceless vector field in three-dimensional space.

It was a perfect day.

Rorvik's War

A SPAZ LAUNCHER LIES BESIDE PRIVATE RORVIK, broken in the lee of a crushed building. The air is crisp with the tang of smokeless powder.

He is dying. The hole in his belly leaks blood around his clenched fingers, around the spike of crimson pain that shoots through the core of his being, turning dry Boston dirt into red-brown mud. There is a lot of mud; hours worth. Try to ignore the pain, try to forget you're dying.

He is tired, so tired, but he can't sleep. The pain won't let him move. Each breath stabs like a bayonet into his stomach. His fear is gone, along with hope, and he is left with only pain.

The sky is blue, impossibly blue for a day so grey, brilliant burnished blue, the blue of boredom, babbling burning broken blue, bright baking burning bleeding... Stop it. Stop it stop it stop it. Think of something else. There is a taste of copper in his mouth. Maybe he would be rescued. The sounds of battle as the Russians are driven back, the rumble of microtanks. The purple glint of sunlight off a video lens, peeking around the corner, the shout of discovery: "Hey! There's somebody alive here!" Soldiers—Americans, thank God! Scurrying people all around, a ripping sound as someone pulls the tab of a smoke grenade and tosses it into the clear area behind him, boiling red smoke twisted like an insubstantial genie to guide the helicopter into the hot zone. "You all right there? Hang on, we've called for medics. Help is coming. You'll be okay, just hang on." Whop whop whop as the chopper comes in, and a stab of pain as the medevac team lifts him up, the pain is there but it's distant because it's going to be all right. He grins stoically and the men cheer at his bravery. The chopper takes off, Russian stingers swarming after it but the decoys and the door-gunner get them all, it's going to be all right, it's going to be all right, it's going to be . . . Stop it.

You're dying. There will be no rescue. The American forces are in retreat. The best you can hope for is the Russian advance.

Think of something else. Think of your family. Think about Lissy. He tries to recall his daughter's face, but can't. Brown hair, freckles, pixie nose. It means nothing to him. How she used to beg him for rides on his knee, pretending it was a pony, no, a *horse*, Daddy, ponies are for *children* and suddenly he sees her there, right in front of him, she is really there and he tries to smile for her and tell her it is all right and that he loves her more than anything but his smile turns into a grimace and all he can do is croak. When he tries to reach out to her the pain hits him in his belly like 50 millimeter cannon fire. He clenches his jaw to keep from screaming, then spits the blood out of his mouth. She isn't there, she has never been there at all and he will never see her again.

And then he can hear them, a low rumbling throbbing of the dirt beneath him, treads and six-legged walkers rumbling across the broken pavement of the city. But this isn't a hallucination; this is real. God! Could it be?

He tries to move, to look, but the pain is too much. Something winks in the corner of his vision, and he slowly turns his head. Indicators on the broken spaz launcher suddenly glow to life. The IFF light flickers, on and off, red. Foe. And another light insistently green: targets acquired and locked, warheads armed and ready.

The spaz launcher is still working! Somehow the advancing Russians have missed it; the broken building must have shielded it from their surveillance drones. Guessing from the rumbling in the distance, the advancing mechs must be a whole division. He could put a big hole in their advance, if he gives the launch command.

And then their drones will home in on him and blow him away.

Or he could wait, he could disable the launcher, he could wait for them to find him. Surely they take prisoners of war? They would bring him to a hospital, fix him up, and maybe someday in a POW exchange he'll be sent home, disabled but still alive. A hero. Nobody would have to know about the launcher. Nobody would ever know . . .

He looks at the launcher. Go away, he thinks. I don't want you. I didn't ask for you. I never asked to be a soldier.

. . . He could go home a hero, but inside he would know. And the Russians would advance, they would take Boston, and Worcester, and Springfield. Lissy would grow up speaking Russian, she would go to Russian schools, and after a while she would learn to hate him.

He can hear a scrabbling, something coming up the hill. A lens pokes around the corner, just as he'd imagined it, but it is a Russian lens, attached to a camera on six spidery metal legs, an unarmed battlefield surveillance unit. It looks at him, humming softly to itself.

They've found him. It is now or never.

He pulls his hand away from the wound in his belly and tries to sit up. The hole opens up afresh, and a new flow of blood wells into his lap. He tries not to look at it. He tries to ignore the pain. The drone—unarmed, thank God!—continues to watch him.

He reaches out to the panel and hits ACTUATE. The launcher shudders and vibrates like an epileptic having a seizure, as armor-piercing hunter-seekers chuff from the aperture. The hum of the drone watching him changes pitch and he knows that the Russians are zeroed in, but it is too late; too late for them, too late for him. He leans back and gasps. For a moment, the world goes purple-black. Far away, he can hear the chumpf of explosions as his missiles find their targets, and closer, much closer, the rising whistle of incoming shells.

The first shell explodes a few meters away, and the ground swells up like a wave and tosses him casually against the broken building. He opens his eyes, and after a moment, they focus. In a frozen moment of perfect clarity, he sees the shell that will kill him swell in an instant from a speck into an absolutely perfect circle, deadly black against the blue, blue sky.

And then there is nothing at all.

Rorvik remembered the day his draft notice had come as clearly as if it had happened yesterday. It had been seven-thirty in the morning, and Angela was about ready to head for work. As she kissed him, promising to hurry home, there was a knock on the door.

Angela pulled away from him and turned. "Who could that be, at this hour?"

"Probably a salesman." The knock came again, three measured raps. He was annoyed. The few minutes in the morning while Lissy was still asleep and before Angela went off to work was about the only time he had Angela to himself. "I'll get it." He jerked open the door, ready to give somebody an earful. "Yes?"

It was a balding man in a plain blue suit. Standing just behind him, flanking him on either side, were two larger men. The man looked at a piece of paper. "Mr. Davis C. Rorvik?"

"What do you want?"

"Excuse me. You *are* Mr. Rorvik?"

"Yes, but—"

The man glanced toward Angela, and then back. "May we speak to you alone for a moment, Mr. Rorvik?"

"You may not," Angela said sharply, coming up behind him. "If you have something to tell him, you can say it right here." She made a show of looking at her watch. "And quickly."

The man shrugged, and addressed Rorvik. "Mr. Rorvik, as a duly authorized agent of the United States Selective Service, it is my duty to inform you that as of this moment, you are a member of the United States Armed Forces."

"Wait one moment—"

The man opened a folder and removed a stack of photocopied papers. He ran his finger down the top page to the signatures, and then showed it to Rorvik. An ancient student loan application. "This is your signature?"

He didn't remember the particular document, but the signature was clearly his. It had seemed a good bargain at the time: tuition money for college in return for a promise to serve if needed, and they probably wouldn't even need him anyway. With the collapse of communism across the globe, there was no prospect of war in sight. "Yes, but. . . ."

The man nodded at one of the goons, who pulled something out from under his jacket.

"I'm too . . ." There was a hiss, and Rorvik felt a cool sting at the back of his neck. ". . . too. . . ." His knees suddenly buckled, and he slid slowly to the ground. Inside the house, he could hear Angela begin to scream.

He couldn't move. His muscles felt like warm pudding; his

head felt like somebody had swathed it in lint. The man continued to speak; presumably to Angela. "Under the provisions of Emergency Order 09-13A, you are forbidden under penalty of law to discuss this draft notice or to divulge any information concerning the whereabouts of Mr. Rorvik." One of the men wrapped his arms under Rorvik's armpits. The other picked up his legs. "This includes discussing the matter with any agents of the press." Angela had stopped screaming, and was, as far as he could tell, listening in silence. "The provisions of the Emergency Order allow for full compensation for any inconvenience occasioned by Mr. Rorvik's service." The two men picked him up and started to take him away to the grey station wagon idling at the curb. As the two men swung him around, he could see his next-door neighbor Jack on his way to the subway stop, briefcase in hand. He was taking an intense interest in the weeds poking out through the cracks in the sidewalk. He didn't once look in Rorvik's direction.

As they bundled him into the car, Rorvik managed to complete the phrase he had started, hours ago ". . . too old to be drafted. I'm thirty-eight years old. . . ."

"It's the Eff-En-Gee. What's your name, FNG?"

"Rorvik."

"That Swedish?"

"Close enough. It's Norwegian."

"Wrong answer, FNG." The big corporal tapped him on the chest. "Start counting. I'll tell you when you can stop."

Rorvik dropped down and began doing push-ups. "One! Two! Three!"

"Either you're an American or you're meat. Got it?"

"Heard and understood."

The corporal—Driscott, his name-tag had said—watched him for a few moments. "You may think your name's Rorvik, but I think your name is FNG. You mind that, FNG?"

"No, sir."

"Good. You learn fast, FNG. You know what FNG stands for?"

"No, sir."

"Stands for Fuckin' New Guy. Means you're dangerous, FNG. You're going to get us all killed. Forget yourself, go outside. Feel good to get outside for a few minutes, wouldn't it, FNG?"

"No, sir."

"Good answer. Get yourself specced by a flying Bear eyeball, and you realize you made a fuck-up when you get pounded to dust

by arty. One tremendous ker-powie is the last thing you're going
to hear. Now, that wouldn't bother me a bit—nobody much cares
if the Army's got one FNG more or less—but that same arty fire
is gonna spread *me* across a few acres of landscape too, and I
wouldn't like that very much, no.

"—Count real quiet there, Private FNG, I want you to hear me
and hear me good.

"Reason we call you FNG is so that we don't forget, even for
a moment, that you're not to be trusted. One FNG is as dangerous
as a dozen bear-eyes. Live 'til the next new guy comes in, maybe
you deserve a name of your own, and *he's* the FNG."

Driscott put his foot on Rorvik's back and pressed him against
the ground. " 'Til then, you don't do nothing outside of rules, and
maybe we all live a little longer. Got it?"

"Heard and understood."

"Good. I think I'm gonna get along with you, FNG. I think
we're gonna get along fine."

There had been no air travel, of course—Russian microsats
could spot an airplane and their SAMs would blow it out of the
sky from a thousand miles away. Rorvik, along with half a dozen
other draftees, dazed and scared, had been taken across the inter-
diction zone in an armored convoy that dashed from hardpoint to
hardpoint, screened with chaff, decoys, jammers. At first he
wondered why it was necessary to get to the battle zone at all; later
he was taught that radio relays were weak links in a battle, and
that a critical half of their communications was by line-of-sight
microwave and laser links that required proximity. No communications link was entirely secure, but the shorter the link, the
more reliable it was.

Later yet he realized that it didn't matter where the soldiers
were actually located. The fire zone could move a hundred miles
in the blink of an eye when the Russian computers made a new
guess at the American command location. The front lines were
everywhere.

Driscott took his foot away and reached down a hand. It took
a moment before Rorvik realized that Driscott was offering him
a hand up. "You're gonna learn about this war fast, FNG. First
thing you gonna learn, we don't get the information here. They
don't tell us nothing."

"Yes, sir."

"You married, FNG? Got a family?"

"Yes."

"Too bad. Forget 'em. War first started, the soldiers stayed back from the lines and let the metal take the fire. Sometimes even got to go home on weekends. That got stopped real quick. Fuckin' Russkies didn't know the rules; too many civvies killed when the Russkies targeted the ops. You're here for the duration, got it?"

"Understood." The funny thing was, he could barely even remember the war starting. He was old enough to remember watching CNN with his parents by the hour during the breakup of the Soviet Union, remembered the sense of relief as the world stood down from the brink of nuclear annihilation. But the rise of the Russian junta and the new cold war had seemed to occur in the blink of an eye when he hadn't been paying attention. In hindsight, it was inevitable—though nobody had predicted it at the time—that a strongman would take over control from the ruins of the Soviet system. It was funny how something so important could seem so distant. He had been too busy marrying, trying to start a family, trying to keep a job in an economy going sour year by year. He knew it intellectually, could quote the headline statistics, but the threat of war had never seemed real to him, even as the cold war turned into a war of hot steel.

And the new threat of war wasn't like the old. It was to be a war of computers, not missiles. "I don't even understand why we're here," Rorvik said to Driscott. "They'd told us that the computers made war obsolete. That battlefield simulations can predict the outcome of every battle, so nobody would actually fight any more."

"Yeah?" Driscott seemed amused. "Tell me about it, new guy."

"If our battlefield simulations say the same thing the Russian ones do, and they know the outcome of a battle before the first shot is fired, why are we fighting? They said that whoever was going to lose would know, and back down. What happened?"

"You got sold a bill of goods, FNG. Lissen to too many of those TV commentators." Driscott shook his head. "Just goes to show. Nah, them computers don't know everything. Ya can't predict the psy-fucking-cology of the guys in the field. You can put in the numbers, but can you put in morale? Can you put in fuckups?" He tapped Rorvik's chest. "It's you and me, buddy, you and me make the difference. We aren't just fighting a war. No, what we're doing is showing them Russian computers that they don't got a clue about just how tough the American soldier really is. No matter what they throw at us, no matter how tough things get, even if all we have left is rocks, we just keep coming. We never give up. Never. Got it?"

"Got it."

For a moment after he wakes, his dream of being a civilian seems like it had been only yesterday, the memories of civilian life stronger and more alive than those of the war. The feeling fades. It was just that the war had started so *fast,* and his life had changed so quickly and completely, it sometimes feels like he had been a civilian just hours before.

Rorvik is a tactical operator on the fly-eyes, one of the best. A fly-eye is a tiny infrared-visible camera with an encrypted radio transmitter, hung under a plastic flex-wing with a miniature propeller and motor, the whole thing folding up to a streamlined package about the size of a pencil that fits into a rifle. It is up to him to find targets for the artillery, located somewhere in a secured hiding place fifty miles or more distant.

The war is a huge game of hide and seek. When the enemy is found, the smart shells pound cracks through his armor to incinerate the meat within.

Somewhere in the city below, a grunt hiding in the deserted city fires him into the sky. Rorvik knows nothing about the soldier who launches him, nor cares, but waits with a rising sense of anticipation until he hits apogee and spreads his wings. Deployed, silent, nearly radar invisible, he soars over darkened buildings looking for movement, flying in slow zigzags to present a less predictable target. His motor gives him about five minutes of power, but it is a point of pride with the fliers not to use it, but to soar the tiny flexwing on thermals and on the ridge lift from rooftops, prolonging his flights for hours before he has to return to the drab world of concrete and first sergeants and smelly underwear and MRE packages eaten cold to avoid unnecessary IR signature. He hates cold water shaves and the endless pinochle game the E-5 sergeants play in their den; he hates the smell of stale piss that washes over the room whenever one of the men opens up the latrine canister to take a leak, and the rotten-fruit smell of unwashed bodies the rest of the time. (There is a perennial rumor that the enemy is developing an odor-sensitive homing bomb, and that when it is developed the field troops will be subject to a smell discipline as strong as the IR discipline is now. God, he wishes they'd hurry.)

But, flying his eye, he is far from all that. He flies above the city, the flier's electronic eyes becoming his own eyes, heedless of his body controlling the flier far below.

He soars over the darkening city. It is spring, but the few trees left in the city provide scant obstruction to his cameras. A flutter of movement attracts his attention, and he wheels around. Nothing. No, there! He zooms in. A piece of paper blowing in the wind. He circles for a minute, hoping to catch something else, but nothing moves. MI will examine his snapshot of the paper, he knows, trying to determine where it came from, if it is ours or theirs.

"Little Eagle? Word from Uncle Henry that they've seen Bear footprints north in sector Tiger three-niner. They want you to eyeball it for them. Do you need a new bird?"

Tiger 39. He flashes up a map. About a kilometer north of him, in the area that once used to be north Cambridge. "Negative, unless they're in some real rush about it. I can get there in five minutes."

"Roger. We're standing by."

He can see the pink warmth of a thermal off to his left, and banks around. He increases speed until his wings begin to ripple and lose lift, then backs off a hair.

Four minutes later he is circling the area.

The sky is muddy brown in the falsecolor of his IR display. "It's an evac zone," the voice in his earphones says. "Anything you see will be Bears."

He hears the slight riffle of air behind him. He snap-rolls instantly, and the diving hawk misses him by inches. He pushes into a dive to gain airspeed, with one eye watching the Russian hawk pull up to come around at him again, with the other flashing to his map to find if he is near a sector where he had fire support from the ground. Negative. He flips his mike on.

"Load up another birdy, Wintergreen. I've drawn a hawk."

"No can do, Little Eagle. A couple of bear-eyes moved in too close to our guys on the ground. Advise you run for the green in sector X-ray niner."

The Russian hawk, abandoning stealth, has lit its tiny pulsejet and is coming at him from below. "Negative, negative. It's too far. Blow the eyes away."

"Sorry, Sport. Too many eyes. We don't want to risk the Bears getting a fix on our artillery. You're on your own."

"Fuck you very much, Wintergreen." He starts an evasion pattern. No way he can outrun a hawk; he pushes the stick forward to the edge of flutter and heads in zigzags toward the turbulence of a fragged building.

He'd been hoping he could ride the turbulence, but the gusty wind is too much for him. The wind-rotor grabs him, flips him upside down. He rolls out inches away from smashing against the concrete, pulls out hard, and stalls. Hanging dead in the air for the instant before falling, he feels more than sees the hawk coming at him. He is dead meat.

And in the next instant the hawk flies apart, ripped to shreds by gunfire. He pushes forward, regains flying speed, and hightails down-wind, at the same time keying his mike. "What the hell was that? Flechette?"

"Birdshot. I found a grunt dumb enough to step outside to take a shot. You owe me one, Sport. Can you make it now?"

"Affirmative."

"Keep your eyes peeled. Local support arty is pinned down, but we have some long-range shoot 'n' scoot that can wipe the Bear HQ if you happen to find it in your travels."

"Rog." He finds some lift, gains altitude, and heads for Tiger.

He flies over territory that is familiar to him. He had worked near here once, before he was married. For a moment he wonders why the Russians had invaded. Arming for war had shored up a failed economy, but did it make any sense for the Bears to actually hold territory? They must have had a reason, or at least a pretext for one, but for the moment Rorvik can't remember what it was. But then, who could ever psych out the Russians? Leave that to the professionals, with their super-computers and tactical models. Not to the soldiers.

Tiger three-niner. Circling the area, he finds a cluster of relatively undamaged buildings, apparently the remains of an old housing project. A bit exposed for a fire base, but still . . . He circles lower, looking for signs of habitation. Nothing. There! Traces of body heat lingering in the still air, a yellowish fog in the IR. He zooms out and follows the heat trace across the city as it brightens into lime green and then the pale blue of recent passage. There, under an overhang, the scarlet flash of a warm body. He checks his map. This is an evac area; a free-fire zone. A flash of movement. "Think I got something here. Hold five." He banks around.

"Standing by to fire."

He comes in low, stalls, fights the building's turbulence.

Another flash of movement; a foot. "Got it! Bogeys, could be a Bear fire-control post." He flashes his IR range finder. "My coords plus 5 at 22 surface, mark. I'm coming around to guide your fire." He rides out and into some slope lift from the breeze flowing up over the facade.

A different voice, the slight echo of multiple radio relays. "Roger. Outgoing, one, two, three." His vision flickers static for a moment from the EM pulse used to dazzle any Bear radars from tracing back the rising shells. It takes a moment for the shells to clear far enough to aero-maneuver, a moment in which he is suddenly aware of sitting in a concrete bunker with a flickering television helmet on his head, and then his vision sharpens back to normal and he is flying again.

The fire support base is miles away; it will be a minute before the shells came in and need his terminal guidance. Something about what he'd seen bothers him. He flicks back to his last photo. A foot shows in the shadow of an overhang. He zooms in, enhances contrast. Barefoot. The Russians are that far out of discipline? He circles back, penetrating upwind slowly, searching for a good view. There. He hovers for a moment into the wind, panning his eye around behind him. Shapes move, but the shadow is too deep to distinguish them in visual. He turns up contrast and sharpens his gain. There.

The instant before he stalls out, he gets a good shot.

Three children circle around an object suspended from above. The oldest is perhaps fourteen, the youngest perhaps nine. One, blindfolded, holds a broken mop handle like a club. In a corner a scruffy yellow dog watches them. He looks closer at the suspended object. He recognizes it as the throw-away cardboard transport tube for an 80-mm Russian antiaircraft missile. It has been decorated, painted bright colors, given old buttons to serve as eyes, four painted cardboard legs and long floppy ears. A crude caricature of a donkey. A piñata.

The voice in his earphones says, "Twenty seconds to incoming. Ready for terminal guidance."

"Abort your rounds! Abort!"

"Say again, Eagle?"

"Abort your rounds! Civilians!"

"Roger." Three sharp cracks in the air above him as the lifting bodies detonate. "Rounds aborted." There is a pause, and then, "Do you have a vector on the target that can avoid the civilians?"

He feels like ash, like he had been burned and there is nothing left. Shooting at shadows is common enough, but it won't endear him to his superiors. "Negative. False alarm. Sorry, guys."

There is a long pause, and then, "Operations wants to talk to you, Rorvik."

Using his name instead of his code is a bad sign. "Acknowledged."

"That means now, Private."

"Roger." He scrambles and finds some lift, prolonging the flight, knowing it might be his last. "I'll be there as soon as I'm down."

Another pause. "Negative, Rorvik. Ops wants to talk to you pronto. Advise you blow the bird and get your butt down here before you get marks for insubordination."

"Heard and understood." No help for it. The critical chips on his bird are set to melt when they lose the carrier wave for more than a few seconds, or if he gives the coded signal. The rest of the bird is just sticks and plastic; no more than a toy. He flicks the cover off the toggle, caresses it for a second, and then presses it with his thumb. His eye screens flash black for an instant, and then there is nothing left of the world but the whisper and swirl of static.

He pops his helmet, and is in a grimy concrete bunker crammed with equipment and stinking of sweat and hot electronics. Next to his contoured seat, two other fliers sit, faceless in the white plastic of surround helmets, oblivious to him and the rest of the world, except for their birds. His muscles ache from the body English he gave his bird while flying, but the bunker is too cramped for him to stretch. He unpins the throat mike, and goes to explain.

They are kept in the dark about the overall course of the war, but from the consistent, slow retreat, and the way that replacements—men and materiel both—are getting scarcer and scarcer, by the end of the summer Rorvik knows that the war is not going well.

Some of the men from Rorvik's unit keep a Russian lieutenant tied up in a remote bunker, nominally an auxiliary command post but actually just an abandoned garage that hadn't been shelled, with a roof thick enough to mask IR signature. They call her Olga—nobody knows her real name; it had been written on her uniform way back when she'd had one, but none of the gang could read Cyrillic, and she either can't or won't speak English.

Rorvik's unit is all male. Equality be damned, the Army is still segregated by sex. Only Headquarters units and reserves mix genders; every operational unit Rorvik has served in has been all male. There are all-female units too, the subject of a good deal of unlikely stories and rude speculation, but Rorvik's unit rarely meets them, except on the field, where the drones are sexless and the operators invisible, hidden behind labyrinths of encrypted radio relays. The Russian lieutenant is the only female any of them has seen for weeks—some of them, months.

And they know that there is little chance that they will survive the war anyway.

As Rorvik passes by, one of the boys yells out an invitation for him to join them. Rorvik walks faster, and they snicker. "Ol' Davey's too good for us." "No, it's just that he's waiting until we capture a *boy*." "Maybe he's got his own nookie stashed away somewhere, some pretty Russky major."

Their lieutenant pretends not to notice, but he knows. No way he could miss it. They were supposed to turn prisoners over to the authorities—they desperately needed Russians for their simulations—but, for the moment, that is impossible. No doubt as soon as they rejoined their Battalion the prisoner would be "found," and rescued from the civilian "partisans" who had so cruelly mistreated her.

Could he do anything? Informing headquarters about the prisoner would result in her disappearance, and possibly his own, long before any inspection might get to them. Still, the thought that there could be something he might do chews at Rorvik's conscience and worries him at the odd moments when battle duty or his eight-hour watch leaves him free to think.

As the battle eddies and stalls, with movement by lightning air deployment and half the battle fought by remotes, it is almost pointless to mark battle lines. Most of the Boston area is controlled by neither the Russians nor the American forces, but watched by both. To the extent that anybody can say, though, Rorvik's unit is temporarily behind enemy lines. Or at least, they are cut off from support.

Their control bunker is buried under Dorchester. When the battle moved closer, his unit had to stay inside; but now, with the battle line off in Roxbury, some outside mobility is possible. At work, of course, he is right in the thick of battle, wherever it is.

Rorvik had been taken off of tac surveillance to become a drone runner. He alternates with Drejivic, six hours on, six off, controlling four robot warriors. The warriors are intelligent; if the coded remote signal is jammed, they will keep fighting until the interference clears, and their IFF signals — changed hourly — keep them from shooting each other. But remotes work best if an actual human watches over them to make decisions. In a hard fire-fight, it is best to let them on their own; human reaction time only slows them down. He'd interfere only when indecision about a questionable IFF (identify, friend or foe) threatens a gridlock. Occasionally he'll have to call in Rick, who runs another four, to take one of his drones; or Rick will call him in. It is a point of pride not to do this too often.

Angie, Lissy, Gumby, and Pokey, he calls them. Drejivic has other names.

He hooks into the computer. When he is running drones, his body stays in the bunker, but *him* — the important part of him — is the drone. He flits back and forth from one viewpoint to another. When he wears one body, the views from the other three cameras are always visible in the edge of his vision.

When he concentrates on one drone, the other ones fight on their own initiative.

Angie and Lissy, the fliers, are the ones he likes best. These aren't the disposable surveillance flexies he had flown when the war was young; these are armed fighting drones. The fliers are pigs for energy use, though, and have to conserve their time aloft. On the ground they are clumsy. More than once he's had to use his rocket-assisted take-off to haul ass out of fire too hot for them to handle. The rasstos are one-shot units; use one up and you have to bring the drone home and wait for a replacement. Like everything else, they are running low. He's been chewed out several times, the sarge drilling in that we are *not* to get into situations where we have to rassto out.

Unfortunately, Angie is waiting for a replacement rassto, and Lissy is out of action. She'd taken a couple of rounds of small-caliber fire. The maintenance tech has her now, trying to scrounge parts to put her back together.

Gumby and Pokey are his two bipedal walkers. Running them feels almost like wearing a robot suit. Gumby is the most flexible of his drones. His problem is that they'd long ago run out of ammo for the 3 mm skittergun that is Gumby's utility weapon. He still has the 10 mm armor piercers and rockets, but on his own, Gumby's first move in a fire-fight is still to bring up the skittergun. The slight hesitation it takes for Gumby's tiny processor to remember it didn't work could be fatal. The unit is supposed to be adaptable enough to remember, but Rorvik guesses that that part of his programming has been shot out.

Pokey is operational, but weaponless until parts become available, after the unit rejoins the main army. Mostly Rorvik stays out of Gumby's viewpoint, and lets the drone move around on auto while he scouts from Pokey.

What the drones fight, mostly, are other drones. There are human infantry in the field, on both sides, but they tend to be dug into stealth emplacements, mobile and heavily protected, only popping out for missions too delicate to be run by drones.

In the distance, the ruins of Boston burn red on the horizon.

The status bulletin has given them a clear for an hour. It is rare that their computers can predict a clear for that long; somewhere far away one side or the other must have ferreted a major command center, and a battle must be drawing all of the resources available. For now, Rorvik's area is clear of Russian eyes, and they can move around outside. Drone runners have to take rest shifts of a minimum of three hours to stay at peak effectiveness; the regulations demand it, and so he knows he won't be called back except for a serious emergency.

A block from their bunker is a square that still has a few trees in it; the closest thing to a park within the defense perimeter. He decides to go there for as long as the clear lasts.

Someone else has gotten there before him.

The woman in the park has a SISI gun grafted right to her shoulder, and the eye-shaped barrel turns to aim at him at the same time she raises her head. He takes an involuntary step back; the gun unnerves him. See it, shoot it: he could be dead with a single thought. She must have volunteered to have the gun grafted into her nervous system; the regulations don't allow them to modify you without consent. It means that she is from a live-combat unit, and that is unusual as well, especially for a woman. Women had to volunteer for front-line duty.

He had been in a live-combat unit once, during the first battle for Boston. He remembers — but that was early in the war; there is no point in dredging up those memories.

Her insignia shows her to be a Spec-4. He has heard that a female infantry company had temporarily moved into an area south of them, but hadn't realized that their clear areas would overlap. The gun moves like something alive on her shoulder, pivoting minutely as she shifts her eyes, jerking from target to target with the unblinking attention of a snake.

She watches him eyeing her gun. "It's no safer behind the lines, soldier. I'd rather have it be up front, where I can fight back, than where you are, buried in some concrete bunker and never hear it coming, you know?"

"Doesn't the gun make you a target?"

"Makes me dangerous." She smiles. "I like to be dangerous."

She is too tall, too many muscles and too few curves, and wears a wrinkled jumpsuit made of fireproof fabric that masks what feminine lines she has. She is desirable as all hell.

She can tell he is thinking about that, too, and she laughs. "Soldiers think any woman out here is sex-crazed, you know it? I'm not like that. I've got a husband, and two kids. They're what I'm fighting for."

"I know."

"You married, soldier?"

He nods.

"Happily? Got any kids?"

"A girl."

She nods. "Then you do know." As she unzips the jumpsuit, she says, "They're back at home, and we're here." She runs the tip of one finger along the gun barrel for a second, then does something to it with the other hand, and it stops tracking her gaze. "This didn't happen, you know? It's the war. No commitments, no promises, no looking each other up, after."

"No." He doesn't believe there will ever be an after, not any more. He has seen the craters where houses had been, the lines of refugees, miles long, trudging endlessly out of the cities toward areas they believed might be safe. He has seen the ruins of the area where his house had been, where his wife and girl had once lived.

But he still believes in now.

Her name is Westermaker, she whispers. She kneels down to unzip his pants. He strokes her hair—short, dark and very slightly curled—as she runs her lips along the underside of his cock.

A confused jumble of thoughts crowds through his head all at the same time. He feels himself already beginning to dribble, and wonders if he will be able to hold back, or if he will come the in-

stant she takes him in her mouth. Wonders if he will ever be able
to tell Angela about this, and whether she could possibly understand. Wonders if the Army issues female grunts birth control.
Wonders if she will stay long enough for him to take her twice.

He reaches down to slide his pants off. She cups his buttock
in a palm as she delicately touches the end of her tongue to the
tip of his cock, and the burst of machine-gun fire takes her low in
the chest. Her mouth opens to scream as her lungs spatter out the
side of her shredded uniform and across the jagged ends of her
splintered ribs. An instant later, without a sound, she dies.

He staggers back, his ears ringing with the report, tries to turn
around, and trips on the pants tangled around his knees. He rolls
over and looks right into the lens of a Russian walker. With the
soft whir of servos, the machine gun tracks to his face.

He squeezes his eyes shut. The smell of blood is very strong.
Nothing happens.

After a long moment he opens his eyes. The machine is still
there, unblinking; the gun still aimed right for him. It is heavier
and clumsier than the American units Rorvik is familiar with, all
angles and graceless ceramic armor-plate, and very deadly. Surreptitiously, he reaches behind him and gropes for a rock. The
machine does nothing. It takes an eternity to find a rock loose
enough to pull out of the ground. When he finally pries one loose
he waits for an instant, gauging the distance, and then, with a
quick, smooth motion, hurls it at the machine.

It dodges easily, still watching him, still tracking him with the
gun, still holding back its fire. The gun must have jammed, he
thinks, and then, an instant later, God, it's already called in
artillery on me.

But the gun killed Westermaker easily enough, and the remote
is making no effort to get clear of incoming artillery.

He should have never gone out, not even to a clear zone,
without his sidearm. But he is a drone runner; he isn't supposed
to fight face to face. Holding his pants up with one hand, he
scrambles to his feet, preparing to make a run for it, and hears the
hydraulics start up behind him. He freezes. Suddenly he realizes
what the remote is up to.

Where can he go?

It had shot Westermaker. Westermaker had been armed,
though her SISI gun had done no good against a threat she had
never seen. He is no threat. The operator—somewhere miles

away—can shoot him any time he wants. But his very presence means that there must be a command post somewhere nearby. Why not let him go, and watch where he goes?

The tell-tale on his wrist has started to blink urgently red: return to secure area immediately. A warning that does him no good at all.

A block of ice has formed in his lungs. It is suddenly impossible for him to breathe. He doesn't dare go back, it would lead the Bears right into his post.

There is no way he can warn his unit, but if he doesn't return they will know, and take measures. Either way, it is too late for him.

The smell of blood has vanished, but the acrid smell of spent powder etches his nostrils, filled the entire world. Slowly, slowly, he turns and starts to walk, then run. Crosswise and down hill; in a wide loop away from his bunker, away from safety, away from hope.

In the ruins of Worcester, the triumphant Russian troops are coming up Belmont Street from Boston. The resistance waits for them. Rorvik's unit has managed to find a gas station that had been shelled to rubble early in the war; its buried storage tank is almost untouched. They'd filled a dumpster with gasoline, poured in five dozen bags of nitrate liberated from an old greenhouse supply, and then melted in styrofoam to make it gel. At the bottom of the dumpster is a pound of black powder, with a detonator made from a light bulb filament.

The dumpster is hidden inside the bricked-up front of an abandoned apartment block, just another forgotten piece of debris in a city full of rubble.

Russian air cover is too complete and the computer triangulation and jamming too swift for Rorvik's unit to trust a radio link, even with encrypted relays. They lost two men learning that lesson. Rorvik had been odd man out on the coin toss. He has found a concealed niche, across the street from the bomb, and waits, nervous, sweat dripping down his back. Through a tiny hole drilled in the wall, he watches the enemy as it walks, crawls, rolls up the street on jointed steel legs and armor-plated wheels.

Wondering if he will be able to get away, after.

Now.

The explosion is huge, an orgasm in orange and black and glorious rolling thunder. The blast picks up one of the ceramic-armored high-mobility one-man tanks and flips it against the wall. It struggles to right itself, but the move is pointless. As planned, the blast has undermined the stone facade of the building, and a slow-motion avalanche of Fitchburg granite rumbles down over the column. Five tanks and about a dozen mechanicals are swept up in the river of boiling stone, then tossed aside and buried by rubble.

The Russian commander is sharp, and in control. Before the dust has started to settle, Rorvik hears the amplified voice booming out in clipped Russian. "They left a man behind to detonate it! Find him! Squadron A, left side of the street! B, right!"

He should have scrambled the instant he pressed the button, not stayed to see what he accomplished. He could hide forever from ordinary eyes, but to infrared sensors the plume of his breath must glow like a beacon. He has only moments. He dashes through the streets, and can hear the clatter of armored soldiers entering the street behind him.

He dodges down an alley, hoping to stay out of sight of the sky for a few more moments, and only after he enters it sees that the shelling has completely blocked it with rubble. It is too late to turn back the way he came; troops are too close behind him. He spots a window into the basement of a dime store, and miraculously the iron grill over the window has been shaken loose, but the glass is still intact. He smashes the glass with a piece of asphalt and drops into the darkness.

He lands awkwardly, bruising his leg. In a few moments his eyes adjust to the dimness. The basement is empty save for rubbish; the cement floor damp and glistening. Across from the window, a stairway once rose up to the main level. It is now just a pile of splintered wood. The door hangs above empty space, and through bullet holes he can see sky.

This, then, will be his last stand. There is nowhere left to run.

Turning, he sees the shadow of an articulated leg fall across the empty window. He limps away from the window, crouches back against the wall and pulls out his automatic. The remote stops, hesitates by the window while the operator queries for directions, and then a lens pokes in through the window.

It swivels left, the wrong way. Rorvik aims, but holds his fire, waiting for a better shot. The body of the remote starts to press in through the window at the same time the camera pans right, and an instant before it fixes on him, Rorvik fires.

His shot is aimed at one of the vulnerable hydraulic lines, and the spray of hot fluid tells him he damaged it. Before he can shoot again, two more shatter the door above. He hears the shot an instant after he feels it hit him in the chest. The second shot, an instant later, he never hears: the one that blows apart his skull.

Then he awoke. The memory of being drafted was fresh in his mind, as it always was when he awoke from a long sleep. All that had been long ago. He'd been captured; the US had fallen. He was, like many others, in a reeducation camp. Since he'd been drafted, not volunteered, the camp bureaucracy had considered him a victim of the imperialist aggressors, rather than a war criminal. That fact had earned him a chance at reeducation, instead of the bullet in the back of the head that had awaited most of his fellow soldiers.

As he stood in the line for the "voluntary" evening reeducation lecture, a man behind him put a hand on his shoulder and whispered.

"Resistance meeting tonight. Strike a blow for freedom!"

How crazy were they? Didn't they know that the Bears had stoolies and paid informants everywhere? Hey, he could even earn brownie points — maybe even a chance to see Angela and Lissy — by passing along what he'd heard.

The lecture was about economics and simulation war. Very little of the war, he discovered, had actually been fought; most of it had been simulation. Both sides' tactical computers could model the outcome of every battle, and the side that would have lost would always withdraw without actually fighting.

In theory.

"What the capitalist computers failed to take into account," said the lecturer, a tall Hispanic man with a Stalin mustache and a habit of nervously looking over his shoulder, "was that the loyal soldiers of the Hegemony have the force of history with them. Citizens of a democracy are by nature unable to act in harmony. Knowing that history is invincible, the soldiers of the Hegemony are unswerving. Purity of ideology gives them strength. How could the computers of an obsolete political system calculate this? Only with the data from actual battles, showing the staggering battlefield superiority of Hegemony troops. Victory of the Hegemony was inevitable. Even now, with algorithms bolstered with actual battle data, the computers of the aggressor capitalist governments have correctly calculated their inevitable defeat. The capitalist government has surrendered unconditionally to the provisional government, and asked all its soldiers to lay down arms. Resistance of any sort is treason, and will be dealt with as such."

Rorvik listened to it sleeping with his eyes open, automatically noting phrases to parrot back in the group-reeducation sessions the next morning. Attending the lecture would earn him points, maybe a second piece of toast at breakfast the next time supplies came to the camp.

Later, after the official lecture, the lecturer—who had been a high-school history teacher before the war—casually gathered interested parties for the second talk, this one quite unofficial. The Americans had a clandestine school system of their own in the camps, and whenever the Russkies' lecturers gave any information from the disputed territories or talked on how the resistance was going, they tried to sort out the kernel of truth from the shell of propaganda. The resistance was still alive, they said, and the Russians were having a tough time trying to govern the territory they had captured. If they could hold out, frustrate their captors at every turn, soon the alleycats would . . .

"Resistance" was a forbidden word, and anyone caught using it could be shot without hesitation. The slang for the day was to call the remnants of the armed forces who had escaped capture "alleycats."

But nothing changed, and if there really were alleycats, he'd heard plenty of talk but seen no real signs of them in the camp. Until now.

As the man spoke, barely loud enough to hear, Rorvik's attention drifted. The talk was about the necessity for computer models to be grounded in data, something Rorvik had no need to be taught again. His mind was running on another track. He couldn't actually remember being captured, and suddenly that had struck him as odd. Surely that was an important moment in his life; he ought to have vivid memories, or at least some recollection of how it had happened. He must have blacked out, that was it. The time he had been wounded, bleeding to death in the rubble . . . but no, he hadn't been captured then, he remembered it vividly, remembered the artillery, remembered dying.

No, that was impossible, he had survived, joined the resistance, set off the bomb and been chased into . . . no, that couldn't be. He had died then, too. There was something wrong with his memory. Had he hallucinated it? But it had been real, he was sure of it, as real as the barbed wire and concrete surrounding him.

One of the other men in the camp, Povelli, brushed past him

on the way to the latrine. Rorvik looked up, and Povelli, without looking at him, bent over, untied his shoe, and then carefully retied it. "Wait a few minutes, then get up and make like you gotta go to the crapper," Povelli said softly. Rorvik glanced around. No one was paying attention to them. "Past the crapper, you know the tool shed? Ten minutes. Whistle once when you approach."

Rorvik nodded slightly, as if agreeing with something the Professor said, and Povelli finished tying his shoe and got up.

The lecture was breaking up anyway; it was dangerous to gather in groups of more than two or three for very long. Rorvik stretched and looked around. Nobody was paying particular attention to him. He strolled toward the latrine.

Before he got halfway to the meeting, just outside the prefab, Khokhlov stopped him. They had two reeducation counselors to assist them in learning correct political thought. Khokhlov was the nicer of the two, and spoke British-accented English with a bare trace of guttural Slavic vowels.

He offered Rorvik a cigarette. The Russians all smoked heavily. Rorvik accepted it, but only puffed on it enough to show that he appreciated the courtesy.

"You have come very far in your thinking, Mr. Rorvik," Khokhlov said. "I believe you are one of my best students."

Rorvik nodded and gave him a wide smile. "Thank you. I have been doing my best."

"Are you dissatisfied at all?" Khokhlov waved his hand. "Of course, I know that food here is not as plentiful as it could be. I assure you that we all are under the same conditions, even guards."

Rorvik wondered what Khokhlov could be after. Did he know about the meeting? "No, no—everything is fine," he said. He knew quite as well as Khokhlov that complaining was a sure sign of regressive-thinking. "Really."

"Perhaps we could chat a bit?" said Khokhlov. He took Rorvik by the arm. "I have been very disturbed by something I heard, my friend. One of the people I have been chatting with—you won't object if I don't mention his name?—said that he believed you were sympathetic to the resistance. I, of course, told him this could not be correct, but he quite insisted on the point."

"No, no," Rorvik said hastily. "Absolutely not. I steer quite clear of them, let me assure you."

Khokhlov looked interested. "Really? Then you know who they are?"

He wanted to kick himself for speaking without thinking, but tried to keep his expression innocent and candid. "Well, no—that is, not really. I've heard rumors, of course—"

"I am quite interested in rumors."

"It wouldn't be fair—"

Khokhlov cut him off. "I am judge of fairness in this camp, Mr. Rorvik. Please, we are not barbarians here. Let me give you my assurance that I am here to help people adjust to scientific society, not to punish them for retrograde thinking. If you are hearing rumors, I should be aware of them. If people are spreading tales— gossips, this is correct word?—spreading the gossips without foundation, I should know this, in order to better guide people to correct thinking. Please, do not hesitate to speak completely candidly with me."

Rorvik smiled ingratiatingly, trying to assume the puppy-dog expression of a convert to correct-thinking. "I don't know any specific names."

"I am afraid that you are not being completely open with me, Mr. Rorvik," Khokhlov said, his face expressing deep sorrow mixed with sternness, the expression of a teacher with a willfully disobedient pupil. "Perhaps I have been overly hasty in evaluating your progress toward objective political thought. You are aware, I am sure, that this camp is quite the luxury dacha. You are guests here, not prisoners. In other places food is not quite so plentiful, and discipline is a bit more . . . severe. Please, I beg of you, tell me some names." He smiled. "I do believe that we could . . . work together."

"I'm afraid not, sir."

Khokhlov frowned. "I am not stupid, Mr. Rorvik. Let me point something out to you. I know that there are resistance sympathizers in this camp, and I know something is going on. I can feel it in the air, and I also have my . . . sources. I suspect that you know what is going on. Now, consider. We have been talking for quite the while. Ten minutes? Don't think we haven't been noticed. Now, what are these resistance sympathizers to think, as they watch us talk? Even if you assure them you told me nothing, how can they trust you? Talk to me, and I will see to your safety— I have my means in this camp, I assure you—or else. . . ." He shook his head. "It is not me you should be afraid of. You are tagged for being a pigeon whether you talk or not."

Khokhlov was right, he realized. Even though he hadn't joined the resistance, he knew too much. Had there been any way he could have avoided talking to Khokhlov? No; the reeducation counselors were all-powerful within the boundary of the camps. Even the guards feared them, and a prisoner who deliberately refused to talk when asked politely could expect to be denounced, or even shot. But it was the wrong night to be talking to him. He wouldn't survive the night without Khokhlov's protection.

His muscles were knotted up, and he had to force himself to breath normally. He knew the feeling intimately; it was the feeling of having hostile, invisible eyes watching from the sky, the feeling of being a target for inevitable death.

But just what, really, did he have to live for? If he talked, other people would die. It wasn't fair—he'd never even joined the camp resistance!—but he understood war very well by now. He shook his head slowly. "I'm sorry. I really am."

The muscles in his neck didn't loosen, but he realized that he could breathe again.

"I am too, Mr. Rorvik." Khokhlov waited for one more moment, then shook his head and strode briskly away, as if he wanted to have nothing more to do with Rorvik, abandoning him to his fate. "I am too."

Rorvik knew that his one chance was to find Povelli—or somebody, anybody with a line to the resistance—and try to explain. There was a bare possibility that they might take a chance on him, if he went to them immediately, showing he had nothing to hide.

He didn't move.

There was something wrong. He desperately needed to find somewhere to think. There was nowhere; standing here by the barbed wire was as good as anywhere.

He squeezed his eyes tightly shut. Where the hell was he?

In a camp.

Was he?

The memory of the draft was still fresh in his mind. His biceps still ached from the pushups that Driscott had made him do, back when he was still a FNG, what, two years ago?

That was impossible.

He had died. Unambiguously, totally. Shot in the chest, shot in the head, blown to pieces by artillery.

That was impossible, too.

Simulations. That was the key. He remembered that from his civilian days, as the superpowers of Europe and Japan and America jockeyed and maneuvered for position, watching their simulations of what would happen in every possible attack scenario, each waiting until they found one where they'd have the advantage. Much of battle was mathematical, a matter of strategy and tactics, faceless forces fighting other faceless forces.

But in some situations, the people mattered. They would need to know how real troops react in battle before they could believe the computer models. God, Driscott had told him that, right out; Driscott had told him everything, and he had been too dumb to understand.

He opened his eyes, and tried to disbelieve what he saw. There was no camp; no war. When he'd been drafted, there had been no war. How long ago was that? A few days? A month? It was ridiculous to think that the Russians would invade the United States; what would they get out of it? The whole war made no sense, not unless it was a scenario, an elaborate set-up to probe how soldiers would act in wartime.

He even knew the technology; it wasn't that much more sophisticated than what he had used to run his drones, except that the resolution would be higher. *Was* higher.

It looked real. There would be micro-lasers somewhere, rastering the image directly onto his retina. If the resolution were high enough, there would be no possible way to tell the difference between real and simulated. He would be drugged, strapped into a contour-couch somewhere, maybe in Washington? Paralytic drugs certainly, to keep his motions from causing problems, while SQUID pickups read the nerve impulses to his muscles. Maybe hypnotics to make him suggestible, make it easier for him to mistake the simulation for reality.

He pinched himself, then punched his arm as hard as he could force himself to. It hurt, but that proved nothing. That could be simulated.

There must be other real people in the simulation, too. Who? Westermaker? Driscott? Who was real, and who simulated? Westermaker, he thought. She had to be real. Somewhere she was still alive. Someday she would go back to her husband, back to her kids. In a few days she would be wondering if he had been real or a simulation. And an incident that had been innocent and decent would turn into a pornographic sideshow for some Washington desk-jockeys.

It took him a moment to realize that if this was true, then somewhere—maybe not even far away—Angela and Lissy were alive too, waiting patiently for him at home, oblivious of the non-existent war. Not starving to death in a relocation camp, not buried in unmarked graves hidden under mountains of rubble. Alive.

God, now he knew what he had been drafted for. Not to be a real soldier, but to play out simulations, perfect computer simulations of possible battle scenarios. The people he'd fought, the ones he'd fought with, weren't real. They needed to know how he'd hold up under stress, how any average American would hold up. They needed the data to make their computer simulations work. He was fighting this war so that, in the real life, no one would ever have to fight a war. He was a pawn.

But was he a pawn of the Americans? Or the Russians? What if the Russians needed to know the reactions of American soldiers, too? What if they really were planning an invasion?

That was ridiculous.

He started to shake his head, first left, then right, watching for a time-lag in the video response. It started making him dizzy, but he refused to stop. "Let me out!" He shook his head harder, faster. The other prisoners in the camp were starting to stare at him. "Stop the simulation! I quit, I tell you! I'm quitting!"

His head was hurting, and the world was no less real. He clenched his teeth and slapped himself on the side of the head, ignoring the pain. Blood started to flow down his cheek on the third or fourth punch, but now he thought he could see something, a blur of black-anodized aluminum, out of focus in front of his eyes, the raster-head of a retinal laser-scanner. He shook his head more violently, left and right, up and down, and he could see it more clearly now, with the lenses and sensors that kept it focused on his eyes. It had slipped slightly off to the side, and the reeducation camp was the part out of focus now, two-dimensional, the view from each eye skewed. He tried to pull it off his head, but his hands felt nothing. He shook his head harder. The moment before he passed out, the head-mounted display slipped entirely away, and he could see the room, and the computers, and the figures of three doctors bending over him with expressions of alarmed concern.

The man from the selective service thanked him, reminded him of the penalties for talking to any person at any time about his service experiences, and then shook his hand. He could see Angela waiting for him at the door. The house looked different; smaller, the paint dingier than he remembered. He'd only been gone a week.

Stop that. If it were a simulation, they would have used photographs of the house; it would be perfect in every detail.

He scanned the bushes automatically, looking for the glint of sun from drone lenses, wishing he had his IR augmented vision. Then he caught himself, forced his muscles to relax. There was no war, no hiding drones.

The government car drove off, and then Lissy darted out from behind Angela and scampered out to greet him. He spread his arms to receive her, and she almost knocked him over with her enthusiasm. "Daddy! You're home! I missed you!"

He picked her up and swung her around. She was bigger than he remembered. Could she have grown so much in a week? Her hair was darker, her face thinner and more ordinary than in his memories.

"I missed you too, Tiger-cub," he said.

She looked up at him, growling like a tiger but with a wide smile, and he hugged her. Then he nuzzled his face up under her ponytail, and purred at her as loud as he could. She giggled and purred back.

They couldn't possibly simulate that. He opened up his arms. Angela joined them, and he hugged them both at the same time. "I missed you too, Daddy-cat," Angela whispered.

It was real this time.

He was home.

Real.

Approaching Perimelasma

THERE IS A SUDDEN FRISSION OF ADRENALINE, A surge of something approaching terror (if I could still feel terror), and I realize that this is it, this time I am the one who is doing it.

I'm the one who is going to drop into a black hole.

Oh, my god. This time I'm not you.

This is real.

Of course, I have experienced this exact feeling before. We both know exactly what it feels like.

My body seems weird, too big and at once too small. The feel of my muscles, my vision, my kinesthetic sense, everything is wrong. Everything is strange. My vision is fuzzy, and colors are oddly distorted. When I move, my body moves unexpectedly fast. But there seems to be nothing wrong with it. Already I am getting used to it. "It will do," I say.

There is too much to know, too much to be all at once. I slowly coalesce the fragments of your personality. None of them are you. All of them are you.

A pilot, of course, you must have, you must be, a pilot. I integrate your pilot persona, and he is me. I will fly to the heart of a darkness far darker than any mere unexplored continent. A scientist, somebody to understand your experience, yes. I synthesize a persona. You are him, too, and I understand.

And someone to simply experience it, to tell the tale (if any of me will survive to tell the tale) of how you dropped into a black hole, and how you survived. If you survive. Me. I will call myself Wolf, naming myself after a nearby star, for no reason whatsoever, except maybe to claim, if only to myself, that I am not you.

All of we are me are you. But, in a real sense, you're not here at all. None of me are you. You are far away. Safe.

Some black holes, my scientist persona whispers, are decorated with an accretion disk, shining like a gaudy signal in the sky. Dust and gas from the interstellar medium fall toward the hungry singularity, accelerating to nearly the speed of light in their descent, swirling madly as they fall. It collides; compresses; ionizes. Friction heats the plasma millions of degrees, to emit a brilliant glow of hard x-rays. Such black holes are anything but black; the incandescence of the infalling gas may be the most brilliantly glowing thing in a galaxy. Nobody and nothing would be able to get near it; nothing would be able to survive the radiation.

The Virgo hole is not one of these. It is ancient, dating from the very first burst of star-formation when the universe was new, and has long ago swallowed or ejected all the interstellar gas in its region, carving an emptiness far into the interstellar medium around it.

The black hole is fifty-seven light years from Earth. Ten billion years ago, it had been a supermassive star, and exploded in a supernova that for a brief moment had shone brighter than the galaxy, in the process tossing away half its mass. Now there is nothing left of the star. The burned-out remnant, some thirty times the mass of the sun, has pulled in space itself around it, leaving nothing behind but gravity.

Before the download, the psychologist investigated my—your—mental soundness. We must have passed the test, obviously, since I'm here. What type of man would allow himself to fall into a black hole? That is my question. Maybe if I can answer that, I would understand ourself.

But this did not seem to interest the psychologist. She did not, in fact, even look directly at me. Her face had the focusless abstract gaze characteristic of somebody hotlinked by the optic nerve to a computer system. Her talk was perfunctory. To be fair, the object her study was not the flesh me, but my computed reflection, the digital maps of my soul. I remember the last thing she said.

"We are fascinated with black holes because of their depth of metaphor," she said, looking nowhere. "A black hole is, literally, the place of no return. We see it as a metaphor for how we, ourselves, are hurled blindly into a place from which no information ever reaches us, the place from which no one ever returns. We live our lives falling into the future, and we will all inevitably meet the singularity." She paused, expecting no doubt some comment. But I remained silent.

"Just remember this," she said, and for the first time her eyes returned to the outside world and focused on me. "This is a real black hole, not a metaphor. Don't treat it like a metaphor. Expect reality." She paused, and finally added, "Trust the math. It's all we really know, and all that we have to trust."

Little help.

Wolf versus the black hole! One might think that such a contest is an unequal one, that the black hole has an overwhelming advantage.

Not quite so unequal, though.

On my side, I have technology. To start with, the wormhole, the technological sleight-of-space which got you fifty-seven light years from Earth in the first place.

The wormhole is a monster of relativity no less than the black hole, a trick of curved space allowed by the theory of general relativity. After the Virgo black hole was discovered, a wormhole mouth was laboriously dragged to it, slower than light, a project that took over a century. Once the wormhole was here, though, the trip is only a short one, barely a meter of travel. Anybody could come here and drop into it.

A wormhole—a far too cute name, but one we seem to be stuck with—is a shortcut from one place to another. Physically, it is nothing more than a loop of exotic matter. If you move though the hoop on this side of the wormhole, you emerge out the hoop on that side. Topologically, the two sides of the wormhole are pasted together, a piece cut out of space glued together elsewhere.

Exhibiting an excessive sense of caution, the proctors of Earthspace refused to allow the other end of the Virgo wormhole to exit at the usual transportation nexus, the wormhole swarm at Neptune-Trojan 4. The far end of the wormhole opens instead to an orbit around Wolf-562, an undistinguished red dwarf sun circled by two airless planets that are little more than frozen rocks, twenty-one light years from Earthspace. To get here we had to take a double wormhole hop: Wolf, Virgo.

The black hole is a hundred kilometers across. The wormhole is only a few meters across. I would think that they were overly cautious.

The first lesson of relativity is that time and space are one. For a long time after the theoretical prediction that such a thing as a traversable wormhole ought to be possible, it was believed that a wormhole could also be made to traverse time as well. It was only much later, when wormhole travel was tested, that it was found that the Cauchy instability makes it impossible to make a wormhole lead backward in time. The theory was correct—space and time are indeed just aspects of the same reality, spacetime—but any attempt to move a wormhole in such a way that it becomes a timehole produces a vacuum polarization to cancel out the time effect.

After we—the spaceship I am to pilot, and myself/yourself—come through the wormhole, the wormhole engineers go to work. I have never seen this process close up, so I stay nearby to watch. This is going to be interesting.

A wormhole looks like nothing more than a circular loop of string. It is, in fact, a loop of exotic material, negative-mass cosmic string. The engineers, working telerobotically via vacuum manipulator pods, spray charge onto the string. They charge it until it literally glows with Paschen discharge, like a neon light in the dirty vacuum, and then use the electric charge to manipulate the shape. With the application of invisible electromagnetic fields, the string starts to twist. This is a slow process. Only a few meters across, the wormhole loop has a mass roughly equal to that of Jupiter. Negative to that of Jupiter, to be precise, my scientist persona reminds me, but either way, it is a slow thing to move.

Ponderously, then, it twists further and further, until at last it becomes a lemniscate, a figure of eight. The instant the string touches itself, it shimmers for a moment, and then suddenly there are two glowing circles before us, twisting and oscillating in shape like jellyfish.

The engineers spray more charge onto the two wormholes, and the two wormholes, arcing lightning into space, slowly repel each other. The vibrations of the cosmic string are spraying out gravitational radiation like a dog shaking off water—even where I am, floating ten kilometers distant, I can feel it, like the swaying of invisible tides—and as they radiate energy the loops enlarge. The radiation represents a serious danger. If the engineers lose control of the string for even a brief instant, it might enter the instability known as "squiggle mode," and catastrophically enlarge. The engineers damp out the radiation before it gets critical, though—they are, after all, well practiced at this—and the loops stabilize into two perfect circles. On the other side, at Wolf, precisely the same scene has played out, and two loops of exotic string now circle Wolf-562 as well. The wormhole has been cloned.

All wormholes are daughters of the original wormhole, found floating in the depths of interstellar space eleven hundred years ago, a natural loop of negative cosmic string ancient as the Big Bang, invisible to the eyes save for the distortion of spacetime. That first one led from nowhere interesting to nowhere exciting, but from that one we bred hundreds, and now we casually move wormhole mouths from star to star, breeding new wormholes as it suits us, to form an ever-expanding network of connections.

I should not have been so close. Angry red lights have been flashing in my peripheral vision, warning blinkers that I have been ignoring. The energy radiated in the form of gravitational waves had been prodigious, and would have, to a lesser person, been dangerous. But in my new body I am nearly invulnerable, and if I can't stand a mere wormhole cloning, there is no way I would be able to stand a black hole. So I ignore the warnings, wave briefly to the engineers, though I doubt that they can even see me, floating kilometers away, and use my reaction jets to scoot over to my ship.

The ship I will pilot is docked to the research station, where the scientists have their instruments and the biological humans have their living quarters. The wormhole station is huge compared to my ship, which is a tiny ovoid occupying a berth almost invisible against the hull. There is no hurry for me to get to it.

I'm surprised that any of the technicians even see me, tiny as I am in the void, but a few of them apparently do, because in my radio I hear casual greetings called out: how's it, *ohayo gozaimasu*, hey glad you make it, how's the bod? It's hard to tell from the radio voices which ones are people I know, and which are only casual acquaintances. I answer back: how's it, *ohayo*, yo, surpassing spec. None of them seem inclined to chat, but then, they're busy with their own work.

They are dropping things into the black hole.

Throwing things in, more to say. The wormhole station orbits a tenth of an astronomical unit from the Virgo black hole, closer to the black hole than Mercury is to the sun. This is an orbit with a period of a little over two days, but, even so close to the black hole, there is nothing to see. A rock, released to fall straight downward, takes almost a day to reach the horizon.

One of the scientists supervising, a biological human named Sue, takes the time to talk with me a bit, explaining what they are measuring. What interests me most is that they are measuring whether the fall deviates from a straight line. This measures whether the black hole is rotating. Even a slight rotation would mess up the intricate dance of the trajectory required for my ship. However, the best current theories predict that an old black hole will have shed its angular momentum long ago, and, so far as the technicians can determine, their results show that the conjecture holds.

The black hole, or the absence in space where it is located, is utterly invisible from here. I follow the pointing finger of the scientist, but there is nothing to see. Even if I had a telescope, it is unlikely that I would be able to pick out the tiny region of utter blackness against the irregular darkness of an unfamiliar sky.

My ship is not so different from the drop probes. The main difference is that I will be on it.

Before boarding the station, I jet over in close to inspect my ship, a miniature egg of perfectly reflective material. The hull is made of a single crystal of a synthetic material so strong that no earthly force could even dent it.

A black hole, though, is no earthly force.

Wolf versus the black hole! The second technological trick I have in my duel against the black hole is my body.

I am no longer a fragile, fluid-filled biological human. The tidal forces approaching the horizon of a black hole would rip a true human apart in mere instants; the accelerations required to hover would squash one into liquid. To make this journey, I have downloaded your fragile biological mind into a body of more robust material. As important as the strength of my new body is the fact that it is tiny. The force produced by the curvature of gravity is proportional to the size of the object. My new body, a millimeter tall, is millions of times more resistant to being stretched to spaghetti.

The new body has another advantage as well. With my mind operating as software on a computer the size of a pinpoint, my thinking and my reflexes are thousands of times faster than biological. In fact, I have already chosen to slow my thinking down, so that I can still interact with the biologicals. At full speed, my microsecond reactions are lightning compared to the molasses of neuron speeds in biological humans. I see far in the ultraviolet now, a necessary compensation for the fact that my vision would consist of nothing but a blur if I tried to see by visible light.

You could have made my body any shape, of course, a tiny cube or even a featureless sphere. But you followed the dictates of social convention. A right human should be recognizably a human, even if I am to be smaller than an ant, and so my body mimics a human body, although no part of it is organic, and my brain faithfully executes your own human brain software. From what I see and feel, externally and internally, I am completely, perfectly human.

As is right and proper. What is the value of experience to a machine?

Later, after I return—if I return—I can upload back. I can become you.

But return is, as they say, still somewhat problematical.

You, my original, what do you feel? Why did I think I would do it? I imagine you laughing hysterically about the trick you played, sending me to drop into the black hole while you sit back in perfect comfort, in no danger. Imagining your laughter comforts me, for all that I know that it is false. I've been in the other place before, and never laughed.

I remember the first time I fell into a star.

We were hotlinked together, that time, united in online-realtime, our separate brains reacting as one brain. I remember what I thought, the incredible electric feel: ohmigod, am I really going to do this? Is it too late to back out?

The idea had been nothing more than a whim, a crazy idea, at first. We had been dropping probes into a star, Groombridge 1830B, studying the dynamics of a flare star. We were done, just about, and the last-day-of-project party was just getting in swing.

We were all fuzzed with neurotransmitter randomizers, creativity spinning wild and critical thinking nearly zeroed. Somebody, I think it had been Jenna, said, we could ride one down, you know. Wait for a flare, and then plunge through the middle of it. Helluva ride.

Helluva splash at the end, too, somebody said, and laughed.

Sure, somebody said. It might have been me. What do you figure? Download yourself to temp storage and then uplink frames from yourself as you drop?

That works, Jenna said. Better: we copy our bodies first, then link the two brains. One body drops; the other copy hotlinks to it.

Somehow, I don't remember when, the word "we" had grown to include me.

"Sure," I said. "And the copy on top is in null-input suspension; experiences the whole thing real-time."

In the morning, when we were focused again, I might have dismissed the idea as a whim of the fuzz, but for Jenna the decision was already immovable as a droplet of neutronium. Sure we're dropping, let's start now.

We made a few changes. It takes a long time to fall into a star, even a small one like Bee, so the copy was reengineered to a slower thought rate, and the original body in null-input was frame-synched to the drop copy with impulse-echoers. Since the two brains were molecule by molecule identical, the uplink bandwidth required was minimal.

The probes were reworked to take a biological, which meant mostly that a cooling system had to be added to hold the interior temperature within the liquidus range of water. We did that by the simplest method possible: we surrounded the probes with a huge block of cometary ice. As it sublimated, the ionized gas would carry away heat. A secondary advantage of that was that our friends, watching from orbit, would have a blazing cometary trail to cheer on. When the ice was used up, of course, the body would slowly vaporize. None of us would actually survive to hit the star.

But that was no particular concern. If the experience turned out to be too undesirable, we could always edit the pain part of it out of the memory later.

It would have made more sense, perhaps, to have simply recorded the brain-uplink from the copy onto a local high-temp buffer, squirted it back, and linked to it as a memory upload. But Jenna would have none of that. She wanted to experience it in realtime, or at least in as close to realtime as speed-of-light delays allow.

Three of us, Jenna, Martha, and me, dropped. Something seems to be missing from my memory here; I can't remember the reason I decided to do it. It must have been something about a biological body, some a-rational consideration that seemed normal to my then-body that I could never back down from a crazy whim of Jenna's.

And I had the same experience, the same feeling then, as I, you, did, always do, the feeling that my god I am the copy and I am going to die. But that time, of course, thinking every thought in synchrony, there was no way at all to tell the copy from the original, to split the me from you.

It is, in its way, a glorious feeling.

I dropped.

You felt it, you remember it. Boring at first, the long drop with nothing but freefall and the chatter of friends over the radio-link. Then the ice shell slowly flaking away, ionizing and beginning to glow, a diaphanous cocoon of pale violet, and below the red star getting larger and larger, the surface mottled and wrinkled, and then suddenly we fell into and through the flare, a huge luminous vault above us, dwarfing our bodies in the immensity of creation.

An unguessable distance beneath me, the curvature of the star vanished, and, still falling at three hundred kilometers per second, I was hanging motionless over an infinite plane stretching from horizon to horizon.

And then the last of the ice vaporized, and I was suddenly suspended in nothing, hanging nailed to the burning sky over endless crimson horizons of infinity, and pain came like the inevitability of mountains—I didn't edit it—pain like infinite oceans, like continents, like a vast, airless world.

Jenna, now I remember. The odd thing is, I never did really connect in any significant way with Jenna. She was already in a quadrad of her own, a quadrad she was fiercely loyal to, one that was solid and accepting to her chameleon character, neither needing nor wanting a fifth for completion.

Long after, maybe a century or two later, I found out that Jenna had disassembled herself. After her quadrad split apart, she downloaded her character to a mainframe, and then painstakingly cataloged everything that made her Jenna: all her various skills and insights, everything she had experienced, no matter how minor, each facet of her character, every memory and dream and longing: the myriad subroutines of personality. She indexed her soul, and she put the ten thousand pieces of it into the public domain for download. A thousand people, maybe a million people, maybe even more, have pieces of Jenna, her cleverness, her insight, her skill at playing antique instruments.

But nobody has her sense of self. After she copied her subroutines, she deleted herself.

And who am I?

Two of the technicians who fit me into my spaceship and who assist in the ten thousand elements of the preflight check are the same friends from that drop, long ago; one of them even still in the same biological body as he had then, although eight hundred years older, his vigor undiminished by biological reconstruction. My survival, if I am to survive, will be dependent on microsecond timing, and I'm embarrassed not to be able to remember his name.

He was, I recall, rather stodgy and conservative even back then.

We joke and trade small talk as the checkout proceeds. I'm still distracted by my self-questioning, the implications of my growing realization that I have no understanding of why I'm doing this.

Exploring a black hole would be no adventure if only we had faster than light travel, but of the thousand technological miracles of the third and fourth millennia, this one miracle was never realized. If I had the mythical FTL motor, I could simply drive out of the black hole. At the event horizon, space falls into the black hole at the speed of light; the mythical motor would make that no barrier.

But such a motor we do not have. One of the reasons I'm taking the plunge—not the only one, not the main one, but one—is in the hope that scientific measurements of the warped space inside the black hole will elucidate the nature of space and time, and so I myself will make one of the innumerable small steps to bring us closer to a FTL drive.

The spaceship I am to pilot has a drive nearly—but not quite—as good. It contains a microscopic twist of spacetime inside an impervious housing, a twist that will parity-reverse ordinary matter into mirror-matter. This total conversion engine gives my ship truly ferocious levels of thrust. The gentlest nudge of my steering rockets will give me thousands of gravities of acceleration. Unthinkable acceleration for a biological body, no matter how well cushioned. The engine will allow the rocket to dare the unthinkable, to hover at the very edge of the event horizon, to maneuver where space itself is accelerating at nearly lightspeed. This vehicle, no larger than a peanut, contains the engines of an interstellar probe.

Even with such an engine, most of the ship is reaction mass. The preflight checks are all green. I am ready to go. I power up my instruments, check everything out for myself, verify what has already been checked three times, and then check once again. My pilot persona is very thorough. Green.

"You still haven't named your ship," comes a voice to me. It is the technician, the one whose name I have forgotten. "What is your call sign?"

One way journey, I think. Maybe something from Dante? No, Sartre said it better: no exit. "*Huis Clos,*" I say, and drop free.

Let them look it up.

Alone.

The laws of orbital mechanics have not been suspended, and I do not drop into the black hole. Not yet. With the slightest touch of my steering engines—I do not dare use the main engine this close to the station—I drop into an elliptical orbit, one with a perimelasma closer to, but still well outside the dangerous zone of the black hole. The black hole is still invisible, but inside my tiny kingdom I have enhanced senses of exquisite sensitivity, spreading across the entire spectrum from radio to gamma radiation. I look with my new eyes to see if I can detect an x-ray glow of interstellar hydrogen being ripped apart, but if there is any such, it is too faint to be a visible with even my sensitive instruments. The interstellar medium is so thin here as to be essentially non-existent. The black hole is invisible.

I smile. This makes it better, somehow. The black hole is pure, unsullied by any outside matter. It consists of gravity and nothing else, as close to a pure mathematical abstraction as anything in the universe can ever be.

It is not too late to back away. If I were to choose to accelerate at a million gravities, I would reach relativistic velocities in about thirty seconds. No wormholes would be needed for me to run away; I would barely even need to slow down my brain to cruise at nearly the speed of light to anywhere in the colonized galaxy.

But I know I won't. The psychologist knew it too, damn her, or she would never have approved me for the mission. Why? What is it about me?

As I worry about this with part of my attention, while the pilot persona flies the ship, I flash onto a realization, and at this realization another memory hits. It is the psychologist, and in the memory I'm attracted to her sexually, so much so that you are distracted from what she is saying.

I feel no sexual attraction now, of course. I can barely remember what it is. That part of the memory is odd, alien.

"We can't copy the whole brain to the simulation, but we can copy enough that, to yourself, you will still feel like yourself," she said. She is talking to the air, not to you. "You won't notice any gaps."

I'm brain damaged. This is the explanation.

You frowned. "How could I not notice that some of my memories are missing?"

"The brain makes adjustments. Remember, at any given time, you never even use one percent of one percent of your memories. What we'll be leaving out will be stuff that you will never have any reason to think about. The memory of the taste of strawberries, for example; the floor-plan of the house you lived in as a teenager. Your first kiss."

This bothered you somewhat—you want to remain yourself. I concentrate, hard. What do strawberries taste like? I can't remember. I'm not even certain what color they are. Round fruits, like apples, I think, only smaller. And the same color as apples, or something similar, I'm sure, except I don't remember what color that is.

You decided that you can live with the editing, as long as it doesn't change the essential you. You smiled. "Leave in the first kiss."

So I can never possibly solve the riddle, what kind of a man is it that would deliberately allow himself to drop into a black hole. I cannot, because I don't have the memories of you. In a real sense, I am not you at all.

But I do remember the kiss. The walk in the darkness, the grass wet with dew, the moon a silver sliver on the horizon, turning to her and her face already turned up to meet my lips. The taste indescribable, more feeling than taste (not like strawberries at all), the small hardness of her teeth behind the lips—all there. Except the one critical detail: I don't have any idea at all who she was.

What else am I missing? Do I even know what I don't know?

I was a child, maybe nine, and there was no tree in the neighborhood that you could not climb. I was a careful, meticulous, methodical climber. On the tallest of the trees, when you reached toward the top, you were above the forest canopy (did I live in a forest?) and, out of the dimness of the forest floor, emerged into brilliant sunshine. Nobody else could climb like you; nobody ever suspected how high I climbed. It was your private hiding place, so high that the world was nothing but a sea of green waves in the valley between the mountains.

It was my own stupidity, really. At the very limit of the altitude needed to emerge into sunlight, the branches were skinny, narrow as your little finger. They bent alarmingly with your weight, but I knew exactly how much they would take. The bending was a thrill, but I was cautious, and knew exactly what I was doing.

It was further down, where the branches were thick and safe, that I got careless. Three points of support, that was the rule of safety, but I was reaching for one branch, not paying attention, when one in my other hand broke, and I was off balance. I slipped. For a prolonged instant I was suspended in space, branches all about me, but I reached out and grasped only leaves, and I fell and fell and fell, and all I could think as leaves and branches fell upward past me was, oh my, I made a miscalculation; I was really stupid.

The flash memory ends with no conclusion. I must have hit the ground, but I cannot remember it. Somebody must have found me, or else I wandered or crawled back, perhaps in a daze, and found somebody, but I cannot remember it.

Half a million kilometers from the hole. If my elliptical orbit were around the sun instead of a black hole, I would already have penetrated the surface. I now hold the record for the closest human approach. There is still nothing to see with unmagnified senses. It seems surreal that I'm in the grip of something so powerful that is utterly invisible. With my augmented eyes used as a telescope, I can detect the black hole by what isn't there, a tiny place of blackness nearly indistinguishable from any other patch of darkness except for an odd motion of the stars near it.

My ship is sending a continuous stream of telemetry back to the station. I have an urge to add a verbal commentary—there is plenty of bandwidth, but I have nothing to say. There is only one person I have any interest in talking to, and you are cocooned at absolute zero, waiting for me to upload myself and become you.

My ellipse takes me inward, moving faster and faster. I am still in Newton's grip, far from the sphere where Einstein takes hold.

A tenth of a solar radius. The blackness I orbit is now large enough to see without a telescope, as large as the sun seen from Earth, and swells as I watch with time-distorted senses. Due to its gravity, the blackness in front of the star pattern is a bit larger than the disk of the black hole itself. Square root of twenty-seven over two—about two and a half times larger, the physicist persona notes. I watch in fascination.

What I see is a bubble of purest blackness. The bubble pushes the distant stars away from it as it swells. My orbital motion makes the background stars appear to sweep across the sky, and I watch them approach the black hole and then, smoothly pushed by the gravity, move off to the side, a river of stars flowing past an invisible obstacle. It is a gravitational lensing effect, I know, but the view of flowing stars is so spectacular that I cannot help but watch it. The gravity pushes each star to one side or the other. If a star were to pass directly behind the hole, it would appear to split and for an instant become a perfect circle of light, an Einstein ring. But this precise alignment is too rare to see by accident.

Closer, I notice an even odder effect. The sweeping stars detour smoothly around the bubble of blackness, but very close to the bubble, there are other stars, stars which actually move in the opposite direction, a counterflowing river of stars. It takes me a long time (microseconds perhaps) before my physicist persona tells me that I am seeing the image of the stars in the Einstein mirror. The entire external universe is mirrored in a narrow ring outside the black hole, and the mirror image flows along with a mirror of my own motion.

In the center of the ring there is nothing at all.

Five thousand kilometers, and I am moving fast. The gravitational acceleration here is over ten million gees, and I am still fifty times the Schwarzschild radius from the black hole. Einstein's correction is still tiny, though, and if I were to do nothing, my orbit will whip around the black hole and still escape into the outside world.

One thousand kilometers. Perimelasma, the closest point of my elliptical orbit. Ten times the Schwarzschild radius, close enough that Einstein's correction to Newton now makes a small difference to the geometry of space. I fire my engines. My speed is so tremendous that it takes over a second of my engine firing at a million gravities to circularize my orbit.

My time sense has long since speeded up back to normal, and then faster than normal. I orbit the black hole about ten times per second.

My god, this is why I exist, this is why I'm here.

All my doubts are gone in the rush of naked power. No biological could have survived this far; no biological could have even survived the million-gee circularization burn, and I am only at the very beginning. I grin like a maniac, throb with a most unscientific excitement that must be the electronic equivalent of an adrenaline high.

Oh, this ship is good. This ship is sweet. A million-gee burn, smooth as magnetic levitation and I barely cracked the throttle. I should have taken it for a spin before dropping in, should have hot-rodded *Huis Clos* around the stellar neighborhood. But it had been absolutely out of the question to fire the main engine close to the wormhole station. Even with the incredible efficiency of the engine, that million-gee perimelasma burn must have lit up the research station like an unexpected sun.

I can't wait to take *Huis Clos* in and see what it will *really* do.

My orbital velocity is a quarter of the speed of light.

The orbit at nine hundred kilometers is only a parking orbit, a chance for me to configure my equipment, make final measurements and, in principle, a last chance for me to change my mind. There is nothing to reconnoiter that the probes have not already measured, though, and there is no chance that I will change my mind, however sensible that may seem.

The river of stars swirls in a dance of counterflow around the blackness below me. The horizon awaits.

The horizon below is invisible, but real. There is no barrier at the horizon, nothing to see, nothing to feel. I will be even unable to detect it, except for my calculations.

An event horizon is a one-way membrane, a place you can pass into but neither you nor your radio signals can pass out of. According to the mathematics, as I pass through the event horizon, the directions of space and time change identity. Space rotates into time; time rotates into space. What this means is that the direction to the center of the black hole, after I pass the event horizon, will be the future. The direction out of the black hole will be the past. This is the reason that no one and nothing can ever leave a black hole; the way inward is the one direction we always must go, whether we will it or not: into the future.

Or so the mathematics says.

The future, inside a black hole, is a very short one.

So far the mathematics has been right on. But nevertheless, I go on. With infinitesimal blasts from my engine, I inch my orbit lower.

The bubble of blackness gets larger, and the counterflow of stars around it becomes more complex. As I approach three times the Schwarzschild radius, 180 km, I check all my systems. This is the point of no rescue: inside three Schwarzschild radii, no orbits are stable, and my automatic systems will be constantly thrusting to adjust my orbital parameters to keep me from falling into the black hole or being flung away to infinity. My systems are all functional, in perfect form for the dangerous drop. My orbital velocity is already half the speed of light. Below this point centrifugal force will decrease toward zero as I lower my orbit, and I must use my thrusters to increase my velocity as I descend, or else plunge into the hole.

When I grew up, in the last years of the second millennium, nobody thought that they would live forever. Nobody would have believed me if I told them that, by my thousandth birthday, I would have no concept of truly dying.

Even if all our clever tricks fail, even if I plunge through the event horizon and am stretched into spaghetti and crushed by the singularity, I will not die. You, my original, will live on, and if you were to die, we have made dozens of back-ups and spin-off copies of myselves in the past, some versions of which must surely still be living on. My individual life has little importance. I can, if I chose, uplink my brain-state to the orbiting station right at this instant, and reawake, whole, continuing this exact thought, unaware (except on an abstract intellectual level) that I and you are not the same.

But we are not the same, you and I. I am an edited-down version of you, and the memories that have been edited out, even if I never happen to think them, make me different, a new individual. Not you.

On a metaphorical level, a black hole stands for death, the blackness that is sucking us all in. But what meaning does death have in a world of matrix back-ups and modular personality? Is my plunge a death wish? Is it thumbing my nose at death? Because I intend to survive. Not you. Me.

I orbit the black hole over a hundred times a second now, but I have revved my brain processing speed accordingly, so that my orbit seems to me leisurely enough. The view here is odd. The black hole has swollen to the size of a small world below me, a world of perfect velvet darkness, surrounded by a belt of madly rotating stars.

No engine, no matter how energetic, can put a ship into an

orbit at 1.5 times the Schwarzschild radius; at this distance, the orbital velocity is the speed of light, and not even my total-conversion engine can accelerate me to that speed. Below that there are no orbits at all. I stop my descent at an orbit just sixty kilometers from the event horizon, when my orbital velocity reaches 85 percent of the speed of light. Here I can coast, ignoring the constant small adjustments of the thrusters that keep my orbit from sliding off the knife-edge. The velvet blackness of the black hole is almost half of the universe now, and if I were to trust the outside view, I am diving at a slant downward into the black hole. I ignore my pilot's urge to override the automated navigation and manually even out the trajectory. The downward slant is only relativistic aberration, nothing more, an illusion of my velocity.

Eighty-five percent of the speed of light is as fast as I dare orbit; I must conserve my fuel for the difficult part of the plunge to come.

In my unsteady orbit sixty kilometers above the black hole, I let my ship's computer chat with the computer of the wormhole station, updating and downloading my sensor's observations.

At this point, according to the mission plan, I am supposed to uplink my brain state, so that should anything go wrong further down the well, you, my original, will be able to download my state and experiences to this point. To hell with that, I think, a tiny bit of rebellion. I am not you. If you awaken with my memories, I will be no less dead.

Nobody at the wormhole station questions my decision not to upload.

I remember one other thing now. "You're a type N personality," the psychologist had said, twitching her thumb to leaf through invisible pages of test results. The gesture marked her era; only a person who had grown up before computer hotlinks would move a physical muscle in commanding a virtual. She was twenty-first century, possibly even twentieth. "But I suppose you already know that."

"Type N?" you asked.

"Novelty-seeking," she said. "Most particularly, one not prone to panic at new situations."

"Oh," you said. You did already know that. "Speaking of novelty seeking, how do you feel about going to bed with a type N personality?"

"That would be unprofessional." She frowned. "I think."

"Not even one who is about to jump down a black hole?"

She terminated the computer link with a flick of her wrist, and turned to look at you. "Well—"

From this point onward, microsecond timing is necessary for the dance we have planned to succeed. My computer and the station computer meticulously compare clocks, measuring Doppler shifts to exquisite precision. My clocks are running slow, as expected, but half of the slowness is relativistic time dilation due to my velocity. The gravitational redshift is still modest. After some milliseconds—a long wait for me, in my hyped-up state—they declare that they agree. The station has already done their part, and I begin the next phase of my descent.

The first thing I do is fire my engine to stop my orbit. I crack the throttle to fifty million gees of acceleration, and the burn takes nearly a second, a veritable eternity, to slow my flight.

For a moment I hover, and start to drop. I dare not drop too fast, and I ramp my throttle up, to a hundred megagee, five hundred, a billion gravities. At forty billion gravities of acceleration my engine thrust equals the gravity of the black hole and I hover.

The blackness has now swallowed half of the universe. Everything beneath me is black. Between the black below and the starry sky above, a spectacularly bright line exactly bisects the sky. I have reached the altitude at which orbital velocity is just equal to the speed of light, and the light from my rocket exhaust is in orbit around the black hole. The line I see around the sky is my view of my own rocket, seen by light that has traveled all the way around the black hole. All I can see is the exhaust, far brighter than anything else in the sky.

The second brightest thing is the laser beacon from the wormhole station above me, shifted from the original red laser color to a greenish blue. The laser marks the exact line between the station and the black hole, and I maneuver carefully until I am directly beneath the orbiting station.

At forty billion gravities, even my ultrastrong body is at its limits. I cannot move, and even my smallest finger is pressed against the form-fitting acceleration couch. But the controls, hardware interfaced to my brain, do not require me to lift a finger to command the spacecraft. The command I give *Huis Clos* is: down.

Inward from the photon sphere, the bright line of my exhaust vanishes. Every stray photon from my drive is now sucked downward.

Now my view of the universe has changed. The black hole has become the universe around me, and the universe itself, all the galaxies and stars and the wormhole station, is a shrinking sphere of sparkling dust above me.

Sixty billion gravities. Seventy. Eighty.

Eighty billion gravities is full throttle. I am burning fuel at an incredible rate, and only barely hold steady. I am still twenty kilometers above the horizon.

There is an unbreakable law of physics: incredible accelerations require incredible fuel consumption. Even though my spaceship is, by mass, comprised mostly of fuel, I can maintain less than a millisecond worth of thrust at this acceleration. I cut my engine and drop.

It will not be long now. This is my last chance to uplink a copy of my mind back to the wormhole station to wake in your body, with my last memory the decision to upload my mind.

I do not.

The stars are blueshifted by a factor of two, which does not make them noticeably bluer. Now that I have stopped accelerating, the starlight is falling into the hole along with me, and the stars do not blueshift any further. My instruments probe the vacuum around me. The theorists tell that the vacuum close to the horizon of a black hole is an exotic vacuum, abristle with secret energy. Only a ship plunging through the event horizon would be able to measure this. I do, recording the results carefully on my ship's on-board recorders, since it is now far too late to send anything back by radio.

There is no sign to mark the event horizon, and there is no indication at all when I cross it. If it were not for my computer, there would be no way for me to tell that I have passed the point of no return.

Nothing is different. I look around the tiny cabin, and can see no change. The blackness below me continues to grow, but is otherwise not changed. The outside universe continues to shrink above me; the brightness beginning to concentrate into a belt around the edge of the glowing sphere of stars, but this is only an effect of my motion. The only difference is that I have only a few hundred microseconds left.

From the viewpoint of the outside world, the light from my spacecraft has slowed down and stopped at the horizon. But I have far outstripped my lagging image, and am falling toward the center at incredible speed. At the exact center is the singularity, far smaller than an atom, a mathematical point of infinite gravity and infinite mystery.

Whoever I am, whether or not I survive, I am now the first person to penetrate the event horizon of a black hole. That's worth a cheer, even with nobody to hear. Now I have to count on the hope that the microsecond timing of the technicians above me had been perfect for the second part of my intricate dance that might, if all goes well, allow me to survive this feat.

Above me, according to theory, the stars have already burned out, and even the most miserly red dwarf has sputtered the last of its hydrogen fuel and grown cold. The universe has already ended, and the stars have gone out. I still see a steady glow of starlight from the universe above me, but this is fossil light, light that has been falling down into the black hole with me for eons, trapped in the infinitely stretched time of the black hole.

For me, time has rotated into space, and space into time. Nothing feels different to me, but I cannot avoid the singularity at the center of the black hole any more than I can avoid the future. Unless, that is, I have a trick.

Of course I have a trick.

At the center of the spherical universe above me is a dot of bright blue-violet; the fossil light of the laser beacon from the orbiting station. My reaction jets have kept on adjusting my trajectory to keep me centered in the guidance beam, so I am directly below the station. Anything dropped from the station will, if everything works right, drop directly on the path I follow.

I am approaching close to the center now, and the tidal forces stretching my body are creeping swiftly toward a billion gees per millimeter. Much higher and even my tremendously strong body will be ripped to spaghetti. There are only microseconds left for me. It is time.

I hammer my engine, full throttle. Far away, and long ago, my friends at the wormhole station above dropped a wormhole into the event horizon. If their timing was perfect—

From a universe that has already died, the wormhole cometh.

Even with my enhanced time sense, things happen fast. The laser beacon blinks out, and the wormhole sweeps down around me like the vengeance of God, far faster than I can react. The sparkle-filled sphere of the universe blinks out like a light, and the black hole—and the tidal forces stretching my body—abruptly disappears. For a single instant I see a black disk below me, and then the wormhole rotates, twists, stretches, and then silently vanishes.

Ripped apart by the black hole.

My ship is vibrating like a bell from the abrupt release of tidal stretching. "I did it," I shout. "It worked! God damn it, it really worked!"

This was what was predicted by the theorists, that I would be able to pass through the wormhole before it was shredded by the singularity at the center. The other possibility, that the singularity itself, infinitesimally small and infinitely powerful, might follow me through the wormhole, was laughed at by everyone who had any claim to understand wormhole physics. This time, the theorists were right.

But where am I?

There should be congratulations pouring in to my radio by now, teams of friends and technicians swarming over to greet me, cheering and shouting.

"*Huis Clos,*" I say, over the radio. "I made it! *Huis Clos* here. Is anybody there?"

In theory, I should have reemerged at Wolf-562. But I do not see it. In fact, what I see is not recognizably the universe at all.

There are no stars.

Instead of stars, the sky is filled with lines, parallel lines of white light by the uncountable thousands. Dominating the sky, where the star Wolf-562 should have been, is a glowing red cylinder, perfectly straight, stretching to infinity in both directions.

Have I been transported into some other universe? Could the black hole's gravity sever the wormhole, cutting it loose from our universe entirely and connect it into this strange new one?

If so, it has doomed me. The wormhole behind me, my only exit from this strange universe, is already destroyed. Not that escaping through it could have done me any good—it would only have brought me back to the place I escaped, to be crushed by the singularity of the black hole.

I could just turn my brain off, and I will have lost nothing, in a sense. They will bring you out of your suspended state, tell you that the edition of you that dropped into the black hole failed to upload, and they lost contact after it passed the event horizon. The experiment failed, but you had never been in danger.

But, however much you think we are the same, I am not you. I am a unique individual. When they revive you, without your expected new memories, I will still be gone.

I want to survive. I want to return.

A universe of tubes of light! Brilliant bars of an infinite cage.

The bright lines in the sky have slight variations in color, from pale red to plasma-arc blue. They must be similar to the red cylinder near me, I figure, but light-years away. How could a universe have lines of light instead of stars?

I am amazingly well equipped to investigate that question, with senses that range from radio through X-ray, and I have nothing else to do for the next thousand years or so. So I take a spectrum of the light from the glowing red cylinder.

I have no expectation that the spectrum will reveal anything I can interpret, but oddly, it looks normal. Impossibly, it looks like the spectrum of a star.

The computer can even identify, from its data of millions of spectra, precisely which star. The light from the cylinder has the spectral signature of Wolf-562.

Coincidence? It cannot possibly be coincidence, out of billions of possible spectra, that this glowing sword in the sky has exactly the spectrum of the star that should have been there. There can be no other conclusion but that the cylinder *is* Wolf-562.

I take a few more spectra, this time picking at random three of the lines of light in the sky, and the computer analyzes them for me. A bright one: the spectrum of 61 Virginis. A dimmer one: a match to Wolf-1061. A blue-white streak: Vega.

The lines in the sky are stars.

What does this mean?

I'm not in another universe. I am in our universe, but the universe has been transformed. Could the collision of a wormhole with a black hole destroy our entire universe, stretching suns like taffy into infinite straight lines? Impossible. Even if it had, I would still see far-away stars as dots, since the light from them has been traveling for hundreds of years.

The universe cannot have changed. Therefore, by logic, it must be me who has been transformed.

Having figured out this much, the only possible answer is obvious.

When the mathematicians describe the passage across the event horizon of a black hole, they say that the space and time directions switch identity. I had always thought this only a mathematical oddity, but if it were true, if I had rotated when I passed the event horizon, and was now perceiving time as a direction in space, and one of the space axes as time—this would explain everything. Stars extend from billions of years into the past to long into the future; perceiving time as space, I see lines of light. If I were to come closer and find one of the rocky planets of Wolf 562, it would look like a braid around the star, a helix of solid rock. Could I land on it? How would I interact with a world where what I perceive as time is a direction in space?

My physicist persona doesn't like this explanation, but is at a loss to find a better one. In this strange sideways existence, I must be violating the conservation laws of physics like mad, but the persona could find no other hypothesis and must reluctantly agree: time is rotated into space.

To anybody outside, I must look like a string, a knobby long rope with one end at the wormhole and the other at my death, wherever that might be. But nobody could see me fast enough, since with no extension in time I must only be a transient event that bursts everywhere into existence and vanishes at the same instant. There is no way I could signal, no way I can communicate —

Or? Time, to me, is now a direction I can travel in as simply as using my rocket. I could find a planet, travel parallel to the direction of the surface —

But, no, all I could do would be only to appear to the inhabitants briefly as a disk, a cross-section of myself, infinitely thin. There is no way I could communicate.

But I can travel in time, if I want. Is there any way I can use this?

Wait. If I have rotated from space into time, then there is one direction in space which I cannot travel. Which direction is that? The direction that used to be away from the black hole.

Interesting thoughts, but not ones which help me much. To return, I need to once again flip space and time. I could dive into a black hole. This would again rotate space and time, but it wouldn't do me any good: once I left the black hole — if I could leave the black hole — nothing would change.

Unless there were a wormhole inside the black hole, falling inward to destruction just at the same instant I was there? But the only wormhole that has fallen into a black hole was already destroyed. Unless, could I travel forward in time? Surely some day the research team would drop a new wormhole into the black hole —

Idiot. Of course there's a solution. I can travel either direction in time now, forward or back. I need only to move back to an instant just after the wormhole passed through the event horizon, and, applying full thrust, shoot through. The very moment that my original self shoots through the wormhole to escape the singularity, I can pass through the opposite direction, and rotate myself back into the real universe.

The station at Virgo black hole is forty light years away, and I don't dare use the original wormhole to reach it. My spacetime-rotated body must be an elongated snake in this version of space-time, and I do not wish to find out what a wormhole passage will do to it until I have no other choice. Still, that is no problem for me. Even with barely enough fuel to thrust for a few microseconds, I can reach an appreciable fraction of lightspeed, and I can slow down my brain to make the trip appear only an instant.

To an outside observer, it takes literally no time at all.

"No," says the psych tech, when I ask her. "There's no law that compels you to uplink back into your original. You're a free human being. Your original can't force you."

"Great," I say. Soon I'm going to have to arrange to get a bio-logical body built for myself. This one is superb, but it's a disad-vantage in social intercourse to being only a millimeter tall.

The transition back to real space worked perfectly. Once I figured out how to navigate in time-rotated space, it had been easy enough to find the wormhole and the exact instant it had pene-trated the event horizon.

"Are you going to link your experiences to public domain?" the tech asks. "I think he would like to see what you experienced. Musta been pretty incredible."

"Maybe," I said.

"For that matter," the psych tech added, "I'd like to link it, too."

"I'll think about it."

So I am a real human being now, independent of you, my original.

There had been cheers and celebrations when I had emerged from the wormhole, but nobody had an inkling quite how strange my trip had been until I told them. Even then, I doubt that I was quite believed until the sensor readings and computer logs of *Huis Clos* confirmed my story with hard data.

The physicists had been ecstatic. A new tool to probe time and space. The ability to rotate space into time will open up incredible capabilities. They were already planning new expeditions, not the least of which was a trip to probe right to the singularity itself.

They had been duly impressed with my solution to the problem, although, after an hour of thinking it over, they all agreed it had been quite obvious. "It was lucky," one of them remarked, "that you decided to go through the wormhole from the opposite side, that second time."

"Why?" I asked.

"If you'd gone through the same direction, you'd have rotated an additional ninety degrees, instead of going back."

"So?"

"Reversed the time vector. Turns you into antimatter. First touch of the interstellar medium—Poof."

"Oh," I said. I hadn't thought of that. It made me feel a little less clever.

Now that the mission is over, I have no purpose, no direction for my existence. The future is empty, the black hole that we all must travel into. I will get a biological body, yes, and embark on the process of finding out who I am. Maybe, I think, this is a task that everybody has to do.

And then I will meet you. With luck, perhaps I'll even like you.

And maybe, if I should like you enough, and I feel confident, I'll decide to upload you into myself, and once more, we will again be one.

What We Really Do Here at NASA

$\mathcal{E}$ VERY MORNING I BRING IN THE TWO BRIEFCASES, packed with a hundred sets of freshly shuffled playing cards each. I hate having to take work home, but hey—if I didn't, who would?

After punching in, we cut cards to see who goes down into the vault. First deuce has to check the vault to make certain nobody sneaked in during the night. When you get past the last of the six steel doors, the perpetual motion machines are an awesome sight, whirring away softly behind the armored glass. Every few years some high management busybody asks why we don't destroy them, instead of keeping them locked up where somebody might someday break in and discover just how easy it is to make one, and we have to patiently explain that you can't destroy a perpetual motion machine once it's running—if you could stop it, it wouldn't be perpetual, now would it?—and if you try, it's a real mess. Trust me. So every day we check the locks and the deadfall traps. You have to be careful that you've memorized exactly where the land mines are—security changes them every week—and that you respond with the password promptly when security challenges you. We lose more civil servants who have trouble remembering a simple, fifteen syllable nonsense-word when

221

they're looking down the barrel of a machine gun. It's a shame, but you just can't be too careful.

After checking the vault we have to waste time doing real work. We all complain about it, but somebody has to read all those scientific journals. We get them sent to us before printing, and what we do is to check that nobody's doing the type of research that might lead to a magnetic spaceship, inertia-free field, or— worst of all!—an antigravity, warp-capable stardrive. Every now and then we see a line of research which, although seemingly innocent, could set people to thinking, and then we have to call up the editors, make sure the paper gets accidentally shredded and an innocuous one substituted, and then call the dean of the relevant university (universities are the worst; government and industrial labs know where their money comes from) to offer a few million dollars to start a research grant on something we know is safe. Works every time.

Occasionally some of our special-effects people drop by. It's always fun to go to the movie room to look at the takes of one of their space shuttle "launches" and offer suggestions on how to make it look more realistic. One time when we were having a party, somebody accidentally spilled marshmallow fluff on the film. We tried to wipe the mess off with vodka, but that only blotched out the image even worse, until there was nothing but a big white blur where the space shuttle should have been. You wouldn't believe how much of a fuss everybody made over that, even though the film we ruined wasn't even the liftoff—it was a minute or two after, when only the real space nuts were watching anyway.

Of course, we have toilets here. Next to each toilet is a big bin full of paper money. It's taxpayer money; which is cheaper and more abundant than toilet paper, and softer on your backside. I like to use fiftys, myself; I think the hundred dollar bills don't circulate enough and are too crinkly, but some people even prefer thousands. No accounting for taste.

We get lunch flown in on the NASA jets. I usually get the caviar and lark's tongues in aspic for an appetizer—with French champagne, of course—and a main course of jellied eyeball of baby seal, depending on my mood.

Afternoons are mostly free. We can't go home early, because that would look bad to the public, so we mostly just nap or play pinochle or watch the Mars Observer broadcasts. It's really too bad that NASA had to pretend to a public failure (I wish I knew

what half-wit had the bright idea to actually announce the launch)
but we really couldn't let outsiders see what Mars is *really* like. I
mean, this thing is a spy-satellite, just like the ones that the CIA
uses to keep tabs on Madonna's dressing room. You can look right
into the windows of the aliens' house-domes if you want. They
have outdoor methane baths, right by the Mars pyramids next to
the grand canal, you can watch 'em in the nude just like you were
right in with 'em. The pale slimy ones with the bulging craniums
are nothing to look at — kinda sexless, I can't even figure out which
are the girls — but those green ones, Zow-whee! You know, they
got six pairs of bazongas, and absolutely no shame at all. Sometimes they . . . well, you can't put that on TV, even if we *did* admit
that they exist, which would cause a worldwide panic, widespread
looting, the collapse of democracy, and several weeks of decreased
revenues for major corporations.

When we get bored with the tube, we play pinochle with the
space aliens from the crashed saucers. Some of the guys get to
feeling sorry for them, stranded so many jillions of light-years from
home, with their huge liquid brown eyes, but I figure, hell, the
youngest damn one of those guys is a million years old, why get
maudlin? And they cheat, too. That's why we have to take the
cards home to shuffle them — if you shuffle the cards at work, they
gimmick the cards around with their minds.

They can read minds, also — that's what management says —
but it's funny, they never seem to use that ability to cheat. I asked
once, and one of 'em said "How would you feel about sharing your
mind with a slug or a jellyfish?" I never can figure those aliens out,
always going on about jellyfish, evolution, cosmic oneness, crap
like that. Screw 'em.

Sometimes the alert buzzer sounds. That means the Air Force
is trying a commando raid. They claim that *we* stole the aliens
from *them*, when everybody knows that we saw them first. And
besides, they had their own aliens to do experiments on, and if
they used theirs up already, is that our fault? So every so often we
have to zap 'em good, until they finally get the lesson and skedad-
dle back home. The Air Force guys never quite figured out the
trick of making an effective ray-gun — good thing they aren't on
speaking terms with the CIA! — so they never get as far as the
inner sanctum. You'd think they'd learn.

Every now and then, the lights flicker and the TV goes on the
fritz. That means that the mother ship is buzzing us, trying to
annoy us into giving the aliens back. It's huge, at least a mile

across, with lots of blinky lights and shiny stuff. (That's why we have the NASA center in Cleveland: the boss figures that even if somebody reports it to the papers, nobody pays attention to news from Cleveland anyway.) Usually the mother ship just buzzes around. Luckily they have a thing about not blasting us into jelly; something to do with being a superior form of life, I guess. But occasionally the buzzing gets annoying, and we have to send somebody out to spray it with Windex until it goes away. They hate Windex.

And then, at five, the whistle blows, we gather up the cards to take home to shuffle, check that the vaults are all locked and nothing suspicious is out in plain sight, and then punch our time clocks and head home.

So that's what it's like to work at NASA. About like working anywhere, I suppose. It's a tough job, but, hey—somebody has to do it.

So, what's it like working for the phone company?

Dark Lady

SHE DRIVES AN ANCIENT MERCEDES CONVERTIBLE. The car is in wretched shape, the body battered and nearly rusted through, chrome pitted and discolored, the seat covers ripped and the stuffing popping out. But the engine is in racing condition. Every Saturday she tunes it up, working slowly, methodically: the engine, then the brakes, the tires. The task takes all morning.

She never takes the car out, except for the two-mile drive to the University each day.

The student scheduled to defend his thesis next, a plasma-physics experimentalist named Li, brought the case of beer. Somebody shot the cork from the first bottle of champagne. It arced across the seminar room and rebounded off a blackboard, and suddenly Caroline's party was in full swing.

Esteban didn't know Caroline very well. She'd kept to herself. He had never seen Caroline look so happy, smiling and laughing as people came up to shake her hand. He couldn't remember seeing her happy at all. Esteban pressed his way through the crowds. "Congratulations, Caroline!" He shook her hand. "Or perhaps I should say Doctor Caroline?"

She laughed. "By all means. I worked hard enough for it."

"So when will you be leaving for Caltech?"

"First thing in the morning."

"So soon? I'd think you'd stay around for a while, relax a bit."

"The sooner I get out of this place, the better."

"Hey, that's some attitude! But I guess it can get to you after a while." Esteban looked around. "Say, where's Doctor Hawke? Isn't she here to say goodbye and congratulate her latest?"

Caroline shrugged. "Jenny. She'll come if she feels like it. Or not. Who knows?"

"Don't you care?"

"Not really." She looked at him for a moment. "So you're her new student, aren't you?"

"Yes, it's all settled. I'll be starting Monday."

She looked down at the ground. "Maybe . . . have you thought about finding another advisor?"

"Why?"

"No reason." She made an irritated gesture with one hand. "This and that. She's not the only theorist in the physics department, you know. She's not easy to work with."

"But she's the best, isn't she?"

"Yeah." She didn't sound very enthusiastic. "I guess."

"Hey, nobody said it would be easy."

Caroline laughed cynically. "They sure didn't."

"So, any words of advice for the fresh meat?"

"Yeah." She paused. "No. You'll find out. Excuse me, I ought to wander around more."

Esteban watched her walk away. "Now what does she mean by that?" he asked, but no one listened, or, at least, no one answered.

The Taproom was dim, Friday-night crowded, and it took a few moments for Esteban's eyes to adjust to the murky blue light. He saw no one he knew. It was a mistake to come here, he thought suddenly. He would sit alone, pour down beers, and then at closing time go back to the student housing with a spinning head. The prospect seemed dismal, but the idea of going back to his apartment to study seemed equally bleak and uninviting.

"I thought I might find you here."

Esteban looked up. The slender man in the wool jacket stood awkwardly, a peculiar expression on his face. He had a short beard, with white hairs twisting together with dark brown ones. It took Esteban an instant to remember who he was. "Doctor Taggart." He suddenly remembered that Taggart was said to be a friend of his advisor, Dr. Hawke. Her only friend.

Taggart nodded toward the bar. "Join me?"

They drank in silence, and Esteban wondered why Taggart was there; had, apparently, particularly sought him out. But Taggart seemed to have no interest in conversation. Finally Esteban turned to him. He looked him over before speaking. "Tell me about Professor Hawke."

"Jenny? You don't even know what to ask, do you?"

"Tell me."

"Not today." Taggart got up without saying anything and crossed the room to the jukebox in back. When he got back to the table he sat down, lifted his head back, and closed his eyes. "Tell me, how do you feel about the blues?"

Esteban shrugged. "Okay, I guess."

In the distance, the jukebox started up; a saxophone yowling blues, a single deep voice wailing:

> *My lover is a lady, purer than the snow*
> *Yes, I've got a lady, I love her like the snow*
> *She'll show me up to heaven, the heavens up above,*
> *yes the heavens up above me, and the hells so far below.*

Taggart said, "You'll learn."

"In the beginning, in the end, there is only one question: what is the universe? What is this stuff, that the world is made of? But the more we learn, the more we understand the workings of the universe we live in, the more subtle and elusive the answer to the question becomes." Professor Hawke was silent for a long moment, standing with eyes focused blankly at some invisible object drifting slowly near the back of the room. Finally she continued, her voice so soft that it was almost a whisper. "We chase, and old theories fall discarded along the wayside, but the goal remains forever elusive."

She looked up, and seemed almost surprised to find the physics students still in the classroom. Not one of them moved. She flicked a wrist. "Dismissed."

Esteban fell into the habit of coming over to her house on Saturdays when she worked on the car. While she went through the long ritual of tuning it up, he worked on the body, sanding off rust, applying primer, covering over with fiberglass the places where the body had rusted through.

There was an odd physical satisfaction to be found in sanding: the smooth, repetitive motion, starting with coarse grit, the texture almost like gravel, and progressively moving through ever finer grits to polishing compound, finer than toothpaste, rubbed on by hand. Professor Hawke raced the engine, producing a cloud of faintly blue engine smoke. He looked up. She was grinning at him, wrapped up in her overalls, shouting over the roar of the engine. "The old beast sounds pretty good, eh, Esteban?"

He nodded, pulled down his dustmask for a moment and shouted back. "Not bad. Burning a little oil, no?"

She tapped the accelerator again in response, and the engine roared. "Yeah. It's the number two cylinder. Next week I'm going to pull the rings."

There were good days and bad days. Sometimes she would be brusque and uncommunicative, hollow-eyed as if she had forgotten how to sleep, silently starting to work on the engine with an odd grim determination, ignoring him. Other days she would laugh with exuberant energy and contagious good spirits.

All during the fall they worked together; on physics during the week, on the car Saturdays. The asphalt driveway was ankle-deep in yellow leaves. As it got colder he had to keep stamping his feet and moving about to avoid freezing. Late in November they moved inside, the garage door blocked halfway open with the handle of an old rake to let out the deadly perfume of the engine. Gusts of early snow blew in through the opening to battle with the warmth from the kerosene heater glowing in the corner. Afterwards, on the days when she was in high spirits, they would go inside and sit by the radiator, warming up, drinking coffee, talking physics.

"So few people ever learn to think," Dr. Hawke said. "Don't memorize, think! Think, think, think! First, last, and always. Use your brainpower."

It was an old house in the middle of the city, with a high ceiling of elaborately sculpted plaster. On the floor, beneath layers of dirt, Esteban could faintly distinguish the wood parquet. Fifty years ago the house, and neighborhood, had been the height of fashion. Now both were deteriorating.

Stacks of paper covered every surface. Scribbled notes, pages of calculations, unfinished scientific papers, piles of journals and conference proceedings, review copies of books, reams of experimental result summaries. He was amazed that she could ever find anything in the disorder, but more often than not she knew exactly which pile had the paper she was looking for. Occasionally one would not be where she thought it should be, and she would rage through the house overturning piles and scattering them across the floor, or else she would go silent and withdraw into herself, refusing to speak or acknowledge Esteban's existence until he left her alone and walked back the two miles to his own small apartment in the student housing.

Slowly Esteban discovers that he is drifting into deeper waters, where he doesn't know how to swim, is not even certain how to float. Esteban feels that he is drowning. He doesn't understand what he is doing. Oh, he understands the mechanics — although it is difficult, he can do the mathematics well enough — but the meaning eludes him. To him, it seems as if he is manipulating obscure symbols according to obscure rules toward some even more obscure goal that recedes from him further the more he strives. He fills notebooks with calculations, attempting to reduce complicated expressions to simplicity, and failing. When he gets stuck he comes to her. Often she points out an approach or an approximation he can try. Other times, though, she cannot find a way through the thicket of symbols, and says, simply, okay, now we can abandon *that* approach.

But when Esteban tries to ask her what it all means, she only shakes her head. We are pathfinders, she says. When — if — we find a path, then we can look back and understand where we've gone.

He remembers when physics used to be easy. God, he understood it then. When had it started to get hard?

Esteban tries not to show his desperation, not to let anyone know that he is terrified that he will be found out to be a fraud, that everyone except him understands it clearly. Taggart is the only one he confesses his fears to, and Taggart only laughs. "Everybody feels that way," he says. "After a while you get a feel for it, and bit by bit it begins to make sense."

He pauses, and then says, "Or else it doesn't."

Esteban saw it in the newspaper, buried several pages back in the metro-area section. Late last night she had been out walking over by the Projects, and she had been assaulted. She put two neat holes in the man with a .22 caliber Beretta, then calmly waited for the police to arrive. The assailant had been taken to the hospital, but was released when she declined to press charges.

But what, wondered Esteban, what she had been doing in that part of town at midnight? There was nothing there; no stores, just graffiti-covered burned out-cars, drug-dealers, and the blank brick walls of the housing projects.

And nobody in the department was even curious. Why wouldn't anybody talk about it?

The saxophone cried out in staccato rhythm, while a thin voice quavered softly over, between the notes:

Oh my lady love is strong and cruel, she serves a jealous god
Yes, my love's a jealous lady, she serves an evil god—

Doctor Taggart went to the bar, bought two mugs of beer, and brought them back to the booth. He handed one to Esteban.

"It was 1962," he said softly. "You have to remember that things were different then. It was the winter of our second year in grad school. That fall we'd taken our comprehensives, and we were still basking in the glow that comes with knowing that we made the grade. None of us so much as Jennifer, of course. She'd been the only one to get a perfect score."

Esteban took a sip of his beer. Her eyes had been unfocused today, and he had thought she was sick, although she'd denied it. Her nose had been dripping, but she didn't bother to wipe it. She'd just stared at the car, not even bothering to start it up. After half an hour of staring, with her wrist and forearm twitching erratically, she'd abruptly told him to go home. It had scared him.

He took another gulp of beer. "Go on," he said.

"It's a long story." Taggart sighed. "Maybe—no, forget it. It's been a long day. We should probably both go home."

Neither one of them made a move. "Go on," Esteban said.

Taggart picked up his beer. "1962," he said, shaking his head slowly. "Yeah. Well, I was a little put off by the fact that she'd out-done me, to tell you the truth. Until then, I'd thought of myself as pretty hot stuff. I have to admit that I wouldn't have minded so much if it had been any of the other students—but to be beaten by a girl! Yes, I know—it seems rather petty now. We were pretty damn narrow-minded back then, and nobody thought any-thing of it. Nobody even noticed. From then on, I made a point of ignoring her. That was easy. She didn't try to attract attention, or try to make friends, and back then any kind of camaraderie between men and woman students were quite discouraged. Women students had nine o'clock curfews — yes, grad students too. They didn't make any distinction."

"You weren't worried about prelims?" Esteban asked.

"Prelims? No. We'd passed the comps, and the prelims seemed just infinitely far in the future.

"There was an intense rivalry between the grad students right then. We had to choose research advisors, and there was keen competition to work for the big names in the department. I don't think that Jenny even noticed it. She went right in to see Lermontov, told him she was going to work for him, just like that."

Esteban smiled. "That's her, all right."

"Lermontov was a bear of a man, with a huge bushy brown beard. I think he hardly even noticed whether his students were men or women. All he cared about was whether they could do physics, and, man, Jenny could do physics in spades. She was the best. I guess that was another way Lermontov was ahead of his time.

"She awed us, just walking in and telling Lermontov how it was going to be. Didn't make her any friends, but it set her apart."

Taggart stopped talking and cocked his head sideways. The song ended on a long lonely note almost impossibly high. It slowly warbled upward and then faded into the air like smoke. After a moment of silence the gabble of voices in the bar started up again, and then the heavy bass rhythm of a rock song beat across the room.

"We were all still taking classes," Taggart said. "Professor Saxon gave us a final exam with just one problem, to prove a certain theorem. Instead of proving it true, the two of us — Jenny and I — found a counter-example, and proved it false. We were the only ones in the class who did.

"If only one of us had given that answer, I'm sure he would have ignored it, given out zero credit, and gone on. But with two of us, he had to try to follow the reasoning to show us where we'd gone wrong. Of course, he couldn't; we were right, and he — and the rest of the class — were wrong.

"When he finally convinced himself that we were right, Saxon went up to the department chairman and accused Jenny of cheating. The argument was so subtle, he told the chairman, a single brilliant student could possibly have stumbled across it, but not two. Jenny must have copied it from my paper, he said, 'most likely without even realizing it was a remarkable piece of work.'

When Jenny was called in, she denied the accusation of cheating and pointed out her score on the comps. He accused her of cheating on those, too.

"So the next day she came bursting into my room and accused me of trying to sabotage her career. This was the first I'd heard anything about it. There was a big scene, but after a bit of shouting back and forth—I did my share of shouting, too—we figured out what had happened, and I convinced her that I had nothing to do with it. It ended up with her crying in my arms. That was the only time I ever saw her cry. Later, she understood not to expect fairness out of the world.

"Enough people in the class had remembered that we'd sat on opposite sides of the room, and at last Saxon stopped pushing the matter. It was allowed to drop, although as far as I know he never withdrew the accusation, or apologized to either one of us.

"That incident broke the barrier between us. From then on, if we weren't exactly best friends, at least we were companions-in-arms. We would work problems together, and I tried to get her interested in other things, like hiking—I was an avid woodsman in those days—and jazz." He shook his head. "Yeah, I listened to a lot of jazz back then. I was still too young to appreciate the blues." He took a sip of his drink. "She'd listen carefully to whatever I played for her, but the only composer she ever really respected was Bach.

"Myself, I picked up a little of her dream, and maybe a little of her dedication. I'd sort of drifted into physics. It was not yet twenty years after the atom bomb, and a lot of people still thought of physicists as heroes who'd won the war and saved a lot of lives." He laughed grimly. "Heroes, yeah. Shows how things change, doesn't it? I went into physics because it was fashionable. She showed me that it was beauty, and truth, as well."

"And so you started sleeping with her," Esteban said.

Taggart looked up. "You're kidding, right?" He chuckled, without any particular humor to it. "This was 1962. Nice girls didn't. Everybody knew that. I did make a pass—a rather tentative pass, since I was rather inexperienced at such things myself—and she ignored it. Maybe she didn't even notice it in the first place. She just didn't think that way.

"We were together a lot. It was about the happiest time of my life.

"In the spring we both took Eisenstern's course on quantum field theories. Field theory was rather new then, the cutting edge of science, and Eisenstern was one of the best. I'd thought I'd seen Jenny work before, but she took to that course like she'd been walking all her life, and just learned she could run. She left us all behind. Me, too, I'm afraid. Oh, I followed her as well as I could, and saw a bit of the elegance of the theory reflected in her work. She tore apart problems as if they held some priceless treasure.

"That was when I made the decision to become an experimentalist. I'd always thought I wanted to do theory, but after watching her approach field theory, I realized I'd never be able to do more than follow along behind. I wanted to make my own trails, even if I had to explore less important territory.

"Eisenstern really took an interest in Jenny. He invited her over to his house for special sessions. He was a young professor, maybe forty, divorced, with a big stone house on the outskirts of town.

"The first time she was invited, she took me along. When I got there he was a little taken aback. I could tell that he hadn't expected her to bring company. We sat around his fireplace, drinking brandy, the two of them talking physics, with me jumping in occasionally with stupid comments. It got to be eight o'clock, and then nine. I finally managed to drag her away. I don't know how she got in past the housemother after curfew."

"Last call!" the bartender shouted. Esteban walked up to the bar and bought two more beers.

When he got back, Taggart continued. "Next time he invited her over I couldn't go. I had a hike already scheduled. She went; she never even considered that there might be anything untoward about it.

"She never told me the details, although over the years I've pretty much figured out what happened. He sat beside her, and leaned in close—still talking physics—and then started to caress her. She should have left then, but she didn't really know what was happening. She was terribly innocent in some ways, for all her mastery of theory. When she realized what he wanted, and started to object, he called her a tease, accused her of leading him on, and called her a lot of other things as well. She was so confused, she didn't know what to do."

"He raped her," said Esteban.

"He . . . was insistent." Taggart shook his head. "I don't know the details. He showed up in class the next day with a bit of a bruise on one cheek. She didn't come to class at all. I didn't think anything about it at the time. She had missed classes before, though usually not without calling me up to ask me to make a carbon of my notes for her. But she didn't come to the next class, or the next, or the next, and I didn't see her around campus, either. I finally went to see her in her room—which was not at all an easy proposition in those days—but she avoided the subject, and wouldn't tell me anything was wrong."

"Closing!" cried the bartender, twisting the dimmer switch to full. The overhead lights brightened, showing the empty glasses and stained bar tables in harsh, ugly glare. "Drink 'em up!"

Esteban does his work in the bullpen, a large open office on the fifth floor of the physics building, side by side with half a dozen other grad students, each one hooked up to earphones and huddled over a stack of papers. He labors until midnight over Feynmann diagrams, a bootleg tape of Buddy Guy in New Orleans blasting in his ears, summing up the histories of elementary particles, hopelessly trying to cancel infinity against itself. He sits alone.

Some days he covers for her when she doesn't come in. He teaches her introductory physics class unasked, and suddenly remembers that Caroline, long since gone, had often done the same. Hawke is sick a lot recently, sometimes for days on end, and then suddenly she is vigorous and full of energy.

"The most important question in the world," said Doctor Hawke, "is this: why is there *something* instead of nothing?"

"I don't know," said Esteban. She is well today, and at the peak of her form. "Why?"

"We can't answer that one. We don't have the tools yet. The next most fundamental question is this: why is that something countable? Why is there quantization? We can track that one, Esteban, we can follow in its footsteps and hunt it down.

"Quantization of energy levels, that we understand pretty well. But why are particles quantized? Why can you have one electron, or two electrons, but never half an electron, or the square root of two electrons?"

Esteban thought for a moment. "The result of an observation has to be an eigenvalue of the hermitian operator. . . ."

"Good! But is that an explanation? Why do the operators have to be hermitian? Why do the eigenvalues have to be integers?"

"Well, since the appropriate field operator is the number operator, the spectrum is that of a harmonic oscillator."

"You're not thinking, Esteban. The number operator was chosen *because* it produces integer eigenvalues. That's a description, not an explanation. It's frightening. Or it should be. People think in integers because people come in integers. We don't measure how *much* people, we count how *many* people. But nature knows nothing of integers. Even in quantum mechanics, nature is continuous. Waves. But electrons come in integers! You count them, you don't measure them. Why? What comes in integers, Esteban?"

"Apples?"

"Very good. Are electrons made of apples?"

"No."

"Right. Apples come in integers, but the stuff of which apples are made is continuous. We have to search for a basic principle. For some reason, the structure of the universe requires that the fundamental particles be countable. Why? Let us consider what mathematical objects are integrally quantized."

Esteban leaned back and pulled out his pad. This was going to be worth taking notes on.

"First, there are topological objects: the number of holes in a torus. . . ."

But it was rare when she was that sharp, that focused. Often she nodded through her classes, barely responded to his questions. He had all the facts, but he didn't want to put them together into the only picture they would make.

She was brilliant, she was in pain, the world was too intense to her. She needed it. She was still in control, wasn't she? She was capable of anything; she was crazy, she was above rules. How could he confront her?

How could he not?

Every day, after work, he would go to the bar and drink until closing.

Esteban waited in the corridor outside her office. Doctor Hawke was half an hour late, but that wasn't unusual. She was often late. Finally he heard her car pull up outside, and a few minutes later she walked in. Today she was bright and chipper, full of energy. He wet his lips. His mouth felt unusually dry. All of a sudden he wasn't sure if he could say it.

"Hello, Esteban. Sorry I'm late."

His chest was so tight that he could hardly breathe, but he had to know for sure. He concentrated on the words, speaking each one separately, not thinking what they meant. "You're using, aren't you?"

She stopped abruptly and looked at him. "I don't think that's any of your business," she said coldly.

"That's not an answer, is it? You're a junkie."

She spoke very softly. "So?"

"Why?"

"What can I say? Do you think there's a simple reason?" She crossed her arms, uncrossed them, crossed them again, and then shrugged. "I do what gets me through the day. Do you think it's easy, Esteban? Do you want to tell me how to run my life?"

She reached across him and opened her office. "Conference today is canceled. Get out of here, Esteban."

As he turned around, the door slammed shut. He could see her silhouette against the frosted glass. "Dr. Hawke?"

"Go!"

He could see her reach up, and then the light went out and there was silence.

> She don't want your heart, but she'll take your soul
> You may try to stay in charge, but she'll always take control,
> You may hate yourself in the light of day
> But it's nighttime now and you'll do what it takes
> Yes, tonight you'll take your pleasure and forget
>   tomorrow's pain.

"So you found out about Jenny." Taggart sat down next to Esteban. "All of her students do, sooner or later. She hardly even tries to cover up any more. It affects them all in different ways. Some quit. Some keep working for her, but turn bitter, like Caroline. Some don't give a damn."

"What does it matter to you what they think?" said Esteban bitterly.

"I care about all of her students. Somebody has to."

"You're her friend. Why don't you get her to stop?"

"I would if I could, Esteban. It's not that simple. What do you want me to do? Kidnap her, lock her up until she changes? Even if I could, she'd go right back to using. Should I call the police? Do you really think that would help her?"

"Don't you care about her?" Esteban said, fighting to keep from shouting. "She's killing herself, slowly. Don't you even care at all?"

"It's her life, Esteban. She's been on the road for a long time, and she knows where it leads. If she's going to change, she has to do it herself. I can't do it for her."

Esteban pushed his chair back abruptly and walked to the bar. The air was thick and blue with cigarette smoke. He got two more mugs of beer, and cleared off an area on the table to set them on. "Mind if I ask a personal question?"

"Yes," said Taggart, "as a matter of fact, I do."

"You ever been married?"

"And what business is that of yours?" Taggart looked at Esteban until Esteban finally looked away, and then answered softly. "No. I guess I should have. Get a wife, a house in the suburbs, kids, all of that . . ." his voice trailed off.

"So how come you never did?" There was no answer. "Are you in love with Doctor Hawke?"

"In love with Jenny? No. Well, only a little, now." Taggart picked up his beer, turned it around in his fingers, and put it down again. "No. I know her too well for that. Once. For a long, long time. But you can't love her, Esteban. She won't let you. It would hurt too much, to love her and watch her destroy herself, and know you are helpless."

"Do you buy for her?" asked Esteban in a bitter voice.

"Esteban, I'd do anything for her. Almost anything. But not cop for her. I wouldn't do it, and she wouldn't ask me to."

Taggart put his beer down and turned his back on Esteban. His voice was soft, speaking to the brick wall. "Yeah, guess I should have gotten married, moved away, gotten away from this damn place. I should have done it a long time ago."

"Can't you do anything?" Esteban said, speaking to Taggart's back. "Send her to a clinic, or something?"

"You think she hasn't been to clinics? Those things won't help, unless she wants them to help."

"Science," she said. "There's nothing else worth doing, Esteban. It's all there is.

"Heroin. That's pleasure, pure; almost as good as the thrill of discovery. And the pain, that's pure, too. It's pain, but it's pure pain."

Esteban nodded. He didn't like to see her like this. He didn't know what to say.

"It's not like people. People. It's not that they're so complex, it's that they're so simple. So trivial, lusting after trivial things. I hate them, I hate them all. So petty, they are so petty to tarnish something so beautiful, so pure, with petty lies and politics and scheming. Can't they see? Don't they care at all?

"I always wanted to have a baby. It's so lonely, knowing there is nothing you can give all your being to. Don't you think it's lonely? Don't you?"

Esteban nodded again, not trusting himself to speak.

"Do you think I'm pretty? I was, you know, I was pretty. But I didn't care, I never cared. It doesn't matter. Looks don't matter. Do you think I should have cared? I had a head of gold, but feet of clay.

"We were never meant for this world, you and I. The stars, they are so beautiful from the gutter. So beautiful."

Esteban got up. "I have to go now, Doctor Hawke. It was nice talking to you." He practically ran out of the room. He didn't want her to see him cry.

Tuesday was a slow night for the Taproom. Esteban and Taggart had it all to themselves. Taggart bought a pitcher, and filled both glasses.

"That can't be all," said Esteban. "How did it come out? How did it finally end?"

"End?" Taggart paused, as if he had never considered the concept before. "Does it end? I suppose it must."

Esteban picked up his beer. He didn't sip it, but just looked across the empty barroom in silence, not bothering to look at Taggart. He knew by now that he would talk. Taggart had his own compulsions, no less demanding than those that tore at Hawke.

Taggart shook his head. "Well. End, eh? Jenny showed up for the final exam, took it, and then hurried away before I even got a chance to talk to her. I saw her again when it was time to pick up the exams. Even though she'd been the best in the class, Eisenstern gave her a C in the course. I told her she should protest to the department head.

"She just sort of shrugged. 'It doesn't matter.'

"I couldn't believe she wouldn't protest. 'But you were the best in the class. You deserve more than—'

"It doesn't matter, she said. 'Let it be, Richard. Just let it be.' She saw Eisenstern coming down the hall. I have to run, she said. 'Talk to you later, okay? Bye.' She left before I could say anything more.

"I don't think she ever did tell Eisenstern. She wouldn't give him the satisfaction. The university pressured her to drop out, or get married, but she refused. So they did the next best thing. Abortions weren't legal then, but, well, in an Ivy League university, certain exceptions can be made, in the face of overriding health reasons. The healthy reputation of the university, for example. Officially, I don't think she ever was pregnant. Right after finals she stayed a week in the infirmary, and certainly she wasn't pregnant when she left.

"The doctors at the infirmary were oh so sympathetic to what she was going through, having lost a child. They gave her pills to help her get over her grief; and told her to take one every two hours, without bothering telling her what she was taking. For her own good, of course.

"So after getting out of the infirmary, she tried to put her life back together and get started on her research. And she couldn't do it. She couldn't concentrate on physics.

"They prescribed stronger sedatives, and she started having real trouble. I think that she must have started to think she had lost her edge, and that unnerved her more than anything else possibly could have. When the doctors at the infirmary thought she was starting to get hysterical, they increased the dose. She started falling asleep in conferences, nodding out at her desk. By now she was addicted to the pills. We all knew that something was wrong, but she wouldn't tell anybody what it was. There was talk that she'd lose her fellowship.

"And then she disappeared.

"Doctor Lermontov was the only one who stood up for her. Ya, I am not vorried, he'd say. Miss Hawke, she vill take care of herself. He was right. Two months later she returned. She had a gaunt and hollow-eyed look. She never said where she went. Somewhere there she learned cynicism. But she'd beaten her habit, or at least learned to keep it under control.

"She had to work hard to keep her fellowship, but she did it. She still knew how to do physics. For the next couple of weeks she worked twenty hours a day, and by the beginning of September she had a prelim presentation that was at least as good as any of ours."

"So Lermontov was the only one she could depend on," said Esteban.

"Well, yes. But in the end, he betrayed her, too. By then she didn't expect anything better."

"Closing time!" called the bartender, one hand on the light switch, the other on a rag. "That's it, boys, you've been here long enough. Finish 'em up and get on home to your families."

*   *   *

"You must have been talking with Doctor Taggart." She shook her head softly. "Ah, dear Richard, where would I be without him? Yes, he has his ideas about me. Stuff that happened long ago, that he thinks is important. The romantic heroine, the dark lady, striving for greatness, fated for tragedy." She picked up a stack of papers on her desk and, without even glancing at them, dropped them into a drawer and slammed it shut. "Nuts. I live the way I do because I choose to. If I'm a junkie, Esteban—and I don't like that word—but if I am, it's my own damn business."

"But don't you get, ah, needle marks and all that? Hepatitis?"

"Don't be ridiculous. What the hell do you think I am, some damn street junky fixing in an alley? You won't get needle tracks if you use a sterile needle and clean the skin with alcohol before fixing. Junkies who get needle tracks are plain stupid. I get sterile needles from lab supplies."

"Here? Don't they ask what you want them for?"

She shrugged. "I'm a professor. They may wonder, but they won't ask.

"Now, let's quit talking about me, and get to work. Have you gotten any results out of the perturbation expansion you were working on yet?"

Esteban nodded. "Yes, I've gotten some results, but I'm not sure about a couple of things. First. . . ."

Still, he couldn't help thinking, why? Why you? And through it all, he could even still marvel at the diamond clarity of her thinking, the beautiful, simple precision of the way she could attack a problem.

They were on the track of something. He could feel it hiding in the mathematics, looming huge just outside the corner of his vision, a great truth that would make it all fit together, but whenever he turned his head it is gone, and he wondered if it was there at all, or an illusion of his desperate wanting.

He told her about it, but she just shook her head and smiled. "Don't look for the great truth yet, Esteban. Do the details. Do the math, fill out the blank spots, and if some great truth is there, it will be waiting there for you. Okay?"

> *But you know you'll never leave her, though she's killing*
> *   you so slow*
> *The blood runs fire in your veins and the hells they wait*
> *   below.*

"There is one thing," Taggart said. "You see, she could have ruined Eisenstern's career. A little bit of fooling around was something the university might turn a blind eye to, but when a professor actually gets a student pregnant, they'd take notice. If she'd complained into the right ears, he would have found that there were plenty of positions available at somewhat lesser universities. If she wanted vengeance, she could have gotten it. But she chose to stay silent; to stick it out, instead.

"There's not much more to say. The year she finished her thesis research, there was a major conference on high-energy physics theory in Stuttgart. She and Lermontov coauthored an abstract on her work and sent it off. It got accepted. Unfortunately, Lermontov told her, there wasn't enough money to pay her way to the conference. Since she didn't have money of her own, Lermontov went to present the paper in both their names.

"Somehow, he never happened to mention that the conference committee had been so impressed by the work that they scheduled it as the lead paper and offered to pay both their ways over. Strangely enough, when he presented the paper, her name mysteriously got left off."

"She didn't object?"

"She didn't know about it. It wasn't her first paper, but it was — should have been — an important one. She didn't even find out until a year later, when she listed the paper on her resume, and one of the people she interviewed called her out on it. By then she had already been a postdoc for a year, a thousand miles away. There wasn't much she could do."

Estaban was listening, but not with all his attention. He was sketching out topological manifolds on one of the napkins from the bar. She had been talking about knot theory recently, and suddenly he understood how it connected to field theory. It had been obvious to her from the start, of course . . . but if you think about the four-dimensional manifold *this* way. . . .

And, slowly, it was starting to make sense. He was beginning to stay even with her, even though he still couldn't see the picture that she seemed to feel intuitively, the theory that the pieces were coming together to form. It was an exhilaration, a feeling of power like a drug, the first time that he realized that he understood something she said so completely that he broke in and finished her sentence for her. She sat back, a smile on her face.

It even seemed to him that she was using less. Maybe? Could

it be? But then he came in for a conference and she was nodding, her pupils tiny pinpricks of dark, sitting at her desk with a dreamy expression, oblivious to him or anything. He walked out — she didn't change position — and walked around the campus, once, twice, a third time, then came back to her office and entered without knocking.

"Why did you go back?" he said, almost shouting at her. "You kicked once. Dr. Taggart said you kicked it once."

She pulled him close and brought her face right up against his, forehead to forehead, so that her two grey eyes were a single cyclopean eye in the middle of her face. Her voice was a hot whisper against his lips.

"Richard likes to talk. Richard likes to tell stories, he likes explanations, likes everything to make sense. Richard doesn't know a damn thing about it. Talk to Richard if it helps you, boy, but don't you ever come up and tell me about it."

She held him, stared into his eye for a long moment, then released him and leaned back in her chair. She picked up a paper from the pile, looked at it without focusing on it. Slowly the hard look on her face relaxed. She sat there for several minutes, until Esteban wondered if she wanted him to leave, wondered if she had forgotten he was there.

"There are some who open up whole new fields; the grand architects like Einstein, Maxwell, Galileo," she said. "And there are others who do the dirty work, who painstakingly fill in the details, who lay the bricks and shine their flashlights into areas of the grand cathedrals that the architects have only briefly mentioned. Don't let anybody tell you that this is less important. For all that there are a thousand bricklayers for each of the architects, that bricklaying is what builds up the body of science, bit by bit.

"But still, I always wanted to be one of the trailblazers, one who looked at what others have looked at before and saw what none have ever seen.

"Maybe it's an accident of luck, to be in the right place at the right time. Maybe there is no fundamentally new physics left, that all is done except filling in the details. Maybe it's me.

"I've tried, Esteban, I've tried. I've gotten piles of honors and citations for things I've done, and it's all shit. Bricklaying. I know that I never did more than that, although I've done it well, as well as I could. I've always just filled in the details of work that others had originated.

"I've had the dream, Esteban. I've had the dream ever since I can remember. And dreams die hard."

* * *

"You love her too, Esteban, don't you?"

He nodded mutely.

"It's hard, isn't it?"

"Yes."

"You can't change her, you know. She's a diamond, and we are just rocks. You can only grind yourself down."

"I know."

And the saxophone said,

> *Maybe God's above, but I'll never know*
> *I've sold my soul to the devils down below*
> *To take my pleasure of my lady love,*
> *white and cold like the deadly burning snow.*

And then she showed him what she had done, how all the pieces that the two of them together had hammered into shape fit together into a theory. It came as a shock to Esteban to find that she had abandoned field quantization. Her first paper—the very first one, the one that she had done so long ago with Lermontov—had been on methods of field quantization.

"But how do you deal with photons?"

"We have no need for photons. Look."

And it was everything he had learned, seen in a new way, all topsy-turvy. But it worked. God, it worked!

"But why? It's so *complicated*."

"Calculationally complicated," she said. "But conceptually, neater."

It didn't look neater to him. It looked like the back side of a magician's stage, all scaffolding and hooks and wires, with ad hoc assumptions to make things come out.

"It was always like that, Esteban. This way the theory just shows it clearly."

It was crazy, a patchwork quilt of a theory, but it all hung together. "That explains everything," he whispered. "It's incredible!"

"Not everything," she said. "But a lot." She crumpled the piece of paper in her hand, and Esteban jerked back as if he'd been shot. "And it's wrong."

"What?"

"Wrong!" she shouted. She threw the ball of paper across the room. It bounced off the blackboard and skittered to a stop out in the hall. "In error. Factually incorrect. False."

"Why? How?"

She grabbed a sheet of paper—a student's final exam—and started scribbling on it, oblivious to what was already written there. "Look! You can solve for the mass of the electron—"

He stared at it. "How? To do that you need to know the coupling coefficient—"

"No! Can't you see? All those terms drop out! You get a Hankel function; the infinities cancel and you can integrate it exactly."

Esteban shook his head. "I can't integrate a Hankel function in my head."

"You don't have to. That's why God invented Russians." She pulled Rhyzhik and Gradshteyn from her bookshelf. "Look!"

It took him half an hour to convince himself she was right, another hour to go through it again, this time looking for some adjustable parameter he could jigger to make the numbers come out right. There weren't any. He went back into the derivation then, trying to find where the error came in. Hawke had gone away—to fix up, he guessed, he had been too busy to notice her leaving—and when she finally came back, he was staring at the wall.

He looked up, and was surprised to notice that it was almost midnight. He'd been working for almost six hours. "The standard model is wrong," he said.

"Obviously."

Esteban let out a sigh of relief. Until he had heard her confirm it he hadn't realized how much on edge he'd been. "But—that's a breakthrough!" he said. The standard model had been used to explain elementary particle physics for over two decades, and their work showed that it was wrong, just like that. "Don't you see—"

"Do you really think I care?" she snapped. "We're back at square zero." She rested her forehead on the desk. "I can't start over again, Esteban, I just can't. That was everything I had, everything, and it wasn't enough." Then she raised her head and looked at him. "Go home, Esteban. Tomorrow will be soon enough for you to write this up for publication."

"But we should celebrate—"

"Go on home, Esteban." She shook her head. "I prefer to do my celebrating alone, and I don't need any help from you. Get some sleep. You can be famous tomorrow."

It was enough. He could see it now, see the whole thing completely—or maybe it was just his own tiredness making him think he could see it all—but he knew that he would get a thesis out of it, and more. Even if they shared the credit—even though Jenny would claim the major portion of the credit, which rightfully was hers—it would still be a major result. His part of the work would be worth a professorship.

But Jenny? On a sudden impulse he hugged her. It was the first time he had ever dared touch her, and she went rigid for a moment. Then for just a brief instant she relaxed, and he felt the crumpled cotton of her blouse, felt her body heat and bunched muscles and quickly beating heart, and suddenly realized she was a human being like any other, with her own fears and sadness and a vulnerability that he could never know, and then she pushed him away.

Her voice was tired now. "Home, Esteban." She pushed him gently out her office door, and closed it behind him. He waited there, alone in the silent corridor, and heard the click of the lock, and waited until at last her light went out.

He drives a beat-up Mercedes convertible. Every morning at nine it comes screeching into the faculty parking lot with the deep, frustrated roar of a powerful engine whose only outlet is through twin racing mufflers. The body has been painstakingly restored with fiberglass patches, sanded into smooth curves and lovingly painted with a deep, hand-rubbed grey, the grey of an overcast winter's dawn, the grey of forgotten hopes.

The body is patched and sanded, but the engine is in racing tune.

Outsider's Chance

A NUCLEAR THERMAL ROCKET IS A TOUCHY BEAST. IT cares what you feed it.

Hydrogen is best. Anything you feed into a nuclear rocket will give you thrust, but the lower the molecular weight of your reaction mass, the better your fuel efficiency is—the best impulse for the input, as it were. But you pay for that; the thrust goes down. Feed it something heavier, say nitrogen, and you don't get as good fuel efficiency. But you get more thrust.

I was feeding *Bessie* lithium this year. I would have preferred hydrogen, but I flat-out couldn't afford it. Hydrogen is expensive in the inner system; you have to haul it up from Earth, tank it in from the outer belt, or else dredge it out of the lunar soil molecule by molecule. Lithium is cheap, a by-product of fluorosilane production from regolith. And I had a little trick I could use, if I had to. Would have worked best with hydrogen, but it would still work with lithium.

Nuclear thermal is about the simplest type of rocket engine there is. The reactor core is an oven. You pump your reaction mass through the reactor core, it gets hot, and you exhaust it out a nozzle to get thrust. Working on a nuclear engine is what I do best, so I won't say it's trivial, but in essence it's no more than an exercise in plumbing.

Lithium's decent reaction mass, don't mistake me. It's great if you don't care much about performance: it's solid for transport, so it doesn't need to be pressurized for storage, but you heat it a little and you can inject it as easy as water. And it's nice and dense — well, compared to hydrogen. But to really get acceptable performance out of lithium, you have to run your core at about four thousand degrees, which is a damn sight hotter than hell. *Bessie* couldn't get those kinds of temperatures even when she was new, and she was long years from being new.

So I was at a double disadvantage; running cold, running heavy. Reactors get old. It's not like a chemical engine, that either works or it doesn't: when a reactor gets old, it still works, but you can't get it quite as hot, can't run quite as much reaction mass through it.

That's probably why I attracted attention. Anybody with a spectroscope could tell I was feeding lithium, could tell from the Doppler that my exhaust velocity was low and that my reactor core was old. It was obvious that I couldn't run fast.

I didn't have much of a choice. *Bessie* was mortgaged up to my eyeballs.

One of the previous owners had tagged the freighter *Bessie*, figuring it was a good name for a mule. Slow and ugly, but good enough for hauling ore. I'd bought her at auction after her last owner had been unable to haul enough cargo to pay the mortgage, and now the ship and the mortgage were both mine. I didn't bother renaming her.

Bessie had a crew of one, Ulysses Ahmed Tabibzadah: me.

The freight this run was oxygen. Oxygen's not a glamorous freight, not like the platinum-group metals from some wildcatter in the way-out, but it's a steady paycheck. I was hauling twenty thousand tons, three tanks of solidified oxygen, one tank of solidified nitrogen. And everybody uses oxygen.

Bessie's design was rather typical of a second-generation nuclear thermal rocket. The reactor and thrust chamber, with its oversized bell nozzle and maze of plumbing, sat at one end of a long truss of aluminum-lithium girders, with the spherical crew compartment at the other end. The truss served to put the nuclear reactor two hundred meters away from me, allowing the radiation shielding to be kept to a minimum. Behind the crew compartment was a utility room, which also served as the airlock. The tanks for the lithium were at the back, right ahead of the engine, close enough to the engine for heat-pipes to efficiently transfer waste heat to liquefy the fuel, and incidentally adding some additional radiation shielding. The engine also had feed-lines for cryogenic fuel, since the engine was designed originally for hydrogen, but at the moment nothing was flowing through these. And strapped to the outside of the main truss, like a cluster of mangoes strapped to an oversized pencil, was the payload, along with a sun-shield of crinkled foil to keep it cool and a refrigerator to recondense the boil-off.

I was boosting a load from a processing plant at Hermes, pull-ing a steady twenty milligees. Time is money in the outer reaches as well as on Earth, but twenty milligees was as hot as I could push the engine. Still, a few weeks of twenty milligees would get me some respectable speed. As long as I didn't get hijacked.

The first intimation I had of trouble was the radar proximity alarm. At first I was surprised, then I was frightened. A proximity alarm shouldn't ever go off in the middle of a haul; space is empty. There are maybe a thousand ships spread across the outside haul-ing freight and ore between the asteroids and the Earth; consider-ing the distances involved, after I'd boosted from the processing factory, it was an incredible coincidence to find another ship within a million kilometers. And yet, the tone of the Doppler told me that a ship was here, and not merely flashing by on another orbit, but less than a kilometer away, and matching trajectory. It was closing with *Bessie* slowly, a few meters per second.

The radio was silent.

Hellfire and damnation!

How had it slipped in so close without a whole tabernacle choir of warning alarms? This was not good news.

Once I was aware of the other ship, it was easy enough to spot. With my good hand I cranked around one of the external cameras to zoom in for a look, while with my foot I punched my rendez-vous beacon. There was no chance that they were unaware of me—there was nothing stealthy about *Bessie*, and the other ship's parallel trajectory couldn't be a coincidence. Nevertheless, pru-dent flight operations dictated that I squawk my position—mis-takes in piloting were usually fatal.

With my beacon squawking, it was obvious to them that I knew they were there, and after a few seconds, the unknown ship's beacon also lit up. I read out the ship's details encoded on their beacon transmission. There was damn little to learn. Ship's name: *Love's Labors Lost*. Registration: [blank]. Ship type: [blank] Owner: [Not in data bank].

A pirate.

I'd heard stories of piracy before; who hadn't? Ships that came to port minus their cargoes, other ships that never made it back. I'd never been sure how much credence to give the story; it would be easy for a crew to divert their own cargo, split the profits, and claim piracy.

Now I knew.

The external camera showed me something interesting. Between the pirate ship and *Bessie*, struts held a sheet of metal mesh fixed to the pirate. It was nearly transparent in the visible, but I knew that in microwave frequencies, it must be operating as a phased array antenna. When the antenna detected pulses from *Bessie*'s radar, it analyzed them, calculated the radar reflection, and synthesized a signal exactly 180 degrees out of phase. The result would be that *Bessie*'s radar would detect nothing, up until the point where the pirate was too close to do anything about.

The pirate ship, or at least the side facing *Bessie*, was polished metal. The reactor in particular was shiny with layers of thermal blanket insulation. I had little doubt that the side I couldn't see would be black, radiating waste heat in all directions except mine. When I was a kid dreaming of space, I drew pictures of rockets with fiery tongues of flame licking out behind them. The reality is less spectacular. If a drive works right, the exhaust is *cold*. That should be obvious, right? The whole purpose of a rocket is to turn heat energy into kinetic energy. If the exhaust is hot, then there's still some heat you're not using. Tune it right, and the exhaust from a rocket should be cryogenic. So the ship wasn't radiating heat my direction. Result, stealthy in the infrared, too.

No communication from the pirate ship yet, although my squawk was broadcasting my receive frequency. The pirate ship was matching my 1/50 gee acceleration with ease, possibly waiting to see what I would do.

Not that I had very many options. In the big empty, twenty million kilometers from anywhere, there was nobody to call for help. And *Bessie* was, of course, unarmed. She was a freighter, not a warship.

I could run, but with a top acceleration of twenty milligees, they could easily match anything I could do. Loaded as she was, *Bessie* was about as agile as an ant towing an elephant—a lot of momentum once it got moving, but not much ability to turn quickly.

I studied the pirate ship with additional care. With a longer look, I could see that their ship was even older than mine. Like me, they were also running lithium, and the fuzzy Doppler I could get from their exhaust gave a lousy value for exhaust velocity. The reactor shielded behind that insulation must be at least twenty years old. The only reason they could match course with me was that I was loaded, and they were empty. I could drop my cargo and run. Unloaded, *Bessie* would run at over a gee of acceleration. This was probably what they were hoping I would do—it would save them the trouble of taking it away from me.

All this time the pirate was drifting closer. Now their stealth blanket retracted, rolling up and folding back against the ship, and their RCS thrusters slowed the rate of closure, preparing to rendezvous.

They were simply going to sever the struts holding the oxygen tanks, I realized, stealing my cargo without even bothering to talk to me.

There was little I could do about it. I could cut thrust, of course, but that would drop me behind their ship. Rocket exhaust may be cryogenic in temperature, but a supersonic stream of cryogenic exhaust will make tatters out about anything less than a thick steel plate. If I allowed *Bessie* to drop behind them, their exhaust plume would shred my crew compartment.

In fact, now that I thought about it, it was clear that they had no intent to harm me. If they had wanted to kill me and cripple the ship, they could have done it in a fly-by, probably killing me before I'd even known that they were there. Then they could pick what they wanted out of the wreckage. So they were thieves, but they had their honor. That made my job simpler.

They may have no interest in talking to me, but that didn't mean I couldn't talk to them. I set my radio to the space-traffic control frequency, guessing that they would be monitoring even if there wasn't any traffic for millions of kilometers.

"Hello, *Love's Labor Lost*, this is *Bessie*."

An immediate response. "Yeah?" A male voice.

"What are your intentions?"

"We are detaching your cargo. Please hold your vector." I couldn't place the accent.

They were on station now, matching my trajectory perfectly, the two ships barely a meter apart. They would have to cut my fuel flow as well, of course—otherwise I would have the same advantage over them that they currently held over me. A blocked fuel flow would take somewhere between an hour and two days to fix, depending on whether they just crimped a feeder, or seriously crippled it. By the time I fixed it, they would be clear of danger. Even if I tried to chase, they would be ready for me, and there would be no way I could run them down and take the cargo back.

There was little point in protesting, but I did anyway. "Can't have it, it's not mine. Belongs to the company."

"No shit?" The pirate didn't sound very interested. "Well, it's ours now."

I paused to think. I needed time.

"Come on over. Bring your crew. We can talk."

"Don't think we have anything to talk about. We're free. You're a company man."

"Come over anyway. I have coffee." That was a serious inducement. No hab in the solar system had enough agricultural margin to grow coffee beans. Real coffee had to be grown on Earth. Coffee, a hot bath, and bubble-gum: the three luxuries worth taking a trip downside.

"Coffee, sure. And maybe a gun."

"No violence. With your ship shadowing me? You know I don't dare. And, anyway, I don't carry a gun. I'll bond, no violence. Outsider's honor."

"OK." A short pause. "I'll be coming over, then. Just me. The crew will stay here. I'm expendable, and my crew knows it." What he was saying was, if I tried to threaten him, the rest of his crew was ready and willing to shred my crew compartment, him and me together. If it wasn't a bluff, it meant that they were desperate. But I knew that already.

I watched him come out the lock. Only when he was halfway out did it occur to me to ask the same thing of him. "No guns on your part, either."

He unbuckled a belt around his suit and passed it back inside the airlock without protesting. So they weren't bluffing; he really was expendable. Also, this showed that he had at least one crewmate, and probably two: one in the lock, one flying the ship. Maybe more.

It wasn't too surprising that he would take me up on my offer to visit. Outsiders get lonely, spending months and years on trajectory. My one-man ship wasn't all that unusual, but still, it was most common to find a ship had a crew of two or three. On trajectory, you live without privacy, living in the pockets of the other members of your crew, every hour of every day. Other than members of your crew, you may not see a stranger for a year. When ships meet, crews visit. It was ancient custom when the surface-bound whalers of *Moby Dick* met, and, centuries later, it was still custom of the outsiders.

It was unusual for one crew to be a pirate, and unheard-of to meet on trajectory. But on the outside, politeness is as much a reflex as checking your airlock seal. I didn't expect any violence. Pirates or not, they were still outsiders, and outsiders know what it's like to live with a killer. We call it the big empty, and we know it intimately, a killer with no compassion, no compunction, and infinite patience, waiting for each of us. Downsides, they kill each other over honor, over sex, over a handful of smuggled cigarettes. In space, we don't kill each other. We know that death is waiting.

When I was a kid I lived for the day I would be able to go into space. I followed the excruciatingly slow process of building the first habitats, dreaming of how I would live in one; I drew pictures of rockets when I should have been doing English assignments, and floated weightless in my dreams. My father had been a penniless refugee, but he did well enough in his adopted country, and sent me to a school good enough that I could study the engineering that would be my ticket into space. Slowly, the development of space shifted, and instead of governments, the frontier changed to business. There were resources to be harvested upside, fortunes for a few who could develop them. Where fortunes waited, companies followed; and where companies went, banks were there to lend them money.

Getting into space is expensive, and once you're upside, staying alive is expensive. Most of the businesses failed. A few flourished.

There was plenty of work in orbit, if you could pay for the boost and the consumables needed to keep you alive when you got there, and the Kageshima-Sukhoi investment cartel was investing in loans to bring workers upside. I found work overhauling nuclear engines. After a few years, I managed to be paid enough to occasionally chip away at my debt.

If you've never been upside, there's no way to describe it. Imagine living in a three-dimensional maze of aluminum tunnels, a warren crammed and stinking with people, where air is something you pay for, privacy is a luxury, and a hot bath is a forgotten dream. Imagine floating in air softer than any feather mattress ever made. Imagine working in a cramped suit that smells of rotten sweat, your muscles aching from the fact that no suit ever gives you decent leverage and any error could kill you, and imagine fatigue so crushing that every move you make is in slow motion. Imagine looking upward, and seeing the Earth hanging above your head, an ever-changing artwork painted by God in great swirls of white and streaks of green and brown and orange and yellow and all of it surrounded by an achingly thin membrane of atmosphere in the palest eggshell blue. Imagine looking down, and seeing the endless stars hanging below your feet, eternity sparkled with shards of diamond, and knowing that you are the tiniest and least significant part of creation, and yet you *are* part of it, and always will be.

I had a girlfriend. Theresa was in debt too, we all were. We moved from upside to outside: from low orbit into the outer reaches. We learned the outsider's code, and we began to find work. Work was harder to find, but the pay was intense.

And then we made a mistake: Theresa got pregnant.

Instantly she was ineligible for most work. It was a contract labor, and, upside or outside, the only benefits that any job in space offered was a free trip downside when you went broke. Nobody would hire a woman carrying a child—too much could go wrong. Theresa had to chose the child or her job, and she chose the child. I can't fault her. She forfeited on her debt, and Kage-shima-Sukhoi gave her the one-way ticket down to that place we had once called home.

Perhaps it was for the best; she would have had to go downside to have the child anyway, since a fetus needs gravity for the last few months of development, and a child needs gravity to grow.

It was a girl. I never held her, but I've seen pictures. Theresa used to write, for the first few years; on lucky occasions she'd even call. But it's hard to maintain a relationship when we can be a thousand or a million kilometers apart, and time lag wasn't the only thing that made it feel like we're talking past each other. It's been five years since she's called.

Sometimes I wonder what's happened to her.

But I can't go down; I've been too long in microgee. Downside, I would be lucky to be able to stand up without breaking bones.

And, besides, I love it here.

Right up until the day that a company I was under contract to went bankrupt owing me eight months in back salary. Kage-shima-Sukhoi was interested in money, not in excuses. Without a firm contract for work, I was headed downside, and with a record for defaulting loans, I would never get another ride upside, not in my lifetime.

Kageshima-Sukhoi was willing to deal. Nobody was making money overhauling nuclear thermal rockets in those days; new engines were entering service that didn't need as much maintenance, and there were plenty of nuclear plumbers scratching for business. I was barely staying in oxygen. But there were opportunities. Asteroid processing plants were gearing up to produce raw materials. Asteroidal ore was beginning to look like it might have a balance sheet competitive with lunar ore, but the companies doing the processing were bottlenecked on transport. To Kageshima-Sukhoi, that meant investment opportunities: they were pumping billions into asteroid processing and ore freighters.

So I bought myself an ore freighter. I figured I could do most of the maintenance on her myself, saving operating expenses. Kageshima-Sukhoi financed the loan to pay for her, and incidentally refinanced my own loan. It was a good deal for everybody.

Except that, three years later, there were hundreds of independent freighters spread across the outside, doing business between rocks, and half of them with newer and faster rockets than *Bessie*. The market was saturated, and nobody was making money. And my mortgage was due.

While I was waiting for the pirate to come through the airlock, I turned off the power to the oxygen coolers, commanded the solenoids that opened up the check valves, furled the sun-shields, and did a visual check to make sure there wasn't anything loose that would fall under acceleration. There wasn't much more I could do, except to start heating water. Upside, the cost of coffee is mostly the cost of transportation, and so the coffee that I had was a rich Ethiopian mix.

The airlock undogged, and the pirate came through.

His space suit was old. The seals had been replaced, the seams mended, and the overhaul job showed off painstaking care, but that couldn't disguise the pitting in the visor or the outdated fittings. It had no company markings; the places where the company logo should have been had been carefully scraped clean or painted over.

When he removed the visor, he had short dark hair and a beard cropped to about a millimeter, both showing traces of white. I could tell from his thin arms and wasted legs that he had spent years, probably decades in microgee. I could tell from the odor that they were short on clean water. I could tell from his eyes that he didn't entirely trust me.

The outsider's code: the person you meet might be your most deadly rival, but when you meet, you offer hospitality, and you help him if you can. Pirates lived outside even the outsider's code, but I wouldn't break it first. It's a tough universe. "Hello," I said. "Welcome to *Bessie*. Let me get you a cup of coffee."

Twenty milligees of acceleration was enough that on the average we drifted toward the surface that was designated "floor," but wasn't enough to serve coffee in an ordinary cup. I used my free-fall cups, which had a fine mesh over the open end that served to keep the liquid adhered into the cup by surface tension.

Pouring coffee in microgee is an art form. I pulled the pot in one direction, letting a thin sausage of coffee trail out, snapped it off with a flick of my wrist, and before the coffee-worm hanging in the air could contract into a ball, transferred the pot to my other hand and then used my good hand to scoop it up with the cup. Then I let that cup float for a few seconds while I repeated the performance with the other cup. Then I caught the falling cup and offered it to my guest.

"Thanks," he said.

I caught my own cup out of the air, and gave him a few moments to savor the coffee in silence. Eventually he spoke.

"You a plumber?" he said. It was more of a statement than a question.

Pouring coffee, I'd shifted the pot from one hand to the other to scoop the coffee. It had only been an instant, but he'd seen it, and every outsider recognizes the symptoms of radiation-induced neural apoptosis. You get it, if you're careless working on things that are hot, if you forget to pay attention to shielding, if you're young and think you're invulnerable. They call it plumber's syndrome, sometimes, because so many nuclear plumbers have it. It's not fatal, although the dead nerves would never heal, and my arm would be weak for the rest of my life. Think of it as the price you pay, learning not to be careless.

"No secret," I said, although in fact, I would prefer not to have him think about the fact that I was a nuclear plumber too much.

"Why'd you quit?" he said.

I could have told him the whole long story, but I opted for the short version. "Money," I said.

He nodded. "Money," he agreed. "Not enough of it, for sure."

"You're from Anteros," I said.

"No secret," he said.

I knew it would be. There really wasn't any other possibility. Anteros was the breakaway colony. The rock that they had colonized was a good one, as Near-Earth Asteroids went. Close to the resources of the inner solar system, and yet a rock big enough to have resources: carbon, the light metals, veins of nickel-iron, solar-wind volatiles trapped in the regolith. It should have been ideal. And then they declared independence.

Nobody cared whether they called themselves independent or not. Their mistake had been when their new government decided to defer repayment on their start-up loans. The banks, the true masters of the outside, couldn't allow that; they had spent ten trillion European Credits to finance the colony, and they expected a return on their investment.

The breakaway colonists at Anteros had been ready for a fight, ready for a siege, ready for anything except what had happened.

They'd been ignored.

They'd failed at the first lesson of economics: nobody stands alone. Maybe they'd really believed that their little colony could produce all the necessities of survival after trade was cut off. Maybe they'd dreamed that others would stand with them. But there's too much manufactured downside. Earth likes the goods manufactured with space resources, but it can live without them. But a spaceship has two hundred thousand separate parts; a habitat ten million parts. We don't have the industrial base to make them all. Not yet.

They had had the best of intentions.

"I don't suppose," I said, "that I could talk you out of this."

"No," he said. "I'm sorry." He had the grace to look down. "I'm sorry," he said again. "But we need it more than you do."

There was nothing more for me to say. All the while, I was watching the pressure rise as the cargo tanks slowly heated. There was a lot of thermal mass; they didn't heat very quickly. I hooked my toes under loops on the floor, but for courtesy, I waited for him to finish his coffee. Then I cut the thrust.

He wasn't hooked in, but he had space reflexes, and removing a small bit of effective gravity didn't bother his equilibrium. *Bessie* started to drop behind the other ship, twenty centimeter per second squared. I had other things to worry about. A few seconds of this would take us into the danger zone, into the exhaust cone of the pirate ship. I yawed the ship, restarted the lithium flow to the engine, braced myself for gee, and hit the afterburners.

When the acceleration hit, he crumpled to the floor. He couldn't have impacted very hard, since I was accelerating at only half a gee, but I doubt if he'd experienced this much acceleration in years. Even if he'd been expecting it, I'm not sure if he could have stood up. It hurt me to watch him, but I had piloting to do.

In the viewports, the pirate ship was illuminated with a vivid, coruscating light. The exhaust of a nuclear rocket should be invisible; this wasn't. It must have been instantly clear to them that I had a new trick, but any realization on their part was a little too late. *Bessie* leaped forward, and began to run. I killed my yaw and initiated a pitch-up. This wasn't needed — it was obvious to both of us now that I could outrun them — but it was outsider courtesy, to keep their ship out of my exhaust.

I kept the thrust up for about half a minute. That put me at three hundred meters per second, relative velocity. If they chased, it would take them hours to catch up, and this time they wouldn't sneak up unwatched. I cut the thrust.

"Shit," the pirate said. "You were a decoy. You sandbagged us."

I shook my head. "Sorry, no. Just an independent who couldn't afford to lose a cargo."

He was floating now. I think he'd twisted an ankle in the fall, but he didn't seem to have anything broken. Good; I'd hate to have abused hospitality that badly, even if pirates were outside of the outsider's code.

"But why?" he said. "Why did you pretend to be helpless?"

"Lord." I shook my head again. He was asking the wrong question, he should have been asking *how*. "What choice did I have? Hellfire and damnation, do you know what it's like to be an independent? Do you think I could *afford* to lose it? The cargo may be insured, but if I'd once been hijacked, nobody would ever be quite sure that it wasn't an inside job, or that I might not do it again. I'd never get another contract, not a good one. I'd be downside within a year. Shit, look at me. Do you think I could survive downside? Do you think I ever had a choice?"

His eyes looked hurt. "You could join us."

I shook my head.

"Really! I mean it." He was earnest now, almost pleading. "Why don't you join us? We could use you. To tell the honest truth, we could use your ship, and your oxygen . . . but we could use you as well. We're desperate."

"I know." I was tempted. It was a great dream, the dream all the outsiders had — to be free, to be independent, to throw off the mortgages and the debts that kept us tied to the banks and governments of Earth. Yes, I was tempted—but not seriously.

They were going to fail. In space, we're too dependent on Earth's resources, her industrial base. Too many things can fail, too many spare parts are needed, too many trace resources are too expensive to mine in space. The fact that they were reduced to hijacking oxygen—oxygen!—showed that they had reached the point of no return. They had declared independence too soon. There was no way they could survive. "I'm sorry."

I let him jump off the ship. *Love's Labors Lost* would pick him up; it would take them about an hour to rendezvous, and by then I would be long gone. I worried a little about that patched-together suit he used, but he assured me that it had thousands of hours of time on it, and he wouldn't trust anything else anyway.

My drive would have shredded him, if I'd used it, but I had no need for violence. Life is tough out here in the outside.

I'd explained it to him before he jumped. I didn't have to, but I'm sure that they would have figured it out.

I was running lithium in the drive. I was hauling oxygen. I'm a nuclear plumber, by training; a freighter pilot only because I couldn't get work. And, in the long months of coasting across the big empty, I had plenty of time to tinker with the plumbing.

Lithium and oxygen react.

What I had done was to re-wire the plumbing of my cargo so that the boil-off from the liquid oxygen vented into the expansion nozzle of my engine. A chemical reaction is inefficient compared to *Bessie's* nuclear engine, but there was no way to beat a chemical reaction's thrust level. Effectively, I used the oxygen as an afterburner to the nuclear rocket.

That thirty seconds of thrust had used up a bit of my oxygen cargo, but I could tell my clients it was boil-off due to a cooler fault. Using the oxygen would shave my thin profit margin down a little, and make my earnings from the trip somewhere between infinitesimal and zero, but it was the only choice I had.

I had my chance; I could have declared my independence and joined them. They weren't wrong; they were just too early. And for the rest of my life, I will dream about the freedom I might have had.

Beneath the Stars of Winter

*T*HE SKY WAS VAST, AN EMPTY PLAIN EXTENDING TO infinity. Mikhail Petrovitch saw only grey: the sky was grey; the rocks on the distant horizon were grey; the snow on the grey fields was grey. The young guard in his grey uniform jerked the barrel of his gun to point the way, and then turned to trudge back through grey snow toward the guard tower and the distant line of barbed wire.

Mikhail squinted against the cold wind and looked without hope in the direction the guard had pointed. Under rags that had once been blue was a man. His face was thin, almost fleshless, and his nose and his broken-toothed smile were both improbably large. "Ah, a new man! A new man!" He reached out a hand wrapped in grey burlap, only the tips of his fingers showing.

Mikhail took his hand out of his pocket and tentatively offered it. The man took his hand in both of his and shook with vigor. "So glad to see a new face, so very glad! Yes, yes! Not glad for you, no, of course not, it's sad, it's a tragedy, but for us, ah!" The man let go of Mikhail's hand, only to clasp him in a bear-hug. "We love you already." He stepped back to get a better look. "And you are?"

Mikhail answered slowly. "Mikhail Petrovitch. At your service." His breath came out in white puffs.

"Ah, Mikhail Petrovitch, so glad to meet you! Yes! And I am Vasily, Vasily Nikolayev," he took another half step back and made a sweeping bow, almost touching his head to the ground, "at your service, yes."

From behind Mikhail a dry voice spoke. "You can ignore him, Mikhail. He's harmless."

Mikhail turned around. "Fyodor! Oh, my God, Fyodor, is it you?"

Fyodor was much thinner than Mikhail remembered, the once bear-like physique now barely filling the shapeless blue overalls. He had once been clean-shaven; now, like all the men in the camps, he had a full beard. The unkempt copper-red hair had now turned mostly grey. Fyodor opened his arms, and the two men embraced. "Yes, my friend, I'm afraid it is. I'm so sorry to meet you here."

"It's all right."

"It's not all right, but I'm afraid we have little say about it. Oh, Mikhail, I'm sorry. You don't belong here. No one could have been more loyal, more honest."

The smaller man danced around them. "So, have you perhaps already met? Yes? No? Mikhail Petrovitch, meet Doctor Levchenko. Fyodor Danilovich, meet Mikhail Petrovitch."

Fyodor coughed. "We've already met, Vasily."

"Yes, yes, I see! Forgive me, do. But introductions are so important, don't you think so?"

"Of course, Vasily. Perhaps you would be so good as to run and find the rest of the group to let them know we've got a new member? Thank you."

"Of course, of course. Mikhail Petrovitch, so good to meet you! So good! Everyone will be so happy to meet you, I'm sure." He suddenly turned and ran off, his ragged grey coat flapping behind him in the breeze.

Fyodor shook his head. "Wish I knew where he got his energy."

Mikhail watched him go. On the vast tundra, the bounding figure seemed almost insignificant, swallowed by immensity. "Was he always like this?"

Fyodor shrugged. "I don't know," he said. "I never knew him on the outside, not personally. He's been like this since I've been here. Don't let him fool you, though. He's the best we've got."

"Him?"

Fyodor nodded. "A first-rate mathematician. Without him, I don't know where our research would be."

Mikhail's mouth dropped. "Research? You can't be serious, Fyodor! You're doing research? Here?"

Fyodor nodded again. "Ah, my friend, without my research I would die." He coughed. "Not that I won't die soon enough anyway, I'm afraid. But what else is there to do here? Dig ditches, yes, of course, but for that we do not require the head." He laughed, but his laughter abruptly turned to a fit of coughing.

"Fyodor, you're not well."

Fyodor's coughing intensified, and to his horror, Mikhail suddenly realized he was still trying to laugh. "Not well? My friend, none of us here are well. In our brigade there are a hundred fifty prisoners, give or take. On a good day, nobody dies."

"Mikhail, my friend, there are not many good days." He slumped to the ground.

Mikhail squatted down, put his hands on Fyodor's shoulders, and looked into his eyes. His eyes were old, old and weary, eyes that had seen too much. "Are you okay? Is there anything I can do?"

"Oh, my friend, I regret that I'm so happy to see you again before I die. I'm sorry. Can you forgive me?"

"I forgive you."

"Thank you."

Mikhail helped Fyodor to stand, and they walked slowly toward the squat sod huts in the distance.

"You were not the best of my students, Mikhail."

"No."

"But you always tried the hardest. I admired you for that. I still do." The old man looked into Mikhail's eyes. "Don't give up, Mikhail. Will you promise me that? So many people here, they let this place sap their will, suck out their souls. Whatever happens, promise me you'll never give up hope."

"I promise."

"Well, then," said Fyodor. "Let's go."

"Welcome to my dacha," said Fyodor, waving his hand to encompass the low building. It was well after sunset, but the strange arctic twilight lingered, and the snow-covered rocks were luminous with a purple glow. The building Fyodor indicated was almost entirely underground. Only the canvas roof, covered with moss and mud with a tiny smokehole, was visible from outside. "It is such a fine vacation villa that the men have given it their own pet name. They call it 'doghouse.' Please — think of it as your home for as long as you are here." Fyodor held open the canvas flap. "After you."

Mikhail had to crawl through the narrow doorway headfirst. The interior was so dark Mikhail could barely make out the shapes of men, lying in vague lumps like caterpillars, swaddled in thread-bare blankets. The smell was dank and fetid; clearly several of the men had already used the tin parasha in the corner.

"Hey, you lazy goats, is this any way to welcome a visitor?" asked Fyodor. None of the men moved. Fyodor nudged one with his foot to make room for Mikhail. The man grunted, but pressed aside, and Mikhail wedged himself into the space.

They were awakened at four A.M., an hour before dawn. A tiny trickle of watery light seeped in through cracks in the walls. There was little need for more light; there was nothing to see except the dirty, unshaven men covered by thin blankets lying on a straw-covered dirt floor.

LABOR IS A MATTER OF HEROISM, the sign over the barbed-wire gate informed them. "I think that our heroism will be in no danger of question," Fyodor said, blowing on his hands to warm them while the guards made them wait in the cold wind to be counted. The morning was brittle and crystalline, with a low orange sun that shed light but no heat.

"This is the end of the line," Fyodor whispered. "This camp is a special one, just for us politicals with an intellectual background. We are kept separate from the ordinary criminals, even from the less well-educated politicals. Our thinking—the very fact that we do think—the butcher sees as corrupting." He meant Stalin, Mikhail knew. In the cattle-cars and the prisoner transports, Stalin was always referred to as the butcher.

The count had tallied with the sheet, and the guard waved them through the gate.

"But here," continued Fyodor, speaking aloud now that they were on the move, "we are free, more free here than anywhere in Russia." He laughed. "The guards stay back in their birdhouses, and as long as we meet quota, they let us organize ourselves as we will. Oh, not free in our bodies. But here we can talk freely. What more can the butcher do to us? Will he kill us? His best workers? Why should he bother?

"Here in our work camps, things are bad. But not hopeless."

"*Noy. Nicht Arbeitslager.*" The voice was soft and sad, without a trace of hope. Mikhail looked around and spotted him. A short man, sandy hair shaved close to his head. He was walking listlessly, bent over and staring at the ground with dead eyes. "Ist Vernichtungslager."

Mikhail was puzzled. "What did he say?"

"Ah. Mikhail, this is Franz. He can understand Russian, but doesn't speak it very well. Franz, Mikhail." Franz twitched a hand slightly, as if too tired to wave.

"But what did he say?"

Fyodor shook his head slowly. "Not a work camp, he said. A death camp." Fyodor coughed. "I'm afraid he's right. In other camps, the prisoners are sometimes rehabilitated, even sometimes go free after they serve their terms. A mere ten years, in some camps. But here, I don't think anyone is likely to see that happen. No one would last that long. To my knowledge, no one has ever left this camp alive."

Their work was to dig a ditch through the permafrost. For what purpose, Mikhail was not told. He was set to work between morose Franz and a zek named Pavel, a cheerful Uzbeki who spoke little but whistled softly and worked as hard as any two others. At the end of the shift two of the guards would come to inspect what they had done. Their channel was to be exactly three meters deep, five meters wide. The daily quota was to extend the ditch by two meters: thirty cubic meters of iron-solid frozen earth to be moved. In addition, the ground around it was to be leveled. If they failed to meet quota, their meager food ration was cut in half.

Mikhail was given his tool, a piece of crudely forged iron tied to the end of a sapling, to use as a pick-ax to cut the hard soil.

"It's not so bad, Mikhail Petrovitch," Vasily told him. "In the morning we sing, to get our rhythm and get the blood stirring. After an hour, the morning lecture. Then two hours for discussion—"

"Wait. Lecture?"

Fyodor coughed. "Ah. I should explain our system. Each day while we work, one of us gives a lecture on a topic that he is an expert on. Relativity, electromagnetism, economic theory." He laughed. "You will like it, Mikhail. You always complained how everyone was afraid to discuss capitalist economic theories, and how can we make a socialist system work if we were afraid to study capitalism? Here you can discuss the theories of Adam Smith to your heart's content."

So Fyodor knew of his interest in samizdat economic theories.

Fyodor would not have betrayed him, though. Had Mikhail been more discreet in choosing who to share his opinions with, he might not be here. Or likely he would; the NKVD needed no reasons, that had been proved well enough.

"Perhaps you would like to give a seminar next morning?"

"No! Not yet, Fyodor. Let me get my bearings."

Fyodor laughed. "It was a joke. When a new fish arrives, he always gives a lecture. Don't worry, my friend. For this, your first seminar, you will be required only to talk about the outside world. What is the latest news of outside? We learn so little here.

"And in the afternoons, we break into working groups to continue our research."

"Fyodor! Even if you discover something, who do you tell?"

"If? No faith, Mikhail, you have no faith in your old professor. Of course we make discoveries here. Do you think that science can be done only in stuffy lecture halls, with graduate students to do the working and janitors to clean up at night? Who do we tell? We tell each other. Do you think science only a way to make for your own personal glory, Mikhail Petrovitch? I am sorry for you. It is enough to learn, to know what nobody else does."

In the daytime the temperature reached almost zero. In the nights the arctic chill returned, and even the guard dogs huddled together for warmth. "This warm weather will not last," said Fyodor. "Enjoy it while it's here."

They were fed twice a day, a thin gruel with a hunk of black bread in the morning, potato soup with bread and a potato or a piece of salted fish in the evening. Vasily boiled a nail in with the tea, claiming that the iron would ward against anemia, a result of the poor food. Even what the zeks called tea was really nothing of the sort; water boiled with dried leaves, a concoction that Vasily had invented after some experimentation.

Despite Fyodor's promise, they left him alone the first day, alone to understand the enormity of moving seventy tons of rock-hard soil with little more than his bare hands. The first day he could not make the quota, and Pavel and Franz had to work at killing speed to make up for him. They did not complain, but he could feel their eyes upon him. The next day he could hardly work at all. He ached all over. His arms were like wet rags, strengthless and limp. He tried to ignore the pain and work anyway, but barely accomplished half of what he had the first day.

His hands blistered and swelled. The second day the blisters tore open, dripping with sour, clear fluid. Vasily doctored him with surprising gentleness, cleaning Mikhail's hands with tea and then smearing them with an unguent of used tea leaves and a paste of some kind of tree bark that Vasily chewed to softness and spat into his hands. As he worked, Vasily told jokes and assured him that he had the hands of a woman, more specifically a high-class whore in Leningrad that he claimed to have known and done vastly improbable things with. Vasily lifted up Mikhail's hand and gently kissed it, then pressed it against his bearded cheek for a brief moment.

Mikhail pulled it away, embarrassed.

Vasily's potions helped the itching and allowed him to sleep, but didn't stop the tender skin beneath his blisters from itself blistering. The blisters broke, and Vasily tended them again. After two weeks his hands were nearly as thickly callused as any of the workers.

At first he had trouble telling one man in faded blue vatnik from another, but in time Mikhail came to learn the other workers in his squad.

"Ah, Mikhail Petrovitch!" said Vasily, grinning and stamping his feet in the cold. "What a wonderful place our compassionate Uncle Joseph has sent us to! Where else would we ever find such friends as these, to know and love and live and work with? Friends to live and die with, are we not the luckiest of all men?"

And it was indeed quite a varied lot he shared his fate with, no questioning that. Vasily with his instantaneous mood shifts, one moment brooding and morose, the next instant suddenly full of energy and jokes. Sandy-haired Franz, silent but hard-working, who had once been a machinist in Poland. Pavel, the pleasant and round-faced Uzbeki, a peasant accused of being a Kulak, with no education but with a photographic memory for equations and the ability to solve complicated integrals in his head; Fyodor used him as a mobile scratchpad. Gregori, a slender, elegant biologist who would sing in a beautiful tenor voice, sentenced to the camps for teaching Mendelism. Pyotr, short and squat with huge bushy dark eyebrows and a wild beard like a barbarian prince, once an electrician. Georgi, like Fyodor a former academician, a tall experimental physicist with small round glasses perched on a huge nose, who could quote whole volumes of Kafka by memory. Viktor, another of Fyodor's former students, a thin and rabbit-eyed young man with thick square wire-framed glasses.

Here they were all the same, all equal: all zeks.

There was another man, excluded from the group, one that none of the others would talk about. He was a bent, nervous man with thin hair and a toothless mouth, with haunted eyes and a perpetual look of fear, always starting at slight noises. "Don't talk to him," said Pavel reluctantly, after Mikhail had asked about him for the tenth time. He made a motion as if to spit on the ground. "He is an informer."

"He is stooped from having three vertebrae fractured when he was questioned," said Fyodor quietly. "And he left his teeth behind with Uncle Lavrenti's friends." He shook his head. "He is more to be pitied than feared, Mikhail. He cannot make quota. It was a hard choice for him. If he did not talk to earn his rations, he would die. Do not hate him, Mikhail."

"But do not talk to him either," said Pavel bluntly. "If he sits by you, get up and sit elsewhere. When he comes to talk to you, turn your back. When he tells you of his family, walk away."

"Yes," said Fyodor. "It is hard, but it is best."

Mikhail did as he was told, and in a few weeks the camp administration had transferred the informer to another work group where, perhaps, he might find more to tell of. They never talked of him again, and, much later, when the word came to them that he had died, the men were all silent save Vasily, who said softly, "Oh," in a small voice full of wisdom and regret.

Despite his initial skepticism, Mikhail quickly looked forward to the morning lecture series and the discussion that followed as the high point of the day. The lectures were surprisingly effective, and the discussions more lively and uncensored than anything Mikhail had ever known. They had nothing else to think about. Mikhail was called on a few days after his introduction to the camp to talk about news from the outside, and was surprised by the eagerness with which they listened to his every word, asking for elaborations on the finest details of each point. In particular they asked for news of Einstein—had he announced the unified field theory yet? Had he published any new papers at all? Was there any news of what he was working on?

Fyodor in particular was keenly disappointed to hear that Mikhail had no news of what Einstein had worked on in his last years, save a vaguely remembered announcement of a popular lecturing tour. Vasily speculated that this might be the most important news of all: surely the physicist must be working on something. Perhaps the fact that there was no publication meant that the

Americans were keeping the very existence of the work a secret.

But no, said Mikhail. In America, all of the work was on quantum mechanics.

"Then you and I are the last, I fear," said Fyodor to Vasily. "All the others have abandoned Einstein's trails, and follow Heisenberg and Pauli like sheep following a goat."

"Is it possible that they could be right?" wondered Vasily.

"No," Fyodor said bluntly. "The quantum theory is not self-consistent. Einstein proved that long ago."

"But Einstein also proved that travel faster than electromagnetic waves is impossible," Mikhail interjected. "We will never reach the stars following Einstein."

"No!" said Fyodor. His vehemence took Mikhail by surprise, and he stepped back, startled. "The restricted theory says that. His general theory says no such thing."

"They are on a different path," said Vasily. "This quantum theory, even if it is not the truth, certainly has much of truth in it. We will let the Americans find it. The path we follow leads elsewhere."

The next two days Vasily gave the lecture, on the theory of quantum electrodynamics, a new theory of elementary particles that had been claimed by a group of young American physicists to solve the fundamental problems. On the first day he gave a brilliant accounting of the theory, showing how it could be derived from a few simple principles and could be used to solve problems considered impossible by earlier theories. On the second day he demolished the theory, developing a neat mathematical argument based on Einstein's work to show that the new theory did not solve any of the fundamental contradictions inherent in quantum mechanics.

"Quantum mechanics is a dead end," said Fyodor, summing up. "For a unified theory we will have to start with general relativity." He winked at the others. "As, of course, we already knew."

As Mikhail watched Fyodor flitting between the men, passing equations on to Pavel, whispering with Georgi, arguing with Vasily, he realized that Fyodor's statement that he was still conducting research was not just an expression of hope.

In the middle of the Gulag, with a research staff of condemned criminals and political untouchables, Fyodor was continuing his research.

*   *   *

It was almost summer now. The nights were barely an hour long, and never got completely dark. Mikhail found himself confused and disoriented by the nearly continuous light. How could men still live, and never see the stars? But they did.

The camp barber—another prisoner—came through to shave the prisoners' heads in a hopeless effort to prevent lice.

Life settled into a routine.

Mikhail worried for Fyodor's health, but it was Fyodor's young student Viktor, a quiet and hard-working fellow, who died first. One day he was healthy as any of them, but in the night he had cramps and diarrhea. This was nothing new to them; often the whole crew had diarrhea for weeks on end. In the morning he was too weak to work, and when they came back from the shift, cold and weary, he was delirious. The next day he was unconscious, and died before they could summon a doctor.

I never really knew him, thought Mikhail, but could not help from weeping. He was surprised at the way the others, even Fyodor, held back. Surely they knew him better. Yes, Fyodor told him. But if we cry for all the dead, where will we stop? Better not to start.

Franz carefully removed Viktor's glasses, and they stacked his body outside. In the morning it was covered with a layer of frost like a marble statue. They walked past it every day for two weeks before a cart was brought around, pulled by four zeks with hard, impassive faces. They tossed Viktor's body onto the pile of other bodies, all anonymous and grey, to be taken away to be burned.

"Why are we digging this?" Mikhail asked, a week after they had stacked Viktor outside. "So far north—surely they are not planning a city here. What could the purpose possibly be?"

"We are zeks," said Fyodor, shaking his head. "We do not ask questions." He paused. "Several months ago, I was summoned to go see the commissar. I walked down the length of our work, past work done by zeks who died long before I arrived. The sides have fallen in; ten kilometers back the channel is no more than a shallow depression in the ground filled with debris." He shook his head. "I don't know, Mikhail. We work, because we work. There is no reason here."

In the seven-kilometer trot out to the work site Fyodor was busy whispering figures to Pavel and Georgi, and so Mikhail trotted along with Vasily.

"They say that this is prison, that this is punishment!" said Vasily. "Oh, how little they know! How blind! They say that a year in the camps will destroy the very soul! Not so, my friend, not so. Ripped away from the hustle-bustle of everyday life in so absolute a degree that our counting the passing minutes—and I have counted them, Mikhail Petrovitch, every one, each individual instant, they are my friends, my lovers—this puts us intimately in contact with the universe. Is it not so? Your eyes, Mikhail, your eyes are still clouded, still sad. You remember too much. You will be purged of every imperfection, of every passion that has stirred and troubled you in your former life, until your soul is absolutely transparent, and then your thoughts will be so clear, so very clear, you will see to the ends of the universe and beyond, to the innermost void at the center of the atom, and you will begin to glow, Mikhail, your soul will glow with light like the halo of a saint. I can feel it, Mikhail. I can."

And what, thought Mikhail, what could one say to that? Nonsense, surely nonsense, but sometimes Mikhail could feel it too, a terrible and lonely light that surrounded each of the prisoners, too bright to look at. And then he looked again, and the light was nothing but the unearthly, pale light of the unsetting sun, made ethereal by his weariness and inadequate sleep. When he looked again at the men working beside him he saw only corpses, animals in a grotesque parody of human form, but with empty, soulless eyes. And a sudden tremor would pass down his spine, and then he would not think at all.

Better, yes, not to think at all.

The morning lectures continued, not always about science. One day Pavel acted out an entire play by Chekhov, miming the various characters' movements with his hands. The burly electrician Pyotr surprised him by shyly reciting poetry, intricately rhymed villanelles and sonnets written to a dark-haired, elfin woman who—Mikhail was later told—had divorced Pyotr and remarried within days after he had been denounced. The biologist Gregori lectured on the possibility of life in outer space, suggesting that not only might there be life on other planets in the universe, but spores might even survive in the cosmos itself, surviving millennia-long journeys between the stars encysted like seeds buried under the frozen snow of an arctic winter, waiting patiently for a new spring.

"And so," he said, "across the gulfs between the stars, across the galaxies themselves, we are kin to other life in the cosmos. Nature is harsh, and many, most, will die in the empty vastness, but life itself endures."

Mikhail swung his pick, loosened a frozen clod of dirt, and whispered to himself Gregori's words. "Life endures."

In the middle of August, in the middle of the terrible days when the sun never set and sensitive men went mad from the endless light, Gregori collapsed at his digging. He had been coughing blood for weeks, and the others had petitioned to have him removed to the camp infirmary. The petition was denied. With a few days rest, Gregori protested that he was well enough to continue, but on his first day back at work he collapsed again. This time rest did not help him; he died as they carried him back.

The temperature dropped to barely freezing at the lowest point in the sun's orbit above their heads—one could not really call it night. Fortunately the cart came quickly this time, and Gregori's emaciated corpse was taken away before it began to stink.

The lecture series the next week was on the subject of space travel. The bearded electrician Pyotr, Mikhail discovered, had worked on a project to make a missile that could put a radio transmitter into orbit around the Earth. The idea had been around for a century, Mikhail knew, but he was surprised at how close, according to Pyotr's disclosures, it was to being accomplished. Still, the overall tenor of the lecture was discouraging. Vasily delivered the summary discourse, and pointed out how none of the worlds of the solar system were suitable for habitation. The stars hold hope, Vasily said, but quickly destroyed that hope by demonstrating that they were far too distant to reach in a lifetime with any rocket, even one powered by an atomic reaction. But when Vasily said this, he gave a slight glance at Fyodor, who answered with the barest hint of a smile, so brief that Mikhail was not even sure he had seen it.

That night Fyodor woke him at midnight. "Come."

The doghouse had two rooms, the larger room where they all slept, and a cramped room to serve as a tiny kitchen. In the kitchen Mikhail was surprised to find Pyotr and Georgi waiting. Pyotr had in his hands a crudely made wooden cross, and was rhythmically twisting it in his hands, left, right, the muscles in his shoulders straining as he did. Georgi held something in one hand, poking at it with a tiny sliver of wood. With a shudder, Mikhail recognized one of the lenses of Viktor's glasses, bound with a fine wire and attached to various other components—bits of glass, fragments of metal and carefully-twisted coils of wire painstakingly put together into a configuration that seemed to make no sense to Mikhail. Georgi gave him a look.

"He is okay, Georgi," said Fyodor. "I stand for him."

Georgi shook his head. "Few is good."

"I said, I stand for him."

Georgi nodded once. "Then let him work."

Fyodor handed him another cross. Mikhail looked at it and saw that the two pieces of wood were lashed to a lump in the center that joined them together, something that looked like a small crystal of yellow quartz wrapped in the tinfoil from American chewing gum. Mikhail raised an eyebrow.

"Like Pyotr," said Georgi.

"What is it?"

"Like Pyotr," Georgi repeated. Mikhail twisted the two pieces, and Georgi grunted. "Harder, but not so hard as to break the crystal, no? Good."

Mikhail worked at his twisting in silence and listened to the short stutters of conversation between Georgi and Fyodor, whispering so as not to disturb the men sleeping in the other room. It was fragments of numbers and instructions: "A bit more. More. Not so far. Back a half. Good." Trying to tune a radio, Mikhail conjectured. Could they build a radio out of tinfoil and bits of wire? Possibly.

"Good. Try it now." Fyodor reached out a hand, and Pyotr handed him the cross. Georgi took it and removed the crossbars, handling the crystal with two splinters of wood held like chopsticks. He put it into the apparatus and manipulated something.

There was a sudden flash of blue-violet light, and the sharp tang of ozone. The men jumped back. "Damn," said Georgi. "Shorted it." The two men bent over it.

"What do you think?"

Fyodor shook his head. "No." He stood up. "Enough for tonight." He stretched, looking for a moment like an emaciated Christ ready to be nailed to the cross. "It is enough." He pulled a board up from the earthen floor and put the apparatus into a hole gouged into the dirt. "Sleep, my friends. It is time we sleep."

The next morning the news on the camp grapevine came that Stalin had died. The rumors flew: he had died months ago, and only now the news had been reported; he had been assassinated by his doctors; he had been killed by Beria, by Trotskyites, by the CIA; that Beria had ordered that all the political prisoners be killed; that the new secretary (Molotov? Khrushchev? Who the hell was Khrushchev?) had ordered the release of all politicals. They hardly dared to believe any of it.

And none of it affected them. Work went on, day after day, the hard labor of the daytimes and the occasional summons by Fyodor in the dead of night. The area of the camp was nothing but mud and standing pools of muddy water and the stench of thawed feces now; they were constantly dirty and bitten by insects. They would work standing in mud halfway up to their knees, and yet the ground they dug would still be frozen solid.

Around them the tundra was bursting out in a mad spectacle of growth, even the moss blossoming forth with tiny yellow flowers, as if the vegetable kingdom had determined to make up in a month of frantic haste for the long cold darkness of the rest of the year. Pavel told them which of the wildflowers might be pulled up and eaten, and which were deadliest poison. On the rare occasions when the guards failed to pay attention and let them stray off their accustomed trail, they would frantically grab handfuls of vegetation and cram it into their mouths, choking it down roots, dirt, and all.

The afternoon sun was almost warm on Mikhail's back, and under his heavy vatnik he was sweating. He didn't stop to loosen it; he had long since learned to ignore sun as well as cold, to focus his attention on nothing other than what needed to be done.

A generator, Mikhail suddenly thought, swinging his pick. The cross with the crystal in the center, it was an unusual kind of electrical generator. His pick stuck in the hard earth and he wretched it free with a practiced twist, hardly noticing it, not missing a beat. A piezoelectric generator. Swing back, down hard! The rhythmic twisting strains the crystal, and in response to the strain it puts out a high-voltage pulse. A large chunk of frozen soil came loose. Alternating current, twisting both ways. Swing back. With some kind of a rectifier, it could be converted to DC. Hard! Another chunk loose. He couldn't see any particular advantage to such a generator over a standard design. His pick clanged off a buried rock. It would be very inefficient. He chipped carefully around the rock. At all costs avoid blunting his pick. But a standard generator took wire and magnets; where would they get magnets? Enough of the rock showed that he could get a grip on it, wiggle it with his hands. He didn't even know where they'd gotten the tinfoil; he hadn't seen foil like that since the Americans had sent over excess military ration packages after the war. The rock was almost free. A piezoelectric generator would produce extremely high voltages, but not much current. Ah! There it is! Such a generator could be good for some purposes. Yes! Hard to insulate, what the hell would they be using?

With a grunt he carried the rock over to the cart. Almost a full load. He scooped up the fragments of earth he had loosened and piled the cart full, then called to Pavel, his work-mate for the day. The two of them lifted the cart up over the earthen wall and into the mud above.

But what were Fyodor and Georgi building, that required such tremendous voltages? Not a radio, that was for sure.

He explained his reasoning to Fyodor when the brigade changed shifts.

Fyodor smiled. "Ah, Mikhail, so you still do have a brain. I had begun to be afraid for you, that you were one of the lost. Good, Mikhail, think. Thinking will not keep you alive, Mikhail. But it will keep you human."

That night when Georgi took the crystal, there was no flash of blue light, no ozone. Something happened, and Mikhail wasn't even certain what it was. Fyodor and Georgi both were bent over, staring intently into the wire-wrapped lens, into Viktor's dead eye. Mikhail tried to sneak a look over Fyodor's shoulder, but couldn't tell what he was looking at. In the middle of the glass, there seemed to be a tiny speck of darkest black. Dirt, a bit of rock? But suddenly it vanished.

Fyodor and Georgi both released their breath. An air of tension left the room. They exchanged glances. Fyodor looked up at Mikhail.

"Enough for tonight, my friend. We have much to think on. But for now, to sleep."

In September the camp was suddenly visited by a plague of mosquitoes, mosquitoes so thick that the men had to make veils for themselves to be able to breathe without sucking in lungsful of insects with each breath of air. They smeared every centimeter of their exposed flesh with a layer of mud, and still their flesh puffed up from a thousand bites.

When Georgi died it was a surprise. He had been coughing, but no more than Fyodor or half a dozen of the others. One morning he could not be awakened.

Mikhail had seen Fyodor impassive over the earlier deaths, but with Georgi's death, Fyodor was devastated. He had to be encouraged to eat. "He was my experimentalist. Theory is nothing without experiments, less than nothing. I can't go on, I cannot. What shall we do now? What can we do?"

"You must continue," said Mikhail. "You said it yourself. We must go on."

"Did I say it?" asked Fyodor, his expression blank. "I don't remember." But he repeated it at quiet intervals to himself all day: "We must go on."

Winter came at the end of September, with a purga that piled snow half a meter deep over their doghouse. The following day was cold and clear.

That night Mikhail woke up, and Fyodor was not in the doghouse. The kitchen was dark. Suddenly fearing the worst, Mikhail ran outside to search for him.

The night was crisp and cool, the skies brilliant with curtains of ethereal fire. The silence was absolute. Mikhail finally spotted Fyodor's silhouette on the ridgeline.

Fyodor was almost motionless, staring upward over the tangle of barbed wire, at where the northern lights flickered and sparkled against an endless background of stars.

"Come away, Fyodor. It's not good for you to watch them like this. They can suck your soul away."

Fyodor did not turn around, did not make a motion to indicate that he had heard. After a long while he spoke. "Oh, but that is what I most yearn for, my friend."

Mikhail let him watch in silence for a moment. He spoke gently. "What do you see?"

"The universe."

"Please come inside, where it is warm. You know that it is electrons hitting air molecules, nothing more."

"Oh, no," Fyodor whispered. "More, it is much more. See with your heart and mind, Mikhail, not your eyes. Plasma is the stuff of the universe itself. We, cold clumps of rock, are insignificant exceptions. One day, a trillion years hence, we too will be plasma, clothed in our own magnetic fields, free to roam the universe. We shall glow then, Mikhail, in all the colors of infrared and radio. We shall scintillate and coruscate. We shall be free."

"Come to sleep now, Fyodor."

"Just a little while longer."

"No. Come now. In the morning we'll talk."

Fyodor sighed. "Then help me." Fyodor extended an arm, and Mikhail helped him to his feet. "Ah, Mikhail. If you were not here to mother me, what would I do?" He stumbled and almost fell, and Mikhail reached out to pull him up. His movements were awkward, and Mikhail knew he must be nearly frozen from sitting motionless in the deadly cold. Mikhail had to half-carry him back to the cabin. His breathing was light, breath barely visible in the night, and he weighed no more than a bundle of straw in the form of a man.

After a while Fyodor continued his work, although never again with the same enthusiasm.

The camp was on a bare, windswept plain at the edge of the glacial ice. No trees grew there, although the oldest of the zeks told of a time when gnarled, stunted pines could be seen barely outside the barbed wire. These had been long ago cut down, and even the roots dug out of the ground to serve as firewood. The nearest stand of trees was in the taiga ten kilometers away, and once a week a brigade of the prisoners was formed to leave before daybreak and make the journey. They would spend the day, heavily guarded, in cutting down trees and sawing them into logs to be used in the endless battle against the arctic cold. They were strictly ordered not to talk, as any talking would be taken as a planning for escape; but still, the lumbering expeditions were one of the few opportunities Mikhail had to learn, in whispers and snatches, of the inmates of the other work squads.

As the days grew shorter the work grew harder and more dangerous, the demand fiercer and more unyielding.

In October Mikhail and Franz were chosen for the duty.

Franz had always seemed silent and distant to Mikhail, a tough and unstinting worker, but aloof. Working beside him cutting trees, in badly-understood German and badly-spoken Russian, he told Mikhail his story. He had come from German stock, but a family that had lived in Poland for centuries. He had been a fervent communist. Before the invasion in 1939 he published a communist newsletter; after the invasion he became a partisan, hiding in the mountains to secretly aid the anti-Hitler forces. For this his reward was a term in Buchenwald. When the camp was liberated, he asked to be repatriated, not to Germany, nor even to Poland, but to the motherland of communism: Russia. He had thought the triumph over fascism was the beginning of a glorious day for communism, and wanted nothing more than to work his hardest to be the smallest part of it.

He shrugged. "And who would have guessed that my prayer would to be answered in its least particular? I have just exactly what I asked, I think."

Not until long after sunset had they had finally cut their quota and were allowed to pile the logs onto sledges to drag back to the camp. Exhausted and numb from cold, they were clumsy and careless. With the first pull on the sledge, one of the retaining wedges came loose. A log slipped, and as Franz ran up to push it back into place, another one started to roll, and another, and then the entire stack of logs rolled off, rolled over Franz and across the ground.

When they reached Franz and pulled away the logs he was white, but seemed unhurt. He protested in German that he was all right, but when the prisoners tried to lift him to his feet, he screamed in agony. The soldiers ran up, their guns at the ready. They lifted him up again, and once more Franz screamed.

One of the other prisoners translated. "His leg. He says it's his leg."

They pulled away his dirty blue trousers, and in the moonlight it was clear that the shape of his leg was wrong, that his shin jutted at the wrong angle and his foot flopped loosely back. "Broken tibia," said one of the prisoners, the best they had for a medic. "We will have to immobilize him and bring him to the infirmary."

"It's not so bad, Franz," Mikhail whispered. "The hospital will be warm, and you won't have to work. Why, we should envy you! You've found your way out of the camp, and that's a trick even the learned Academician hasn't mastered. Eh?"

Franz didn't answer. His eyes were rolled back into his skull and his face was covered in a fine sweat, a bad sign in the chill arctic night. His teeth were clenched so hard Mikhail was afraid that he would break them. As the guards watched with their guns held ready, the zek who fancied himself a medic ripped his shirt into strips to strap the broken leg to a hastily cut sapling. Franz made a soft, high keening sound between his clenched teeth, the note almost ultrasonic.

As they dragged him back on the pile of logs (they could not leave the logs; it would mean another trip, and they would not be allowed another day of 'vacation' from their work) he lapsed unconscious.

When they got back to the camp the sub-administrator was hastily summoned. He was a stocky man, seeming almost fat in contrast to the sapling-thin zeks. He ordered the wrappings removed and inspected the leg himself, grabbing the foot in both hands and twisting it. Franz whimpered and squeezed Mikhail's hand. "It's okay, Franz. It's okay."

The administrator winced in sympathetic pain. "I'm sorry, fellow. You'd be surprised what some people would try to pull off to take a rest in the infirmary. Okay." The administrator nodded, and they wrapped his leg up again.

Mikhail held Franz's hand until the administrator had finished the transfer order, and two of the soldiers fetched a truck to take him away to the camp infirmary.

For the next two weeks Mikhail would at odd moments stop his work, sometimes in mid-swing, and think of Franz, having a lazy rest in a comfortable bed, with full rations, no less. He would smile, and return to work. It would almost be worth the broken leg, just for that.

It was two weeks later that he heard from the camp grapevine that Franz had died of dysentery six days after arriving in the infirmary.

The apparatus now was a lot more complicated, with a small glass jar acting as some sort of vacuum tube, although Mikhail couldn't figure out how Fyodor could have managed to pump a vacuum. Pavel had taken over the task of making the painstaking adjustments when Fyodor's hands shook too badly. The Uzbeki's hands seemed too improbably huge for such a painstaking task, but surprisingly, he had proven to be good at it. In a night of slowly adjusting tiny screws carved by dead Georgi out of pine splinters, while Mikhail pumped the generator and Fyodor whispered advice, under Pavel's hands the black speck in the center of Viktor's glasses distended slowly to a spot the size of a kopek. With a whisper of satisfaction the peasant put it on the plank they used as a bench. They all hesitated to touch it, fearing it would vanish in a puff of ozone. At last Fyodor crept closer, and put his eye against the glass. He looked in silence, staring into the blackness.

After a minute Mikhail could take the silence no more. "Fyodor? Fyodor, what do you see?"

"The stars."

In November the trucks came with new prisoners to replace the zeks who had died. Mikhail was horrified to see women prisoners among the arrivals. "Have they no decency? What could they be thinking of, sending women to a forced labor camp? We have no facilities for women. What could they have possibly have done so awful that could merit sending them, women, here?"

"Mischa, Mischa," said Fyodor. "Look around you. Tell me, just what have you done so awful? What have any of us done?" He gestured to Pyotr. "He asked why food rationing didn't stop after the war. Anti-Soviet agitation: article fifty-eight, twenty-five years." He indicated Vasily. "Acquaintance with a suspicious individual: article fifty-eight, twenty-five years." Pavel. "His father owned three cows. Article fifty-eight, twenty-five years." Fyodor shook his head. "Women? Why not? In the new regime, we are all equal."

Much to Mikhail's surprise, a woman was even assigned to their brigade, Vera Lvovna. She was an overweight Ukrainian peasant, coarse and muscular, with huge pale blue eyes not yet turned empty by the camp life, and dirty blonde hair shorn close to her skull by the camp barbers. At least she will be able to pull her share of the load, thought Mikhail.

The first day she worked she was the subject of a barrage of crude jokes and propositions. It was surprising that the zeks, after fourteen-hour days at hard labor, could even think such things, Mikhail thought. With an expression of annoyance, Fyodor squelched the talk, telling them that she was under his protection. Vasily and Mikhail quickly backed him up.

Mikhail was disgusted when Fyodor made good on his promise by taking Vera as his special charge, talking to her at each chance during the work shifts, looking only into her eyes when he lectured. Mikhail's disgust was only slightly tempered by the fact that he knew perfectly that, until she arrived, it had been he who had been Fyodor's special pupil. Not jealousy, he told himself. It's just that it is a sad spectacle when a fine man takes after a woman of her sort, a peasant, not even fit to empty his parasha. And he was immediately sorry to think it.

Her sleeping quarters were with the women in a doghouse across the camp, one that the zeks immediately tagged the bitch-house.

*   *   *

Fyodor came to him on the long trek back across the steppe. "You are avoiding me, my friend Mikhail."

Mikhail turned away. "No."

Fyodor caught hold of his shoulder and gently turned Mikhail to face him. "Do not be so distant to me, Mikhail. I am old, and have not so many friends that I can leave them to walk away from me without noticing."

"You . . . and that, woman—"

"Ah, Mikhail." Fyodor shook his head. "The fires of jealousy are hot, but will they boil your tea? You do not even know her, I think. Mikhail, my heart is large. There is room in it for two."

"I am sorry, Fyodor."

"She is coming to us tonight."

Mikhail gasped. "You would—?"

"No, no, Mikhail. How could you think? She has intelligence and imagination. She will help us in our work. Our real work."

Mikhail turned away. "I see."

"Mikhail, Mikhail," Fyodor cried after him, but this time Mikhail would not turn.

Vera silently took the place of Pavel, who had been weak and feverish for a week now, and was unable to take his place in the midnight work. Mikhail refused to look at her as he worked his cross, and tried to avoid listening to them whisper while she and Fyodor worked on poor Georgi's machine. The air in the small kitchen was so cold that every few minutes he had to stop and press his hands into his armpits to get his fingers warm.

Fyodor lay face down on the floor, one eye staring into dead Viktor's lens. They evidently had something, for he could hear the excitement in Fyodor's voice. "Rotate me, more, more."

Vera's hands twitched and fluttered delicately, like a clarinetist's.

"More, good! Stop! Move me in, in more, rotate me a little back, back, stop. Good. Is that the highest setting? Damn. Mikhail, more power!"

Mikhail handed him his cross without saying a word, and Fyodor's fingers shook as he took it. He handed it to Vera, who delicately pulled free the crystal at its heart and placed it carefully into the apparatus. Fyodor got back down and stared into the lens. "We lost it. No, there I have it. Bring me in closer, please."

Vera's hands moved some more. Mikhail tried not to watch them, but he couldn't help it. In the darkness they were not like a peasant's hands, but more like a musician's, almost like his dead wife's. Except that the light was not as dim as it had been. There was a bright glow coming from the apparatus.

Fyodor gave a cry of satisfaction. He was no longer looking right into the lens, but standing back in triumph. "Let there be light!" he cried. "Look!"

Mikhail and Vera both stood up and bent over the apparatus, their heads almost touching. In the center of the lens was a fuzzy spot of brilliance, red as the setting sun but far brighter, bright enough to hurt the eyes. Mikhail squatted down and put his hands out. He could feel the warmth emanating from it like a fire. "Fyodor! This is incredible!"

They all held their hands out to warm them. Slowly the wax holding the wire to the lens softened and turned transparent. "Fyodor?" Mikhail started, "Do you think that—"

With a soft slurping sound the lens slid away to the side. There was a high-pitched whistle, and the glass suddenly shattered.

The fuzzy red spot suddenly sharpened into a marble-sized crimson sphere surrounded by a disk of perfect blackness. There was a whistling roar like the engine of a fighter plane. The disk slowly floated upward. Mikhail stepped back involuntarily, and the bright sphere disappeared, although strangely enough he could still see the red circle of light it cast on the canvas roof. In the sudden wind, dirt whirled up from the floor and made a dust pinwheel around the black disk like a tiny red galaxy.

The disk started to tumble as it continued to rise. The red circle on the roof disappeared. In the blackness of the disk tiny pinpricks of glitter sparkled. The tent roof stretched taut. Mikhail's ears hurt. Cold wind shrieked in.

The disk disappeared, and the roar cut off abruptly. Vera stood up, holding the crystal from Georgi's apparatus.

Fyodor's eyes rolled up, and he slumped. Mikhail ran over to catch him before he fell.

Fyodor's cheek was cold, but he was not shivering. That was a bad sign, Mikhail knew.

Vera came over and felt his forehead. "Blankets," she whispered. "Get some more from the men."

Pavel protested as Mikhail took his blankets, but Mikhail was in no mood for an argument. He told him sharply to go nestle in Pyotr's arms. Vera took the blankets and wrapped them around Fyodor.

"What happened," Mikhail whispered. "What did it do to him?"

"It?" she whispered back. "It didn't do anything to him. He's just overworked, that's all. Take a look at him. I'm surprised he could even stand up, much less labor all day and work all night. Don't you give him any rest? Does he always have to be the strongest one, even when he's stretched to his limits, and beyond?"

"Then he'll be all right?"

Her laugh was an unpleasant barking noise, and Mikhail suddenly remembered that he despised her. "No, Mikhail," she said, her voice sharp with sarcasm, "he is not going to be all right. He's going to die."

With no transition at all, her laugh turned into huge racking sobs, and Mikhail had to restrain himself from putting his arms around her to comfort her. "We're all going to die, didn't you know that? There isn't anything we can do about it."

But Fyodor didn't die. In the morning he was a bit paler than usual, and unusually quiet, but he did his morning labor without complaint. Mikhail and Vasily did their best to help him. On the long trek back from the work site Vera held him up, although Mikhail thought that he didn't seem to need it. That night there was no work on the project, but Vera snuck her way into the doghouse anyway, to check on how he was sleeping.

"He is better, but he will never be well," she whispered to Mikhail.

"Of course he is better," said Vasily, "He is our father, our soul. How could he be sick, and we well?"

"Then you had better prepare to live without a soul," she snapped back. "This coughing he has, it is tuberculosis. He's not going to last forever."

"It couldn't be," said Mikhail, incredulous. "Such a thing—how could he keep it secret? Why would he? He could go to the infirmary."

Vera shook her head. "Don't be naive, Mikhail. He wouldn't last two weeks in the infirmary, and he knows it."

Mikhail buried his head in his hands and began to silently cry.

"I'm sorry, Mikhail," she said. "I'm sorry. I forgot that you are his friend, too."

Fyodor recovered, as much as could be expected. A week later, Pyotr died, when dysentery spread through the camp.

The peasant Pavel, who had been his friend, grieved silently. He refused food for three days, and then one morning he vanished.

It was snowing lightly, but a stiff breeze had swept away any footprints. It was impossible to figure how he might have crossed the three layers of barbed wire and past the patrolling dogs and guards, but apparently he had. The entire camp was under a restricted regimen for ten days, with reduced rations, extra counting, and unscheduled searches. They buried Georgi's apparatus, covered over its hole, and brushed the dirt to eliminate any traces. The guards searched the camp for larger quarry; it was possible that Pavel had not escaped, but was being hidden somewhere in the camp.

The tenth day the restricted regimen was called off. They had found Pavel's body. He had escaped straight north on improvised skis, perhaps hoping that the ocean had frozen enough that he could do the impossible and ski right across the north pole to Canada. His body was intact, the grapevine whispered: he had not been shot.

He had frozen to death, but he died outside the barbed wire, a free man.

The next week, on a day when two of the new men were out on the wood-gathering expedition, a blizzard came. It covered the doghouse with snow well over a meter thick. The men were happy the next day when the snow was so deep that there was no possibility of work, and still the endless snow continued.

In the middle of the day the sky was hardly brighter than at midnight. Vera came over to the doghouse to check on Fyodor; she had wrapped herself in layers of rags with sawdust packed between, but when she got there she was nearly frozen through. Mikhail and Vasily pulled her jacket off and held her between their bodies to warm her, ignoring the coarse comments of the other zeks. Vasily warmed her toes by holding them in his mouth, and was still afraid that she would have frostbite and that they would have to be removed. They wrapped her in as many blankets as could be spared and sat her close to the tiny stove, although they dared not heat the stove to more than a tiny glow, knowing that the wood they had might have to last through a deadly night. They scavenged the sawdust Vera had carried in her clothes and fed that to the stove as well.

The night was bitter cold. Flakes drifted in through cracks in the sod walls too small to see, and did not melt. Even the parasha froze. They fed the stove one tiny stick at a time, hoping to make it last. Vera huddled together with the men, one zek among zeks, dozing and shivering and waking, pressed tightly together in some hope of finding body heat. The last remnants of the fire died around daybreak, but there was no light. The temperature dropped.

An hour or so after dawn Fyodor awoke. "The apparatus," he said, his voice barely more than a croak.

"It is safe, Fyodor," said Mikhail.

"Use it," he whispered. "It is our only hope."

"Of course!"

Vasily and Mikhail worked the crystals frantically, while Vera repaired the central apparatus with the remaining lens of Viktor's glasses. There was no wax to seal it in place.

"No matter," whispered Fyodor. "Hold it in place with your hand. Just prevent it from sliding, and the vacuum on the other side will hold it in place."

They worked the first of the crystals in place, and Vera tweaked the wooden screws until the kopek of darkness appeared. Mikhail shook Fyodor. "What now, Fyodor? What do we do next?"

"Look in the darkness. What do you see?"

"Nothing."

"Your eye right up to the lens, Mikhail. You must nearly touch it with your eye. What do you see?"

"Tiny points of light."

"Find one, Mikhail. Go to a star."

"How?"

"Vera knows how. Guide her, tell her how to go. A bright one, Mikhail. Look for a bright one."

Between the two of them they maneuvered the lens until weak sunshine came through the disk. The men crowded around the lens, but it was not enough to warm the air. "Closer, Mikhail. Bring it in close to the star."

They made the light brighten until it was dazzling, and the lens itself was hot. Any closer and it would be in danger of melting.

It was warmer in the room, slightly but noticeably. Mikhail looked at Fyodor. "There is hope."

"Mikhail," said Fyodor. "I can see something in your eyes. You saw something, looking into the lens."

"Yes."

"What was it?"

"A planet."

Fyodor sat up suddenly. "You saw the Earth?"

Mikhail shook his head. "No. It was no planet ever seen, Fyodor. It had clouds in bands around the planet, but they were orange, stripes like on a cat."

Fyodor laid back down. "I knew it. The constellations I saw were too strange. I don't know how far away we have gone, Mikhail. But it is far." He slumped. "Far."

"Fyodor," whispered Mikhail. "You said that there is vacuum on the other side of the lens. Then this is not just an image, but the other side of the lens is really somewhere else? The last time, the air was sucked through—yes! So we could go through too, could we not? We could escape!"

Fyodor shook his head. "I had that hope too, Mikhail, the very first day that Vasily and I found that there were solutions to the portal equations, the day that Vasily dared to suggest that if we were clever enough, we could forge a hole through space itself. But the energy is too great. If the crystals were shattered and all of the energy discharged at once . . . but the wire could not take it, it would melt.

"And look at the stars, Mikhail. How many they are! How far away is it that we are looking? A thousand light years? A million? To the portal, distance is nothing. We could be looking into another galaxy, or back into time. If you searched for a hundred years, Mikhail, you could not search enough to find the right sun. Or for a thousand times longer." He shook his head. "It is no hope, to escape."

But Fyodor's face did not have a hopeless expression. His eyes, huge and hollow, burned with a liquid brown intensity. "We have looked into the face of another sun, you and I," he whispered. "Is that not enough?"

Mikhail nodded, and held his hand. "It is enough, Fyodor."

They drafted one or another of the men into pumping the crystals continuously. Mikhail watched the lens nervously, worried that it would break like the other one had the prior night, but it held firm. When the light started to drift to one side or the other he called out instructions, and Vera adjusted it in silence with delicate, precise motions of her fingers.

Gathered around the unsteady circle of sunlight, not daring to take their eyes off their work long enough to look at each other, they whispered together. Mikhail unveiled his heart, told her of his former wife, his family, his barely-remembered happiness. Vera told of her life. She had been a plant doctor, educated in Leningrad. She was studying grain diseases in the Ukraine when she learned that her father had been taken by the NKVD. She had gone to Moscow to petition for his release, only to learn that he had died in custody. She should have known then it would be dangerous to take the matter further. She had protested too loudly, and was sent to the camps for it.

Mikhail reached out to touch her hand. "I'm sorry," he said. He wanted to say more, but knew no words that could express the complexity of his feelings. "I'm sorry."

In mid-afternoon something failed in the apparatus. They tried to wake Fyodor, but he would not be awakened. Vasily took his pulse.

"He is alive," he said.

"And?"

Vasily shook his head. "He is alive."

The temperature slowly dropped.

Toward evening the blizzard abated, and not long after a labor team tunneled through to them. They walked out into the snow ˥ uncertain legs, dazzled by the wan grey light and the clean air. None of the men spoke of what they had seen in the dog-

˥n Vera was discovered in their barracks, the guards were ˥ake her away. For being in the wrong barracks, she was ˥days in the punishment cell. Mikhail shuddered. Eight ˥ally a death sentence; only the strongest of men sur- of the men were reprimanded, but not punished. ˥ll afford to lose many more. Fully a third of the to death in the blizzard; a hundred suffered ˥nany were expected not to survive. Of the ˥ the detail chopping wood, there was no

of reprieve. In the morning, wrapped ˥ find to keep warm, they were sent

˥vith Georgi's apparatus. Mikhail ˥ Fyodor would wake. ˥w, Mikhail. Was it beautiful?"

"Yes, Fyodor. It was striped, orange and white and brown, in swirling bands like candy."

"Like a tiger, was it, Mikhail?"

"Yes, like a tiger, big and bright and beautiful. Just like a tiger, Fyodor."

"It is good, Mikhail. If there is one planet, there must be many. Infinitely more than we can count." He had a fit of coughing and then was silent for a moment. "The universe is more wonderful than we ever imagined, Mikhail. Is it not?" Fyodor noticed Mikhail's tears. "Why are you crying, Mikhail? We have seen what no one else has ever seen. We have looked into infinity, and seen what lies beyond. How can you cry, except tears of joy?"

"Yes, Fyodor," said Mikhail, still crying. "Joy. These are tears of joy."

"It is good, Mikhail," said Fyodor. "Good." He lapsed into silence.

Sometime in the night Mikhail dozed. He dreamed that Fyodor was with him, and that they were looking at a planet, a beautiful ringed planet fuzzy and striped like a tiger; and that Gregori was there with them, and all of them, even Vera. And Fyodor said something to him, something important, but just then he woke up and could not remember what it was.

For a moment in the close darkness he could not remember where he was, but then he reached out for Fyodor. "Fyodor? Did you just say something?"

Fyodor did not answer. "Fyodor? I just dreamed —" Suddenly Mikhail noticed the silence. The labored breathing, as familiar t Mikhail as his own heartbeat, had stopped. Fyodor would n answer him, would never answer again.

The pain was too great for Mikhail to bear, too great for to cry. He buried his face into Fyodor's chest and beat his fis the ground.

Vasily came and put his arms around Mikhail's back, b once had the wisdom to be silent.

In the morning they took the body away, and Mik alone. They must have said he was sick, covered for hin sick? He didn't know, no longer cared.

In the evening Vera returned. For an instant he thou a ghost. There was a glow about her; the glow, Mik that Vasily had told him about, the purity that r everything else has been burned away.

Could it have been eight days since the blizzard? Mikhail couldn't remember, had lost all track of the time passing.

Vera looked around. "Where is Fyodor?" she asked. "They wouldn't send him to work—"

Mikhail took her in his arms. For the first time since Fyodor's death, he cried.

Later that night Vasily called them over. His eyes were bright, almost maniacal. He had been working on the apparatus. "Fyodor gave me his notes, did you know that? His notes, and my notes; together what an article we could write, he and I!"

"Good, Vasily," said Mikhail. "Perhaps they will let you free?"

Vasily shook his head. "I have written it in my head, and that is enough. This morning I burned the notes, his and mine. I have been in the camps for eight years." Vasily stopped, shook his head slowly. "Two thousand, nine hundred and fifty days. I no longer remember how to breathe free air; I do not know how to talk to free people. There are seventeen more years in my term. Six thousand days. I do not think I will live to see them all."

"I am sorry, Vasily," said Mikhail.

Vasily shook his head. "No, no! It is nothing. Look!"

He pointed to the lens.

In the lens was green. Mikhail put his eye to it, and for a moment it made him dizzy. The landscape was upside down, drifting slowly past the lens with trees growing downward toward a cloud-spattered blue-grey sky.

Vasily reached out, twisted the lens and pulled it away. A waft of warm, paprika-scented air caressed Mikhail's face. Not trees. Where Mikhail would have expected leaves, the plants grew bulbous green balloons shaped like soccer balls. In the upside-down distance he could see other plants shaped like corkscrews, with delicate flowers like a baby's fingers.

"Green!" said Vasily. "And the shade of green, is it not the most beautiful?"

It seemed ordinary green to Mikhail.

"But that is just the point!" said Vasily. "Chlorophyll, Mikhail! Out of the million, billion light-absorbing molecules that might be, these plants have chlorophyll! Can't you understand what that means? Their biology is like ours, Mikhail. Don't you remember what Gregori said? Like ours.

"I have been here too long, Mikhail. But you, you and Vera, you are still young. You have not yet been broken by the camps.

"Go, Mikhail, go and live my dreams."

Vasily nodded toward the tiny portal.

"But—" said Mikhail.

"We can't—" said Vera.

"You can! You must! I will work the apparatus," said Vasily. "Quickly!" He twisted two wires together, and suddenly the portal grew. It was a meter in diameter. "No time to think! Go!"

Mikhail hesitated.

"Faith, Mikhail! Have faith!" Vasily put a hand on Mikhail's back and pushed gently. "Go!"

Mikhail jumped headfirst into the sunshine of the new world, momentarily disoriented as the alien gravity grabbed him. He tumbled and hit the ground. For a moment he was dazed. Behind him, Vera twisted as she fell.

All around him was a mad chirping of—birds?—squawking warning of intruders. The sounds of life. Floating upside down inside a ring of greyness was Vasily. "Remember me, Mikhail!" His face shrank to the size of a coin, a fuzzy disk of grey drifting slowly into a tangled green thicket. "Remember me, Vera!" The disk shrank to a point. "Live long, and free!" The point flared and vanished.

"Forever," Mikhail whispered. His eyes were wet. To the side he saw Vera stand up, awkward as a kitten in the strangely low gravity. "Good-bye, Vasily," he said, softly. "Good-bye, Fyodor. Good-bye."

Vera stood beside him and took his hand. "Good-bye, Pavel. Good-bye Pyotr." One by one they named them all and said farewell, and when Vera stopped Mikhail continued on, saying good-bye to those who had died before she came, even the ones he had never known himself, saying softly all the farewells that they could never give in the camps.

Finally it was done, the last name remembered, and then, at last, they turned to explore the new world.

The Singular Habits
of Wasps

O F THE MANY ADVENTURES IN WHICH I HAVE PARTICI-
pated with my friend Mr. Sherlock Holmes, none has been
more singularly horrifying than the case of the Whitechapel killings, nor ever had I previously had cause to doubt the sanity of
my friend. I need but close my eyes to see again the horror of that
night; the awful sight of my friend, his arms red to the elbow, his
knife still dripping gore, and to recall in every detail the gruesome
horrors that followed.

The tale of this adventure is far too awful to allow any hint of
the true course of the affair to be known. Although I dare never
let this account be read by others, I have often noticed, in
chronicling the adventures of my friend, that in the process of
putting pen to paper a great relief occurs. A catharsis, as we call
it in the medical profession. And so I hope that by putting upon
paper the events of those weeks, I may ease my soul from its dread
fascination with the horrid events of that night. I will write this
and then secret the account away with orders that it be burned
upon my death.

Genius is, as I have often remarked, closely kin to madness, so
closely that at times it is hard to distinguish the one from the
other, and the greatest geniuses are also often quite insane. I had

for a long time known that my friend was subject to sporadic fits
of blackest depression, from which he could become aroused in
an instant into bursts of manic energy, in a manner not unlike the
cyclic mood-swings of a madman. But the limits to his sanity I
never probed.

The case began in the late springtime of 1888. All who were
in London at that time will recall the perplexing afternoon of the
double cannonade. Holmes and I were enjoying a cigar after lunch
in our sitting room at 221B Baker Street when the hollow report
of a double firing of cannon rang out from the cloudless sky, rattling the windows and causing Mrs. Hudson's china to dance upon
its shelves. I rushed to the window. Holmes was in the midst of
one of those profound fits of melancholia to which he is so prone,
and did not rise from his chair, but did bestir himself so much as
to ask what I saw. Aside from other, equally perplexed folk opening their windows to look in all directions up and down the street,
I saw nothing out of the ordinary, and such I reported to him.

"Most unusual," Holmes remarked. He was still slumped
almost bonelessly in his chair, but I believed I detected a bit of
interest in his eye. "We shall hear more about this, I would venture to guess."

And indeed, all of London seemed to have heard the strange
reports, without any source to be found, and the subject could not
be avoided all that day or the next. Each newspaper ventured an
opinion, and even strangers on the street talked of little else. As
to conclusion, there was none, nor was the strange sound repeated. In another day the usual gossip, scandals and crimes of the
city had crowded the marvel out of the papers, and the case was
forgotten.

But it had, at least, the effect of breaking my friend out of his
melancholia, even so far as to cause him to pay a rare visit to his
brother at the Diogenes Club. Mycroft was high in the Queen's
service, and there were few secrets of the Empire to which
Mycroft was not privy. Holmes did not confide in me as to what
result came of his inquiries of Mycroft, but he spent the remainder of the evening pacing and smoking, contemplating some
mystery.

In the morning we had callers, and the mystery of the cannonade was temporarily set aside. They were two men in simple but
neat clothes, both very diffident and hesitant of speech.

"I see that you have come from the south of Surrey," Holmes
said calmly. "A farm near Godalming, perhaps?"

"Indeed we have, sir, from Covingham, which is a bit south of Godalming," said the elder of the visitors, "though how you could know, I'll never guess in all my born days, seeing as how I've never had the pleasure of meeting you before in my life, nor Baxter here neither."

I knew that Holmes, with his encyclopaedic knowledge, would have placed them precisely from their accents and clothing, although this elementary feat of deduction seemed to quite astound our visitors.

"And this is the first visit to London for either of you," said Holmes. "Why have you come this distance from your farm to see me?"

The two men looked at each other in astonishment. "Why, right you are again, sir! Never been to London town, nor Baxter."

"Come, come; to the point. You have traveled this distance to see me upon some matter of urgency."

"Yes, sir. It's the matter of young Gregory. A farm hand he was, sir, a strapping lad, over six feet and still lacking 'is full height. A-haying he was. A tragic accident t'was, sir, tragic."

Holmes of course noticed the use of the past tense, and his eyes brightened. "An accident, you say? Not murder?"

"Yes."

Holmes was puzzled. "Then, pray, why have you come to me?"

" 'Is body, sir. We've come about 'is body."

"What about it?"

"Why, it's gone, sir. Right vanished away."

"Ah." Holmes leaned forward in his chair, his eyes gleaming with sudden interest. "Pray, tell me all about it, and spare none of the details."

The story they told was long and involved many diversions into details of life as a hired hand at Sherringford Farm, the narration so roundabout that even Holmes's patience was tried, but the essence of the story was simple. Baxter and young Gregory had been working in the fields when Gregory had been impaled by the blade of the mechanical haying engine. "And cursed be the day that the master ever decided to buy such an infernal device," added the older man, who was the uncle and only relation of the poor Gregory. Disentangled from the machine, the young farmhand had been still alive, but very clearly dying. His abdomen had been ripped open and his viscera exposed. Baxter had laid the dying man in the shade of a hayrick, and gone to fetch help. Help had taken two hours to arrive, and when they had come, they had found the puddle of congealing blood, but no sign of Gregory. They had searched all about, but the corpse was nowhere to be found, nor was there any sign of how he had been carried away. There was no chance, Baxter insisted, that Gregory could have walked even a small distance on his own. "Not unless he dragged 'is guts after him. I've seen dying men, guv, and men what 'ave been mere wounded, and young Gregory was for it."

"This case may have some elements of interest in it," said Holmes. "Pray, leave me to cogitate upon the matter tonight. Watson, hand me the train schedule, would you? Thank you. Ah, it is as I thought. There is a 9 A.M. train from Waterloo." He turned to the two men. "If you would be so good as to meet me on the morrow at the platform?"

"Aye, sir, that we could."

"Then it is settled. Watson, I do believe you have a prior engagement?"

That I did, as I was making plans for my upcoming marriage, and had already made firm commitment in the morning to inspect a practice in the Paddington district with a view toward purchasing it. Much as I have enjoyed accompanying my friend upon his adventures, this was one which I should have to forego.

Holmes returned late from Surrey, and I did not see him until breakfast the next morning. As often he was when on a case, he was rather uncommunicative, and my attempts to probe the matter were met with monosyllables, except at the very last. "Most unusual," he said, as if to himself. "Most singular indeed."

"What?" I asked, eager to listen now that it appeared that Holmes was ready to break his silence.

"The tracks, Watson," he said. "The tracks. Not man, nor beast, but definitely tracks." He looked at his pocket-watch. "Well, I must be off. Time enough for cogitation when I have more facts."

"But where are you going?"

Holmes laughed. "My dear Watson, I have in my time amassed a bit of knowledge of various matters which would be considered most *recherché* to laymen. But I fear that, upon occasion, even I must consult with an expert."

"Then whom?"

"Why, I go to see Professor Huxley," he answered, and was out the door before I could ask what query he might have for the eminent biologist.

He was absent from Baker Street all afternoon. When he

returned after supper time I was anxious to ask how his interview with the esteemed professor had gone.

"Ah, Watson, even I make my occasional mistake. I should have telegraphed first. As it was, Professor Huxley had just left London, and is not to return for a week." He took out his pipe, inspected it for a moment, then set it aside and rang for Mrs. Hudson to bring in some supper. "But in this case, my journey was not in vain. I had a most delightful discussion with the professor's protégé, a Mr. Wells by name. A Cockney lad, son of a shop-keeper and no more than twenty-two, unless I miss my guess, but a most remarkable man nonetheless. Interested in a wide variety of fields, and I venture to say that in whatever field he chooses, he will outshine even his esteemed teacher. Quite an interesting conversation we had, and a most useful one."

"But what was it that you discussed?" I asked.

Holmes set aside the cold beef that Mrs. Hudson had brought, leaned back in his chair, and shut his eyes. For a while I thought that he had gone to sleep without hearing my question. At last he spoke. "Why, we discussed the planet Mars," he said, without opening his eyes. "And the singular habits of wasps."

It seemed that his researches, whatever they were, led to no distinct conclusion, for when I asked him about the case the next day, he gave no response. That day he stayed in his chambers, and through the closed door I heard only the intermittent voice of his violin speaking in its melancholy, unfathomable tongue.

I have perhaps mentioned before that my friend would habitually have more than one case on which he worked at any one time. It appeared that over the next few evenings he was about on another one, for I found him dressing to go out at a late hour.

"Another case, Holmes?" I asked.

"As you can see, Watson," he replied. He indicated his less-than-respectable outfit and the threadbare workman's jacket he was pulling on over it. "Duty calls at all hours. I shan't be more than a few hours, I expect."

"I am ready to assist."

"Not in this one, my dear friend. You may stay home tonight."

"Is there danger?"

"Danger?" He seemed surprised, as if the thought hadn't occurred to him. "Danger? Oh, perhaps a slight bit."

"You know that I would not hesitate. . . ."

"My dear doctor," he said, and smiled. "Let me assure you

that I am not worried on that score. No, it is that I go to the East End. . . ."

The East End of London was no place for gentlemen, with slaughterhouses and tenements of the lowest order; a place for drunkards, sailors, Chinese and Indian laborers, and ruffians of all sorts. Nevertheless I was quite willing to brave much worse, if necessary, for the sake of Holmes. "Is that all?" I said. "Holmes, I do believe you underestimate me!"

"Ah, Watson . . ." He seemed to reflect for a moment. "No, it would not do. You are soon to be married, and have your wife-to-be to think of." He raised a hand to forestall my imminent objection. "No, not the danger, my friend. Don't worry for me on that score. I have my resources. It is . . . how to put it delicately? I expect that I shall meet people in places where a gentleman soon to be married would best not be seen."

"Holmes!"

"Business, my dear Watson. Business." And with that, he left.

His business there did not seem to be concluded that evening or the next. By the end of August he was visiting the East End once or twice a week. I had already become used to his odd hours and strange habits, and soon thought nothing of it. But he was so habitual about it, and so secretive, that it soon caused me to wonder whether perhaps he might be calling upon a woman. I could think of nothing that seemed less like Holmes, for in all my time with him he had never expressed a trace of romantic interest in the fairer sex. And yet, from my own medical experience, I knew that even the most steadfast of men must experience those urges common to our gender, however much he might profess to disdain romance.

Romance? Though I myself never frequented such places, as an Army man I knew quite as well as Holmes what sort of women dwelt in Whitechapel, and what profession they practiced. Indeed, he had admitted as much when he had warned me away 'because I was to be married.' But then, a woman of such type could well appeal to Holmes. There would be nothing of romance involved. It would be merely a business proposition for her, and a release of pressure for him. A dozen times I resolved to warn him of the dangers — the danger of disease, if nothing else — in patronizing women of that sort, and so many times my nerve failed and I said nothing.

And, if it were not what I feared, what case could it be that would take him into Whitechapel with such frequency?

*   *   *

One evening shortly after Holmes had left, a message boy delivered a small package addressed to him. The address proclaimed it to be from a John B. Coores and Sons, but gave no clue to its contents. This name seemed to me familiar, but, struggle as I might, I could not recall where I might have seen it before. I left it in the sitting room for Holmes, and the next morning saw that he had taken it. He made no mention of the package or of what it contained, however, and my curiosity over it remained unslaked.

But another event soon removed that curiosity from my mind. The newspaper that morning carried a report of a brutal murder on Buck's Row in Whitechapel. The body of an unidentified woman had been found on the street, and, what was even more grotesque, after her death her body had been brutally sliced open. I read the paper to Holmes as he sat drinking coffee in the morning. As far as I could tell, he had not slept the previous night, although he seemed little the worse for it. He made no comment on the article. It occurred to me that for all its gruesome features, this was the sort of commonplace murder he would have no interest in, since it seemed quite lacking in the singular points that so interested him. I made a comment to him to that effect.

"Not so, Watson," he said, without looking up. "I am quite interested to hear what the press has to say about the Nichols tragedy."

This comment startled me considerably, since the paper had given no name to the victim. I suddenly remembered that East London was exactly where Holmes was going for all these evenings, perhaps to the very place the murder had occurred.

"My God, Holmes! Did you know her?"

At this he looked up, and gave me a long, piercing stare. After a long while he looked away and gave a short laugh. "I do have my secrets, Watson. Pray, inquire no further."

But to me his laughter sounded forced.

It was a week before I saw Holmes prepare for another of his nocturnal sojourns. After napping all afternoon, Holmes was again dressing in faded and tattered clothing. This time I did not ask, but silently dressed to follow.

When he put on his ear-flapped traveling-cap, I was ready as well. I quietly walked to his side, clutching my old service revolver in the pocket of my coat. He looked at me with an expression of utmost horror and put up a hand. "My God, Watson! If you value your life and your honour, don't follow me!"

"Just tell me this, then," I said. "Are you doing something . . . dishonourable?"

"I am doing what I must." And he was out the door and gone in the time it took me to realize that he had in no way answered my question.

As I prepared for bed that night, wondering where Holmes had gone and what he was doing there, it suddenly occurred to me where I had seen the name John B. Coores and Sons before. I crossed the room, thrust open the cabinet where I kept medical supplies, and drew out a small wooden box. There it was. I had looked at the name a thousand times without really seeing it, neatly lettered on the side of the box: John B. Coores and Sons, Fine Surgical Instruments. But what could Holmes want with surgical tools?

And in the next evening's paper, I saw with horror that there had been another murder. The Whitechapel killer had struck again, and once more he had not contented himself with merely killing the woman. Using a surgical knife and a knowledge of anatomy, he had dissected the body and removed several organs.

That Sunday I took my beloved Mary to the theatre. My thoughts were dark, but I endeavoured to allow none of my turmoil to be communicated to her, hoping instead that her sweet presence might distract me from my dire speculations. Events plotted against me, however, for playing at the Lyceum was a most disturbing play, *The Strange Case of Dr. Jekyll and Mr. Hyde.* I watched the play with my mind awhirl, scarcely noticing the presence of my beloved at my side.

After the play I pleaded sudden ill health and fled home. Seeing my ashen face, Mary heartily agreed that I should go home to rest, and it was all I could do to dissuade her from accompanying me back to serve as nurse.

The play had been presented as fiction, but it had hit a note of purest truth. That a single man could have two personalities! Stevenson had been circumspect about naming the drug that would so polarize a man's psyche as to split his being into two parts, but with my medical knowledge I could easily fill in the name, and it was a drug I had intimate knowledge of. Yes. A man could suppress his animal instincts, could make himself into a pure reasoning machine, but the low urges would not wither away, oh no. They would still be there, lurking inside, waiting a chance to break loose.

I had thought that either Holmes was stalking the White-chapel killer, or else that Holmes was the killer. Now I suddenly realized that there was yet another alternative: Holmes the detective could be stalking the Whitechapel killer, completely unaware that he himself was the very criminal he sought.

It was a week before he went out again. The following day I scanned the newspapers in an agony of suspense, but there was no murder reported. Perhaps I was overwrought and imagining things? But Holmes seemed haunted by something, or perhaps hunted. There was something on his mind. When I invited him to confide in me, he looked at me for a long time and then slowly shook his head. "I dare not, Watson." He was silent for a while, and then said, "Watson, if I should suddenly die—"

At this I could take no more. "My God, Holmes, what is it? Surely you can tell me something!"

"This is important, Watson. If I should die . . . burn my corpse. Promise me that."

"Holmes!"

He gripped my shoulder and looked intently into my eye. "Promise me, on your honour."

"I promise."

"On your honour, Watson!"

"On my honour, I promise."

He suddenly relaxed, almost collapsing into his chair. "Thank you."

That night again he went out, and again the next. His face was drawn, as if he were desperately seeking something he had been unable to find on the previous night. Both evenings he seemed upon the brink of saying something to me, only to think better of it at the last moment, and vanish without a word into the London night.

The next evening's papers told of not one, but two murders in the East End. The Whitechapel killer—now dubbed 'Jack the Ripper' by all the papers—had worked double duty. And this time a witness had given a description of the suspected killer: a tall man in a dark cutaway overcoat, wearing a felt deerstalker hat.

I confronted Holmes with the papers and my suspicions. I had hoped, more than I hope for paradise, that he would dismiss my deductions with his soft, mocking laugh, and show me some utterly commonplace alternative explanation of the facts. My hopes were in vain. He listened to my words with his eyes nearly shut, his briar pipe clenched unlit between his teeth. Finally my words ground to a stop against his stony silence. "My God, Holmes, tell me I'm wrong! Tell me that you had nothing to do with those murders, I beg of you."

"I can say nothing, my friend."

"Then give me some reason, some shred of sanity."

He was silent. Finally he said, "Do you intend to go to the police with your suspicions?"

"Do you want me to?" I asked him.

"No." His eyes closed for a moment, and then he continued, "but it doesn't matter. They would not believe you in any case." His voice was weary, but calm. His manner did not seem that of a madman, but I know that madmen can be fiendishly clever in concealing their madness from those about them. "Are you aware of how many letters and telegrams have flooded Scotland Yard in these last few weeks? The Yard is a madhouse, Watson. Landladies and madmen, people claiming to have seen the Ripper, to know the Ripper, to *be* the Ripper. They receive a thousand letters a week, Watson. Your voice would be lost in the madness." He shook his head. "They have no idea, Watson. They cannot begin to comprehend. The Whitechapel horror, they call it. If the true horror of it were known, they would flee the city; they would scream and run in terror."

Despite everything, I should have gone to the police, or at least have confided my suspicions to someone else and asked for counsel. But I knew of no one in whom to confide such an awful suspicion, least of all my Mary, who trusted Holmes nearly as a god and would hear no ill of him. And, despite all, in my heart of hearts I still believed that I must have read the evidence awry, that Holmes could not truly be a culprit of such infamy.

The next day, Holmes made no reference to our conversation. It seemed so strange that I thought to wonder if it had actually occurred, or if I had dreamed the entire thing. I determined that, without giving any outward sign of it to Holmes, I should keep my eyes sharp on him like a hawk. The next time that I saw him making preparations to leave on a nocturnal sojourn, I would follow him, whether he wanted it or no.

Holmes made several trips to Whitechapel during the daytime, and gave no objection when I asked to accompany him. It was no place for decent humans to live. The streets were littered with the filth of horses, pigs, chickens and humans, and the air clamorous with the clatter of delivery wagons and trains, the carousal of children and drunkards, and the cackling of chickens and bawling of pigs which lived side-by-side with people in the basements and doss-houses. Above us, hanging from every window, ragged wash turned dingy grey as it dried in pestilence-ridden air.

During these trips he did little other than inspect the streets and look over the blank, white-washed brick walls of warehouses and blind alleys. On occasion he would stop for a brief chat over inconsequential matters with a charwoman or a policeman he might meet walking the narrow alleyways. Contrary to his nature, he made no attempt to visit the scenes of the crimes. To me this last fact was the most damning to my suspicions. Unless he was involved in some way, surely there would have been no possibility that anything could have kept him away.

But it was all of October and a week into November before he again left upon one of his evening peregrinations. But for an accident of chance, I would have missed it entirely. I had laid out several traps for him, so as to awaken me if he tried to leave in the night, and sat wakeful in the evenings until long after I had heard him retire. One night in early November, after retiring without incident, I was unexpectedly awakened in the middle of the night by some noise. The night was foggy, and through my window I could hear only the most muffled sounds of the street, as if from a tremendous distance, the clopping of a lone set of hooves and the call of a man hailing a hansom. For some reason I was unable to get back to sleep, and so I put on my dressing-gown and descended to the sitting room to take a finger of whisky.

Holmes was gone. His door was ajar, but the bed was empty.

I was determined to know the truth, whatever it might be, and thus in one way or another to bring this adventure to an end. I dressed hurriedly, thrust my service revolver into a pocket of my overcoat, and ran out into the night. At that hour, well after midnight, I had only the most remote hope of finding a cab anywhere near our Baker Street diggings. Sometime during the day Holmes must have surreptitiously arranged for the cab to meet him that night. As I had made no such arrangements, he had quite the head start on me. It was the better part of an hour before I made my way past Aldgate pump and entered the East End slums.

I had suspected that in the wake of the killings the streets of Whitechapel would be deserted, the public houses closed and the citizens suspicious of any strangers. But even at this late hour the streets were far from deserted. It was a busy, populous area. Wandering aimlessly on the streets, I found many open pubs, most all crowded with unemployed workmen and idle women of dubious repute. Everywhere I walked I found that I was not more than a hundred yards from a citizen's patrol or a watchful, armed constable—several of whom watched me with an intent, suspicious gaze. Even the women on the streetcorners, wearing shawls and bonnets to ward against the wet November night, stood in groups of two and three.

Holmes I could find nowhere, and it occurred to me belatedly that if he were in one of his disguises, he could be any of the people about me—one of the unemployed mechanics gambling in the front room of the Boar and Bristle, the aged clergyman hustling down Commercial Street toward some unknown destination, the sailor chatting up the serving girls at the King's Arms. Any of these could be Holmes.

Any of these could be the Ripper.

All around me there were women, in the pubs, in the doorways, walking the streets; pathetic women dressed in cheap finery, with tired smiles and the flash of a stockinged ankle for any passers-by wearing trousers—"you lonely, love?"—or with saucy greetings and friendly abuse for the other women.

I realized that the size of Whitechapel that showed on the map was deceptive. In the fog and the darkness the streets were far more narrow, the shops smaller, and the whole larger and more cluttered that I recalled from the daytime. Even if there were a hundred constables patrolling the streets it would not be enough. The blind alleys, the sparse gas lights, and the drifting banks of fog made the streets a maze in which the Ripper might kill with impunity within a few yards of a hundred or more people.

Twice I thought I caught a glimpse of Holmes, but, when I ran after him, found that I had been deceived. Every drunkard sleeping in a doorway seemed to be a fresh corpse, every anonymous stain on the cobblestones looked like blood, every wandering alleycat seemed the shadow of a lurking killer. Several times I contemplated giving up my hopeless errand and going home, managing to keep on only by promising myself that I would stay on for just one hour more.

In the dark hour before sunrise I found him.

I had come into a pub to warm myself for a while. The barman was surly and uncommunicative, evincing a clear suspicion of my motives that, while perhaps well enough justified by recent events, nevertheless made the atmosphere inside scarcely less chill than that of the night outside. The beer was cheap and thoroughly watered. At first a few of the women had come by to pass time with me, but I found them pathetic rather than alluring, and after a bit they left me in solitude.

After an hour or so of this, I went out into the night air to clear my head of the smoke and stink. A light rain had cleared most of the fog away. I walked at random down the streets and up alleyways, paying no attention to where I headed.

After walking for some time, I was disoriented, and stopped to get my bearings. I had no idea where I was. I turned a corner and looked down into an unmarked court, hoping to descry a street sign, but had no luck. In the darkness I saw something ahead of me; a pair of legs protruding from the arch of an entranceway. I walked forward, my blood chill. It was the body of a woman laid on the cobblestones, skirts awry, half concealed in a doorway. I had seen a dozen such in the last few hours, drunkards too poor to afford a bed, but in the instant of vision a dread presentiment came to me that this one was not merely drunk and asleep. The darkness beneath her body looked darker and more liquid than any mere shadow. I knelt down, and touched her wrist to take a pulse.

Her eyes flew open. It took a moment for her to focus on me. Suddenly she shrieked and stumbled to her feet. "Lord have mercy! The Ripper!" she said in a hoarse whisper. She tripped over her petticoats in a clumsy effort to stand and run at the same time, and fell to her knees.

"My pardons, Miss," I said. "Are you all right?" Without thinking, I reached down a hand to help her up.

"Murder!" she shrieked, scrambling away on all fours like an animal. "Oh! Murder!"

"Madam, please!" I backed away into the alley behind me. It was evident that nothing I could do would calm her. She continued to yell as she clattered away, darting frightened glances back at me over her shoulder. The courtyard I was in was dark and silent, but I was afraid that her cries would wake others. I stepped backwards into a doorway, and suddenly found the door behind me yield to the pressure. It had not been latched. Off balance, I half-fell backwards into the room.

The room was thick with the cloying, coppery odor of blood. The hand I had put down to steady myself came up slick with it. By the wan light of the fire in the grate across the room I could see the bed, and the dark, twisted shape on it, and I had no need to look more closely to know what it was.

The body of the woman on the bed had been so badly muti-
lated that it was hardly recognizable as human. Blood was everywhere. In a daze I reached out a hand to feel for a pulse.

Her hand was already cool.

Her skirt had been removed, her petticoats cut away, and her
body neatly opened from pubes to sternum by some expert
dissector.

I was too late. I gave a low moan. Somewhere before me I
heard a low, steady dripping. I looked up, and stared into the pale
face of Sherlock Holmes.

His eyes were weary, but empty of any trace of the horror that
I felt. He was standing in the room behind the body, and as my
eyes adjusted to the shadow I saw that he held a dissecting knife.
His arms were red to the elbows, and gore dripped in a monotonous rhythm from the knife onto the stone floor. At his feet was
a worn leather shopkeeper's satchel, half open.

"There is nothing you can do for her, Doctor," said Holmes,
and the calm, even voice in which he said this pierced me with
chill. It was not the Holmes I knew. I was not sure if he even
recognized me. He bent down to snap the satchel shut before I
had more than a brief glimpse of the bloody meat within it, then
wiped the scalpel on the canvas apron he wore, put it carefully
back into the small wooden case, and dropped it into an outside
pocket of the bag.

He tugged at his left elbow, and only then did I realize that he
wore full-length gloves. He was well prepared for this venture, I
thought, my mind in a state of shock. He removed the gloves,
tossed them into the fire grate, and pushed at them with a poker.
They smoldered for a moment and then caught fire, with the
heavy charnel stink of burning blood. Beneath his apron he wore
work clothes such as any tradesman might wear.

"My God, Holmes!" I stuttered. "Did you kill her?"

He sighed deeply. "I don't know. Time is short. Please follow
me, Watson."

At least he recognized me. That was a good sign. I followed
him out of long habit, too numb to do anything else. He closed
and locked the door behind him and put the key into his pocket.
He led me through a small gate, down a cluttered alley, then
quickly through two narrow passageways and into a courtyard
behind the slaughterhouses. The key and the apron he discarded
there. I saw he had a cab waiting, the horse tethered to an unlit
lamppost. There was no cabman in sight. "Take me home, Wat-

son," he said. "You should not have come. But, since you are nevertheless here, I confess myself glad of the chance to unburden myself of the awful things that I have seen and done. Take me home, and I shall conceal nothing from you."

I drove and Holmes sat in back, meditating or sleeping, I could not tell which. We passed three constables, but I did not stop. He bade me halt at a certain mews not far from Baker Street. "The cabman will be here in half an hour," he said, as he tended expertly to the horse. "He has been paid in advance, and we need not wait."

"I believe you must think me most utterly mad, Watson," said Holmes, after he had exchanged his rough clothes for a dressing-gown, meticulously cleansed himself of dirt and spattered blood, fetched the Persian slipper in which he kept his tobacco, and settled back in his chair. "You have not loosened your grip on that service revolver of yours for the last hour. Your fingers must be cramped by now, you have been clutching it so strongly — Ah," he said, as I opened my mouth to deny this, "no use in your protesting your innocence. Your hand has not strayed from the pocket of your robe for an instant, and the distinctive weight of your pistol is quite clearly evident in it. I may be mad, my dear Watson," he said with a smile, "but I am not blind."

This was the Holmes I knew, and I relaxed. I knew I had nothing to fear from him.

His hand hesitated over his rack of pipes, selected his clay-stemmed pipe, and filled it with shag. "Indeed, Watson, at times during these last months I would not have disputed it with you myself. It would have been a relief to know myself mad, and that all I have seen and conjectured to be merely the delusions of a maniac."

He teased a coal out of the grate and lit his pipe with it. "To begin, then, with the missing corpse." He puffed the pipe until its glow matched that of the fire behind him. "Or, perhaps better," he said, "I should begin with the London cannonade." He raised a finger at my imminent objection. "I have promised to tell all, Watson, and I shall. Pray let me go about it in my own way.

"My brother Mycroft," he continued, "made a most interesting comment when I discussed the matter of the cannonade with him. He mentioned that when a highly-powered cannon is fired, an observer at the front lines ahead of the artillery and distant from the firing will hear a very distinct report at the instant the shell passes. This is the crack of displaced air. This report comes considerably in advance of the actual sound of the cannon firing. If our ears were but sensitive enough to hear it, he informed me, this report would be heard as two distinct waves, one of the air compressed by the shell, and another of the air rushing inward to fill the vacuum left behind it. An aeroship which traversed faster than the velocity of sound would produce a like crack, and, if it were large enough, the two waves would be heard as distinct reports.

"My brother discussed this only as an abstract but interesting fact, but I know him well enough to understand the meaning behind his words.

"Taking this as a provisional theory, then, and judging by the fact that observers noted the timing between the two reports was briefer in the north than in the south of London, we find that the hypothetical aeroship must have been slowing down as it traveled south."

"But Holmes," I said, my mind in total consternation, "an aeroship? And one which moves faster than an artillery shell? No nation on God's Earth could make such a thing, not to mention the impossibility of keeping it secret."

"Precisely," said Holmes. He took another puff from his pipe. "This brings us to the case of the missing corpse. I had been looking for a reason to investigate south of London, and the case presented by the two farm-hands was quite fortuitous in that respect.

"You know my method, Watson. It was unfortunate that the men in the original searching party had in many places quite trampled the tracks that I needed, but in the few places where they could be clearly distinguished, the tracks told a most puzzling story. Some animals had circled the hayrick, leaving tracks like nothing I had ever seen. I could make nothing of the footprints, save that one side was dragging slightly, as if one of the animals were limping. From the depth of the impressions they must have been the size of small dogs. What was most peculiar about the set of tracks was that the animals seemed to march in precision step. The strange thought occurred to me then, that the tracks of a single animal with eight or more legs might leave exactly such impressions. The steps led to the place where the dying man had lain, and circled about. Of outgoing tracks, there were only those of the men who had tended him and those of the searchers.

"I attempted to follow the tracks backward, but could follow back no more than a mile to where they emerged from a sheep meadow and were obliterated by the hoofprints of innumerable sheep. All that I could determine from this was that the animals had been severely panicked at some time in the last few days, running over and around each other and back and forth across the field.

"I turned my attention back to the impressions made by the dying man, and the tracks of the men away from the spot. I inspected the tracks of the unusual animal further. They were extremely strange, and in some ways rather insect-like. The animal's tracks overlaid two of the other tracks, which I knew to be those of the men who had summoned me. Over these tracks, however, were those of a third man.

"I quickly determined these tracks to be those of the dying man himself. After the other two men had left, he had risen up and walked away, apparently carrying the strange animal with him."

"My God, Holmes," I interjected. The revolver lay forgotten in my pocket. "You can't be serious. Are you suggesting some sort of voodoo?"

Holmes smiled. "No, Watson, I am afraid that it was something far more serious than mere superstition.

"The man had crawled on all fours for a few feet, then stood up and walked in a staggering, unbalanced stride. After a few unsteady moments, however, he found his feet and began to walk quickly and purposefully in a straight line. Soon he came to a hard-packed road, where his traces were obliterated by the traffic and I could track his movements no further. His aim, though was quite clearly toward London, and this I took to be his goal."

Listening to his narrative I had completely forgotten the events of the previous night, the slain streetwalkers, and my suspicion of Holmes.

"At this point," Holmes continued, "I knew that I needed to consult an expert. Mr. Wells, of whom I spoke earlier, was that expert, and I could not have asked for a better source. We discussed the possibility of life on other worlds. Mr. Wells offered the opinion that, since there are millions upon millions of suns very much like our own Sun in the sky, that certainly there must be other intelligences, and other civilisations, some of which must be as far beyond ours as our English civilisation is beyond that of the African savage."

"Then you take this strange aeroship to be a vehicle from

another world?" I asked. While I had heard such ideas discussed in popular lectures on astronomy, I had, heretofore, always dismissed these as purest fancy.

"A provisional hypothesis, to be confirmed or forgotten as further data became available. I went on to ask Mr. Wells whether such citizens of other worlds might be human in shape and thought. At this suggestion he was most frankly contemptuous. Such beings would have no more reason to be shaped in our form, he said, than we in that of an octopus or an ant. Likewise they might take no more notice of our civilisation and our morality than we take of the endeavors and ethics of an ant hill.

"This I had already surmised. I turned the talk to biology, and without tipping my hand, managed to steer the conversation to the unusual life-cycles of other species. One in particular he mentioned struck my attention, the life-cycle of the ichneumon, or solitary wasp."

"Really, Holmes. Wasps? I do believe that you are toying with me."

"I wish that I were, my dear doctor. Pray listen; all of this is germane to the subject at hand. The ichneumon wasp has a rather gruesome life-cycle. When the female wasp is ready to lay eggs, it finds and stings a cicada, often one much larger than itself, and then deposits its egg inside the body of the paralyzed but still living insect. This insect then serves as sustenance for the hatching larva, which forms its home within the living insect, having the instinct to avoid eating the essential organs until the very last, when it is ready to exit into the world to lay eggs of its own.

"This was enough for me to frame my provisional hypothesis. I believed that some strange being from the aeroship had not merely met the fatally injured man, but crawled inside his body and taken control of his gross physical function.

"I was struck by one fact. Of all the people that this . . . alien . . . might have met, it was a dying man who he−it−actually chose. Clearly, then, the . . . thing . . . believed itself unable to subdue an uninjured person."

"I must confess, Holmes, if I were asked to prove your sanity, this story would hardly bolster your case."

"Ah, Watson, always the practical man. Permit me." He got out of the leather chair, crossed the room to where he had put down the leather satchel, and laid it on the table in front of me.

I sat paralyzed. "I dare not, Holmes."

"Your courage has never failed you before, my friend."

With a shudder I touched the satchel, and then, steeling myself, opened it. Inside was some object covered in streaks of gore. I didn't want to look, but I knew that I must.

The two eggs inside were of a translucent purplish white, large as a moderate-sized mango, and slick with a film of blood. Within each one a monstrous coiled shape could be discerned. No Earthly animal ever laid such an egg, of this I was sure. More horrible than the eggs was the other thing. I shuddered and looked away. It was something like a giant prawn, and something like some jungle millipede, with dozens of long barbed feelers and multiply-jointed appendages bristling with hooks and spines. Its head, or what passed for a head, had been nearly severed with a knife, and the wound exuded a transparent fluid rather like whale-oil, with a sharp and unpleasant odor similar to kerosene. Instead of a mouth, it had a sucking orifice rimmed with myriad tiny hooked teeth.

"This is what I removed from her body," Holmes said.

I looked up at him. "My God," I whispered. "And she was not dead?"

"You asked that question before. It is a question of definitions, Watson. All that was left alive in her body was the thing that you see. By removing it, did I kill her?"

I shuddered again, and slammed the satchel shut with my eyes averted. "No." I stood for a moment, trying to regain my composure. "But why Whitechapel?"

"What you saw was a juvenile," said Holmes. "The adult would be much larger. I would not know if it is intelligent, or what we call intelligent, but it is at least very clever. Why Whitechapel? Think, Watson. It had eggs and juveniles it must deposit into a living body. But how is it to approach a complete stranger, embrace him—or her—closely enough to? Ah, you see the picture. It was the perfect place for the thing, Watson; the only place where it could do what it needed.

"I studied the East End in minute detail, tracing the path of the mysterious stranger. Again and again I was too late, sometimes only by minutes. I removed the juveniles from the corpses out of necessity. I say corpses, Watson, for although they still walked upright they were already dead. Had I not killed them, they would have gone to cover until they were mature. I could find the one, I knew, only by concentrating on the one trail. Even then it would be a near thing. Two of them, and I were lost."

"Why didn't you go to the police?"

"And tell them what? To start a man-hunt for a thing they can only find by ripping open bodies?"

"But the letters? The ones from 'Jack the Ripper'—did you write these?"

Holmes laughed. "Why should I need to?" he said. "Fakes, forgeries, and cranks, every one. Even I am continuously amazed at how many odd people there are in London. I daresay they came from newspapers hungry to manufacture news, or from pranksters eager at a chance to make fools of Scotland Yard."

"But, what do we do?"

"We, Watson?" Holmes raised an eyebrow.

"Surely you wouldn't think that, now that I know the danger, I would let you continue alone."

"Ah, my good Watson, I would be lost without you. Well, I am hot on its trail. It cannot elude me much longer. We must find it and kill it, Watson. Before it kills again."

By the next morning the whole episode seemed a nightmare, too fantastical to credit. I wondered how I could have believed it. And yet, I had seen it—or had I? Could I have deluded myself into seeing what Holmes had wanted me to see?

No. It was real. I could not afford to doubt my own sanity, and hence I must believe in Holmes's.

In the next few days Holmes went back to his daytime reconnaissance of the East End, mapping the way buildings abutted and how doorways aligned with alleys, like a general planning his campaign, stopping for conversation with workmen and constables alike.

On the third day, my business in town kept me late into the evening. At the end of it, it was almost certain that I had purchased a practice, and at a price which I could afford, but the sealing of the deal required an obligatory toast, and then there were more papers to be inspected and signed, so that all in all, it was well past ten in the evening when I returned to Baker Street.

Of Holmes there was only a note: "I have gone to see the matter to its conclusion. It is better that you are out of it, and I shall think no less of you if you stay. But if you must follow, then look for me near the blind court at Thrawl Street." I read it and swore. He seemed determined to leave me out of this adventure, no matter how dangerous it was for him alone. I snatched my greatcoat and hat from the hall stand, fetched my revolver out from the drawer where it resided, and went out into the night.

It was the night of the great carboniferous fog. The gas-lights were pale yellow glimmers that barely pierced the roiling brown stink. The cab I hailed almost ran me down before seeing me in the street in front of him.

The fog in Whitechapel was even thicker and yellower than that of Baker Street. The cab left me off in front of the Queen's Head pub, the cabbie warning me of the danger of the neighborhood. The blind court was one which was being resurfaced by the MacAdam method, in which the street was covered with liquid tar, and a layer of gravel rolled into the tar surface. The process results in a surface which is even and far easier to repair than cobblestone. I can see the day when all of London will have such smooth quiet streets.

Earlier Holmes had talked with some of the workmen as they rolled the gravel. Now they were long gone. The half-full cauldron of tar was still at the corner of the alley. Although the oil-pot which heated it to boiling had been removed, the cooling drum of tar still gave out quite a bit of heat.

Three unfortunate women had lit a small fire out of wood-scraps and huddled between the warm cauldron and their fire, with their hands toward the tiny fire and their backs against the cauldron for warmth. The glow of the fire gave a luminous orange cast to the surrounding fog. A tiny pile of additional wood scraps stood waiting to keep the fire going for the rest of the night.

Holmes was nowhere in sight.

The women spotted me looking at them, and whispered amongst themselves. One came up to me and attempted a smile. "Care to spend some money and buy a poor unfortunate a drink, dearie?" She tossed her head toward the end of the street where the pub was invisible in the fog, and at the same time flicked her skirt in such a way as to allow me a clear view of her bare ankle.

I averted my eyes. "I'm looking for a friend."

"I could be a friend, if you wanted me to."

"No. I don't need . . . that sort of comfort."

"Oh, sure you do, dearie." She giggled. "All men do. 'Sides, I h'aint even got money for me doss. Surely a fine gent like yourself has a shilling to spend on a poor lady down on 'er luck, hasn't he? Sure 'e does."

I looked at her more closely, and she preened for my inspection. She might have been a rather pretty woman, striking if not actually beautiful, if she had been given the chance. Instead I saw the lines on her face, the threadbare bonnet she wore, and the unmistakable signs of the early stages of consumption. Such a woman should be resting in bed, not out standing in the chill of a night such as this. I was about to speak to her, to invite her into the public house for the drink she requested, for no other reason than to get her out of the chill and away, perhaps, from the monster that stalked the fog-shrouded night. I could wait for Holmes as well in the pub as in the street.

As I was about to speak, I heard a man approach from the blind end of the court, although I had seen no one there previously. I started to call out, thinking it must be Holmes, but then saw that, while the man was quite as tall as Holmes, he was much bulkier, with a considerable paunch and ill-fitting clothes. As he passed, another of the woman smiled at him and called a greeting. He nodded at her. As she put out her arm for him to take, he dropped his hand to the buttons of his trousers. I looked away in disgust, and as I did so the woman who had spoken to me slipped her arm around mine.

I had lost track of the third woman, and was as surprised as the others when her voice rang out from behind. "Stop, fiend!"

The voice was calm and authoritative. I looked up. The woman was holding a revolver — Holmes's hair-trigger revolver — in an unwavering grip aimed at the man's head. I looked closely at her face and saw, beneath the makeup, the thin, hawk-like nose and the unmistakable intense gaze of Sherlock Holmes.

The other man swiveled with surprising speed and sprang at Holmes. I pulled my hand loose from my lady companion and in an instant snatched my revolver free of my pocket and fired. Our two shots rang out at almost the same instant, and the man staggered and fell back. The two bullets had both hit above the left eye, and taken away the left half of the cranium.

The women screamed.

The man, with half his head missing, reached out a hand and pulled himself to his feet. He came at Holmes again.

I fired. This time my bullet removed what was left of his head. His jutting windpipe sucked at the air with a low sputtering hiss, and in the gaping neck I thought I saw purplish-white tendrils feeling about. The shot slowed him down for no more than an instant.

Holmes's shot took him in the middle of the chest. I saw the crimson spot appear and saw him rock from the impact, but it seemed to have no other effect.

We both fired together, this time lower, aiming for the horror hidden somewhere within the body. The two shots spun the headless thing around. He careened against the cauldron of tar, slipped, and fell down, knocking the cauldron over.

In an instant Holmes was upon him.

"Holmes, no!"

For a moment Holmes had the advantage. He pushed the monster forward, into the spreading pool of tar, struggling for a hold. Then the monster rose, dripping tar, and threw Holmes off his back with no more concern than a horse tossing a wayward circus monkey. The monster turned for him.

Holmes reached behind him and grabbed a brand out of the fire. As the monster grabbed him he thrust it forward, into the thing's chest.

The tar ignited with an awful whoosh. The thing clawed at its chest with both hands. Holmes grabbed the cauldron, and with one mighty heave poured the remainder of the tar onto the gaping wound where its head had once been.

Holmes drew back as the flames licked skyward. The thing reeled and staggered in a horrible parody of drunkenness. As the clothes burned away, we could see that where a man's generative organs would have been was a pulsing, wickedly barbed ovipositor with a knife-sharp end writing blindly in the flames. As we watched it bulged and contracted, and an egg, slick and purple, oozed forth.

The monster tottered, fell over on its back, and then, slowly, the abdomen split open.

"Quickly, Watson! Here!"

Holmes shoved one of the pieces of firewood into my hands, and took another himself. We stationed ourselves at either side of the body.

The horrors which emerged were somewhat like enormous lobsters, or some vermin even more loathsome and articulated. We bludgeoned them as they emerged from the burning body, trying as we could to avoid the oily slime of them from splattering onto our clothes, trying to avoid breathing the awful stench that arose from the smoking carcass. They were tenacious in the extreme, and I think that only the disorientation of the fire and the suddenness of our attack saved our lives. In the end six of the monstrosities crawled out of the body, and six of the monstrosities we killed.

There was nothing remotely human left in the empty shell that had once been a man. Holmes pulled away his skirts and petticoat to feed the fire. The greasy blood of the monstrosities burned with a clear, hot flame, until all that remained were smoldering rags with a few pieces of unidentifiable meat and charred scraps of bone.

It seemed impossible that our shots and the sounds of our struggle had not brought a hundred citizens with constables out to see what had happened, but the narrow streets so distorted the sounds that it was impossible to tell where they had originated, and the thick blanket of fog muffled everything as well as hiding us from curious eyes.

Holmes and I left the two daughters of joy with what money we had, save for the price of a ride back to Baker Street. This we did, not with an eye toward their silence, as we knew that they would never go to the police with their story, but in the hopes—perhaps foolish—that they might have a respite from their hard trade and a warm roof over their heads during the damp and chill months of winter.

It has been two months now, and the Whitechapel killings have not resumed. Holmes is, as always, calm and unflappable, but I find myself unable to look at a wasp now without having a feeling of horror steal across me.

There are as many questions unanswered as answered. Holmes has offered the opinion that the landing was unintentional, a result of some unimaginable accident in the depths of space, and not the vanguard of some impending colonization. He bases this conclusion on the fact of the ill-preparedness and hasty improvisation of the being, relying on luck and circumstance rather than planning.

I think that the answers to most of our questions will never be known, but I believe that we have succeeded in stopping the horrors, this time. I can only hope that this was an isolated ship, blown off-course and stranded far from the expected shores in some unexpected tempest of infinite space. I look at the stars now, and shudder. What else might be out there, waiting for us?

Winter Fire

I AM NOTHING AND NOBODY; ATOMS THAT HAVE learned to look at themselves; dirt that has learned to see the awe and the majesty of the universe.

The day the hover-transports arrived in the refugee camps, huge windowless shells of titanium floating on electrostatic cushions, the day faceless men took the ragged little girl that was me away from the narrow, blasted valley that had once been Salzburg to begin a new life on another continent: that is the true beginning of my life. What came before then is almost irrelevant, a sequence of memories etched as with acid into my brain, but with no meaning to real life.

Sometimes I almost think that I can remember my parents. I remember them not by what was, but by the shape of the absence they left behind. I remember yearning for my mother's voice, singing to me softly in Japanese. I cannot remember her voice, or what songs she might have sung, but I remember so vividly the missing of it, the hole that she left behind.

My father I remember as the loss of something large and warm and infinitely strong, prickly and smelling of—of what? I don't remember. Again, it is the loss that remains in my memory, not the man. I remember remembering him as more solid than mountains, something eternal; but in the end he was not eternal, he was not even as strong as a very small war.

I lived in the city of music, in Salzburg, but I remember little from before the siege. I do remember cafés (seen from below, with huge tables and the legs of waiters and faces looming down to ask me if I would like a sweet.) I'm sure my parents must have been there, but that I do not remember.

And I remember music. I had my little violin (although it seemed so large to me then), and music was not my second language but my first. I thought in music before ever I learned words. Even now, decades later, when I forget myself in mathematics I cease to think in words, but think directly in concepts clear and perfectly harmonic, so that a mathematical proof is no more than the inevitable majesty of a crescendo leading to a final, resolving chord.

I have long since forgotten anything I knew about the violin. I have not played since the day, when I was nine, I took from the rubble of our apartment the shattered cherry-wood scroll. I kept that meaningless piece of polished wood for years, slept with it clutched in my hand every night until, much later, it was taken away by a soldier intent on rape. Probably I would have let him, had he not been so ignorant as to think my one meager possession might be a weapon. Coitus is nothing more than the natural act of the animal. From songbirds to porpoises, any male animal will rape an available female when given a chance. The action is of no significance except, perhaps, as a chance to contemplate the impersonal majesty of the chain of life and the meaninglessness of any individual's will within it.

When I was finally taken away from the city of music, three years later and a century older, I owned nothing and wanted nothing. There was nothing of the city left. As the hoverjet took me away, just one more in a seemingly endless line of ragged survivors, only the mountains remained, hardly scarred by the bomb craters and the detritus that marked where the castle had stood, mountains looking down on humanity with the gaze of eternity.

My real parents, I have been told, were rousted out of our apartment with a tossed stick of dynamite, and shot as infidels as they ran through the door, on the very first night of the war. It was probably fanatics of the New Orthodox Resurgence that did it, in their first round of ethnic cleansing, although nobody seemed to know for sure.

In the beginning, despite the dissolution of Austria and the fall of the federation of free European states, despite the hate-talk spread by the disciples of Dragan Vukadinovic, the violent cleansing of the Orthodox church, and the rising of the Pan-Slavic unity movement, all the events that covered the news-nets all through 2108, few people believed there would be a war, and those that did thought that it might last a few months. The dissolution of Austria and Eastern Europe into a federation of free states was viewed by intellectuals of the time as a good thing, a recognition of the impending irrelevance of governments in the post-technological society with its burgeoning sky-cities and prospering free-trade zones. Everyone talked of civil war, but as a distant thing; it was an awful mythical monster of ancient times, one that had been thought dead, a thing that ate people's hearts and turned them into inhuman gargoyles of stone. It would not come here.

Salzburg had had a large population of Asians, once themselves refugees from the economic and political turmoil of the twenty-first century, but now prosperous citizens who had lived in the city for over a century. Nobody thought about religion in the Salzburg of that lost age; nobody cared that a person whose family once came from the orient might be a Buddhist or a Hindu or a Confucian. My own family, as far as I know, had no religious feelings at all, but that made little difference to the fanatics. My mother, suspecting possible trouble that night, had sent me over to sleep with an old German couple who lived in a building next door. I don't remember whether I said good-bye.

Johann Achtenberg became my foster father, a stocky old man, bearded and forever smelling of cigar-smoke. "We will stay," my foster father would often say, over and over. "It is our city; the barbarians cannot drive us out." Later in the siege, in a grimmer mood, he might add, "They can kill us, but they will never drive us out."

The next few months were full of turmoil, as the Orthodox Resurgence tried, and failed, to take Salzburg. They were still disorganized, more a mob than an army, still evolving toward the killing machine that they would eventually become. Eventually they were driven out of the city, dynamiting buildings behind them, to join up with the Pan-Slavic army rolling in from the devastation of Graz. The roads in and out of the city were barricaded, and the siege began.

For that summer of 2109, the first summer of the siege, the life of the city hardly changed. I was ten years old. There was still electricity, and water, and stocks of food. The cafés stayed open, although coffee became hard to obtain, and impossibly expensive when it was available, and at times they had nothing to serve but water. I would watch the pretty girls, dressed in colorful Italian suede and wearing ornately carved Ladakhi jewelry, strolling down the streets in the evenings, stopping to chat with T-shirted boys, and I would wonder if I would ever grow up to be as elegant and poised as they. The shelling was still mostly far away, and everybody believed that the tide of world opinion would soon stop the war. The occasional shell that was targeted toward the city caused great commotion, people screaming and diving under tables even for a bird that hit many blocks away. Later, when civilians had become targets, we all learned to tell the caliber and the trajectory of a shell by the sound of the song it made as it fell.

After an explosion there is silence for an instant, then a hubbub of crashing glass and debris as shattered walls collapse, and people gingerly touch each other, just to verify that they are alive. The dust would hang in the air for hours.

Toward September, when it became obvious that the world powers were stalemated, and would not intervene, the shelling of the city began in earnest. Tanks, even modern ones with electrostatic hover and thin coilguns instead of heavy cannons, could not maneuver into the narrow alleys of the old city and were stymied by the steep-sided mountain valleys. But the outer suburbs and the hilltops were invaded, crushed flat, and left abandoned.

I did not realize it at the time, for a child sees little, but with antiquated equipment and patched-together artillery, my besieged city clumsily and painfully fought back. For every fifty shells that came in, one was fired back at the attackers.

There was an international blockade against selling weapons to the Resurgence, but that seemed to make no difference. Their weapons may not have had the most modern of technology, but they were far better than ours. They had superconducting coilguns for artillery, weapons that fired aerodynamically-shaped slugs — we called them birds — that maneuvered on twisted arcs as they moved. The birds were small, barely larger than my hand, but the metastable atomic hydrogen that filled them held an incredible amount of explosive power.

Our defenders had to rely on ancient weapons, guns that ignited chemical explosives to propel metal shells. These were quickly disassembled and removed from their position after each shot, because the enemy's computers could backtrail the trajectory of our shells, which had only crude aeromaneuvering, to direct a deadly rain of birds at the guessed position. Since we were cut off from regular supply lines, each shell was precious. We were supplied by ammunition carried on mules whose trails would weave through the enemy's wooded territory by night and by shells carried one by one across dangerous territory in backpacks.

But still, miraculously, the city held. Over our heads the continuous shower of steel eroded the skyline. Our beautiful castle Hohensalzburg was sandpapered to a hill of bare rock; the cathedral towers fell and the debris by slow degrees was pounded into gravel. Bells rang in sympathy with explosions until at last the bells were silenced. Slowly, erosion softened the profiles of buildings that once defined the city's horizon.

Even without looking for the craters, we learned to tell from looking at the trees which neighborhoods had had explosions in them. Near a blast, the city's trees had no leaves. They were all shaken off by the shock waves. But none of the trees lasted the winter anyway.

My foster father made a stove by pounding with a hammer on the fenders and door panels of a wrecked automobile, with a pipe made of copper from rooftops and innumerable soft-drink cans. Floorboards and furniture were broken to bits to make fuel for us to keep warm. All through the city, stovepipes suddenly bristled through exterior walls and through windows. The fiber-glass sides of modern housing blocks, never designed for such crude heating, became decorated with black smoke trails like unreadable graffiti, and the city parks became weirdly empty lots crossed by winding sidewalks that meandered past the craters where the trees had been.

Johann's wife, my foster mother, a thin, quiet woman, died by being in the wrong building at the wrong time. She had been visiting a friend across the city to exchange chat and a pinch of hoarded tea. It might just as easily have been the building I was in where the bird decided to build its deadly nest. It took some of the solidity out of Johann. "Do not fall in love, little Leah," he told me, many months later, when our lives had returned to a fragile stability. "It hurts too much."

In addition to the nearly full-time job of bargaining for those necessities that could be bargained for, substituting or improvising those that could not, and hamstering away in basements and shelters any storable food that could be found, my foster father

Johann had another job, or perhaps an obsession. I only learned this slowly. He would disappear, sometimes for days. One time I followed him as far as an entrance to the ancient catacombs beneath the bird-pecked ruins of the beautiful castle Hohensalzburg. When he disappeared into the darkness, I dared not follow.

When he returned, I asked him about it. He was strangely reluctant to speak. When he did, he did not explain, but only said that he was working on the molecular still, and refused to say anything further, or to let me mention it to anyone else.

As a child I spoke a hodgepodge of languages; the English of the foreigners, the French of the European Union, the Japanese that my parents had spoken at home, the book-German of the schools and the Austrian German that was the dominant tongue of the culture I lived in. At home we spoke mostly German, and in German, "Still" is a word which means quietude. Over the weeks and months that followed, the idea of a molecular still grew in my imagination into a wonderful thing, a place that is quiet even on the molecular level, far different from the booming sounds of war. In my imagination, knowing my foster father was a gentle man who wanted nothing but peace, I thought of it as a reverse secret weapon, something that would bring this wonderful stillness to the world. When he disappeared to the wonderful molecular still, each time I would wonder whether this would be the time that the still would be ready, and peace would come.

And the city held. "Salzburg is an idea, little Leah," my foster father Johann would tell me, "and all the birds in the world could never peck it away, for it lives in our minds and in our souls. Salzburg will stand for as long as any one of us lives. And, if we ever abandon the city, then Salzburg has fallen, even if the city itself still stands."

In the outside world, the world I knew nothing of, nations quarreled and were stalemated with indecision over what to do. Our city had been fragilely connected to the western half of Europe by precarious roads, with a series of tunnels through the Alps and long arcing bridges across narrow mountain valleys. In their terror that the chaos might spread westward, they dynamited the bridges, they collapsed the tunnels. Not nations, but individuals did it. They cut us off from civilization, and left us to survive, or die, on our own.

Governments had become increasingly unimportant in the era following the opening of the resources of space by the free-trade zones of the new prosperity, but the trading consortia that now ruled America and the Far East in the place of governments had gained their influence only by assiduously signing away the capacity to make war, and although the covenants that had secured their formation had eroded, that one prohibition still held. Only governments could help us, and the governments tried negotiation and diplomacy as Dragan Vukadinovic made promises for the New Orthodox Resurgence and broke them.

High above, the owners of the sky-cities did the only thing that they could, which was to deny access to space to either side. This kept the war to the ground, but hurt us more than it hurt the armies surrounding us. They, after all, had no need for satellites to find out where we were.

To the east, the Pan-Slavic army and the New Orthodox Resurgence were pounding against the rock of the Tenth Crusade; further south they were skirmishing over borders with the Islamic Federation. Occasionally the shelling would stop for a while, and it would be safe to bring hoarded solar panels out into the sunlight to charge our batteries—the electric grid had gone long ago, of course—and huddle around an antique solar-powered television set watching the distant negotiating teams talk about our fate. Everybody knew that the war would be over shortly; it was impossible that the world would not act.

The world did not act.

I remember taking batteries from wrecked cars to use a headlight, if one happened to survive unbroken, or a taillight, to allow us to stay up past sunset. There was a concoction of boiled leaves that we called "tea," although we had no milk or sugar to put in it. We would sit together, enjoying the miracle of light, sipping our "tea," perhaps reading, perhaps just sitting in silence.

With the destruction of the bridges, Salzburg had become two cities, connected only by narrow-beam microwave radio and the occasional foray by individuals walking across the dangerous series of beams stretched across the rubble of the Old Stone Bridge. The two Salzburgs were distinct in population, with mostly immigrant populations isolated in the modern buildings on the east side of the river, and the old Austrians on the west.

It is impossible to describe the Salzburg feeling, the aura of a sophisticated ancient city, wrapped in a glisteningly pure blanket of snow, under siege, faced with the daily onslaught of an unseen army that seemed to have an unlimited supply of coilguns and metastable hydrogen. We were never out of range. The Salzburg stride was relaxed only when protected by the cover of buildings or specially constructed barricades, breaking into a jagged sprint over a stretch of open ground, a cobbled forecourt of crossroads open to the rifles of snipers on distant hills firing hypersonic needles randomly into the city. From the deadly steel birds, there was no protection. They could fly in anywhere, with no warning. By the time you heard their high-pitched song, you were already dead, or, miraculously, still alive.

Not even the nights were still. It is an incredible sight to see a city cloaked in darkness suddenly illuminate with the blue dawn of a flare sent up from the hilltops, dimming the stars and suffusing coruscating light across the glittering snow. There is a curious, ominous interval of quiet: the buildings of the city dragged blinking out of their darkness and displayed in a fairy glow, naked before the invisible gunners on their distant hilltops. Within thirty seconds, the birds would begin to sing. They might land a good few blocks away, the echo of their demise ringing up and down the valley, or they might land in the street below, the explosion sending people diving under tables, windows caving in across the room.

They could, I believe, have destroyed the city at any time, but that did not serve their purposes. Salzburg was a prize. Whether the buildings were whole or in parts seemed irrelevant, but the city was not to be simply obliterated.

In April, as buds started to bloom from beneath the rubble, the city woke up, and we discovered that we had survived the winter. The diplomats proposed partitioning the city between the Slavs and the Germans—Asians and other ethnic groups, like me, being conveniently ignored—and the terms were set, but nothing came of it except a cease-fire that was violated before the day was over.

The second summer of the siege was a summer of hope. Every week we thought that this might be the last week of the siege; that peace might yet be declared on terms that we could accept, that would let us keep our city. The defense of the city had opened a corridor to the outside world, allowing in humanitarian aid, black-market goods, and refugees from other parts of the war. Some of the people who had fled before the siege returned, although many of the population who had survived the winter used the opportunity to flee to the west. My foster father, though, swore that he would stay in Salzburg until death. It is civilization, and if it is destroyed, nothing is worthwhile.

Christians of the Tenth Crusade and Turks of the Islamic Federation fought side by side with the official troops of the Mayor's Brigade, sharing ammunition but not command, to defend the city. High above, cities in the sky looked down on us, but, like angels who see everything, they did nothing.

Cafés opened again, even those without black-market connections that could only serve water, and in the evenings there were nightclubs, the music booming even louder than the distant gunfire. My foster father, of course, would never let me stay up late enough to find out what went on in these, but once, when he was away tending his molecular still, I waited for darkness and then crept through the streets to see.

One bar was entirely Islamic Federation Turks, wearing green turbans and uniforms of dark maroon denim, with spindly railgun-launchers slung across their backs and knives and swords strung on leather straps across their bodies. Each one had in front of him a tiny cup of dark coffee and a clear glass of whiskey. I though I was invisible in the doorway, but one of the Turks, a tall man with a pocked face and a dark mustache that drooped down the side of his mouth, looked up, and, without smiling, said, "Hoy, little girl, I think that you are in the wrong place."

In the next club, mercenaries wearing cowboy hats, with black uniforms and fingerless leather gloves, had parked their guns against the walls before settling in to pound down whiskey in a bar where the music was so loud that the beat reverberated across half the city. The one closest to the door had a shaven head, with a spider web tattooed up his neck, and daggers and weird heraldic symbols tattooed across his arms. When he looked up at me, standing in the doorway, he smiled, and I realized that he had been watching me for some time, probably ever since I had appeared. His smile was far more frightening than the impassive face of the Turk. I ran all the way home.

In the daytime, the snap of a sniper's rifle might prompt an exchange of heavy machine-gun fire, a wild, rattling sound that echoed crazily from the hills. Small-arms fire would sound, tak, tak, tak, answered by the singing of small railguns, tee, tee. You can't tell the source of rifle fire in an urban environment; it seems to come from all around. All you can do is duck, and run. Later that summer the first of the omniblasters showed up, firing a beam of pure energy with a silence so loud that tiny hairs all over my body would stand up in fright.

Cosmetics, baby milk, and whiskey were the most prized commodities on the black market. I had no idea what the war was about. Nobody was able to explain it in terms that an eleven-year-old could understand; few even bothered to try. All I knew was that evil people on hilltops were trying to destroy everything I loved, and good men like my foster father were trying to stop them.

I slowly learned that my foster father was, apparently, quite important to the defense. He never talked about what he did, but I overheard other men refer to him with terms like "vital" and "indispensable," and these words made me proud. At first I simply thought that they merely meant that the existence of men like him, proud of the city and vowing never to leave, were the core of what made the defense worthwhile. But later I realized that it must be more than this. There were thousands of men who loved the city.

Toward the end of the summer the siege closed around the city again. The army of the Tenth Crusade arrived and took over the ridgetops just one valley to the west; the Pan-Slavic army and the Orthodox Resurgence held the ridges next to the city and the territory to the east. All that autumn the shells of the Tenth Crusade arced over our heads toward the Pan-Slavs, and beams of purple fire from pop-up robots with omniblasters would fire back. It was a good autumn; mostly only stray fire hit the civilians. But we were locked in place, and there was no way out.

There was no place to go outside; no place that was safe. The sky had become our enemy. My friends were books. I had loved storybooks when I had been younger, in the part of my childhood before the siege that even then I barely remembered. But Johann had no story books; his vast collection of books were all forbidding things, full of thick blocks of dense text and incomprehensible diagrams that were no picture of anything I could recognize. I taught myself algebra, with some help from Johann, and started working on calculus. It was easier when I realized that the mathematics in the books was just an odd form of music, written in a strange language. Candles were precious, and so in order to keep on reading at night, Johann made an oil lamp for me, which would burn vegetable oil. This was nearly as precious as candles, but not so precious as my need to read.

A still, I had learned from my reading—and from the black market—was a device for making alcohol, or at least for separating alcohol from water. Did a molecular still make molecules?

"That's silly," Johann told me. "Everything is made of molecules. Your bed, the air you breathe, even you yourself, nothing but molecules."

In November, the zoo's last stubborn elephant died. The predators, the lions, the tigers, even the wolves, were already gone, felled by simple lack of meat. The zebras and antelopes had gone quickly, some from starvation-induced illness, some killed and butchered by poachers. The elephant, surprisingly, had been the last to go, a skeletal apparition stubbornly surviving on scraps of grass and bits of trash, protected against ravenous poachers by a continuous guard of armed watchmen. The watchmen proved unable, however, to guard against starvation. Some people claim that kangaroos and emus still survived, freed from their hutches by the shelling, and could be seen wandering free in the city late at night. Sometimes I wonder if they survive still, awkward birds and bounding marsupials, hiding in the foothills of the Austrian Alps, the last survivors of the siege of Salzburg.

It was a hard winter. We learned to conserve the slightest bit of heat, so as to stretch a few sticks of firewood out over a whole night. Typhus, dysentery, and pneumonia killed more than the shelling, which had resumed in force with the onset of winter. Just after New Year, a fever attacked me, and there was no medicine to be had at any price. Johann wrapped me in blankets and fed me hot water mixed with salt and a pinch of precious sugar. I shivered and burned, hallucinating strange things, now seeing kangaroos and emus outside my little room, now imagining myself on the surface of Mars, strangling in the thin air, and then instantly on Venus, choking in heat and darkness, and then floating in interstellar space, my body growing alternately larger than galaxies, then smaller than atoms, floating so far away from anything else that it would take eons for any signal from me to ever reach the world where I had been born.

Eventually the fever broke, and I was merely back in my room, shivering with cold, wrapped in sheets that were stinking with sweat, in a city slowly being pounded into rubble by distant soldiers whose faces I had never seen, fighting for an ideology that I could never understand.

It was after this, at my constant pleading, that Johann finally took me to see his molecular still. It was a dangerous walk across the city, illuminated by the glow of the Marionette Theater, set afire by incendiary bombs two days before. The still was hidden below the city, farther down even than the bomb shelters, in catacombs that had been carved out of rock over two thousand years ago. There were two men there, a man my foster father's age with a white mustache, and an even older Vietnamese-German man with one leg, who said nothing the whole time.

The first man looked at me and said in French, which perhaps he thought I wouldn't understand, "This is no place to bring a little one."

Johann replied in German. "She asks many questions." He shrugged, and said, "I wanted to show her."

The other said, still in French, "She couldn't understand." Right then I resolved that I would make myself understand, whatever it was that they thought I could not. The man looked at me critically, taking in, no doubt, my straight black hair and almond eyes. "She's not yours, anyway. What is she to you?"

"She is my daughter," Johann said.

The molecular still was nothing to look at. It was a room filled with curtains of black velvet, doubled back and forth, thousands and thousands of meters of blackness. "Here it is," Johann said. "Look well, little Leah, for in all the world, you will never see such another."

Somewhere there was a fan that pushed air past the curtains; I could feel it on my face, cool, damp air moving sluggishly past. The floor of the room was covered with white dust, glistening in the darkness. I reached down to touch it, and Johann reached out to still my hand. "Not to touch," he said.

"What is it," I asked in wonder.

"Can't you smell it?"

And I could smell it, in fact, I had been nearly holding my breath to avoid smelling it. The smell was thick, pungent, almost choking. It made my eyes water. "Ammonia," I said.

Johann nodded, smiling. His eyes were bright. "Ammonium nitrate," he said.

I was silent most of the way back to the fortified basement we shared with two other families. There must have been bombs, for there were always the birds, but I do not recall them. At last, just before we came to the river, I asked, "Why?"

"Oh, my little Leah, think. We are cut off here. Do we have electrical generators to run coilguns like the barbarians that surround us? We do not. What can we do, how can we defend ourselves? The molecular still sorts molecules out of the air. Nitrogen, oxygen, water; this is all that is needed to make explosives, if only we can combine them correctly. My molecular still takes the nitrogen out of the air, makes out of it ammonium nitrate, which we use to fire our cannons, to hold the barbarians away from our city."

I thought about this. I knew about molecules by then, knew about nitrogen and oxygen, although not about explosives. Finally something occurred to me, and I asked, "But what about the energy? Where does the energy come from?"

Johann smiled, his face almost glowing with delight. "Ah, my little Leah, you know the right questions already. Yes, the energy. We have designed our still to work by using a series of reactions, each one using no more than a gnat's whisker of energy. Nevertheless, you are right, we must needs steal energy from somewhere. We draw the thermal energy out of the air. But old man entropy, he cannot be cheated so easily. To do this we need a heat sink."

I didn't know then enough to follow his words, so I merely repeated his words dumbly: "A heat sink?"

He waved his arm, encompassing the river, flowing dark beneath a thin sheet of ice. "And what a heat sink! The barbarians know we are manufacturing arms; we fire the proof of that back at them every day, but they do not know where! And here it is, right before them, the motive power for the greatest arms factory of all of Austria, and they cannot see it."

Molecular still or not, the siege went on. The Pan-Slavics drove back the Tenth Crusade, and resumed their attack on the city. In February the armies entered the city twice, and twice the ragged defenders drove them back. In April, once more, the flowers bloomed, and once more, we had survived another winter.

It had been months since I had had a bath; there was no heat to waste on mere water, and in any case, there was no soap. Now, at last, we could wash, in water drawn directly from the Salzach, scrubbing and digging to get rid of the lice of winter.

We stood in line for hours waiting for a day's ration of macaroni, the humanitarian aid that had been air-dropped into the city, and hauled enormous drums across the city to replenish our stockpile of drinking water.

Summer rain fell, and we hoarded the water from rain gutters for later use. All that summer the smell of charred stone hung in the air. Bullet-riddled cars, glittering shards of glass, and fragments of concrete and cobblestone covered the streets. Stone heads and gargoyles from blasted buildings would look up at you from odd corners of the city.

Basements and tunnels under the city were filled out with

mattresses and camp beds as makeshift living quarters for refugees, which became sweaty and smelly during summer, for all that they had been icy cold in winter. Above us, the ground would shake as the birds flew in, and plaster dust fell from the ceiling.

I was growing up. I had read about sex, and knew it was a natural part of the pattern of life, the urging of chromosomes to divide and conquer the world. I tried to imagine it with everybody I saw, from Johann to passing soldiers, but couldn't ever make my imagination actually believe in it. There was enough sex going on around me — we were packed together tightly, and humans under stress copulate out of desperation, out of boredom, and out of pure instinct to survive. There was enough to see, but I couldn't apply anything of what I saw to myself.

I think, when I was very young, I had some belief that human beings were special, something more than just meat that thought. The siege, an unrelenting tutor, taught me otherwise. A woman I had been with on one day, cuddled in her lap and talking nonsense, the next day was out in the street, bisected by shrapnel, reduced to a lesson in anatomy. If there was a soul it was something intangible, something so fragile that it could not stand up to the gentlest kiss of steel.

People stayed alive by eating leaves, acorns, and, when the humanitarian aid from the sky failed, by grinding down the hard centers of corncobs to make cakes with the powder.

There were developments in the war, although I did not know them. The Pan-Slavic Army, flying their standard of a two-headed dragon, turned against the triple cross of the New Orthodox Resurgence, and to the east thousands of square kilometers of pacified countryside turned in a day into flaming ruin, as the former allies savaged each other. We could see the smoke in the distance, a huge pillar of black rising kilometers into the sky.

It made no difference to the siege. On the hilltops the Pan-Slavic Army drove off the New Orthodox Resurgence, and when they were done, the guns turned back on the city. By the autumn the siege had not lifted, and we knew we would have to face another winter.

Far over our heads, through the ever-present smoke we could see the lights of freedom, the glimmering of distant cities in the sky, remote from all of the trouble of Earth. "They have no culture," Johann said. "They have power, yes, but they have no souls, or they would be helping us. Aluminum and rock, what do they have? Life, and nothing else. When they have another thousand years, they will still not have a third of the reality of our city. Freedom, hah. Why don't they help us, eh?"

The winter was slow frozen starvation. One by one, the artillery pieces that defended our city failed, for we no longer had the machine shops to keep them in repair, nor the tools to make shells. One by one the vicious birds fired from distant hilltops found the homes of our guns and ripped them apart. By the middle of February we were undefended.

And the birds continued to fall.

Sometimes I accompanied Johann to the molecular still. Over the long months of siege they had modified it so that it now distilled from air and water not merely nitrate, but finished explosive ready for the guns, tons per hour. But what good was it now, when there were no guns left for it to feed? Of the eight men who had given it birth, only two still survived to tend it, old one-legged Nguyen, and Johann.

One day Nguyen stopped coming. The place he lived had been hit, or he had been struck in transit. There was no way I would ever find out.

There was nothing left of the city to defend, and almost nobody able to defend it. Even those who were willing were starved too weak to hold a weapon.

All through February, all through March, the shelling continued, despite the lack of return fire from the city. They must have known that the resistance was over. Perhaps, Johann said, they had forgotten that there was a city here at all, they were shelling the city now for no other reason than that it had become a habit. Perhaps they were shelling us as a punishment for having dared to defy them.

Through April, the shelling continued. There was no food, no heat, no clean water, no medicine to treat the wounded.

When Johann died it took me four hours to remove the rubble from his body, pulling stones away as birds falling around me demolished a building standing a block to the east, another two blocks north. I was surprised at how light he was, little more than a feather pillow. There was no place to bury him; the graveyards were all full. I placed him back where he had lain, crossed his hands, and left him buried in the rubble of the basement where we had spent our lives entwined.

I moved to a new shelter, a tunnel cut out of the solid rock below the Mönchsberg, an artificial cavern where a hundred families huddled in the dark, waiting for an end to existence. It

had once been a parking garage. The moisture from three hundred lungs condensed on the stone ceiling and dripped down on
us.

At last, at the end of April, the shelling stopped. For a day
there was quiet, and then the victorious army came in. There
were no alleys to baffle their tanks now. They came dressed in
plastic armor, faceless soldiers with railguns and omniblasters
thrown casually across their backs; they came flying the awful
standard of the Pan-Slavic Army, the two-headed dragon on a field
of blue crosses. One of them must have been Dragan Vukadinovic, Dragan the Cleanser, the Scorpion of Bratislava, but in their
armor I could not know which one. With them were the diplomats, explaining to all who would listen that peace had been nego-
tiated, the war was over, and our part of it was that we would
agree to leave our city and move into camps to be resettled elsewhere.

Would the victors write the history, I wondered? What would
they say, to justify their deeds? Or would they, too, be left behind
by history, a minor faction in a minor event forgotten against the
drama of a destiny working itself out far away?

It was a living tide of ragged humans that met them, dragging
the crippled and wounded on improvised sledges. I found it hard
to believe that there could be so many left. Nobody noticed a dirty
twelve-year-old girl, small for her age, slip away. Or if they did
notice, where could she go?

The molecular still was still running. The darkness, the smell
of it, hidden beneath a ruined, deserted Salzburg, was a comfort
to me. It alone had been steadfast. In the end the humans who
tended it had turned out to be too fragile, but it had run on, alone
in the dark, producing explosives that nobody would ever use, filling the caverns and the dungeons beneath a castle that had once
been the proud symbol of a proud city. Filling it by the ton, by
the thousands of tons, perhaps even tens of thousands of tons.

I brought with me an alarm clock, and a battery, and I sat for
a long time in the dark, remembering the city.

And in the darkness, I could not bring myself to become the
angel of destruction, to call down the cleansing fire I had so
dreamed of seeing brought upon my enemies. In order to survive
you must become tough, Johann had once told me; you must
become hard. But I could not become hard enough. I could not
become like them.

And so I destroyed the molecular still, and fed the pieces into the Salzach. For all its beauty and power it was fragile, and when I was done there was nothing left by which someone could reconstruct it, or even understand what it had been. I left the alarm clock and the battery, and ten thousand tons of explosive, behind in the catacombs.

Perhaps they are there still.

It was, I am told, the most beautiful, the most civilized city in the world. The many people who told me that are all dead now, and I remember it only through the eyes of a child, looking up from below and understanding little.

Nothing of that little girl remains. Like my civilization, I have remade myself anew. I live in a world of peace, a world of mathematics and sky-cities, the opening of the new renaissance. But, like the first renaissance, this one was birthed in fire and war.

I will never tell this to anybody. To people who were not there, the story is only words, and they could never understand. And to those who *were* there, we who lived through the long siege of Salzburg and somehow came out alive, there is no need to speak.

In a very long lifetime, we could never forget.

Afterword: About the Stories

I ALWAYS FIND IT HARD TO TALK ABOUT MY OWN stories. A story ought to speak for itself, and if there's anything to say, it should be said in the story. I suppose that this is rather contrary of me, since I love to read what other authors have to say about their own stories (in fact, for some authors I like the comments they write about the stories better than I like the stories themselves). But when asked about my own stories, I can never think of anything to say.

Still, if I can't talk about the stories themselves, I can talk about how I came to write the story, and where I was, and some of the science ideas in it.

* * *

"A Walk in the Sun." When I started working for NASA, I worked in a scientific group that did research on solar arrays for spacecraft. Now, solar arrays are critical to almost all space missions, but they have never been particularly important to science fiction stories. One of the things that I worked on was a study of what energy-storage technologies might keep a solar-powered lunar base operating over the 354-hour lunar night. I published this as a scientific paper in 1989 ["Solar Power for the Lunar Night," in *Space Manufacturing 7: Space Resources to Improve Life on Earth,* AIAA, 1989], and shortly afterwards it occurred to me that there might be a story there somewhere.

"A Walk in the Sun" won the Hugo for best story at Magicon, the 50th World Science Fiction Convention, and I was in a daze for a week afterwards.

"A Walk in the Sun" is a story that contains a hidden homework problem for the mathematically inclined. Every now and then a reader asks the question: why not go to the north (or south) pole?

Like the Earth, the pole of the moon receives six months of daylight and six months of night, so one or the other of the lunar poles is always in sunlight. Since the rotation axis of the moon is tilted only 1½ degrees, the "arctic circle" on the moon is very small. (Among other things, this means that a mountain only 600 meters high will actually stick out of the moon's shadow and will always be in the light.)

The basic calculation here is that Trish must walk to the pole, then return to the landing site, where the rescue party will expect to find her. In walking to the pole, she must always stay in sunlight. This means that she cannot head straight north (or south), but must walk at an angle, to keep safely ahead of the terminator. If her average speed is significantly faster than the moon's rotation, or if she starts out well before sunset, then this spiral path is clearly shorter. With no head start, and a speed exactly equal to the rotational velocity, she can never get ahead enough to slant toward the pole. So, here is the math problem: how much speed and head start does she need to make the polar spiral the optimum solution?

Believe it or not, I actually considered putting this discussion into the story, but finally had to leave it out — it just bogged the story down too much. So, the solution is left as an exercise for the reader.

A more mundane point is the fact that at the lunar poles, the sun will never be higher than 1½ degrees off of the horizon — at the lunar equinox, in fact, the sunlight is exactly horizontal. This means that the shadows of even very small mountains will be very, very long. Near the pole, her feet will always be in shadows, so she will never be able to see where she is walking. And she can never go into a crater, or into the shadow of a mountain. This makes the polar terrain rather hazardous. Encountering an adverse slope, one where her only path moves through a down-sun shadow, will be fatal here.

*   *   *

"Impact Parameter." When I lived in Rhode Island, once a month I would drive up to Cambridge, Massachusetts for meetings of the Cambridge Science Fiction Workshop. It was a fun group of people to hang out with, as well as a group of insightful critiquers. During a long social gathering one Saturday, we discussed aliens, and shared-world anthologies. As a result, the CSFW took on a project of writing a braided novel. It was something more ambitious than a shared world, a novel with many viewpoints written by several authors dealing with the way the city of Boston is affected by change in the form of rising oceans and alien contact. I eventually wrote two stories for *Future Boston* (they can be found in *Future Boston*, Tor Books 1994, edited by David Alexander Smith). Part of the scientific background of the story was that the alien contact occurred when an extraterrestrial race brought a faster-than-light "loophole" into the solar system, and I also wrote for the book a short vignette describing the physics behind the faster-than-light travel.

As it happened, shortly before the book came out, Mike Morris and Kip Thorne wrote a paper for *American Journal of Physics* describing a possible real solution of Einstein's equations for a wormhole, a shortcut (or "loophole") through spacetime. One of the interesting features of their solution, as elucidated in a later paper in *Physical Review*, was that from the outside view, it had the same gravitational field as a (charged) black hole. In particular, it occurred to me, if such a wormhole passed in front of a star, you would see the gravitational lensing effect identical to the gravity lens produced by a black hole. Thinking these thoughts, and thinking about the history of *Future Boston*, and how the characters might react when they saw such a gravity lens effect, led to "Impact Parameter," and *Future Boston* gave it the perfect setting.

Some years later I met Mike Morris and another general relativity theorist, Matt Visser, and learned a bit more about the physics of wormholes. Thinking about the gravity lens caused by a wormhole eventually led to another paper that I coauthored with them in *Physical Review*, but that's a different story.

*   *   *

"Elemental." "Elemental" was my first published story.

I have mixed feelings about it now. With sixteen years of hindsight, it seems to me that the story is a little crude, the plot a little naive. But then, when I wrote it, I didn't know what I was doing.

I started this story sometime around 1980, not long after I graduated from MIT, and the character sketches, the main story line, and some of the early scenes were written then. My mother, who is also a science-fiction reader, contributed quite a bit. I had far more extensive biographies of the main characters than the small amount of background that appeared in the story; even now, sixteen years after writing it, I still know the characters in "Elemental" better than the characters in any other story I've written; I know them better than I know many living humans.

I didn't start writing seriously on the story for another three years. At that time I was myself a graduate student in physics at Brown University. I probably should have been working on my own research instead of writing, but somehow, despite spending all too much time writing, I did manage to complete my degree anyway.

The idea that magic could be a form of technology and be used on an equal footing with physics and engineering in a high-tech future world seemed quite fresh and exciting at the time. It's hard to decide if this story should be classified as fantasy or science fiction. Stanley Schmidt, the editor of *Analog,* told me later that he doesn't publish fantasy in Analog, but he decided to make an exception for this story.

"Elemental" came out as the cover story of the December 1984 issue of *Analog,* with a cover by Jack Gaughan. I got the issue and said to myself, wow, this is just so cool—I'm a science fiction writer! I wonder if I could do it again?

Late in the winter of 1985, I received a phone call from Australia informing me that "Elemental" was a Hugo nominee for best novella of 1984, and I was a nominee for the John W. Campbell award for best new writer. In a sense, that call changed my writing career: by writing "Elemental," I proved to myself that I could be a science fiction writer. The Hugo nomination allowed me to think that, perhaps, someday I could become a *good* science-fiction writer.

"Elemental" didn't win any awards. John Varley's "Press Enter ■" won the Hugo that year, and Lucius Shepard won for best new writer. I wasn't to win my own Hugo for another seven years.

Looking back over the story, I can see that I would write it differently now. It seems almost like a story written by a different person. But then, if parts of the story seem a bit awkward to me now, I am a different person now than I was then, and a different writer. So are we all.

But I still think it is a first story I can be proud of.

*   *   *

"Ecopoiesis." Carbon dioxide is odd in that the colder it gets, the more readily it dissolves in water. That seemed like a noteworthy fact to me.

I am quite fond of the scientific puzzle story, where the protagonists of the story must solve the riddle of some strange phenomenon. This is a form of literature that is excruciatingly difficult to write, and I am moderately pleased with my attempt at it. It was a finalist for both the Hugo and the Nebula award.

I was at the terraforming session at one of the "Case for Mars" conferences, and one of the hot topics under discussion was the idea that the planet Mars could be modified to sustain a bacterial ecology. This wouldn't really be "Terra" forming, since the ecology that was formed wouldn't be like that of Terra, but a separate ecology, made for Mars. A new word was needed, a word for creating an ecology from nothing, and the word "ecopoiesis" was suggested, forming an ecosystem without the implication of making a copy of the Earth.

At a later conference, Chris McKay presented a paper by Carl Sagan (who couldn't make it) that said, basically, you guys are proposing seeding Mars with anaerobic bacteria. Are you crazy? You're proposing turning Mars into a sewer!

My working title for this story was "Brown Mars."

I must acknowledge that I sent an early draft of the story to Martyn Fogg (the guy who wrote the book on terraforming). He gave me some very insightful comments, and I apologize for the fact that, where the story demanded it, I completely ignored his advice.

"Ecopoiesis" was the first time I'd ever had a story that continued characters from an earlier story. (Tinkerman, Leah, and Tally had earlier appeared in "Farthest Horizons.") My characters aren't usually interested in appearing in a second story. Who knows, some day I may end up writing more of their story, and it could become a novel.

*   *   *

"Across the Darkness." At the end of my freshman year of college, programmable calculators hit the market, and my slide rule instantly became obsolete. When I got my first calculator, I did what pretty much everybody does with their first calculator: I designed a fusion-powered interstellar spaceship.

A few days of playing around with the rocket equation taught me a powerful lesson: if you were going to make a fusion-powered starship with enough speed to go anywhere interesting, the mass ratio is going to be incredible. The vast majority of the mass of the ship is going to be fuel.

And, conversely, when you need a thousand tons of fuel for every kilogram of payload, you're not going to carry anything you don't absolutely positively need. Forget the thousand-person starships with everything you can possibly want brought along: an interstellar colonization mission is going to be stripped down to barely nothing. I came to the conclusion that men were unnecessary: your interstellar colonization mission would have only women, and a sperm bank.

Thinking these thoughts, I collaborated with a high-school friend on ideas that eventually became an elaborate outline for a science fiction novel, focusing on the colonists raised on the planet: the first generation raised with both sexes. Of course, as a college sophomore, I had no real exposure to life, only theoretical experience of sex, and nothing really deep to say: any novel I might have written would have been just plain awful. Nevertheless, I can still feel the novel that I might have written, a groundbreaking novel if I'd actually written it in 1974; the plot and characters are far more real to me than many novels that actually exist.

"Across the Darkness" is part of the backstory for that never-written novel. I wrote the first draft at Clarion, where it was soundly thrashed in critique. I think that the kindest comment I got was Kate Wilhelm's; she said that she saw what I was trying to do with the story, and admired the intention, but of course the story didn't work. It took me nearly ten more years to get up the courage to do a rewrite, and when I did I tore the original story down to its skeleton and started over.

*   *   *

"Ouroboros." This has always worried me. If we were simulated people in a simulated reality, how could we tell?

*   *   *

"Into the Blue Abyss." I was having lunch with Sheila Williams, the executive editor of *Asimov's Science Fiction.* (One of the perks of selling to a magazine is that sometimes the editors will buy you lunch.) She mentioned that they wanted to do an *Asimov's* solar-system anthology: one story for each planet of the solar system, and only stories originally published in *Asimov's Science Fiction.* The only problem was this: *Asimov's* had never published a story about the planet Uranus. They had a story about every other planet in the solar system, but not Uranus.

Sounded like a challenge to me, so I found my battered old copy of Beatty, Petersen and Chaikin's book *The New Solar System*, and learned what I could about Uranus. I discovered that Uranus is, in fact, a rather fascinating planet. One of the most fascinating things I discovered was that, at least as of 1995, it was not clear that Uranus had any solid core at all—one of the models said that Uranus was a water ocean all the way down, an ocean without a bottom.

A year after I wrote this, a news report mentioned that scientists calculated that the pressure in the oceans of Uranus could be so high that dissolved methane might precipitate out diamonds. An ocean with a rain of diamonds! Truth really is stranger than fiction.

Maybe another story.

*   *   *

"Snow." I was teaching a writing class, and (taking a suggestion from Charlie Oberndorf) I gave to my students an exercise for them to set up, and then subvert, stereotyped characters. I make a point of doing the exercises that I give to my students. The night before the class I was sitting in my study, in front of my computer, thinking about the exercise and watching snow twinkle in the darkness as it fell through the sphere of light cast by the streetlight outside my window. I was thinking how much better it was inside, in front of my nice warm computer, than outside. And thinking about being homeless brought my thoughts around, by subtle curves, to thinking about Paul Erdös, the Hungarian mathematician who was literally homeless, living in the spare bedrooms of other mathematicians, possibly the world's best example of an eccentric genius.

*   *   *

"Rorvik's War." I started this one living in Rhode Island, and finished it living in Cleveland. This story came from a remark by David Alexander Smith. We were discussing a different story, and I put forth the idea that wars are fought for essentially rational reasons, and that therefore no wars would be fought after computer modeling became accurate enough to reliably predict which side would win any possible conflict. He disagreed, saying— among other things—that simulations would never get that good: the skill and morale and decision-making capability of individual soldiers can't be simulated.

The story contains a bit of my thinking about the ways in which a high-tech future war might be fought, with remotely-directed machinery doing much of the actual battle.

*   *   *

"Approaching Perimelasma." I was thinking that most science fiction stories about black holes are pretty much inaccurate about the real physics, and I though, okay, why don't I write one that works hard to actually get the physics right?

Turned out to be harder than you'd think.

I'd been studying the theory of wormholes a little bit since "Impact Parameter," and had learned about Visser portals, which are much slicker solutions of general relativity than Morris-Thorne wormholes. A Visser portal, in principle, can be held open by as little as a single loop of negative-mass cosmic string. Of course, nobody has ever seen a piece of cosmic string, negative or positive, but it's good enough for science fiction. The wormholes in this story are Visser portals.

There is an additional problem, which is that any reasonable black hole would have gravitational forces high enough to rip any real human to spaghetti, but then, I was talking about a post-human future. If you are small — Galileo pointed this out — if you are small enough, your strength to weight ratio becomes extremely good.

I had one additional problem. Rocket scientists call the point of a trajectory that approaches closest to the Earth "perigee," the closest approach to the sun "perihelion," the closest approach to a star "periastron." So what's the closest approach to a black hole? There didn't seem to be a word, so I made one up.

In 1996 the Nebula award banquet was on the Queen Mary in Long Beach California. I was there because one of my stories had made the final ballot (although I didn't win, I'm afraid). An unexpected feature of the event was that when you sat at the bar, bodies would come plummeting out of the sky and fall past the window. On the pier outside the ship was a bungee-jumping spot, and for a fee of eighty-five dollars, you could climb two hundred and twenty feet up in the air, have a rubber band strapped to your legs, and dive off into space, waving at your friends sitting in the bar as you fell.

The average science fiction writer, as it turns out, had the very sensible opinion "you couldn't pay me to do that!" A few of us, however, said "Hey, if you buy me a ticket, I'll jump." A number of friends took up the challenge and collected money, and in the end Martha Soukup, Jenna Felice, and I took the dive. It's remarkable how difficult it is, when you get down to it, to take that step into thin air, even when you've seen hundreds of people do it, and know perfectly well that you're safe. I used some of that feeling as background in the story, and (after asking permission), I put Jenna and Martha into the story as well.

Jenna Felice, who as far as I could tell was afraid of absolutely nothing, died last week. She could dive off a two hundred twenty foot tower with perfect equanimity; but an allergic reaction (and we don't even know to what) did it. I hate to see her go. Life is not fair.

*   *   *

"What We Really Do At NASA." When I wrote the first line of this, I didn't have any idea where it was going. I'd recently started work as a postdoctoral scientist at the NASA Lewis Research Center in Cleveland (now renamed NASA Glenn), and somebody had said something about the crashed flying saucer that was supposedly kept in a secret vault underneath the center. It was amazing to me how many people had no idea what we did at NASA, and I put all of the misconceptions and odd ideas into one place.

Now you know. Don't tell anybody!

*   *   *

"Dark Lady." I wrote this one when I was a graduate student in physics, and it's about being a graduate student in physics. Score one for "write what you know." I was an experimental solid-state physicist, not a theoretical physicist, so my experience wasn't exactly the same. Nevertheless, some of the pieces of this story are autobiographical, but I won't tell you which parts.

The lyrics aren't really blues—more of a free jazz.

I stole the car from my Aunt Jill, although before putting it in the story, I combined it with pieces of a disassembled sports car forever being built by an eccentric landlord I had in Roxbury, Massachusetts.

*   *   *

"Outsider's Chance." I was thinking about pirates, and whether there was any way that there could be space pirates in the real world, and if so, how they could hide, since the sky is transparent, and you can't disappear merely by sailing over the horizon. And I was thinking about nuclear rockets, and how nobody had ever written a story with a really good description of how a nuclear rocket works. I was thinking about a lot of things. One of the people who I run into from time to time at NASA Glenn is Stan

Borowski, who has proposed—among other things—that you could augment the thrust of a nuclear rocket, if you needed high thrust, by dumping liquid oxygen into the exhaust. So there you go.

The hidden background of "Outsider's Chance," the story of the failed rebellion on the asteroid Anteros, is much more detailed than the little piece that shows up in this story. Like the background of "Across the Darkness," this is a setting stolen from yet another novel that I've never actually gotten around to writing.

* * *

"Beneath the Stars of Winter." In *Gulag Archipelago*, Solzhenitsyn made a brief mention of scientists continuing to do research even after being sent to prison camps in Siberia. I don't know if I had ever heard of anything more admirable, more of a perfect example of the indomitable human spirit.

* * *

"The Singular Habits of Wasps." There is a point in the very first of Arthur Conan Doyle's Sherlock Holmes adventures where Watson is surprised to find Holmes ignorant of the fact that the Earth revolves around the sun. After Watson explains this to him, Holmes retorts that now that he knows it, he shall do his best to forget it, as the fact "would not make a pennyworth of difference to me or to my work." I'm sure that every science fiction reader who comes across this passage has had the same immediate urge: to toss Holmes headfirst into a situation where the fact that the Earth is only one of a family of planets revolving around a sun that is itself one of billions in the galaxy, does, indeed, "make a pennyworth of difference."

I had originally intended this story for an anthology edited by Mike Resnick, but as the writing progressed I discovered that the story was a bit longer than I'd anticipated, and would come in within neither the time nor length deadlines. Mike ended up accepting a different (and much shorter) Sherlock Holmes story.

In researching the story, I came across several interesting facts, including the fact that in the summer of 1888, the stage adaptation of Stevenson's "Dr. Jekyll and Mr. Hyde" was the hit of London's Lyceum theatre, and that in the only one of the "Jack the Ripper" killings in which the presumed murderer was seen with the victim, the suspect was described as a tall man wearing a deerstalker hat.

Science fiction did not begin with H.G. Wells, but he did originate many of the concepts we now accept as given. One of these, an insight so simple as to be almost invisible to us now, was his realization that intelligent life originating elsewhere than Earth would differ from humans in ways more fundamental than merely being taller or shorter or with skin of an odd color. Aliens would not be human, or even humanoid. Television writers, please take note.

I am often uncertain whether a story works or not—I can't tell if other people share my fascination with Sherlock Holmes, or whether I had hit the Victorian tone quite exactly right. But Stan Schmidt at *Analog* cheerfully bought it, and, as it happened, it was a finalist for both the Hugo and the Nebula, losing both to David Gerrold.

A final technical note. The life-cycle of the "solitary wasp"— actually a whole category of insects—is as described in the story. However, while I used terminology correct for the nineteenth century, modern entomologists do not classify them as members of the wasp (*vespidae*) family, but as a separate family, the *ichneumonidae*.

*   *   *

"Winter Fire." In Sarajevo, I have been told, when the first mortar rounds exploded, all the bells of the city rang out in sympathy.

I really cannot think of very much to say about "Winter Fire." It is a story about human nature. As science fiction writers, we all would like to hold forth a hope that the future will be better than the past, that the worst is over, and that, somehow, we learn from history. And if this is not possible, we all would like to believe that the anvil of history is hammered in places far away, where we can watch in peace, in places with odd names like Mogadishu or Phnom Penh or Sarajevo.

Science fiction gives us hope.

"Winter Fire" is not really science fiction.

Three thousand copies of this book have been printed by the Maple-Vail Book Manufacturing Group, Binghamton, NY, for Golden Gryphon Press, Urbana, IL. The text type is Elante, printed on 55# Sebago. The binding cloth is Roxitel. Typesetting by The Composing Room, Inc., Kimberly, WI.